Jimmy Gownley's

AMELIA RULES!™

THE TWEENAGE GUIDE TO NOT BEING UNPOPULAR

Atheneum Books for Young Readers
New York   London   Toronto   Sydney

This book is dedicated
with love and gratitude to
Michael Cohen, Harold Buchholz,
and Judy Hansen.

ATHENEUM BOOKS FOR YOUNG READERS
An imprint of Simon & Schuster Children's Publishing Division
1230 Avenue of the Americas, New York, New York 10020
For information about special discounts for bulk purchases, please contact Simon & Schuster Special Sales
at 1-866-506-1949 or business@simonandschuster.com.
The Simon & Schuster Speakers Bureau can bring authors to your live event.
For more information or to book an event, contact the Simon & Schuster Speakers Bureau
at 1-866-248-3049 or visit our website at www.simonspeakers.com.
Also available in an Atheneum Books for Young Readers paperback edition
Book design by Sonia Chaghatzbanian
The text for this book is hand-lettered.
The illustrations for this book are digitally rendered.
Manufactured in the United States of America
0310 WOR
First Edition
2 4 6 8 10 9 7 5 3 1
CIP data for this book is available from the Library of Congress.
ISBN 978-1-4169-8610-2 (hc)
ISBN 978-1-4169-8608-9

Don't Expect Miracles!

(A Note From the Author)

If you've purchased this book, I am sorry.

Sorry that you have had to live your life as an outsider, a nerd, a loser. Sorry that it took you so long to gain access to my wisdom.

But that's okay, because now we've found each other.

Within this book, you will find many helpful tips, exercises, and activities that will help you raise your social standing.

But, before we begin, a word of warning.

Don't expect miracles.

Most of you will never be popular. You will never be prom queens or kings. You will never be class president or voted most likely to, well, do anything positive.

But together, with hard work and dedication, we might be able to prevent you from embarrassing yourself any further.

So remember: Fate and genetics may have already decided that you will never be popular, but at least, with my help, you need no longer be UNpopular.

Dr. Victoria Medeochrias

Dr. Victoria Medeochrias

"Intro to Tweenage Guide"
From the private library of Rhonda Bleenie.

Victoria St. James Medeochrias is a world reknowned author, scholar, and motivational speaker. Her many books have been global bestsellers, and it is assumed that at least one of them helped someone, somewhere.

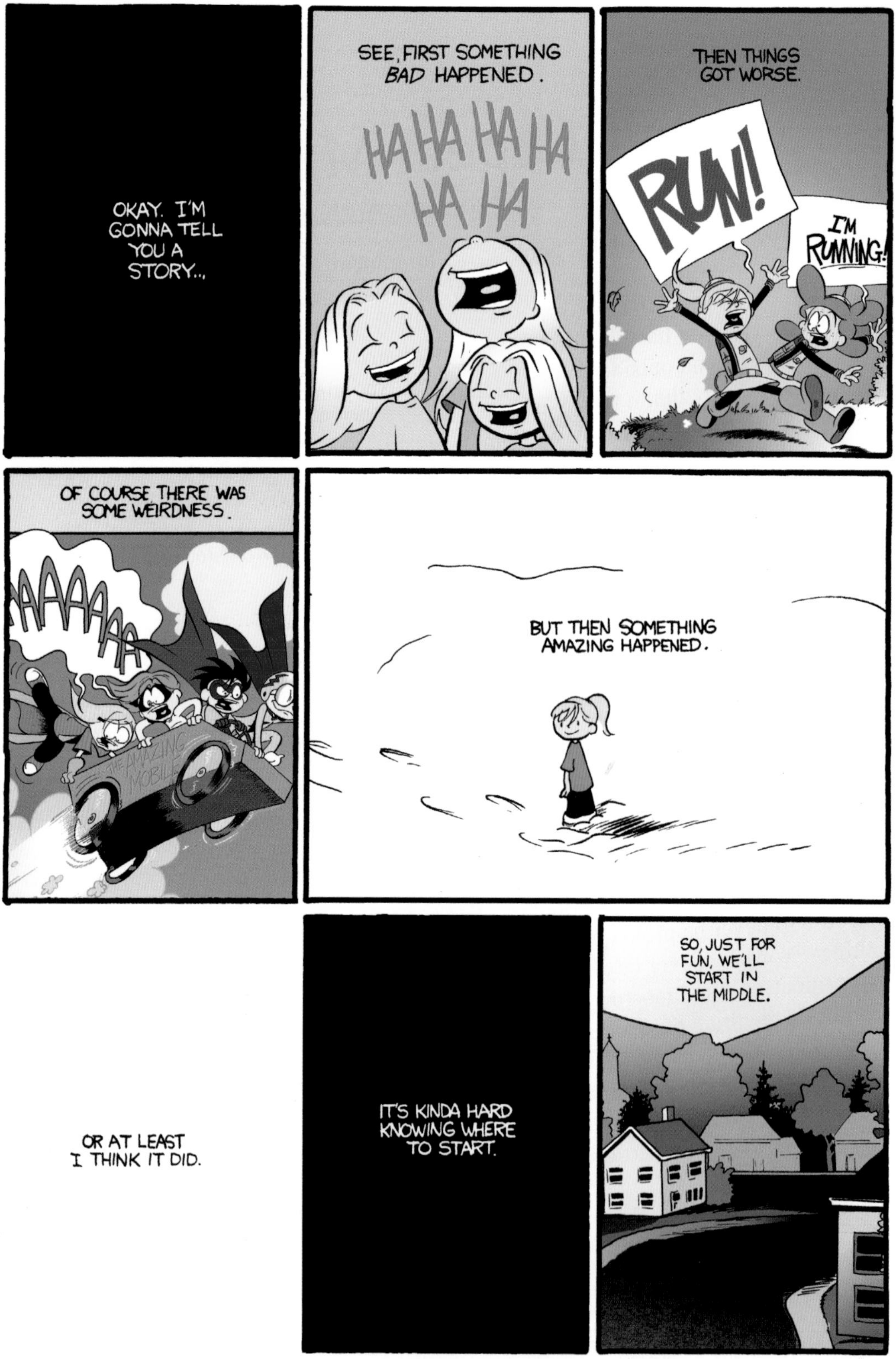
OKAY. I'M GONNA TELL YOU A STORY...
SEE, FIRST SOMETHING *BAD* HAPPENED.
HA HA HA HA HA HA HA
THEN THINGS GOT WORSE.
RUN!
I'M RUNNING!
OF COURSE THERE WAS SOME WEIRDNESS.
THE AMAZING MOBILE
BUT THEN SOMETHING AMAZING HAPPENED.
OR AT LEAST I THINK IT DID.
IT'S KINDA HARD KNOWING WHERE TO START.
SO, JUST FOR FUN, WE'LL START IN THE MIDDLE.

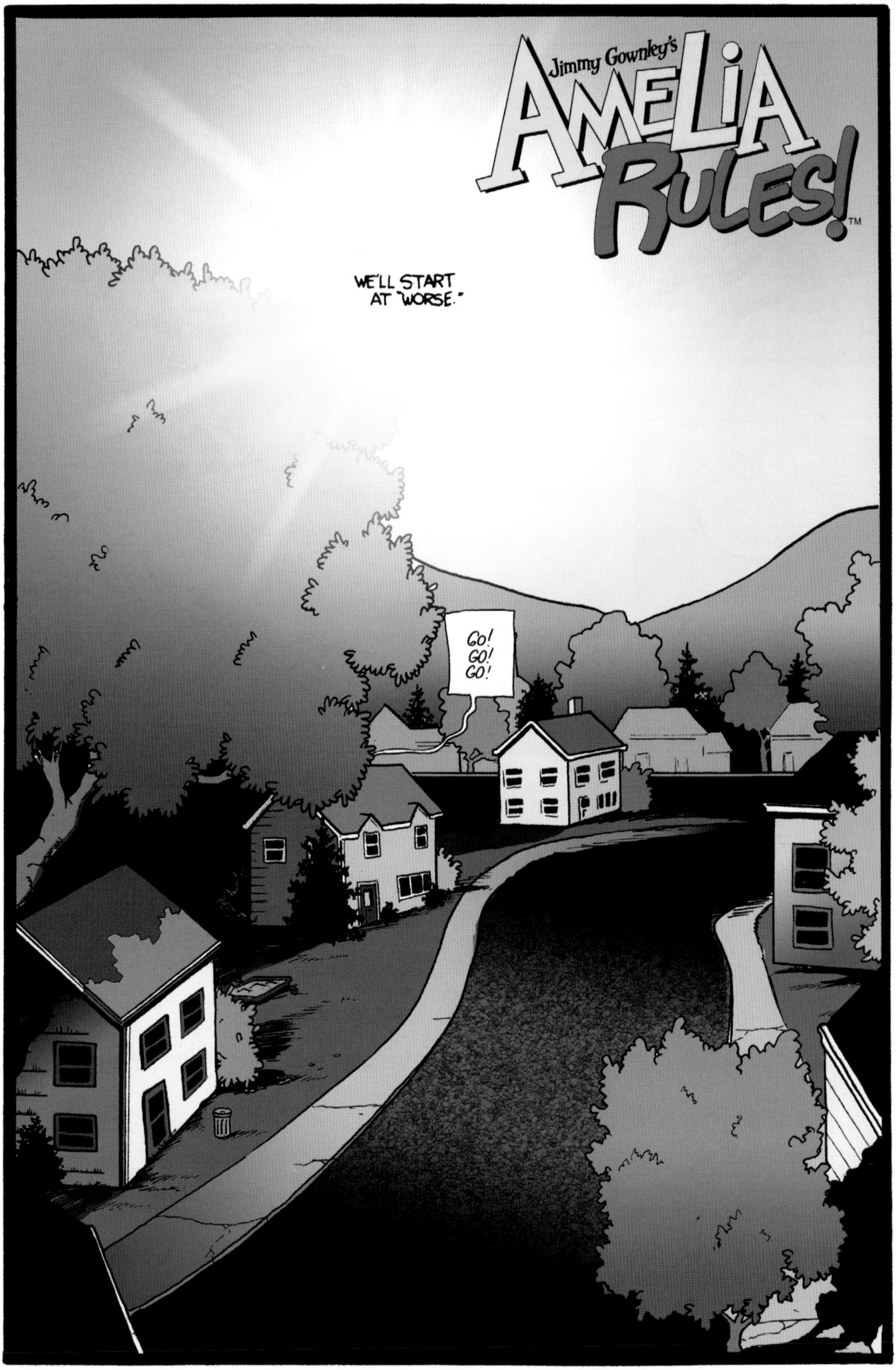
Jimmy Gownley's
AMELIA RULES!
WE'LL START AT "WORSE."
GO! GO! GO!

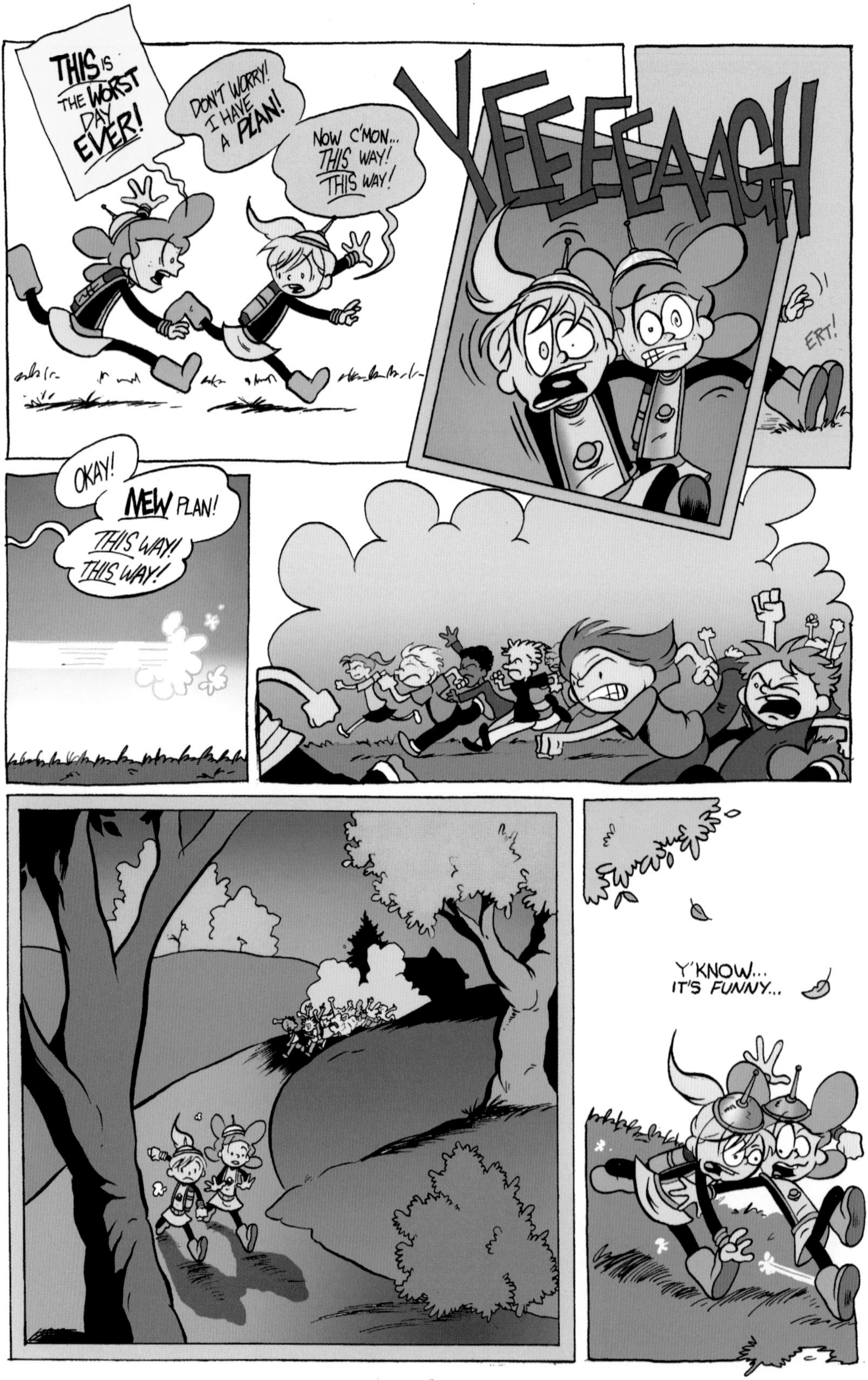
THIS IS THE WORST DAY EVER!
DON'T WORRY! I HAVE A PLAN!
NOW C'MON... THIS WAY! THIS WAY!
YEEEEAAGH
ERT!
OKAY! NEW PLAN! THIS WAY! THIS WAY!
Y'KNOW... IT'S FUNNY...

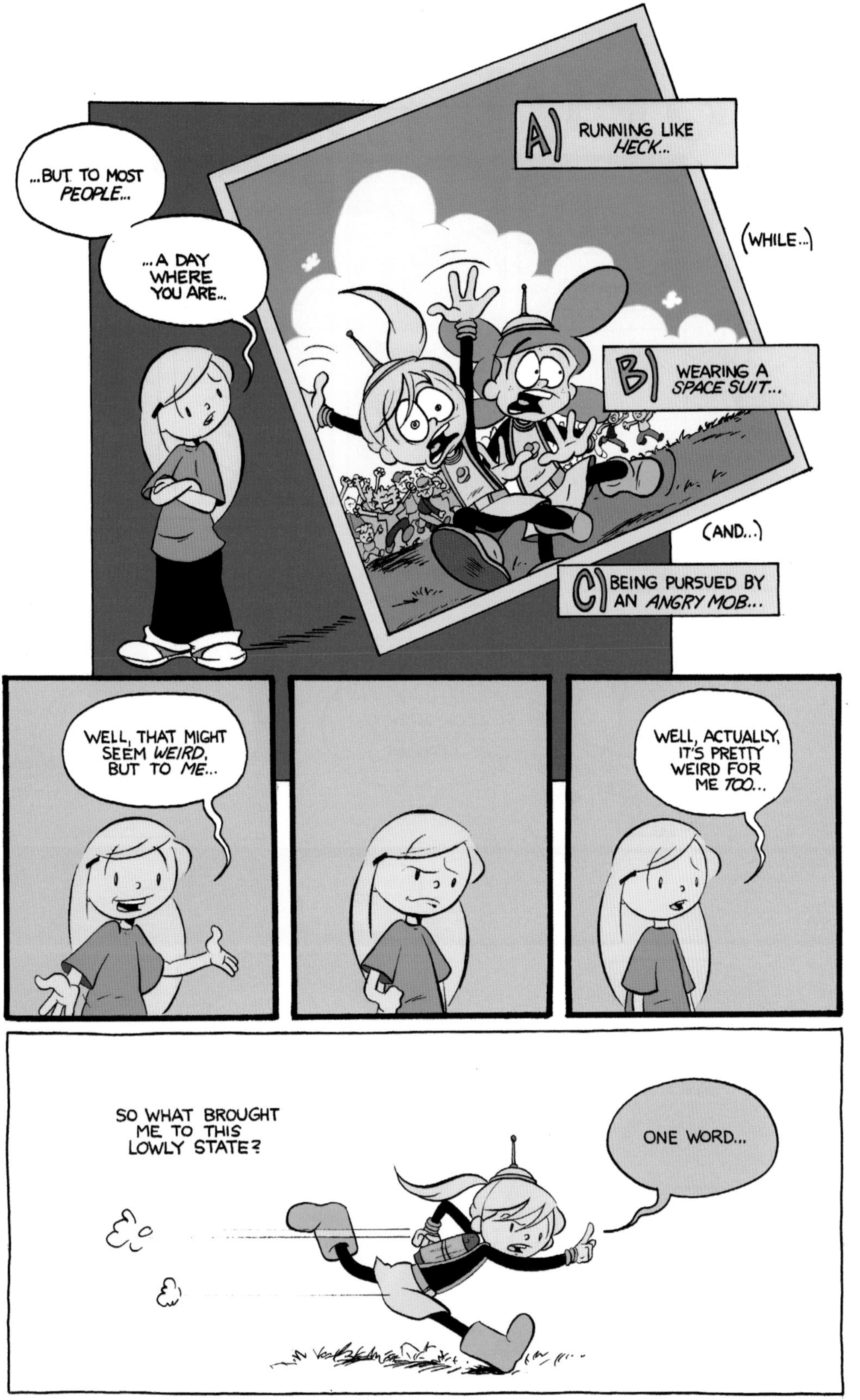

...BUT TO MOST *PEOPLE*...
...A DAY WHERE YOU ARE...
A) RUNNING LIKE *HECK*...
(WHILE...)
B) WEARING A *SPACE SUIT*...
(AND...)
C) BEING PURSUED BY AN *ANGRY MOB*...
WELL, THAT MIGHT SEEM *WEIRD*, BUT TO *ME*...
WELL, ACTUALLY, IT'S PRETTY WEIRD FOR ME *TOO*...
SO WHAT BROUGHT ME TO THIS LOWLY STATE?
ONE WORD...

POPULARITY...

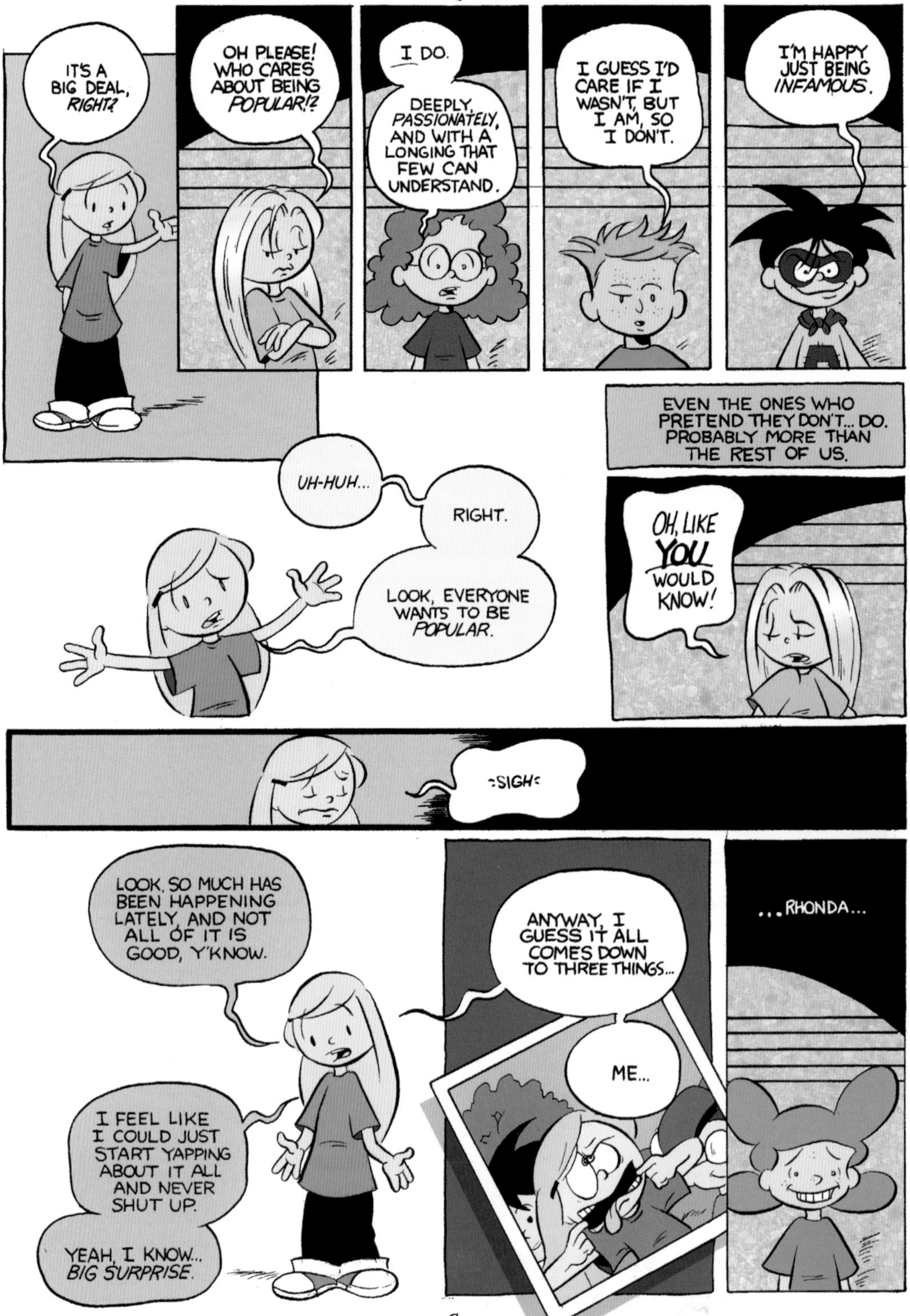
IT'S A BIG DEAL, RIGHT?
OH PLEASE! WHO CARES ABOUT BEING POPULAR!?
I DO.
DEEPLY, PASSIONATELY, AND WITH A LONGING THAT FEW CAN UNDERSTAND.
I GUESS I'D CARE IF I WASN'T, BUT I AM, SO I DON'T.
I'M HAPPY JUST BEING INFAMOUS.
EVEN THE ONES WHO PRETEND THEY DON'T... DO. PROBABLY MORE THAN THE REST OF US.
UH-HUH...
RIGHT.
LOOK, EVERYONE WANTS TO BE POPULAR.
OH, LIKE YOU WOULD KNOW!
:SIGH:
LOOK, SO MUCH HAS BEEN HAPPENING LATELY, AND NOT ALL OF IT IS GOOD, Y'KNOW.
I FEEL LIKE I COULD JUST START YAPPING ABOUT IT ALL AND NEVER SHUT UP.
YEAH, I KNOW... BIG SURPRISE.
ANYWAY, I GUESS IT ALL COMES DOWN TO THREE THINGS...
ME...
...RHONDA...

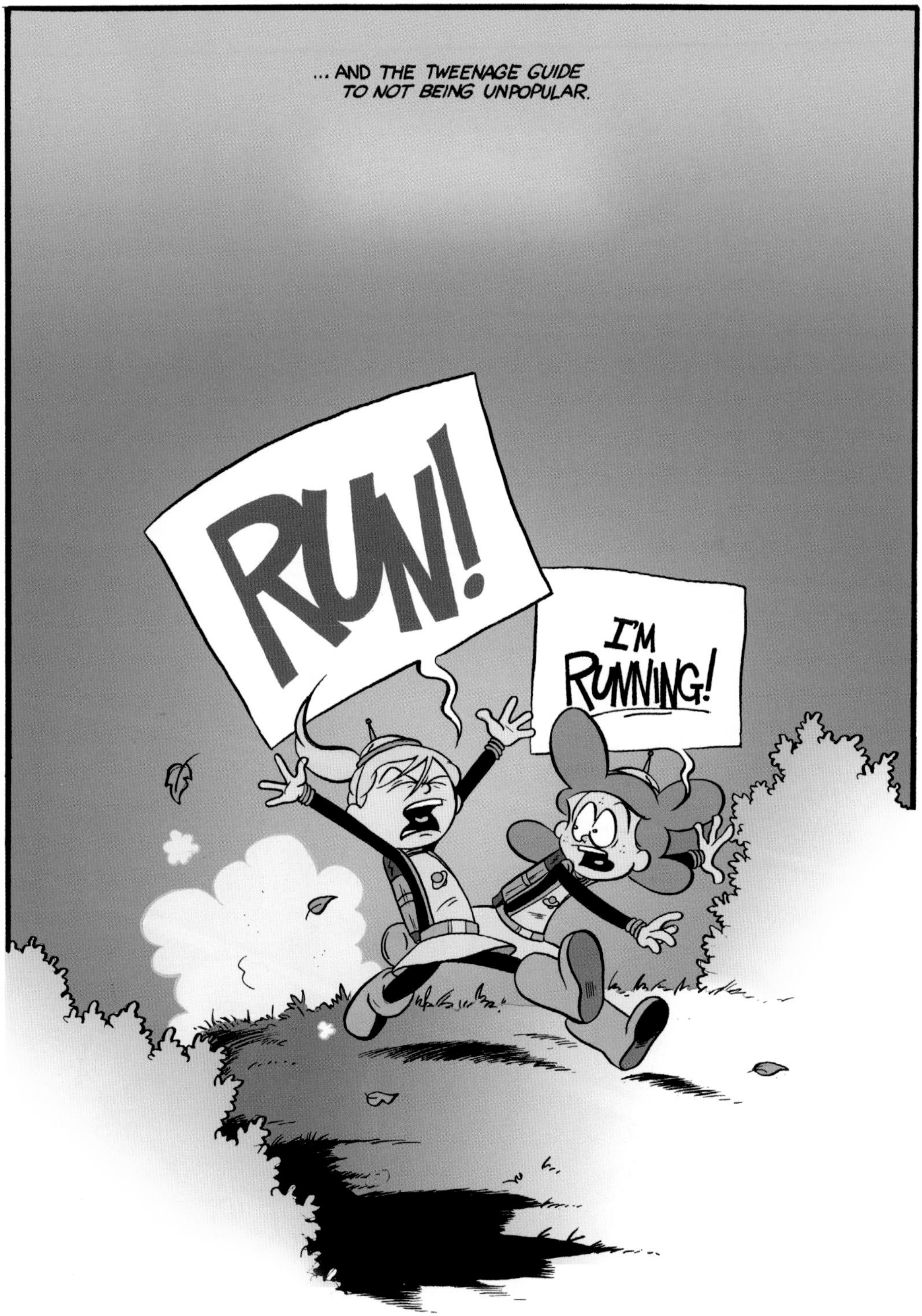
... AND THE TWEENAGE GUIDE TO NOT BEING UNPOPULAR.
RUN!
I'M RUNNING!

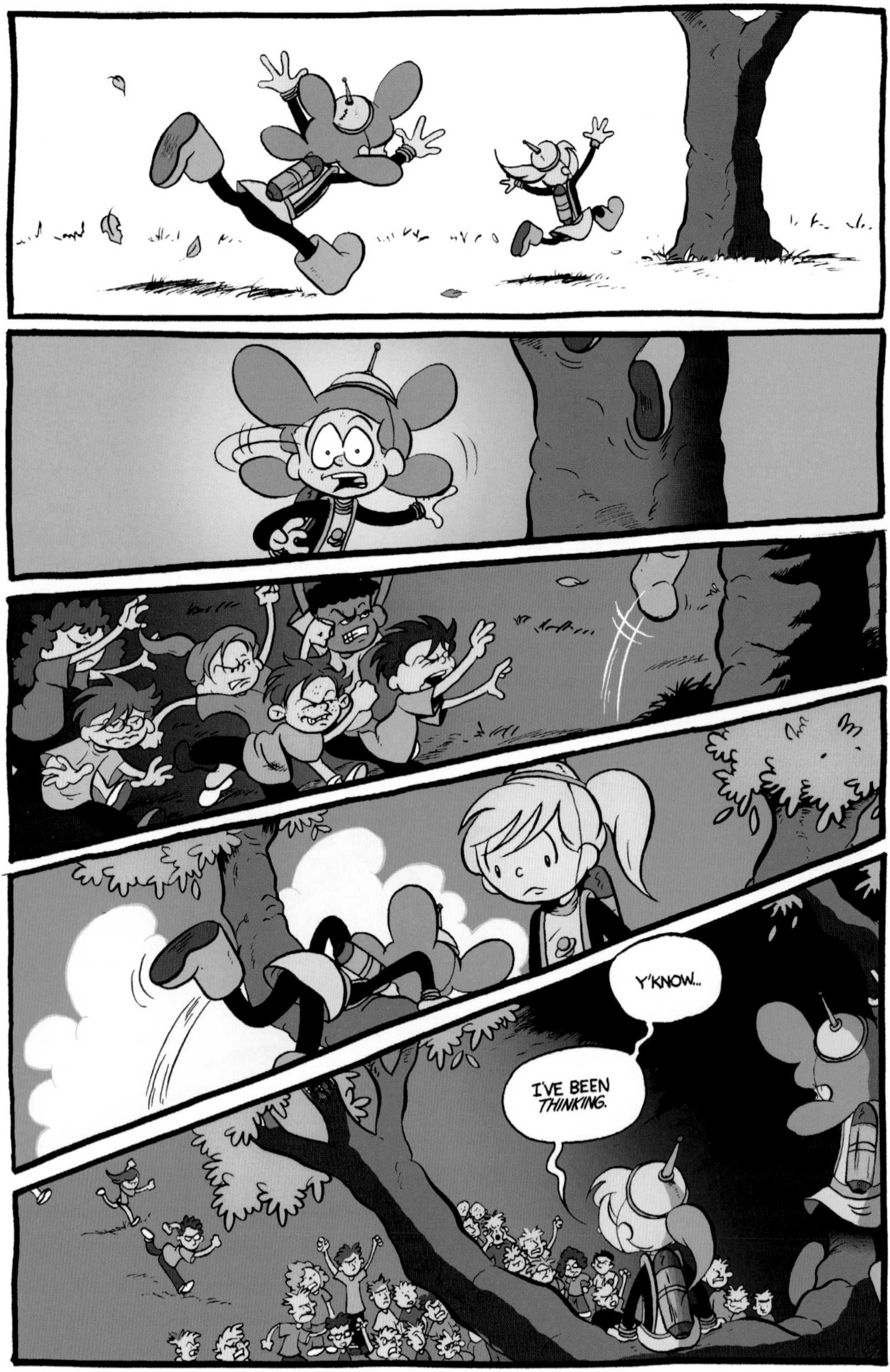
Y'KNOW...
I'VE BEEN THINKING.

SPECIFICALLY

IF I EVER HAVE A DAUGHTER, AND SOMEDAY, SHE WANTS TO HEAR STORIES FROM MY *YOUTH*...
...I THINK I'LL LEAVE THIS ONE OUT!
GOOD IDEA.

NEXT TUESDAY

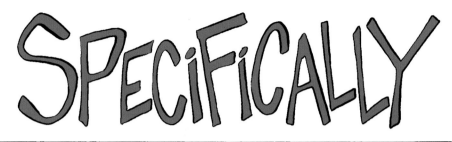

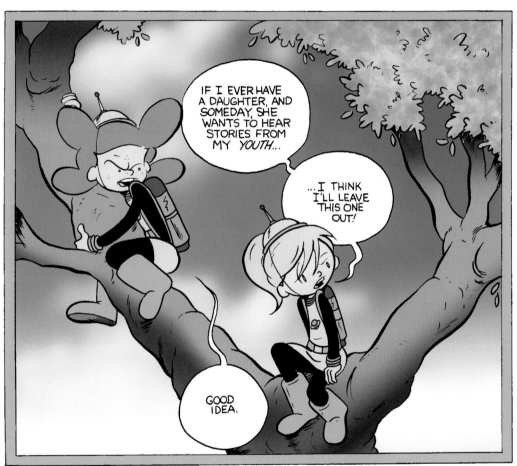

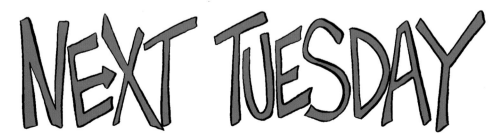

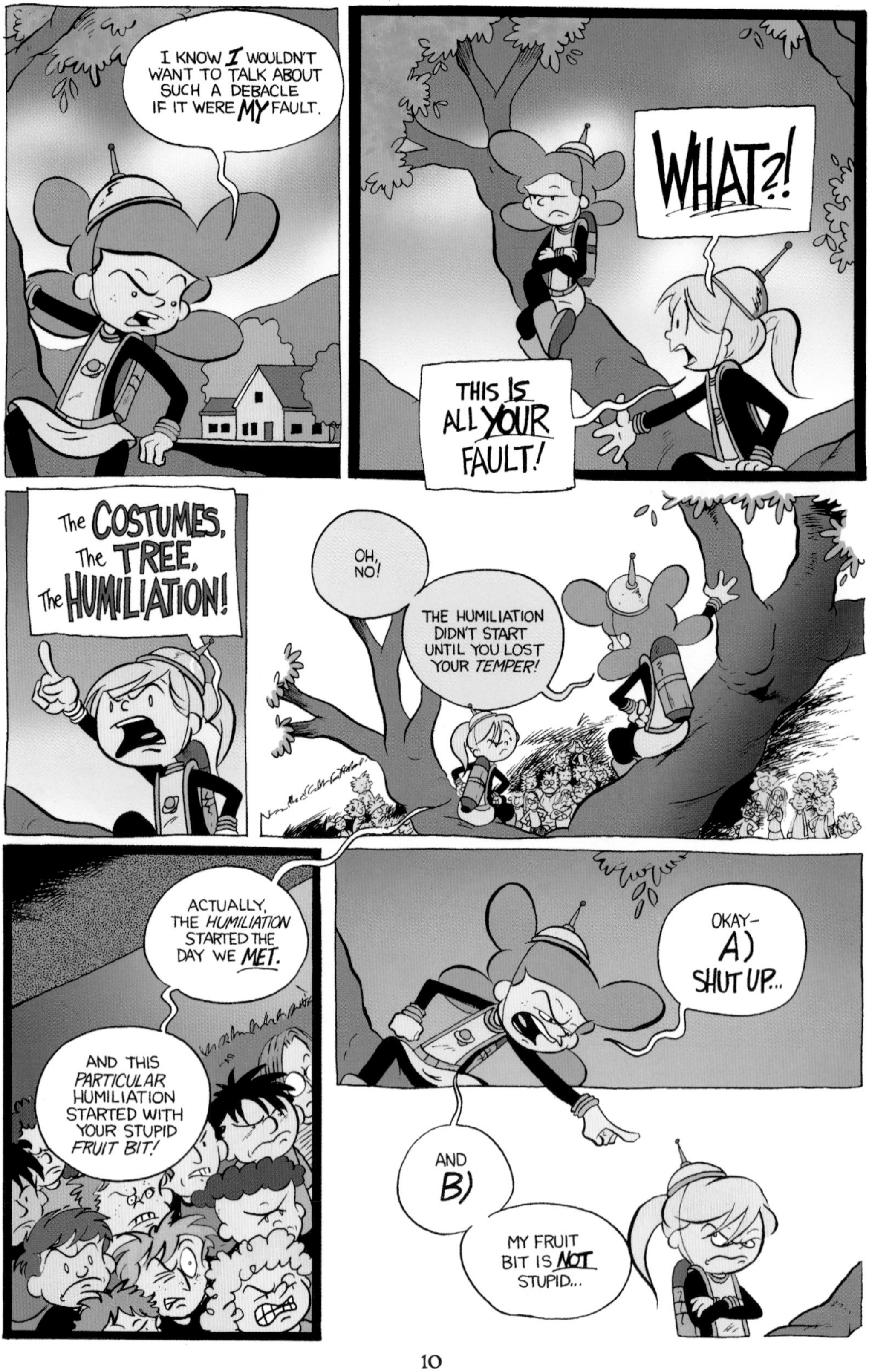
I KNOW I WOULDN'T WANT TO TALK ABOUT SUCH A DEBACLE IF IT WERE MY FAULT.
WHAT?!
THIS IS ALL YOUR FAULT!
The COSTUMES, The TREE, The HUMILIATION!
OH, NO!
THE HUMILIATION DIDN'T START UNTIL YOU LOST YOUR TEMPER!
ACTUALLY, THE HUMILIATION STARTED THE DAY WE MET.
AND THIS PARTICULAR HUMILIATION STARTED WITH YOUR STUPID FRUIT BIT!
OKAY- A) SHUT UP...
AND B)
MY FRUIT BIT IS NOT STUPID...

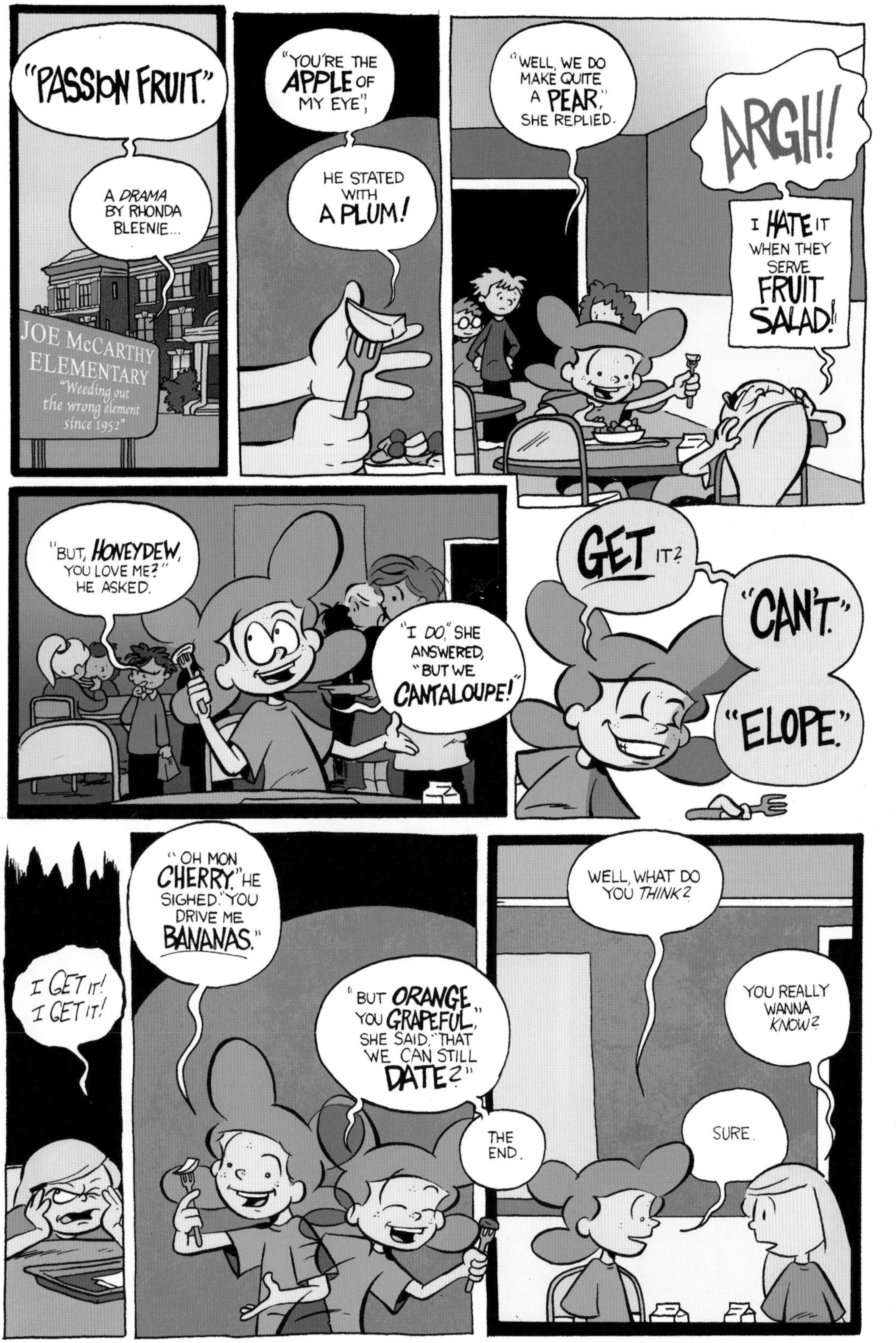
"PASSION FRUIT."
A DRAMA BY RHONDA BLEENIE...
JOE McCARTHY ELEMENTARY
"Weeding out the wrong element since 1952"
"YOU'RE THE APPLE OF MY EYE",
HE STATED WITH A PLUM!
"WELL, WE DO MAKE QUITE A PEAR," SHE REPLIED.
ARGH!
I HATE IT WHEN THEY SERVE FRUIT SALAD!!
"BUT, HONEYDEW, YOU LOVE ME?" HE ASKED.
"I DO," SHE ANSWERED, "BUT WE CANTALOUPE!"
GET IT?
"CAN'T."
"ELOPE."
I GET IT! I GET IT!
"OH MON CHERRY," HE SIGHED. "YOU DRIVE ME BANANAS."
"BUT ORANGE YOU GRAPEFUL," SHE SAID, "THAT WE CAN STILL DATE?"
THE END.
WELL, WHAT DO YOU THINK?
YOU REALLY WANNA KNOW?
SURE.

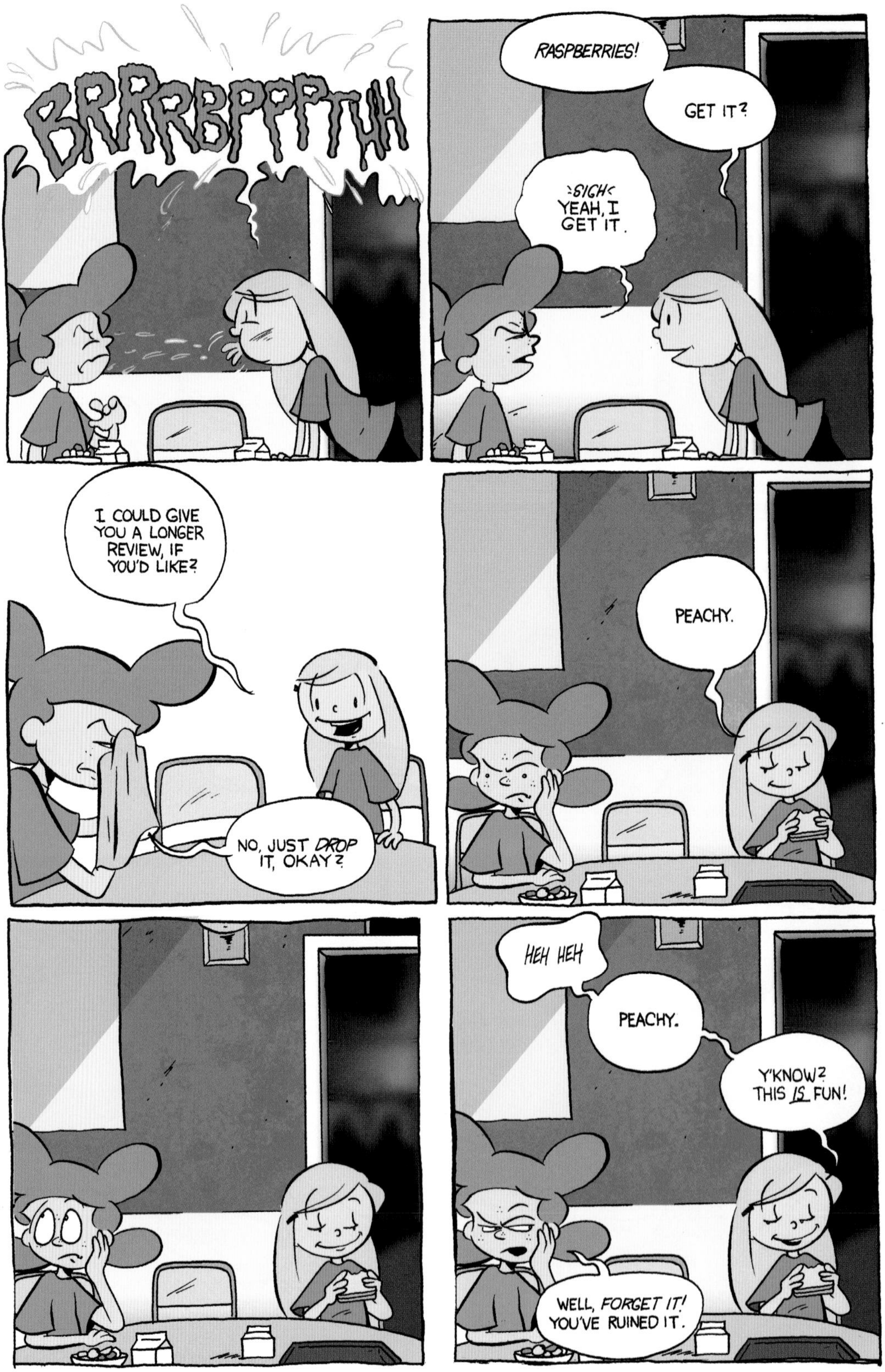
BRRRBPPPTUH
RASPBERRIES!
GET IT?
>SIGH< YEAH, I GET IT.
I COULD GIVE YOU A LONGER REVIEW, IF YOU'D LIKE?
NO, JUST DROP IT, OKAY?
PEACHY.
HEH HEH
PEACHY.
Y'KNOW? THIS IS FUN!
WELL, FORGET IT! YOU'VE RUINED IT.

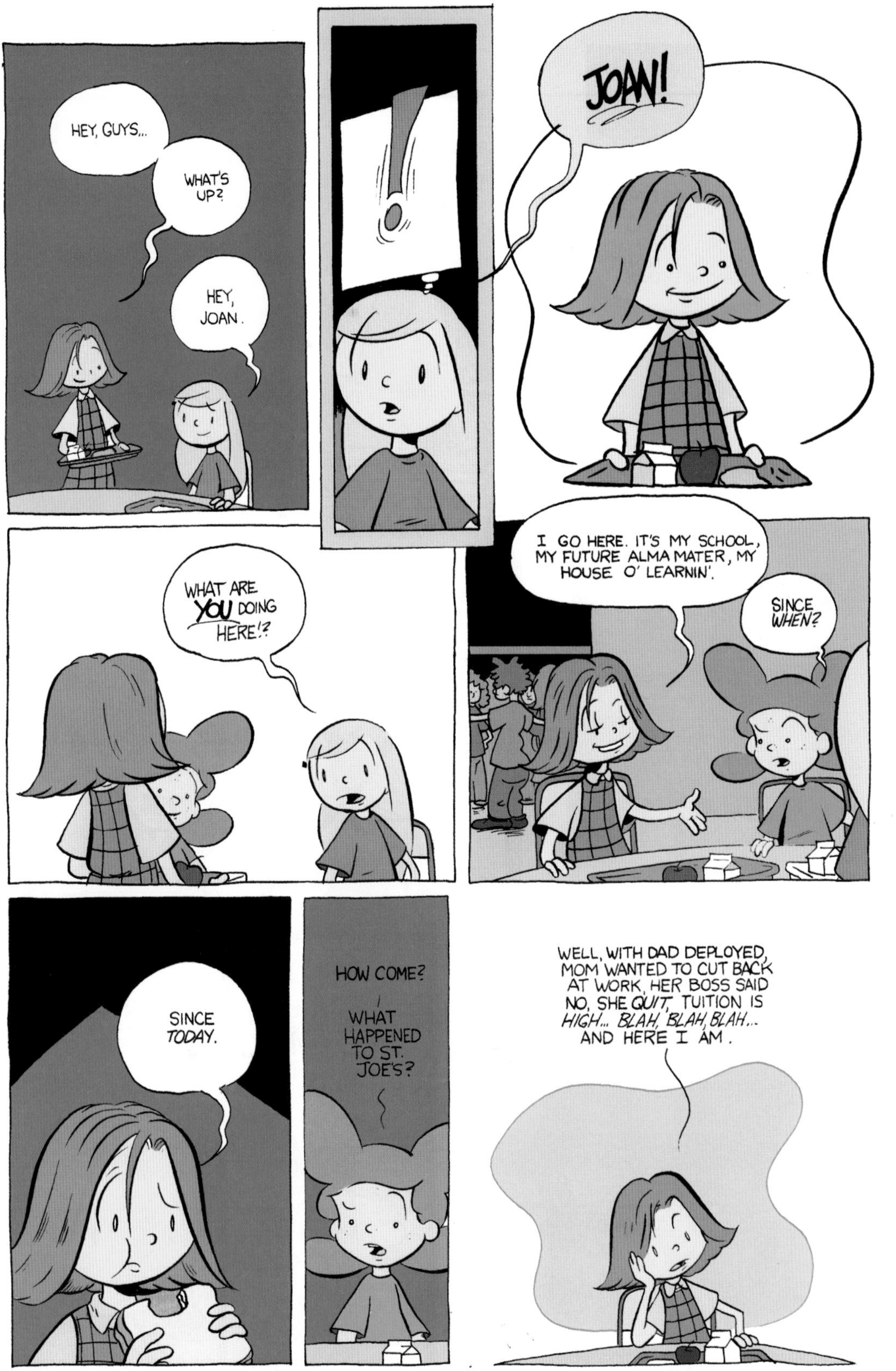
HEY, GUYS...
WHAT'S UP?
HEY, JOAN.
!
JOAN!
WHAT ARE YOU DOING HERE!?
I GO HERE. IT'S MY SCHOOL, MY FUTURE ALMA MATER, MY HOUSE O' LEARNIN'.
SINCE WHEN?
SINCE TODAY.
HOW COME?
WHAT HAPPENED TO ST. JOE'S?
WELL, WITH DAD DEPLOYED, MOM WANTED TO CUT BACK AT WORK, HER BOSS SAID NO, SHE QUIT, TUITION IS HIGH... BLAH, BLAH, BLAH... AND HERE I AM.

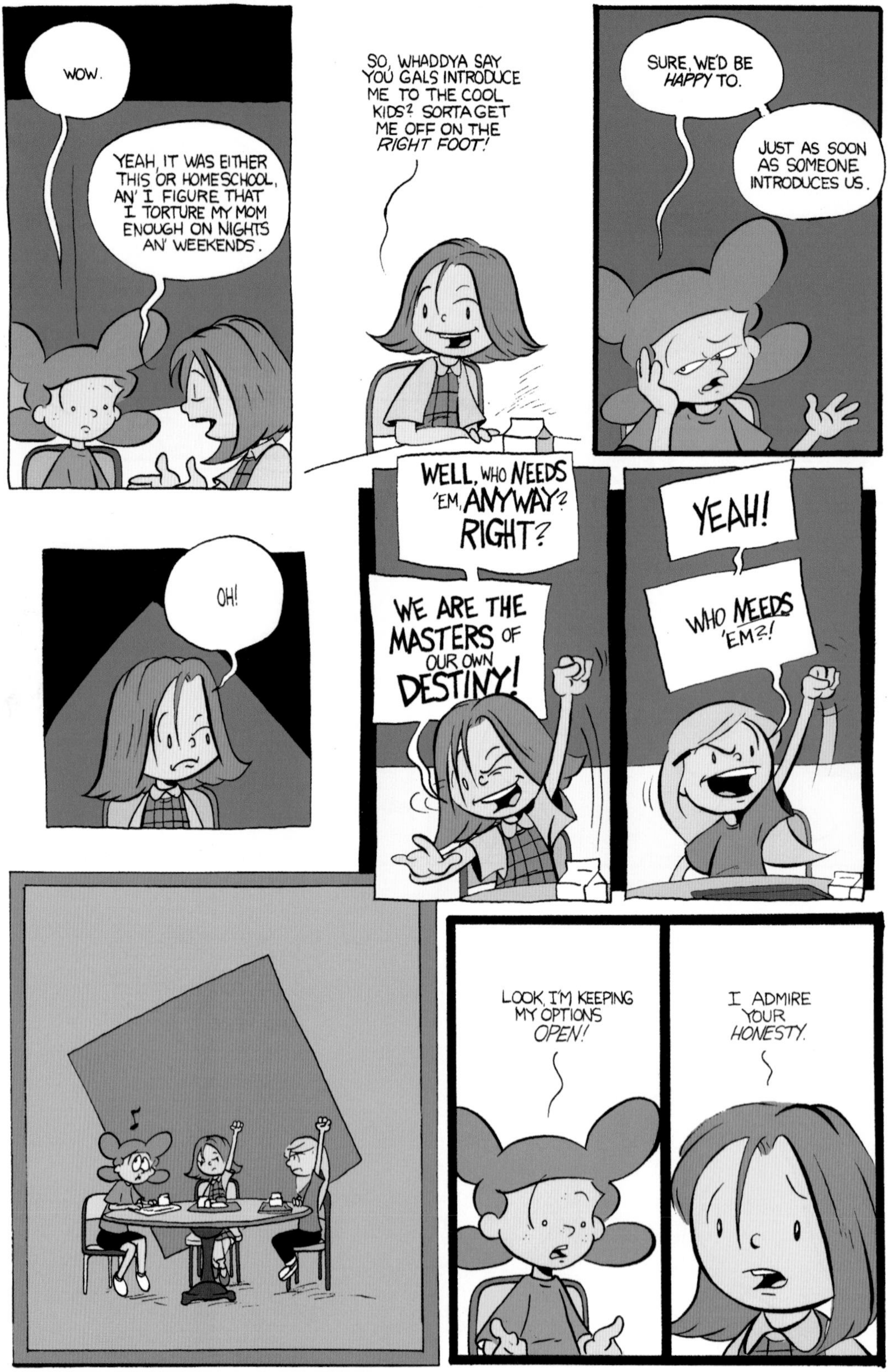
WOW.
YEAH, IT WAS EITHER THIS OR HOMESCHOOL, AN' I FIGURE THAT I TORTURE MY MOM ENOUGH ON NIGHTS AN' WEEKENDS.
SO, WHADDYA SAY YOU GALS INTRODUCE ME TO THE COOL KIDS? SORTA GET ME OFF ON THE RIGHT FOOT!
SURE, WE'D BE HAPPY TO.
JUST AS SOON AS SOMEONE INTRODUCES US.
OH!
WELL, WHO NEEDS 'EM, ANYWAY? RIGHT?
WE ARE THE MASTERS OF OUR OWN DESTINY!
YEAH!
WHO NEEDS 'EM?!
LOOK, I'M KEEPING MY OPTIONS OPEN!
I ADMIRE YOUR HONESTY.

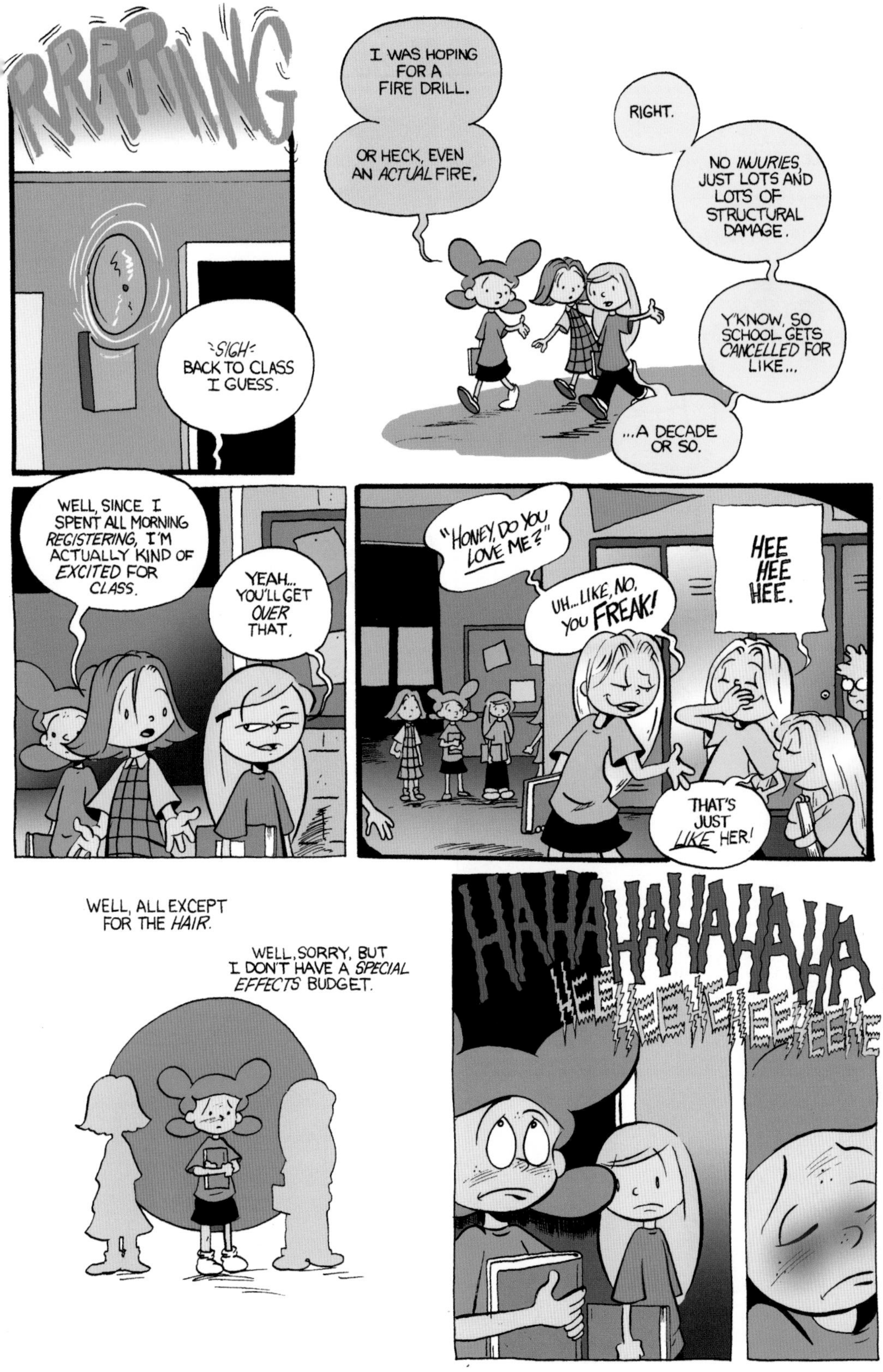
RRRRRRING
I WAS HOPING FOR A FIRE DRILL.
OR HECK, EVEN AN *ACTUAL* FIRE.
-SIGH- BACK TO CLASS I GUESS.
RIGHT.
NO *INJURIES*, JUST LOTS AND LOTS OF STRUCTURAL DAMAGE.
Y'KNOW, SO SCHOOL GETS *CANCELLED* FOR LIKE...
...A DECADE OR SO.
WELL, SINCE I SPENT ALL MORNING *REGISTERING*, I'M ACTUALLY KIND OF *EXCITED* FOR *CLASS*.
YEAH... YOU'LL GET *OVER* THAT.
"HONEY, DO YOU LOVE ME?"
UH...LIKE, NO, YOU FREAK!
HEE HEE HEE.
THAT'S JUST LIKE HER!
WELL, ALL EXCEPT FOR THE *HAIR*.
WELL, SORRY, BUT I DON'T HAVE A *SPECIAL EFFECTS* BUDGET.
HAHAHAHAHAHAHA
HEEHEEHEEHEEHEEHEE

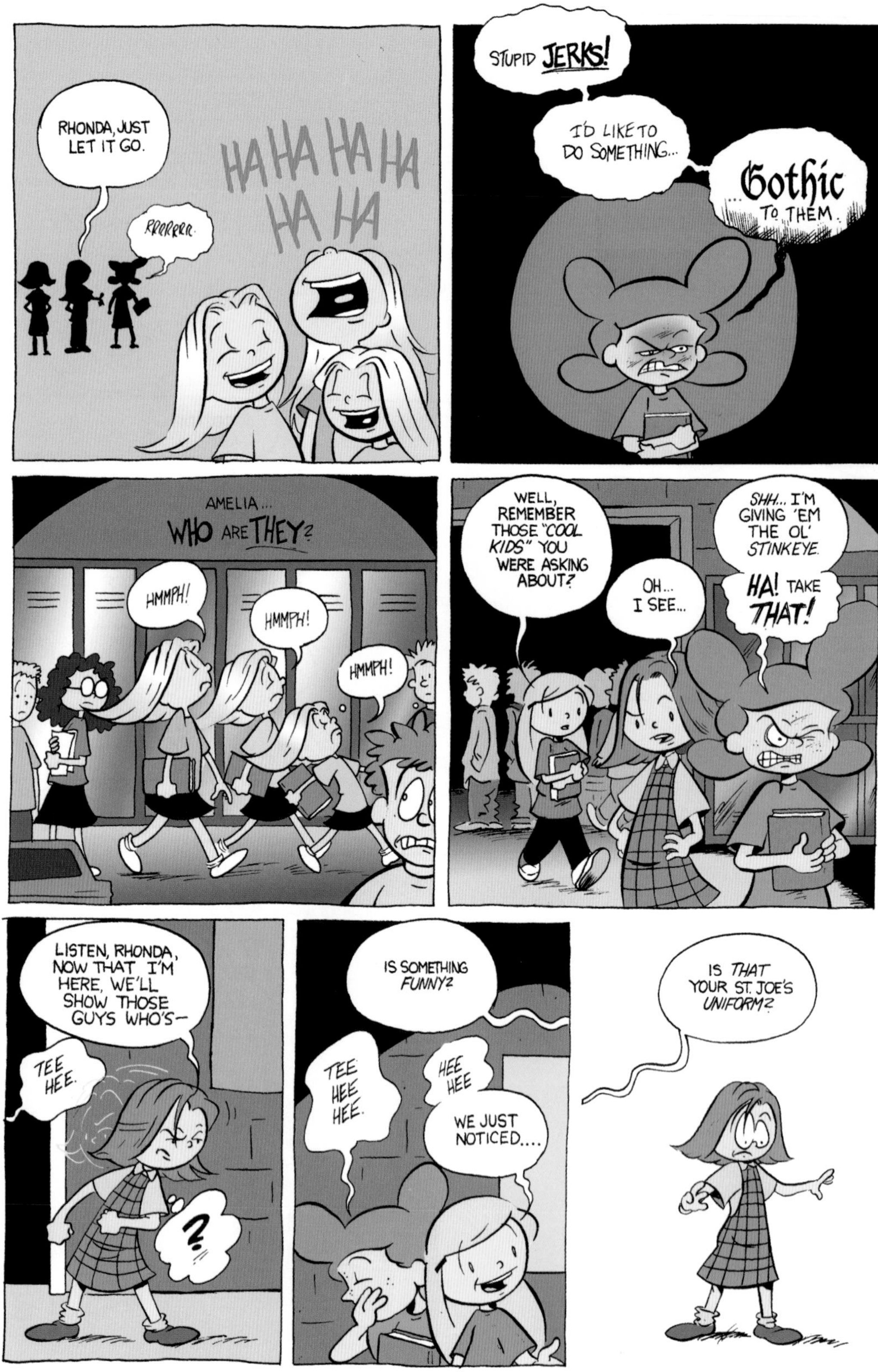
RHONDA, JUST LET IT GO.
HA HA HA HA HA HA
RRRRRRR
STUPID JERKS!
I'D LIKE TO DO SOMETHING...
...Gothic TO THEM.
AMELIA... WHO ARE THEY?
HMMPH!
HMMPH!
HMMPH!
WELL, REMEMBER THOSE "COOL KIDS" YOU WERE ASKING ABOUT?
OH... I SEE...
SHH... I'M GIVING 'EM THE OL' STINKEYE.
HA! TAKE THAT!
LISTEN, RHONDA, NOW THAT I'M HERE, WE'LL SHOW THOSE GUYS WHO'S—
TEE HEE.
?
IS SOMETHING FUNNY?
TEE HEE HEE.
HEE HEE
WE JUST NOTICED....
IS THAT YOUR ST. JOE'S UNIFORM?

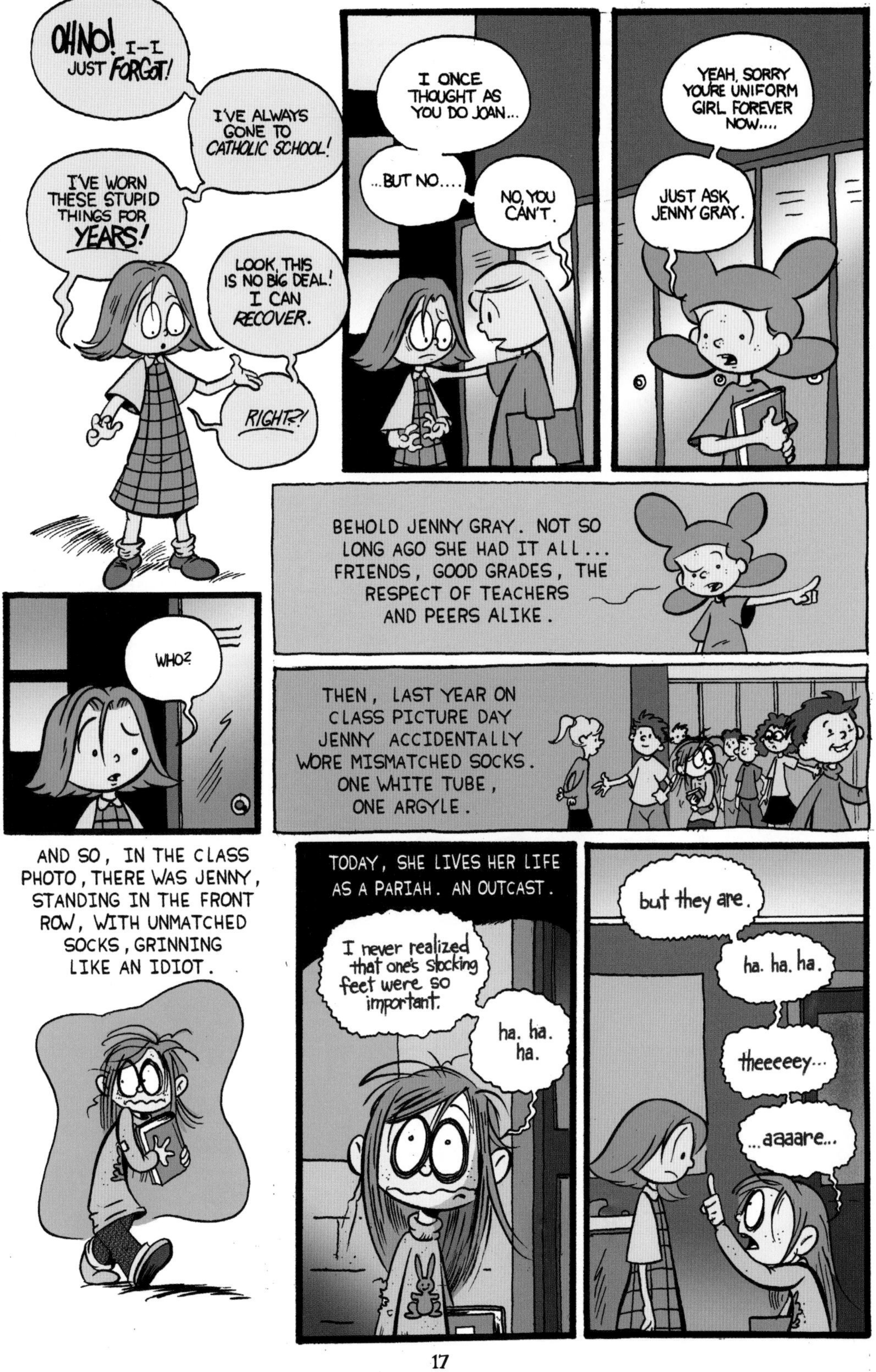
OH NO! I-I JUST FORGOT!
I'VE ALWAYS GONE TO CATHOLIC SCHOOL!
I'VE WORN THESE STUPID THINGS FOR YEARS!
LOOK, THIS IS NO BIG DEAL! I CAN RECOVER.
RIGHT?!
I ONCE THOUGHT AS YOU DO JOAN...
...BUT NO....
NO, YOU CAN'T.
YEAH, SORRY YOU'RE UNIFORM GIRL FOREVER NOW....
JUST ASK JENNY GRAY.
WHO?
BEHOLD JENNY GRAY. NOT SO LONG AGO SHE HAD IT ALL... FRIENDS, GOOD GRADES, THE RESPECT OF TEACHERS AND PEERS ALIKE.
THEN, LAST YEAR ON CLASS PICTURE DAY JENNY ACCIDENTALLY WORE MISMATCHED SOCKS. ONE WHITE TUBE, ONE ARGYLE.
AND SO, IN THE CLASS PHOTO, THERE WAS JENNY, STANDING IN THE FRONT ROW, WITH UNMATCHED SOCKS, GRINNING LIKE AN IDIOT.
TODAY, SHE LIVES HER LIFE AS A PARIAH. AN OUTCAST.
I never realized that one's stocking feet were so important.
ha. ha. ha.
but they are.
ha. ha. ha.
theeeeey...
...aaaare...

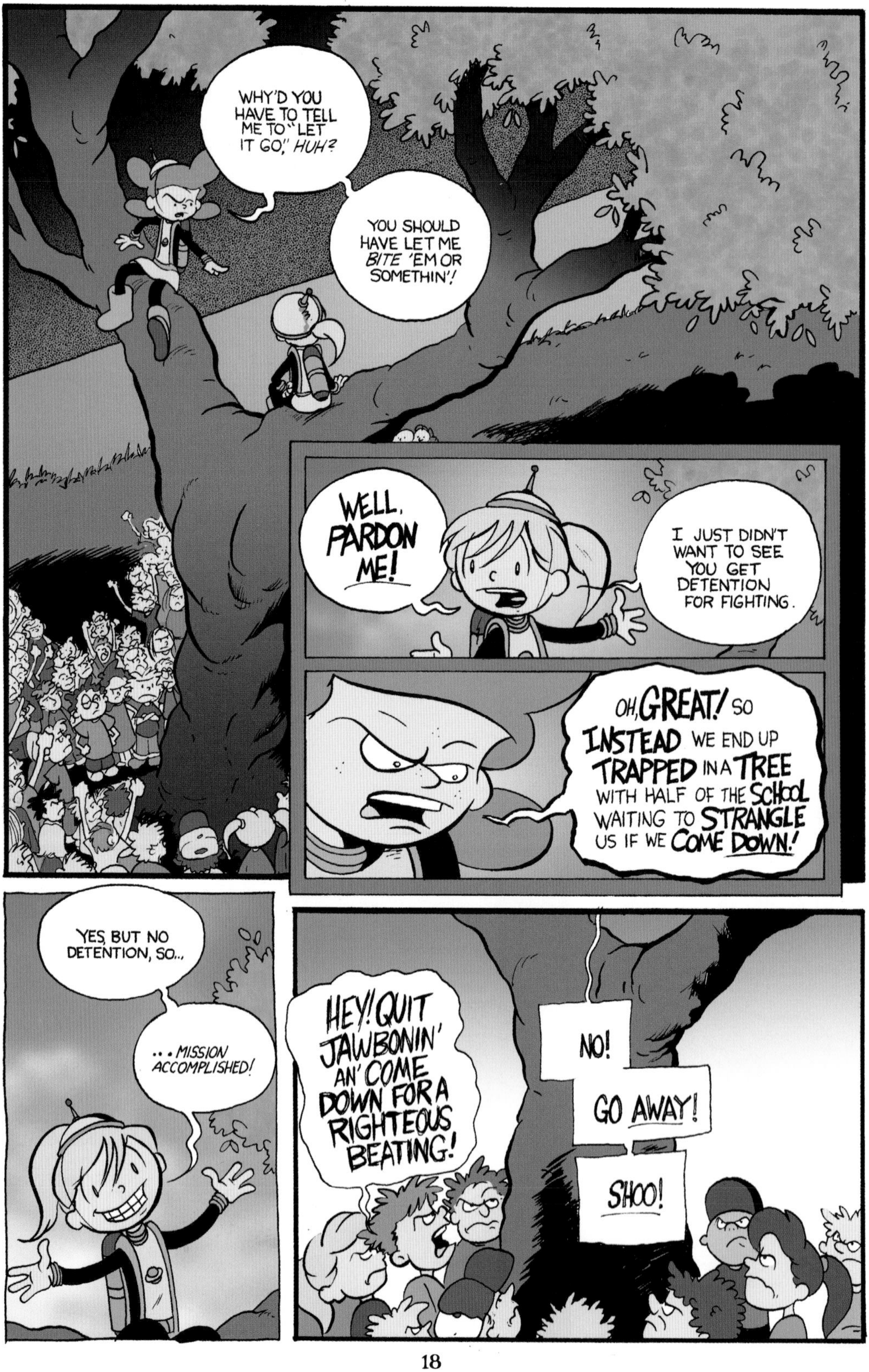
WHY'D YOU HAVE TO TELL ME TO "LET IT GO," HUH?
YOU SHOULD HAVE LET ME BITE 'EM OR SOMETHIN'!
WELL, PARDON ME!
I JUST DIDN'T WANT TO SEE YOU GET DETENTION FOR FIGHTING.
OH, GREAT! SO INSTEAD WE END UP TRAPPED IN A TREE WITH HALF OF THE SCHOOL WAITING TO STRANGLE US IF WE COME DOWN!
YES, BUT NO DETENTION, SO...
...MISSION ACCOMPLISHED!
HEY! QUIT JAWBONIN' AN' COME DOWN FOR A RIGHTEOUS BEATING!
NO!
GO AWAY!
SHOO!

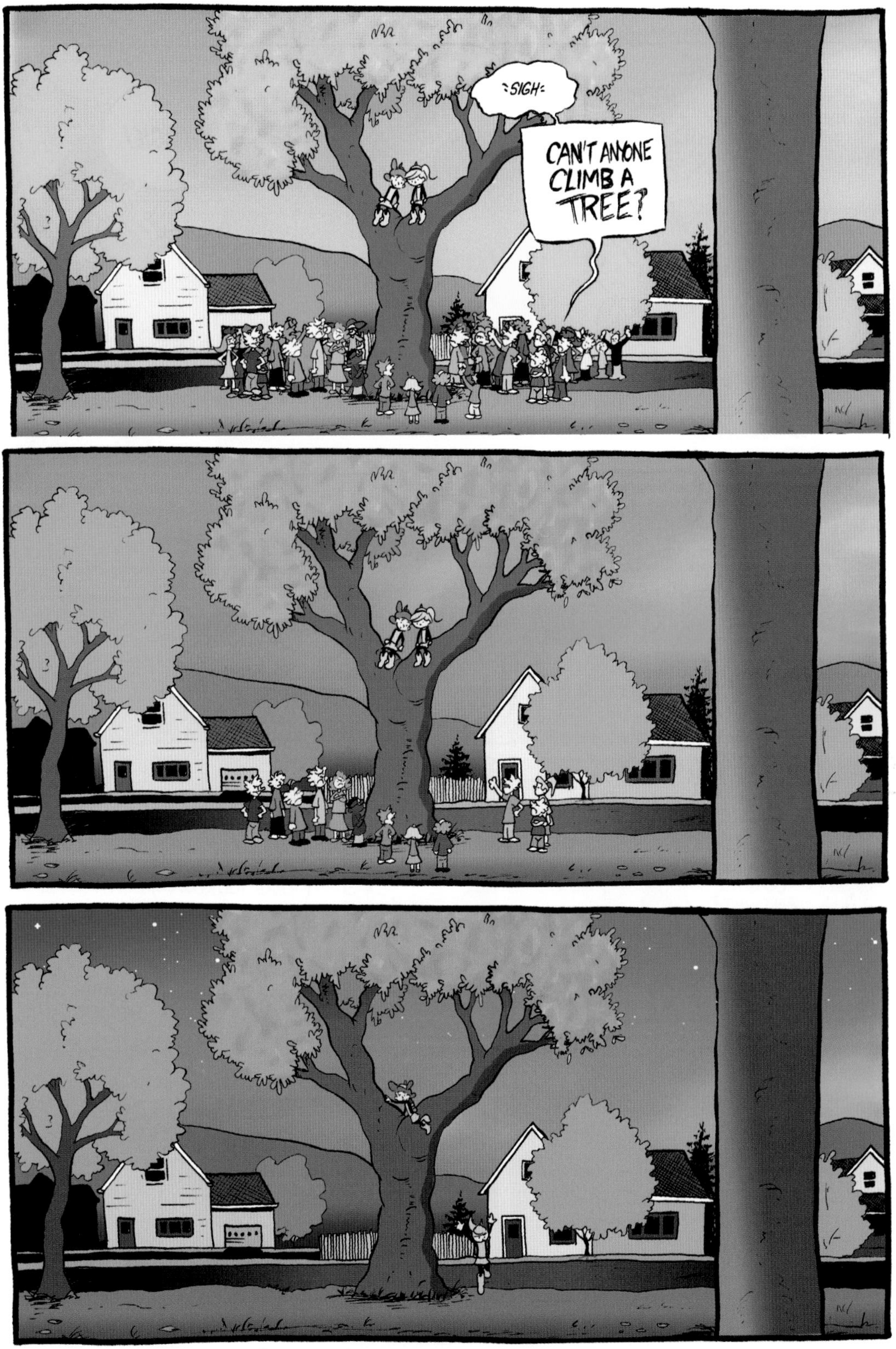
SIGH
CAN'T ANYONE CLIMB A TREE?

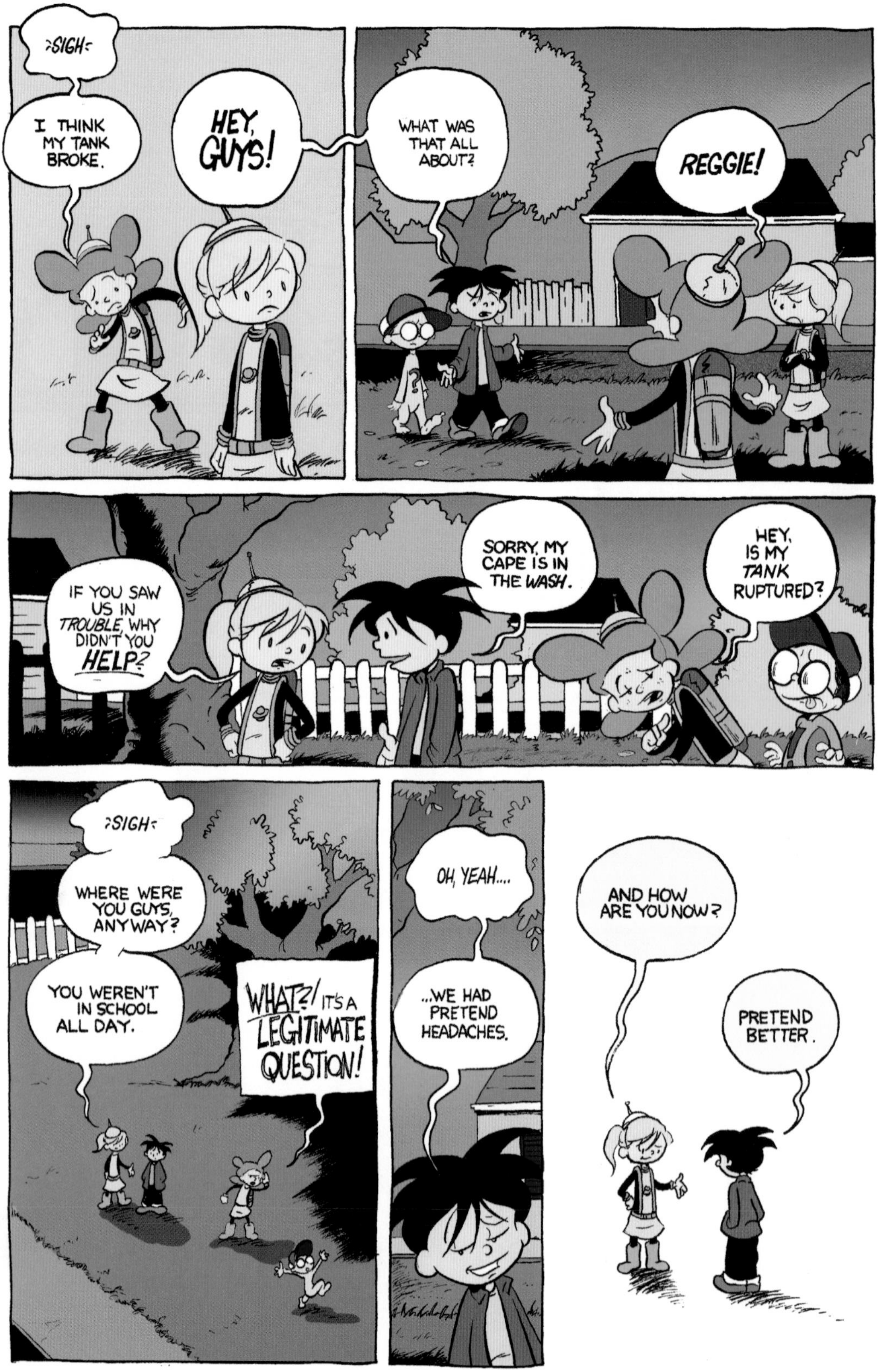

~SIGH~
I THINK MY TANK BROKE.
HEY, GUYS!
WHAT WAS THAT ALL ABOUT?
REGGIE!
IF YOU SAW US IN TROUBLE, WHY DIDN'T YOU HELP?
SORRY, MY CAPE IS IN THE WASH.
HEY, IS MY TANK RUPTURED?
~SIGH~
WHERE WERE YOU GUYS, ANYWAY?
YOU WEREN'T IN SCHOOL ALL DAY.
WHAT?! IT'S A LEGITIMATE QUESTION!
OH, YEAH....
...WE HAD PRETEND HEADACHES.
AND HOW ARE YOU NOW?
PRETEND BETTER.

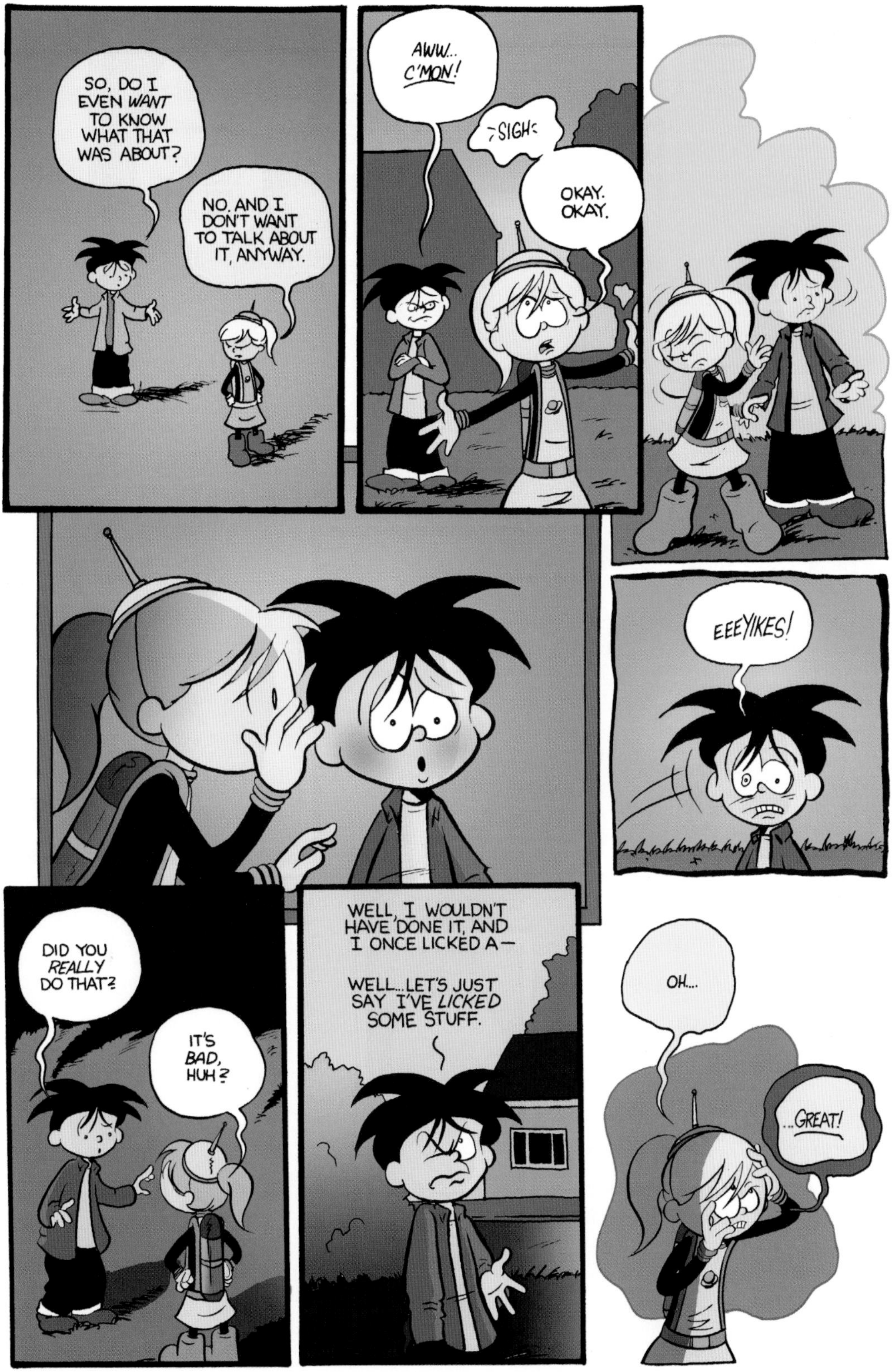
SO, DO I EVEN *WANT* TO KNOW WHAT THAT WAS ABOUT?
NO. AND I DON'T WANT TO TALK ABOUT IT, ANYWAY.
AWW... C'MON!
SIGH
OKAY. OKAY.
EEEYIKES!
DID YOU *REALLY* DO THAT?
IT'S *BAD*, HUH?
WELL, I WOULDN'T HAVE DONE IT, AND I ONCE LICKED A—
WELL...LET'S JUST SAY I'VE *LICKED* SOME STUFF.
OH...
...GREAT!

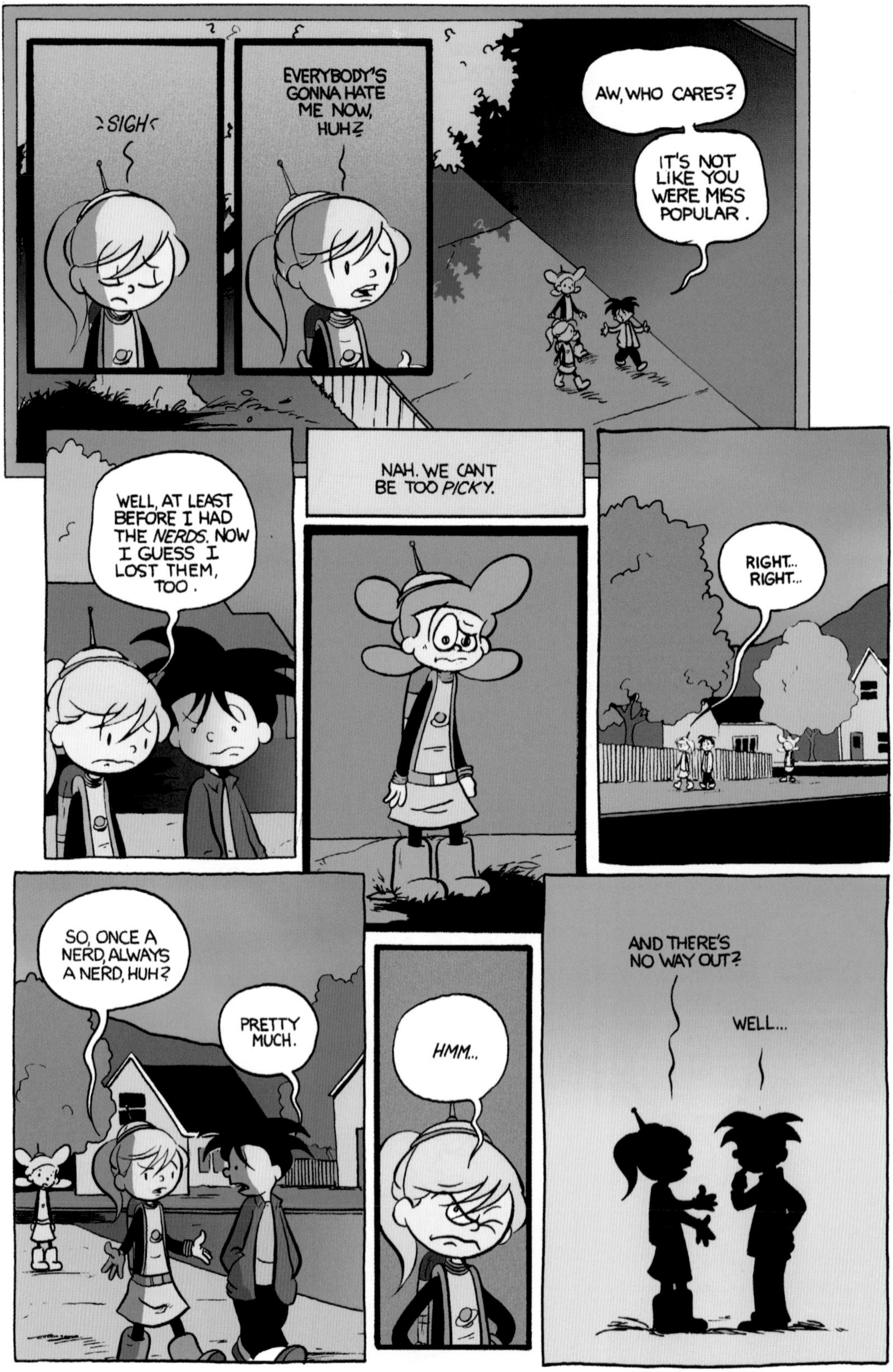

SIGH
EVERYBODY'S GONNA HATE ME NOW, HUH?
AW, WHO CARES?
IT'S NOT LIKE YOU WERE MISS POPULAR.
WELL, AT LEAST BEFORE I HAD THE *NERDS*. NOW I GUESS I LOST THEM, TOO.
NAH. WE CANT BE TOO *PICKY*.
RIGHT... RIGHT...
SO, ONCE A NERD, ALWAYS A NERD, HUH?
PRETTY MUCH.
HMM...
AND THERE'S NO WAY OUT?
WELL...

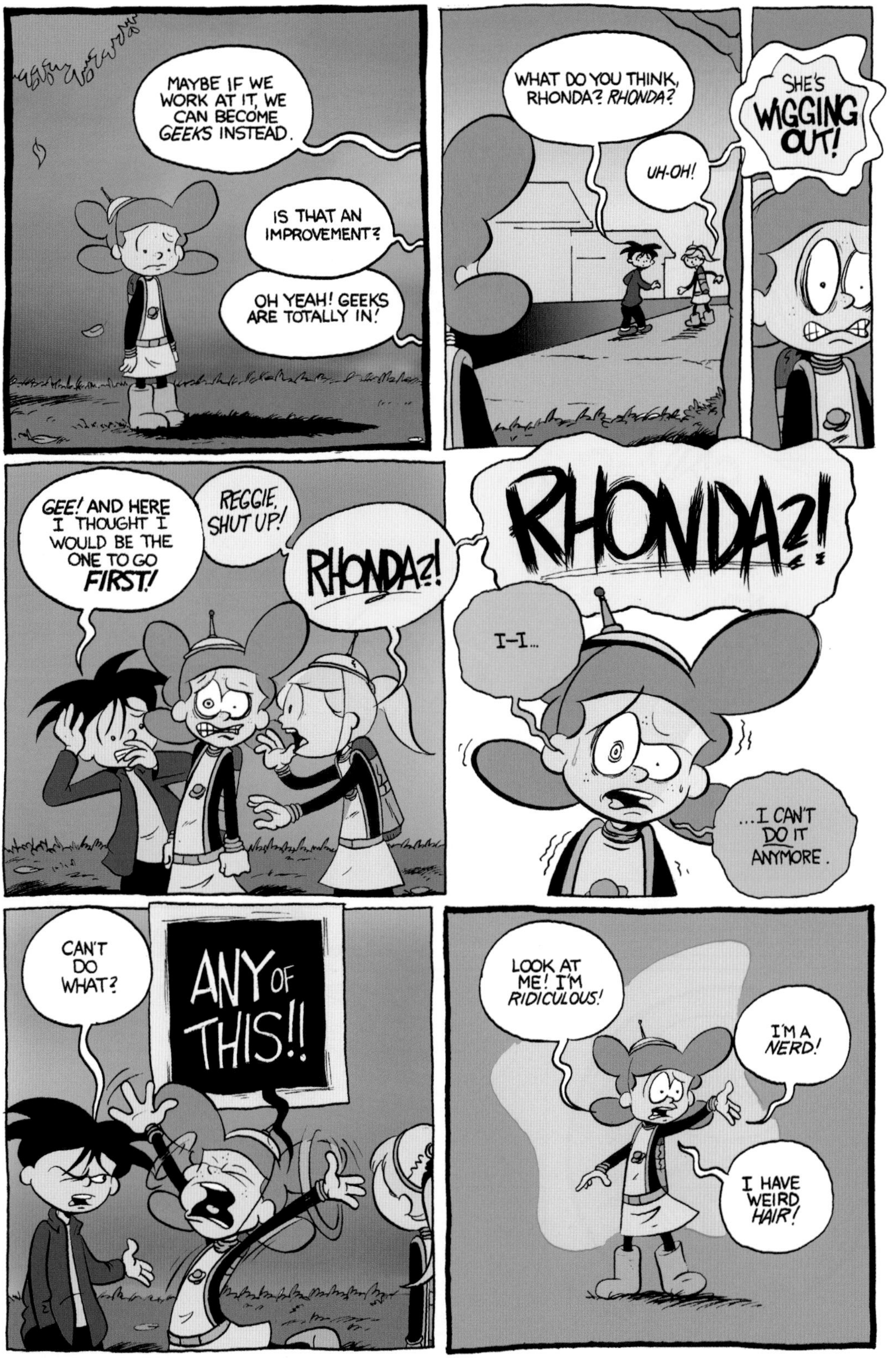
MAYBE IF WE WORK AT IT, WE CAN BECOME GEEKS INSTEAD.
IS THAT AN IMPROVEMENT?
OH YEAH! GEEKS ARE TOTALLY IN!
WHAT DO YOU THINK, RHONDA? RHONDA?
UH-OH!
SHE'S WIGGING OUT!
GEE! AND HERE I THOUGHT I WOULD BE THE ONE TO GO FIRST!
REGGIE, SHUT UP!
RHONDA?!
RHONDA?!
I-I...
...I CAN'T DO IT ANYMORE.
CAN'T DO WHAT?
ANY OF THIS!!
LOOK AT ME! I'M RIDICULOUS!
I'M A NERD!
I HAVE WEIRD HAIR!

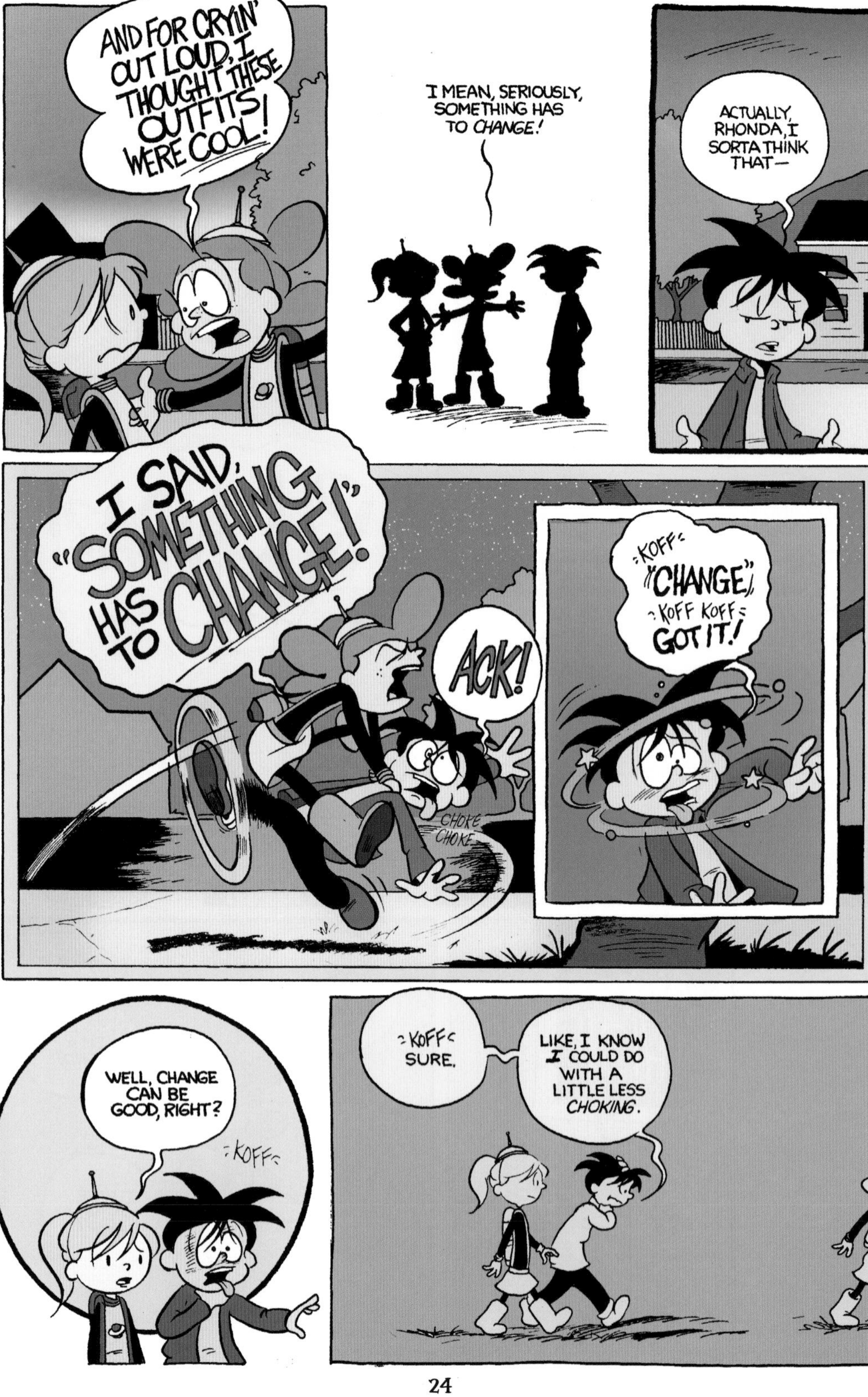
AND FOR CRYIN' OUT LOUD, I THOUGHT THESE OUTFITS WERE COOL!
I MEAN, SERIOUSLY, SOMETHING HAS TO CHANGE!
ACTUALLY, RHONDA, I SORTA THINK THAT—
I SAID, "SOMETHING HAS TO CHANGE!"
ACK!
CHOKE CHOKE
KOFF "CHANGE" KOFF KOFF GOT IT!
WELL, CHANGE CAN BE GOOD, RIGHT?
KOFF
KOFF SURE.
LIKE, I KNOW I COULD DO WITH A LITTLE LESS CHOKING.

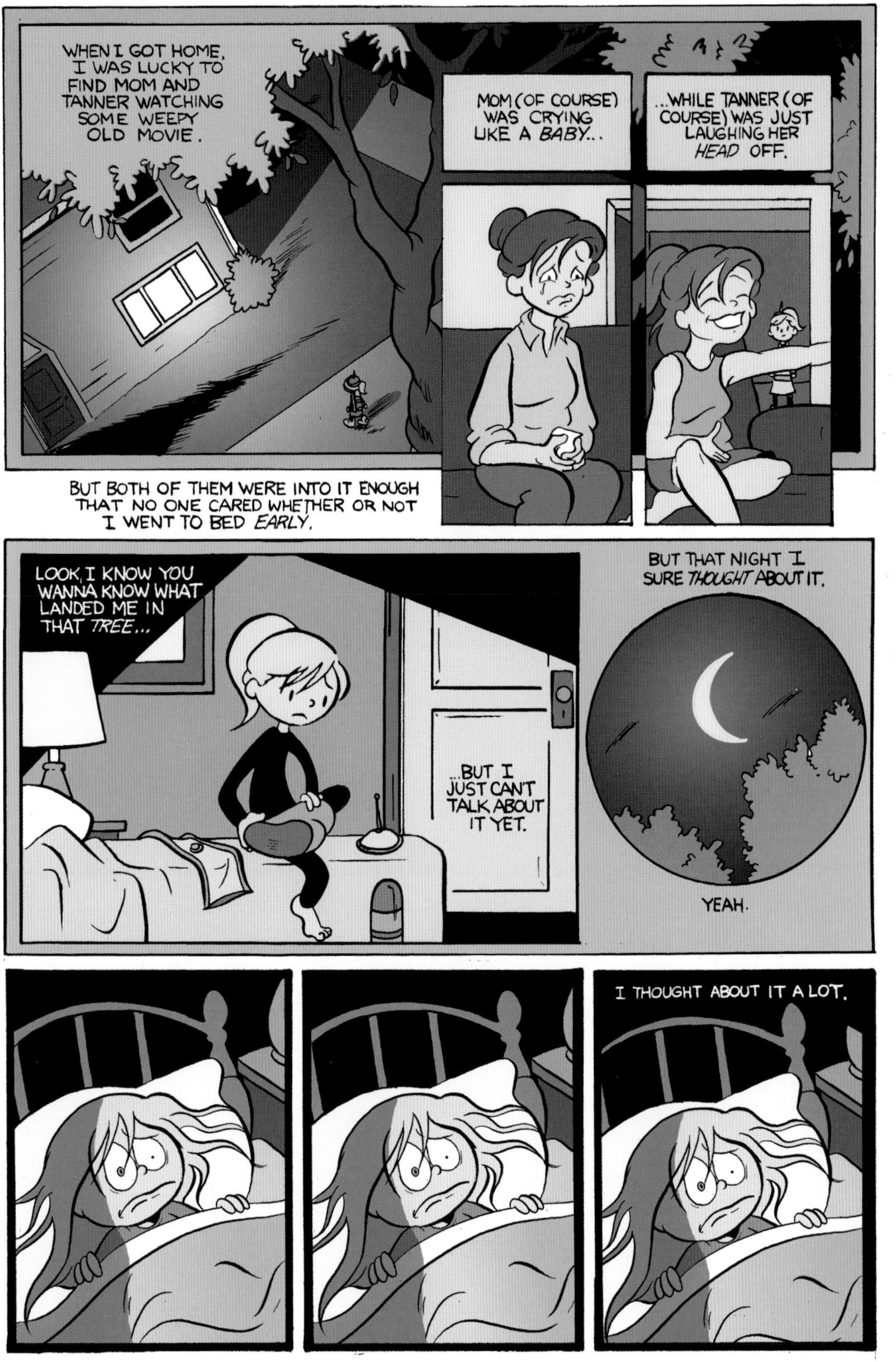
WHEN I GOT HOME, I WAS LUCKY TO FIND MOM AND TANNER WATCHING SOME WEEPY OLD MOVIE.
MOM (OF COURSE) WAS CRYING LIKE A *BABY*...
...WHILE TANNER (OF COURSE) WAS JUST LAUGHING HER *HEAD* OFF.
BUT BOTH OF THEM WERE INTO IT ENOUGH THAT NO ONE CARED WHETHER OR NOT I WENT TO BED *EARLY*.
LOOK, I KNOW YOU WANNA KNOW WHAT LANDED ME IN THAT *TREE*...
...BUT I JUST CAN'T TALK ABOUT IT YET.
BUT THAT NIGHT I SURE *THOUGHT* ABOUT IT.
YEAH.
I THOUGHT ABOUT IT A LOT.

the BLACK MARK

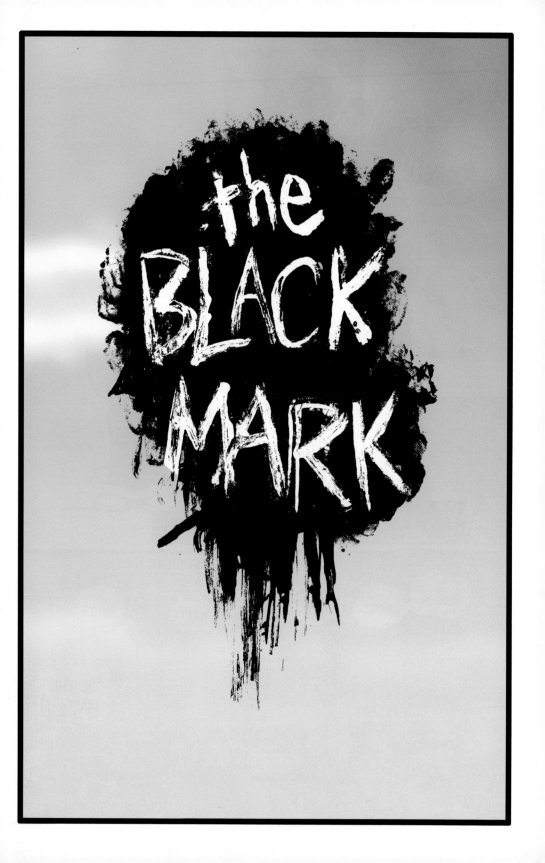

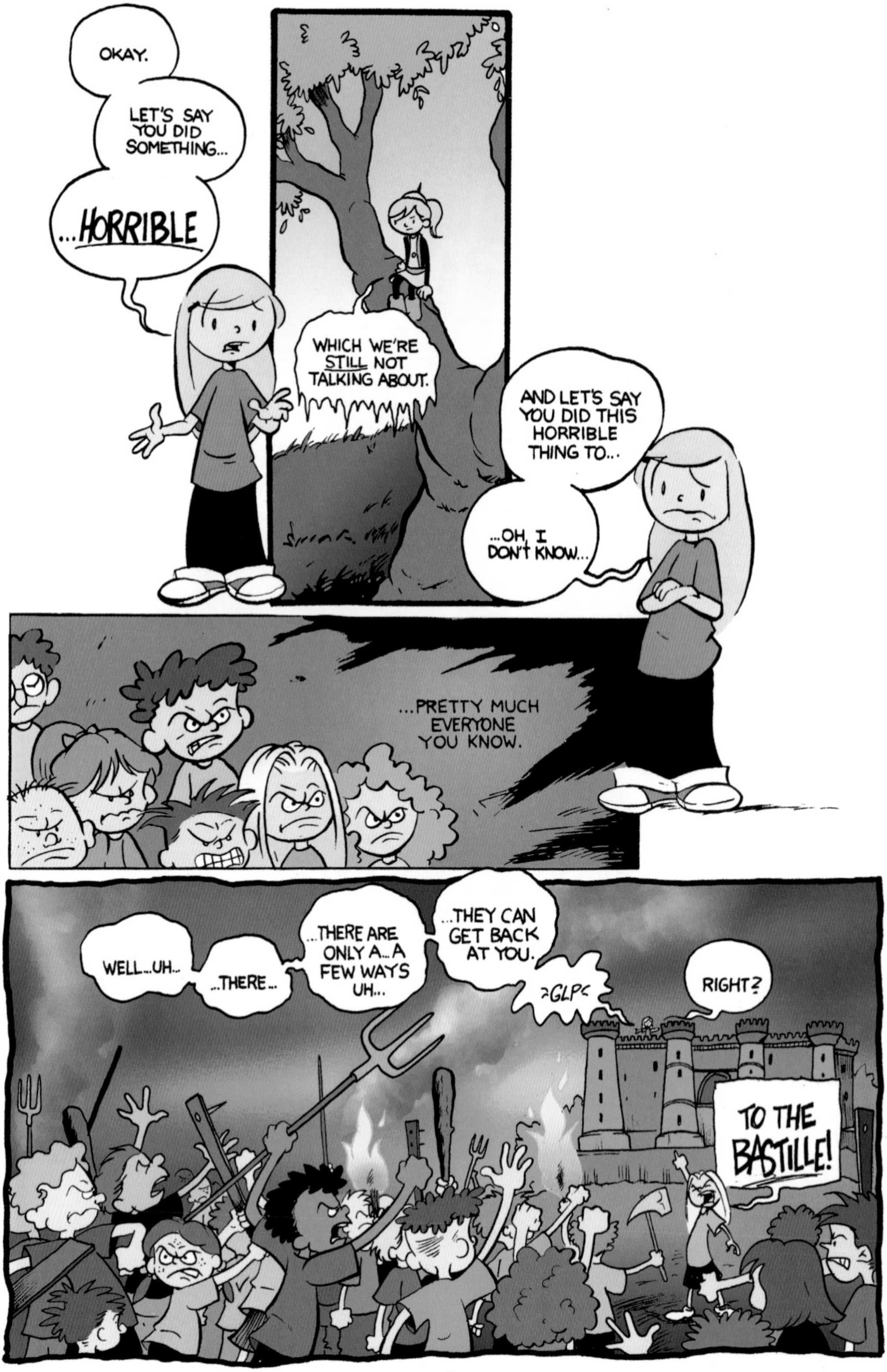
OKAY.
LET'S SAY YOU DID SOMETHING...
...HORRIBLE
WHICH WE'RE STILL NOT TALKING ABOUT.
AND LET'S SAY YOU DID THIS HORRIBLE THING TO...
...OH, I DON'T KNOW...
...PRETTY MUCH EVERYONE YOU KNOW.
WELL...UH...
...THERE...
...THERE ARE ONLY A...A FEW WAYS UH...
...THEY CAN GET BACK AT YOU.
GLP
RIGHT?
TO THE BASTILLE!

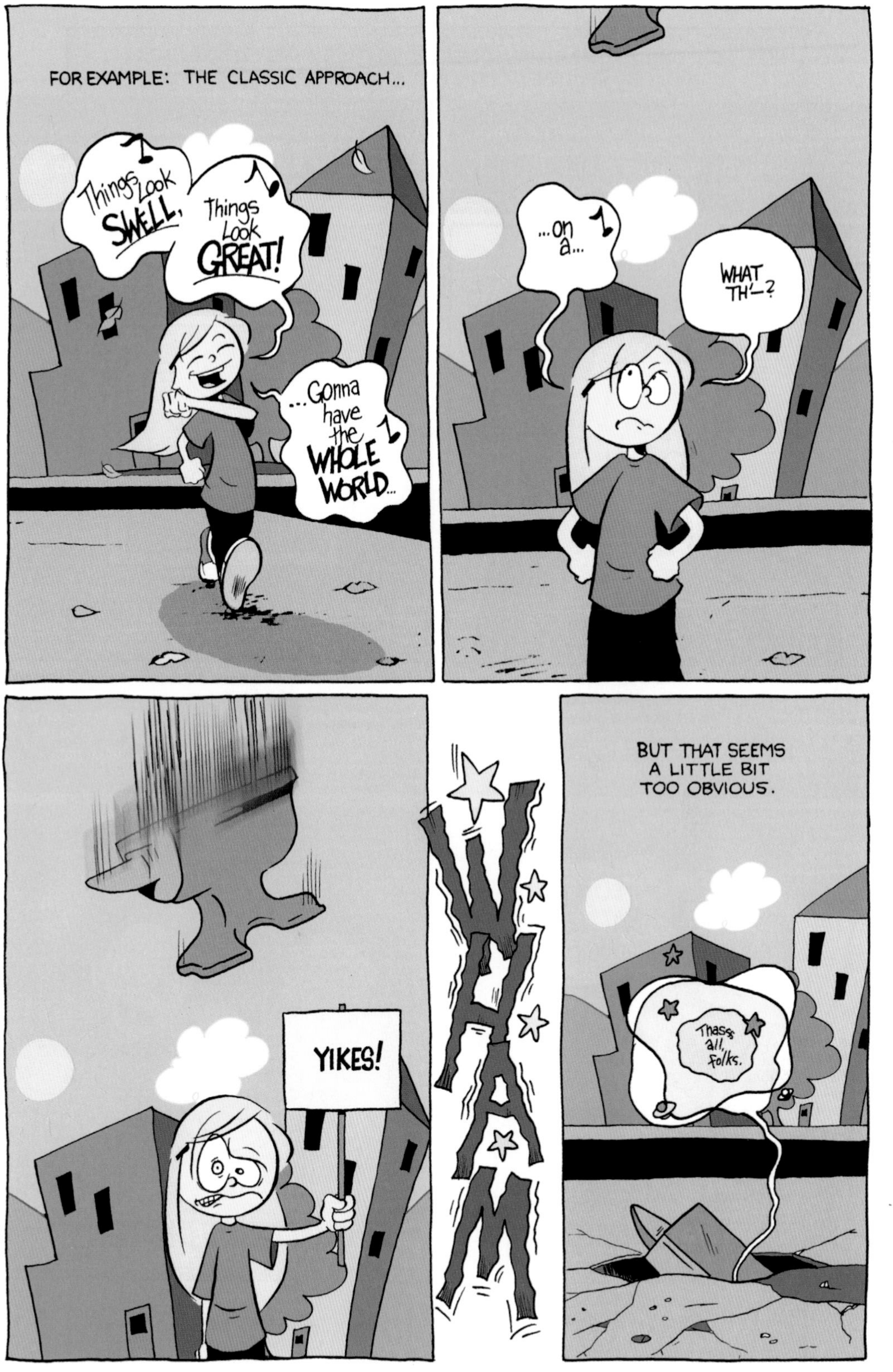
FOR EXAMPLE: THE CLASSIC APPROACH...
Things Look SWELL,
things Look GREAT!
...Gonna have the WHOLE WORLD...
...on a...
WHAT TH'—?
YIKES!
WHAM
BUT THAT SEEMS A LITTLE BIT TOO OBVIOUS.
Thasss all, folks.

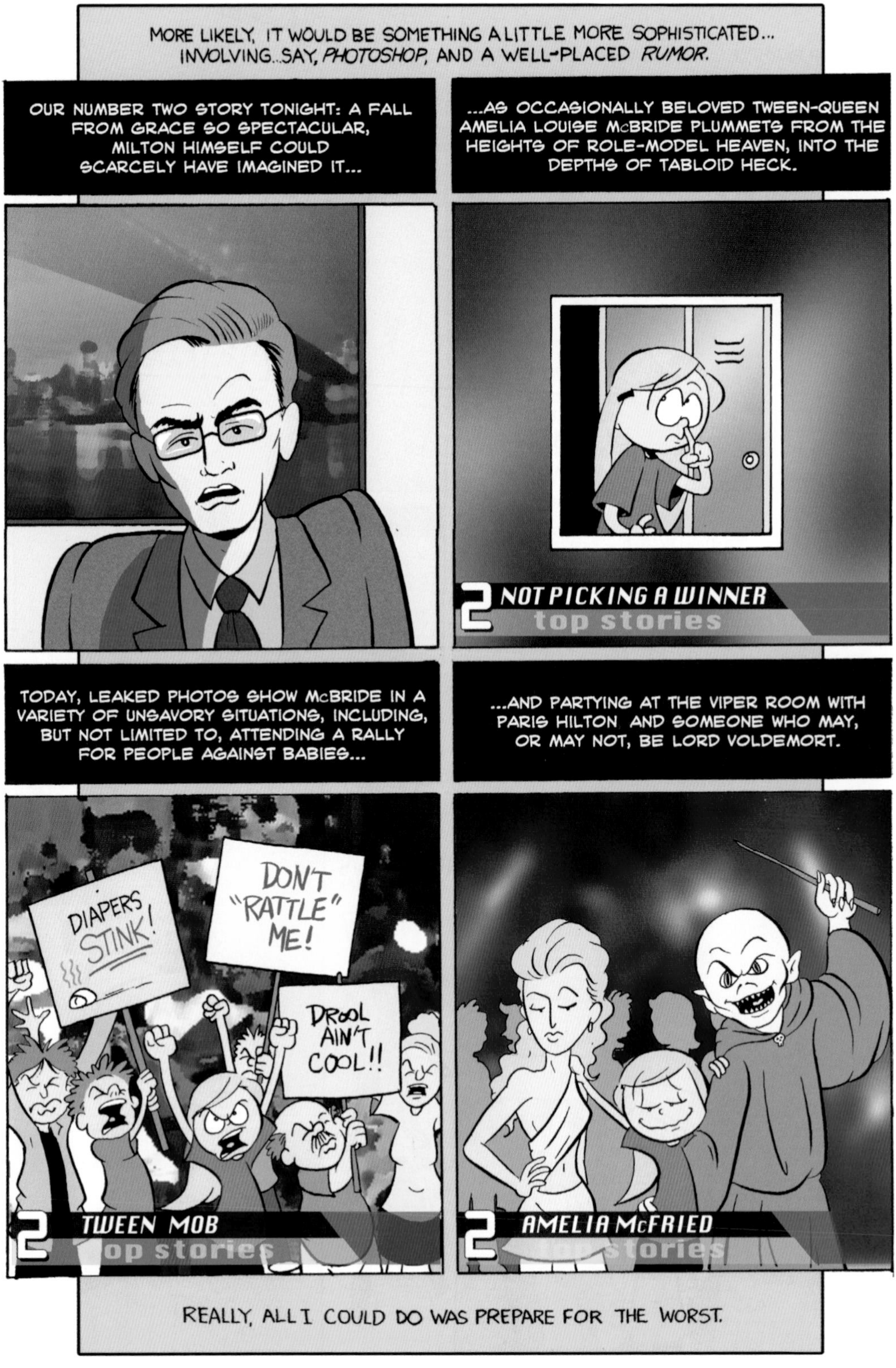
MORE LIKELY, IT WOULD BE SOMETHING A LITTLE MORE SOPHISTICATED... INVOLVING...SAY, *PHOTOSHOP*, AND A WELL-PLACED *RUMOR*.
OUR NUMBER TWO STORY TONIGHT: A FALL FROM GRACE SO SPECTACULAR, MILTON HIMSELF COULD SCARCELY HAVE IMAGINED IT...
...AS OCCASIONALLY BELOVED TWEEN-QUEEN AMELIA LOUISE McBRIDE PLUMMETS FROM THE HEIGHTS OF ROLE-MODEL HEAVEN, INTO THE DEPTHS OF TABLOID HECK.
2 NOT PICKING A WINNER
top stories
TODAY, LEAKED PHOTOS SHOW McBRIDE IN A VARIETY OF UNSAVORY SITUATIONS, INCLUDING, BUT NOT LIMITED TO, ATTENDING A RALLY FOR PEOPLE AGAINST BABIES...
...AND PARTYING AT THE VIPER ROOM WITH PARIS HILTON AND SOMEONE WHO MAY, OR MAY NOT, BE LORD VOLDEMORT.
DIAPERS STINK!
DON'T "RATTLE" ME!
DROOL AIN'T COOL!!
2 TWEEN MOB
top stories
2 AMELIA McFRIED
top stories
REALLY, ALL I COULD DO WAS PREPARE FOR THE WORST.

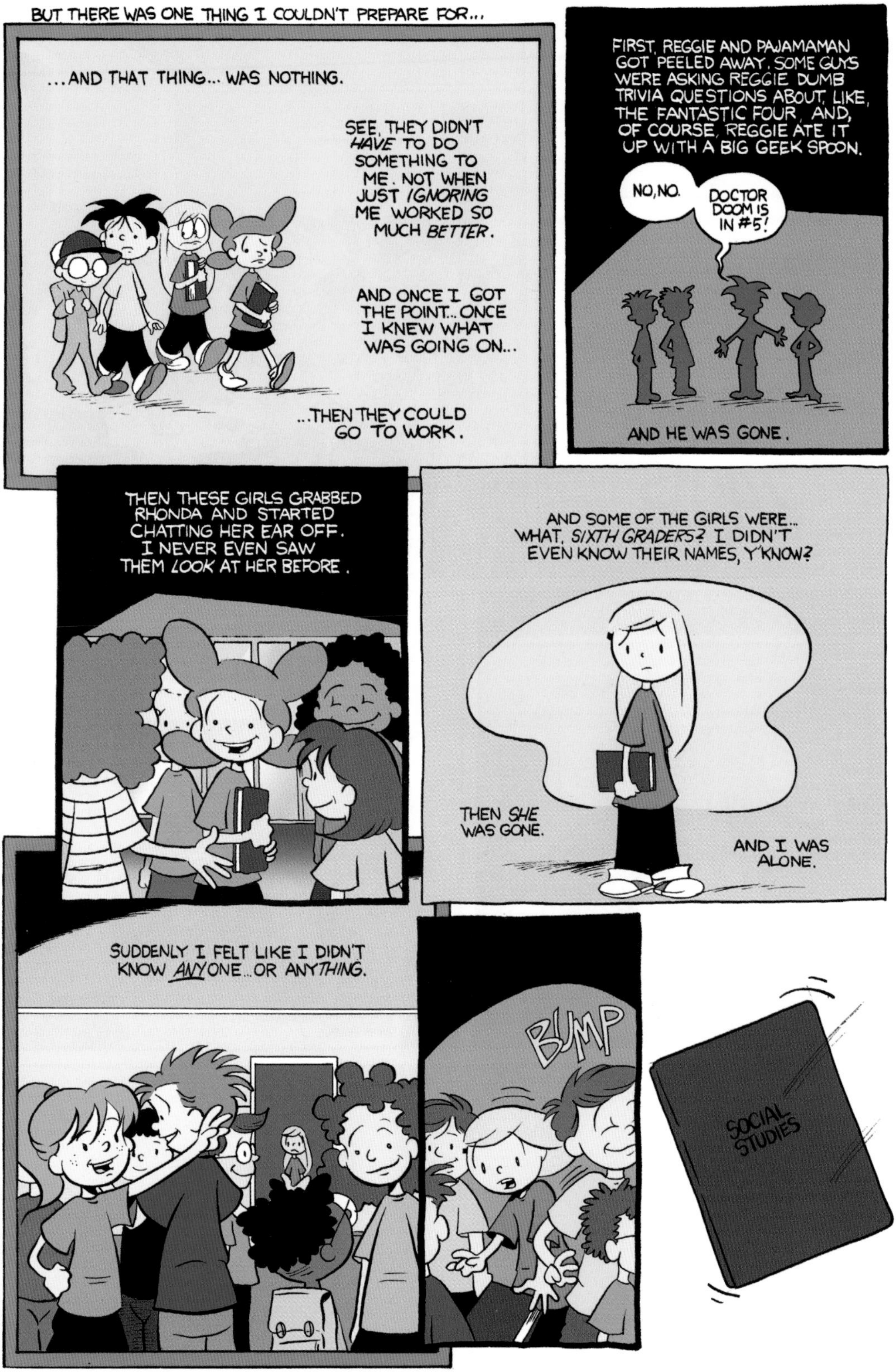

BUT THERE WAS ONE THING I COULDN'T PREPARE FOR...
...AND THAT THING... WAS NOTHING.
SEE, THEY DIDN'T HAVE TO DO SOMETHING TO ME. NOT WHEN JUST IGNORING ME WORKED SO MUCH BETTER.
AND ONCE I GOT THE POINT... ONCE I KNEW WHAT WAS GOING ON...
...THEN THEY COULD GO TO WORK.
FIRST, REGGIE AND PAJAMAMAN GOT PEELED AWAY. SOME GUYS WERE ASKING REGGIE DUMB TRIVIA QUESTIONS ABOUT, LIKE, THE FANTASTIC FOUR, AND, OF COURSE, REGGIE ATE IT UP WITH A BIG GEEK SPOON.
NO, NO.
DOCTOR DOOM IS IN #5!
AND HE WAS GONE.
THEN THESE GIRLS GRABBED RHONDA AND STARTED CHATTING HER EAR OFF. I NEVER EVEN SAW THEM LOOK AT HER BEFORE.
AND SOME OF THE GIRLS WERE... WHAT, SIXTH GRADERS? I DIDN'T EVEN KNOW THEIR NAMES, Y'KNOW?
THEN SHE WAS GONE.
AND I WAS ALONE.
SUDDENLY I FELT LIKE I DIDN'T KNOW ANYONE... OR ANYTHING.
BUMP
SOCIAL STUDIES

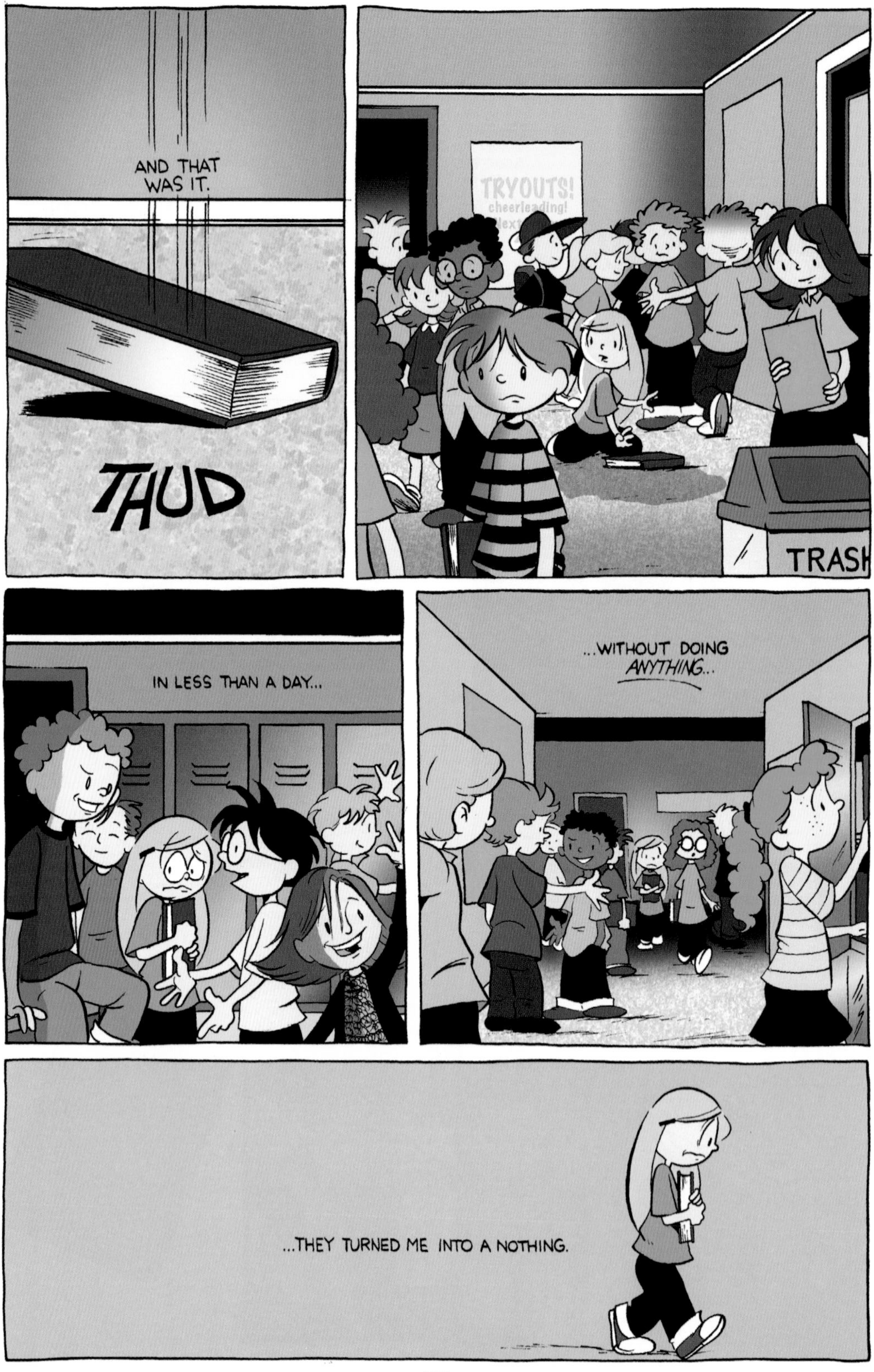
AND THAT WAS IT.
THUD
TRYOUTS!
cheerleading!
TRASH
IN LESS THAN A DAY...
...WITHOUT DOING ANYTHING...
...THEY TURNED ME INTO A NOTHING.

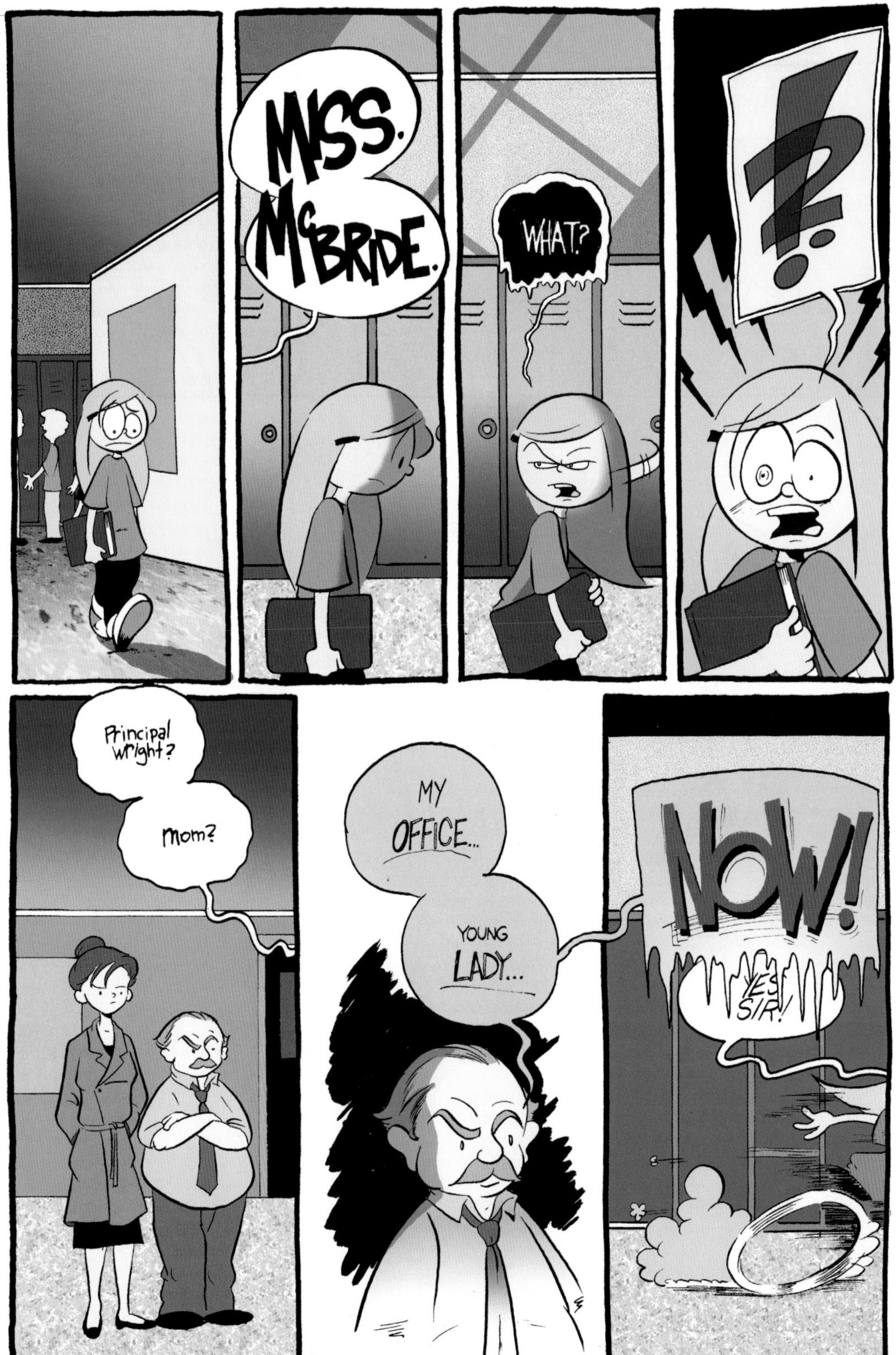
MISS. McBRIDE.
WHAT?
?!
Principal wright?
mom?
MY OFFICE...
YOUNG LADY...
NOW!
YES SIR!

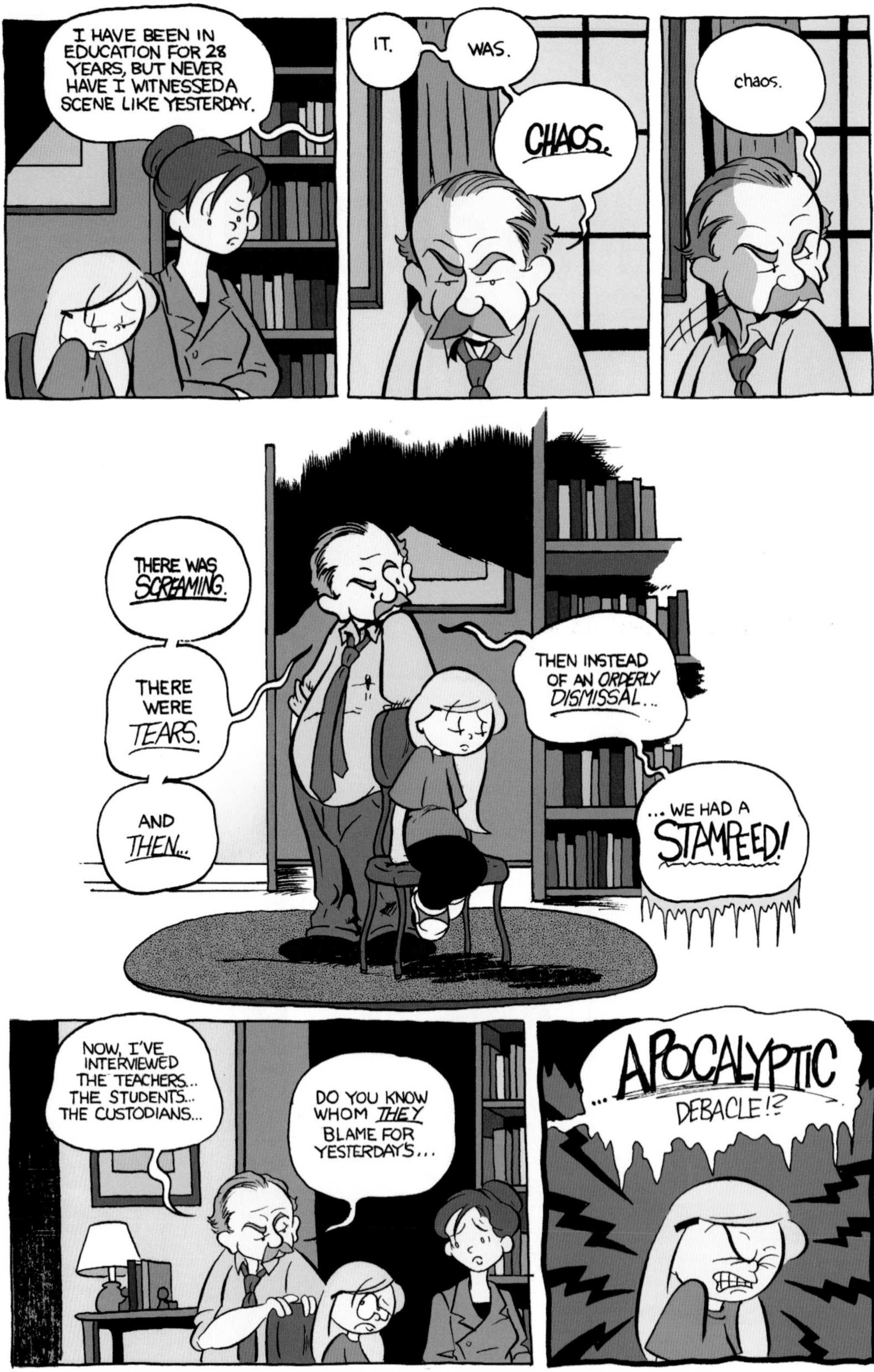
I HAVE BEEN IN EDUCATION FOR 28 YEARS, BUT NEVER HAVE I WITNESSEDA SCENE LIKE YESTERDAY.
IT.
WAS.
CHAOS.
chaos.
THERE WAS SCREAMING.
THERE WERE TEARS.
AND THEN...
THEN INSTEAD OF AN ORDERLY DISMISSAL...
...WE HAD A STAMPEED!
NOW, I'VE INTERVIEWED THE TEACHERS... THE STUDENTS... THE CUSTODIANS...
DO YOU KNOW WHOM THEY BLAME FOR YESTERDAY'S...
...APOCALYPTIC DEBACLE!?

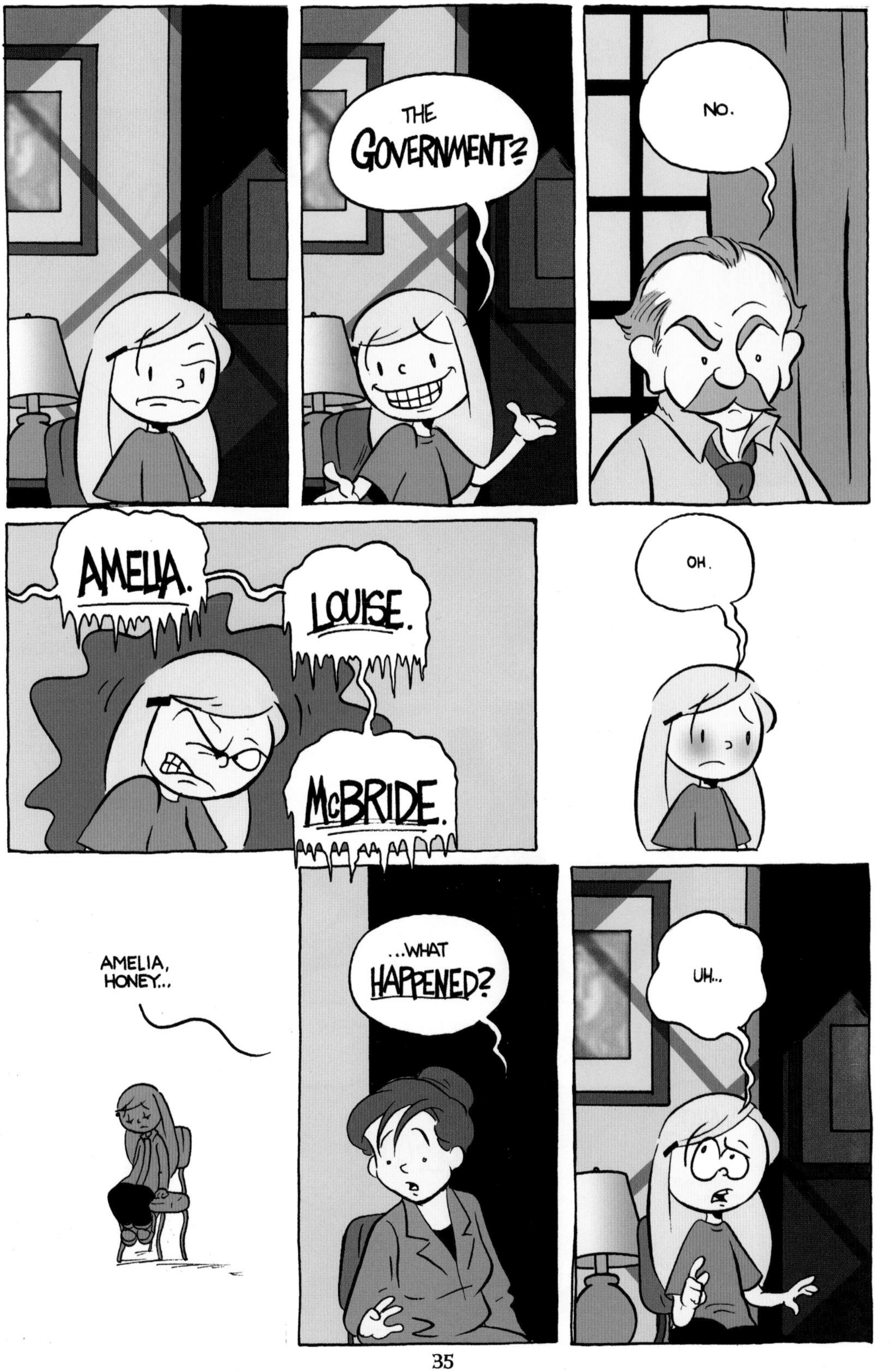
THE GOVERNMENT?
NO.
AMELIA.
LOUISE.
McBRIDE.
OH.
AMELIA, HONEY...
...WHAT HAPPENED?
UH...

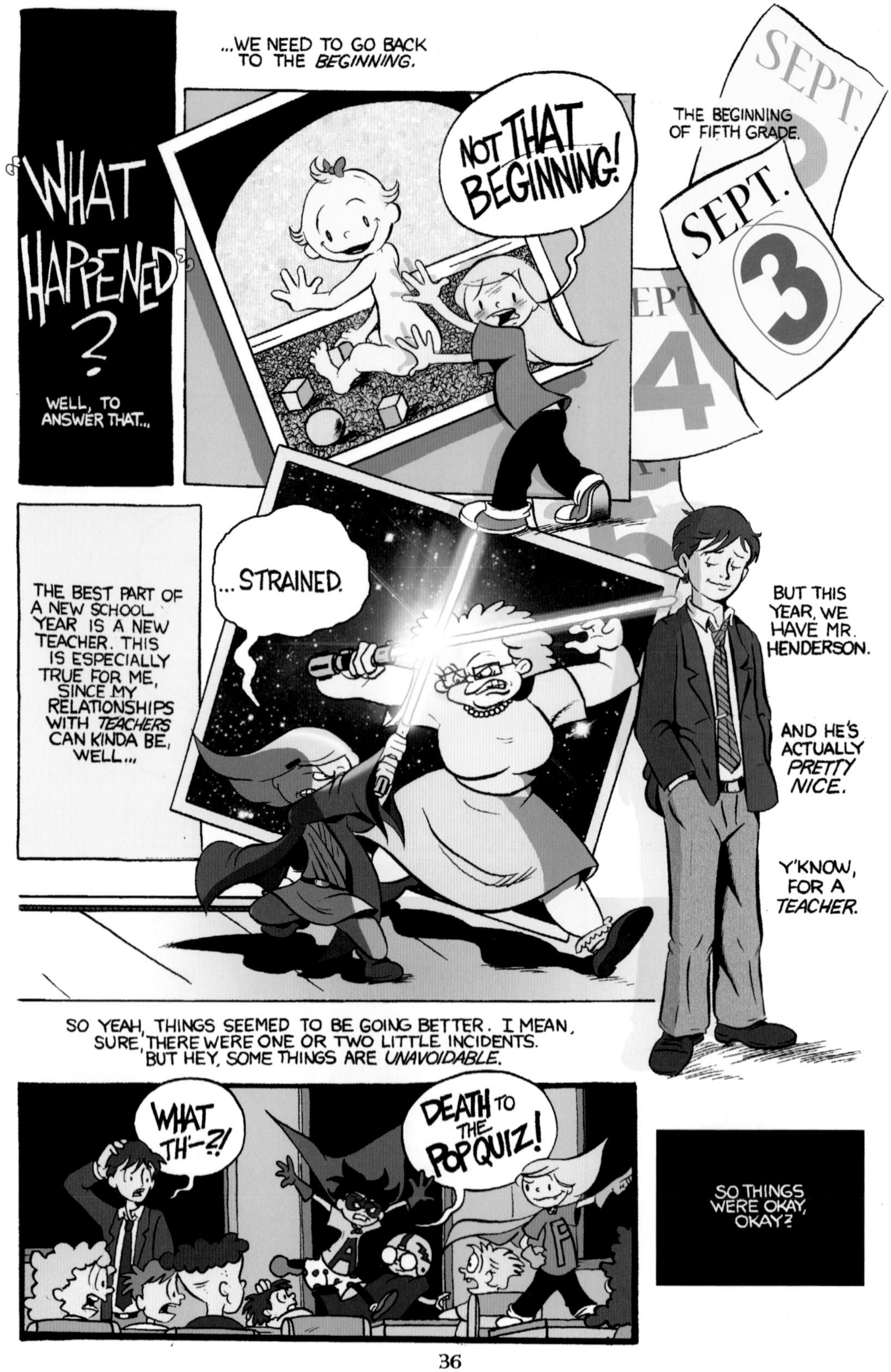
"WHAT HAPPENED"?
WELL, TO ANSWER THAT...
...WE NEED TO GO BACK TO THE BEGINNING.
NOT THAT BEGINNING!
THE BEGINNING OF FIFTH GRADE.
SEPT. 3
SEPT. 4
THE BEST PART OF A NEW SCHOOL YEAR IS A NEW TEACHER. THIS IS ESPECIALLY TRUE FOR ME, SINCE MY RELATIONSHIPS WITH TEACHERS CAN KINDA BE, WELL...
...STRAINED.
BUT THIS YEAR, WE HAVE MR. HENDERSON.
AND HE'S ACTUALLY PRETTY NICE.
Y'KNOW, FOR A TEACHER.
SO YEAH, THINGS SEEMED TO BE GOING BETTER. I MEAN, SURE, THERE WERE ONE OR TWO LITTLE INCIDENTS. BUT HEY, SOME THINGS ARE UNAVOIDABLE.
WHAT TH-?!
DEATH TO THE POP QUIZ!
SO THINGS WERE OKAY, OKAY?

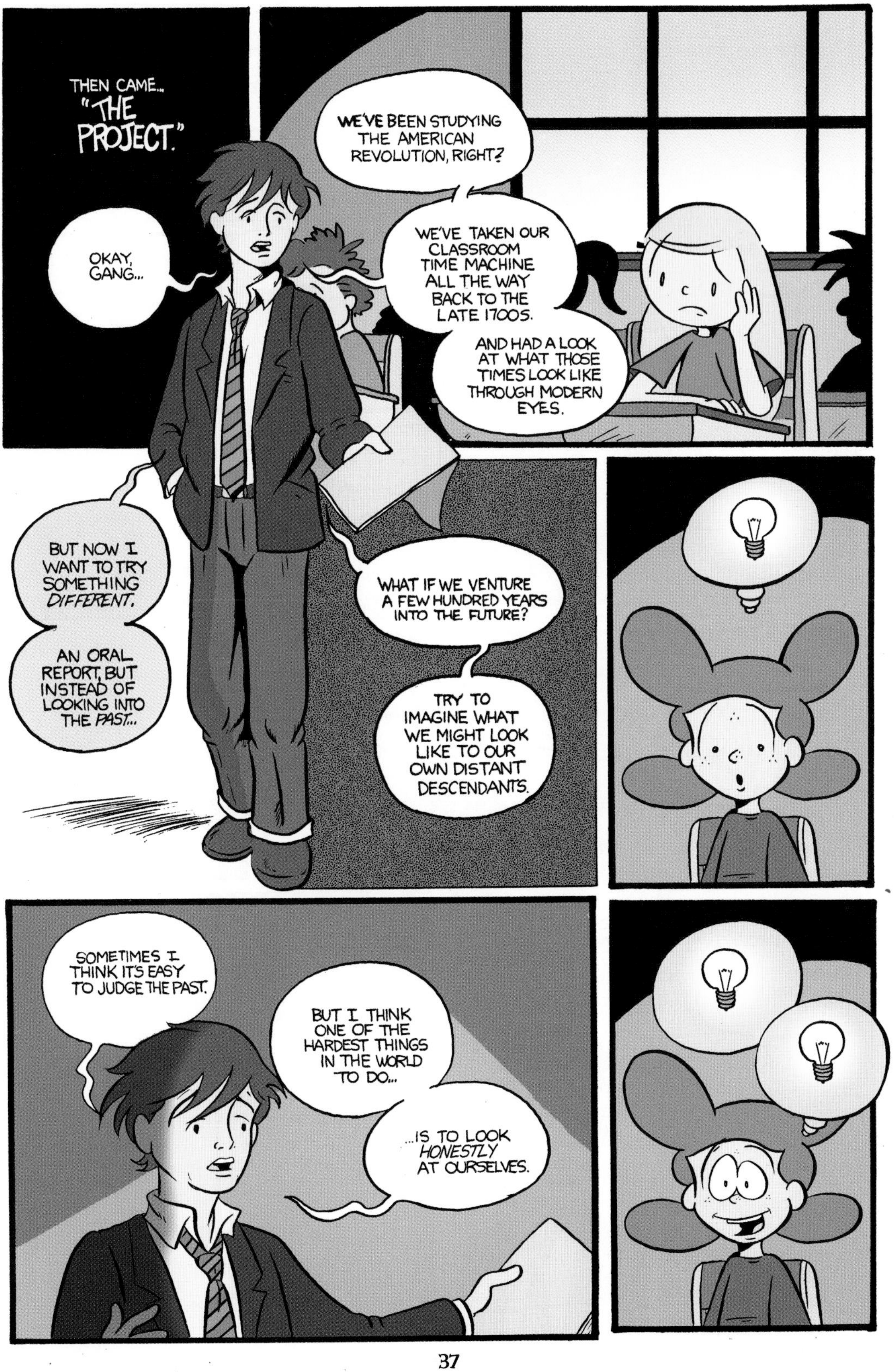
THEN CAME... "THE PROJECT."
OKAY, GANG...
WE'VE BEEN STUDYING THE AMERICAN REVOLUTION, RIGHT?
WE'VE TAKEN OUR CLASSROOM TIME MACHINE ALL THE WAY BACK TO THE LATE 1700S.
AND HAD A LOOK AT WHAT THOSE TIMES LOOK LIKE THROUGH MODERN EYES.
BUT NOW I WANT TO TRY SOMETHING DIFFERENT.
AN ORAL REPORT, BUT INSTEAD OF LOOKING INTO THE PAST...
WHAT IF WE VENTURE A FEW HUNDRED YEARS INTO THE FUTURE?
TRY TO IMAGINE WHAT WE MIGHT LOOK LIKE TO OUR OWN DISTANT DESCENDANTS.
SOMETIMES I THINK IT'S EASY TO JUDGE THE PAST.
BUT I THINK ONE OF THE HARDEST THINGS IN THE WORLD TO DO...
...IS TO LOOK HONESTLY AT OURSELVES.

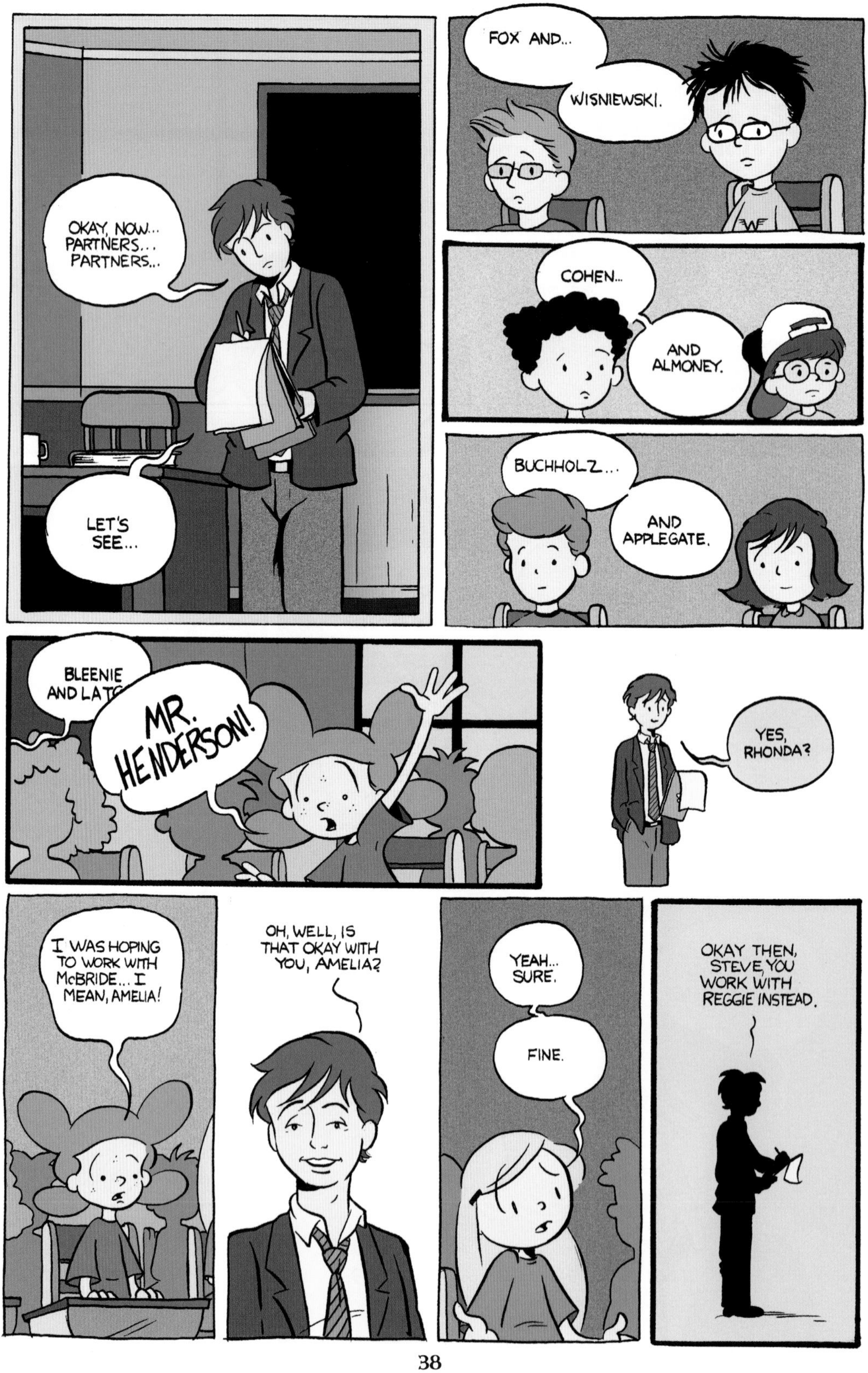
OKAY, NOW... PARTNERS... PARTNERS...
LET'S SEE...
FOX AND...
WISNIEWSKI.
COHEN...
AND ALMONEY.
BUCHHOLZ...
AND APPLEGATE.
BLEENIE AND LAT
MR. HENDERSON!
YES, RHONDA?
I WAS HOPING TO WORK WITH McBRIDE... I MEAN, AMELIA!
OH, WELL, IS THAT OKAY WITH YOU, AMELIA?
YEAH... SURE.
FINE.
OKAY THEN, STEVE, YOU WORK WITH REGGIE INSTEAD.

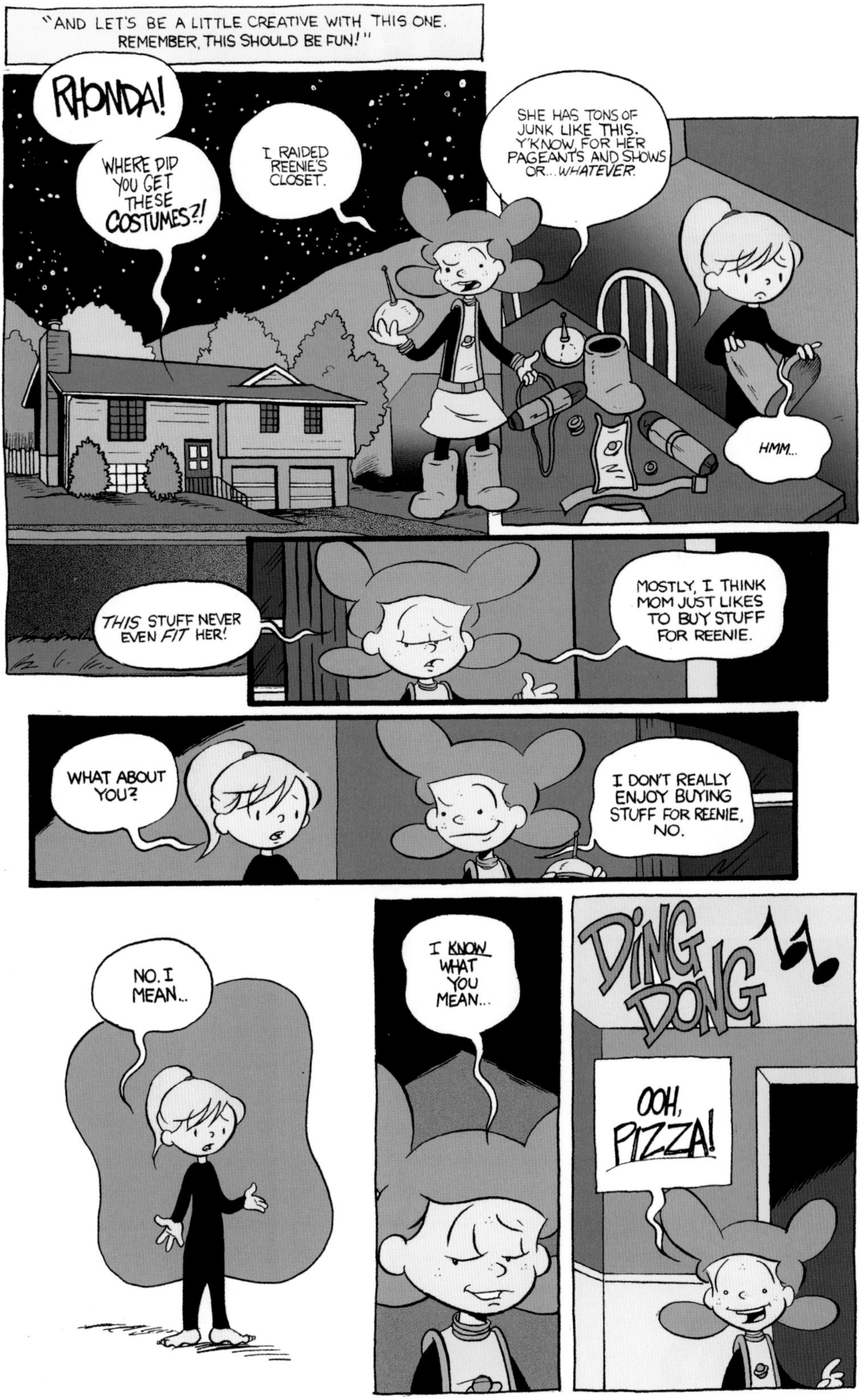
"AND LET'S BE A LITTLE CREATIVE WITH THIS ONE. REMEMBER, THIS SHOULD BE FUN!"
RHONDA!
WHERE DID YOU GET THESE COSTUMES?!
I RAIDED REENIE'S CLOSET.
SHE HAS TONS OF JUNK LIKE THIS. Y'KNOW, FOR HER PAGEANTS AND SHOWS OR... WHATEVER.
HMM...
THIS STUFF NEVER EVEN FIT HER!
MOSTLY, I THINK MOM JUST LIKES TO BUY STUFF FOR REENIE.
WHAT ABOUT YOU?
I DON'T REALLY ENJOY BUYING STUFF FOR REENIE, NO.
NO. I MEAN...
I KNOW WHAT YOU MEAN...
DING DONG
OOH, PIZZA!

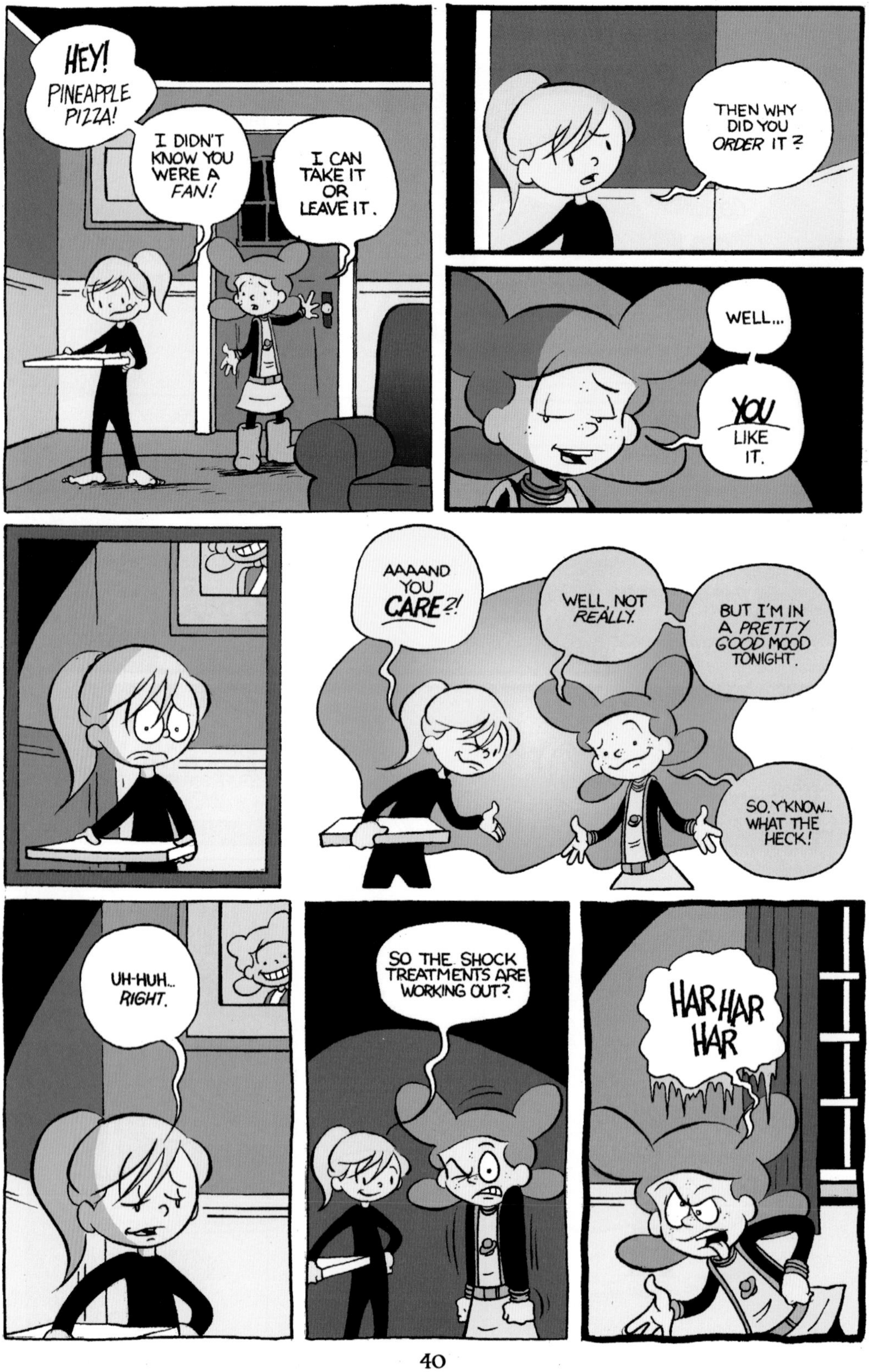
HEY! PINEAPPLE PIZZA!
I DIDN'T KNOW YOU WERE A FAN!
I CAN TAKE IT OR LEAVE IT.
THEN WHY DID YOU ORDER IT?
WELL...
YOU LIKE IT.
AAAAND YOU CARE?!
WELL, NOT REALLY.
BUT I'M IN A PRETTY GOOD MOOD TONIGHT.
SO, Y'KNOW... WHAT THE HECK!
UH-HUH... RIGHT.
SO THE SHOCK TREATMENTS ARE WORKING OUT?
HAR HAR HAR

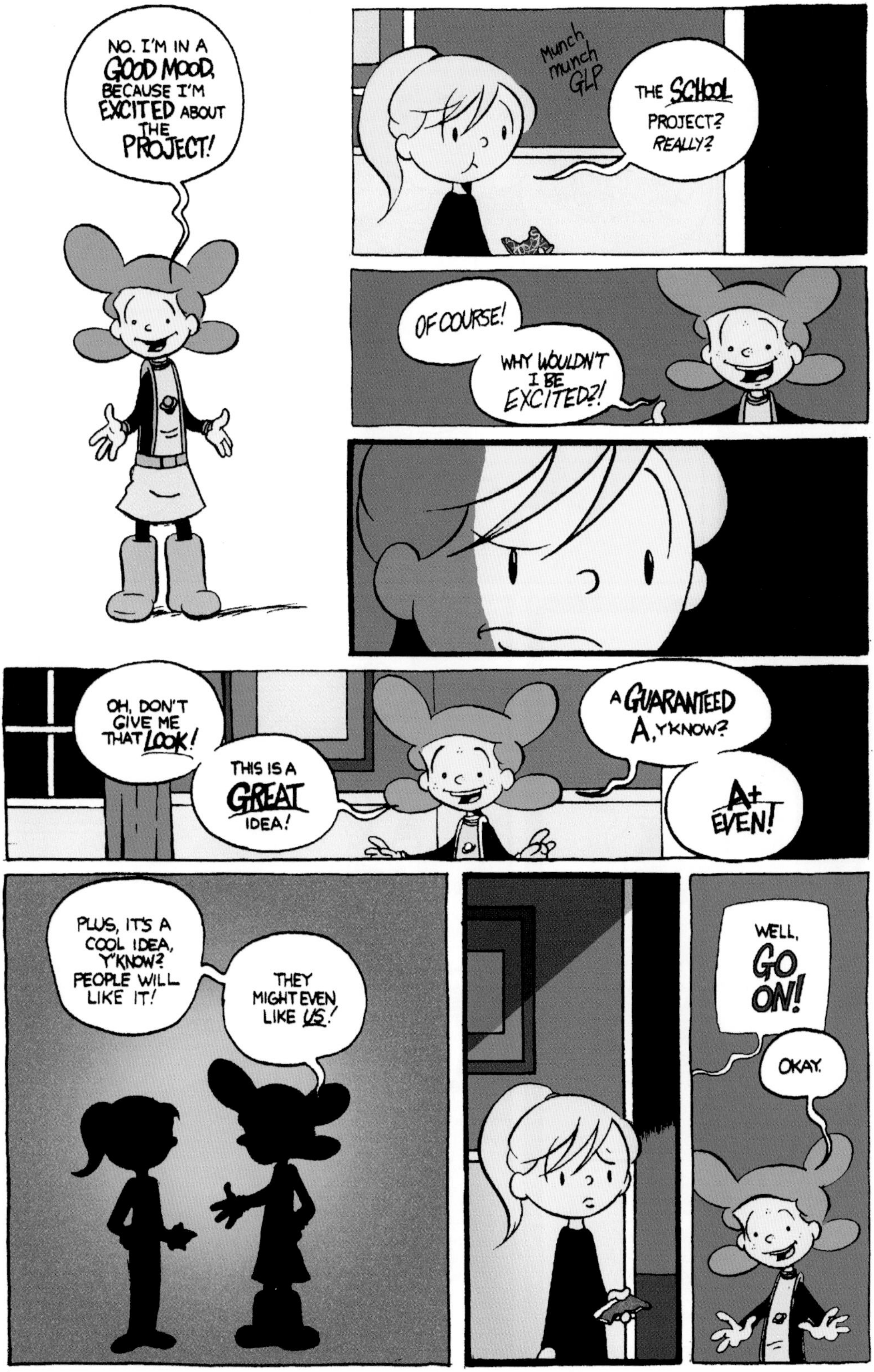
NO. I'M IN A GOOD MOOD, BECAUSE I'M EXCITED ABOUT THE PROJECT!
Munch munch GLP
THE SCHOOL PROJECT? REALLY?
OF COURSE!
WHY WOULDN'T I BE EXCITED?!
OH, DON'T GIVE ME THAT LOOK!
THIS IS A GREAT IDEA!
A GUARANTEED A, Y'KNOW?
A+ EVEN!
PLUS, IT'S A COOL IDEA, Y'KNOW? PEOPLE WILL LIKE IT!
THEY MIGHT EVEN LIKE US!
WELL, GO ON!
OKAY.

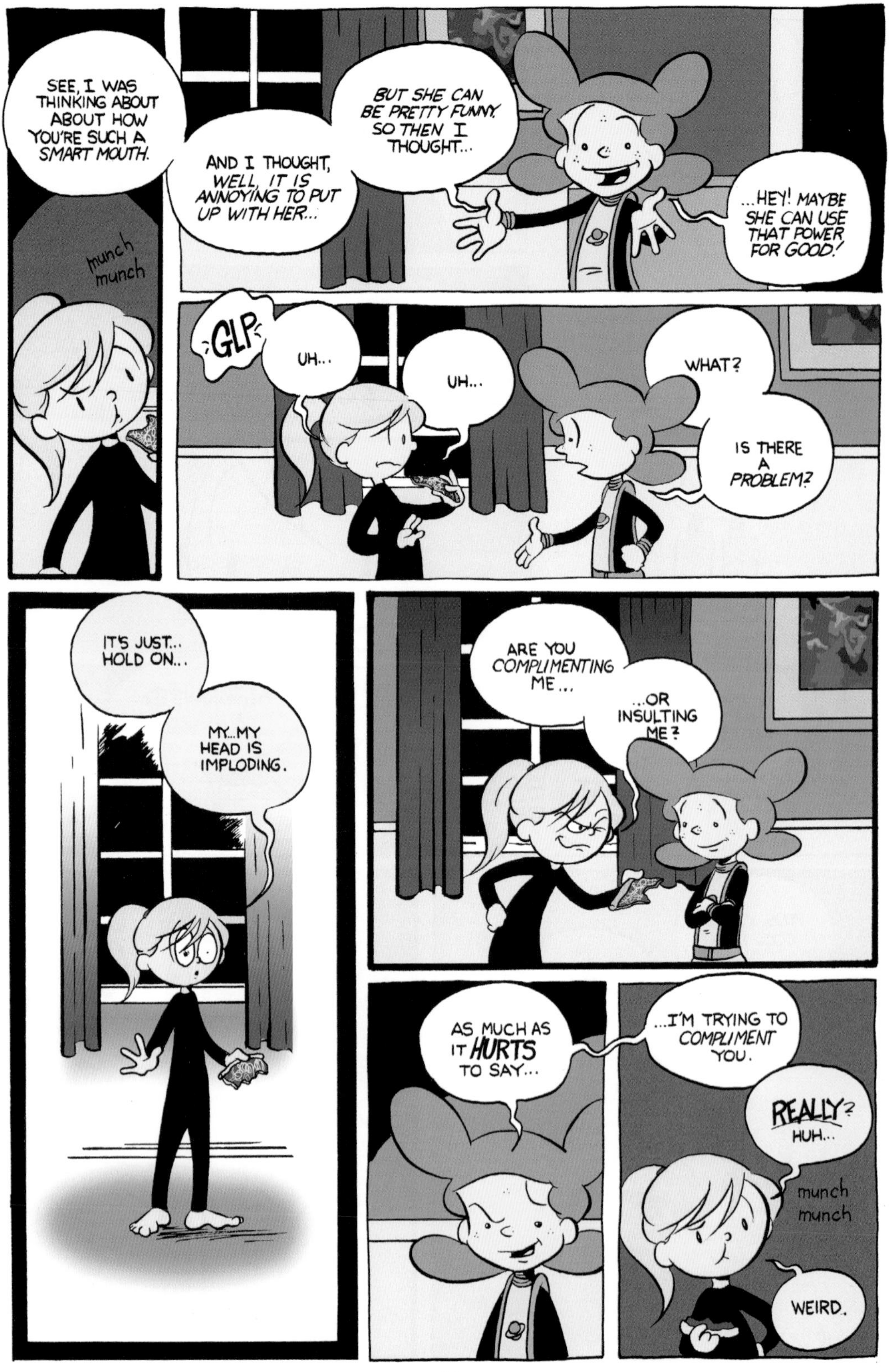

SEE, I WAS THINKING ABOUT ABOUT HOW YOU'RE SUCH A SMART MOUTH.
AND I THOUGHT, WELL, IT IS ANNOYING TO PUT UP WITH HER...
BUT SHE CAN BE PRETTY FUNNY. SO THEN I THOUGHT...
...HEY! MAYBE SHE CAN USE THAT POWER FOR GOOD!
munch munch
GLP
UH...
UH...
WHAT?
IS THERE A PROBLEM?
IT'S JUST... HOLD ON...
MY...MY HEAD IS IMPLODING.
ARE YOU COMPLIMENTING ME...
...OR INSULTING ME?
AS MUCH AS IT HURTS TO SAY...
...I'M TRYING TO COMPLIMENT YOU.
REALLY? HUH...
munch munch
WEIRD.

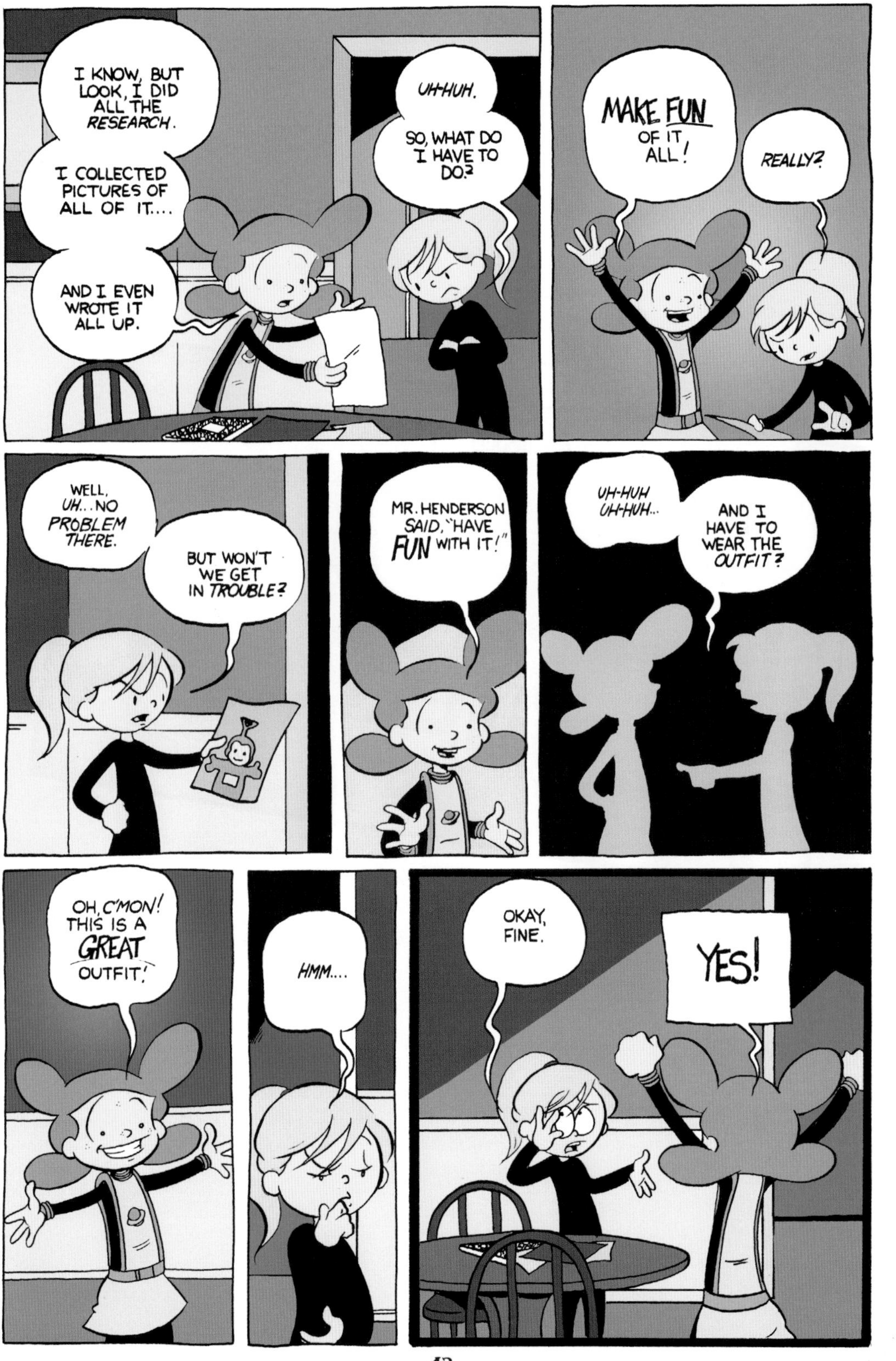
I KNOW, BUT LOOK, I DID ALL THE RESEARCH.
I COLLECTED PICTURES OF ALL OF IT....
AND I EVEN WROTE IT ALL UP.
UH-HUH.
SO, WHAT DO I HAVE TO DO?
MAKE FUN OF IT, ALL!
REALLY?
WELL, UH...NO PROBLEM THERE.
BUT WON'T WE GET IN TROUBLE?
MR. HENDERSON SAID, "HAVE FUN WITH IT!"
UH-HUH UH-HUH...
AND I HAVE TO WEAR THE OUTFIT?
OH, C'MON! THIS IS A GREAT OUTFIT!
HMM....
OKAY, FINE.
YES!

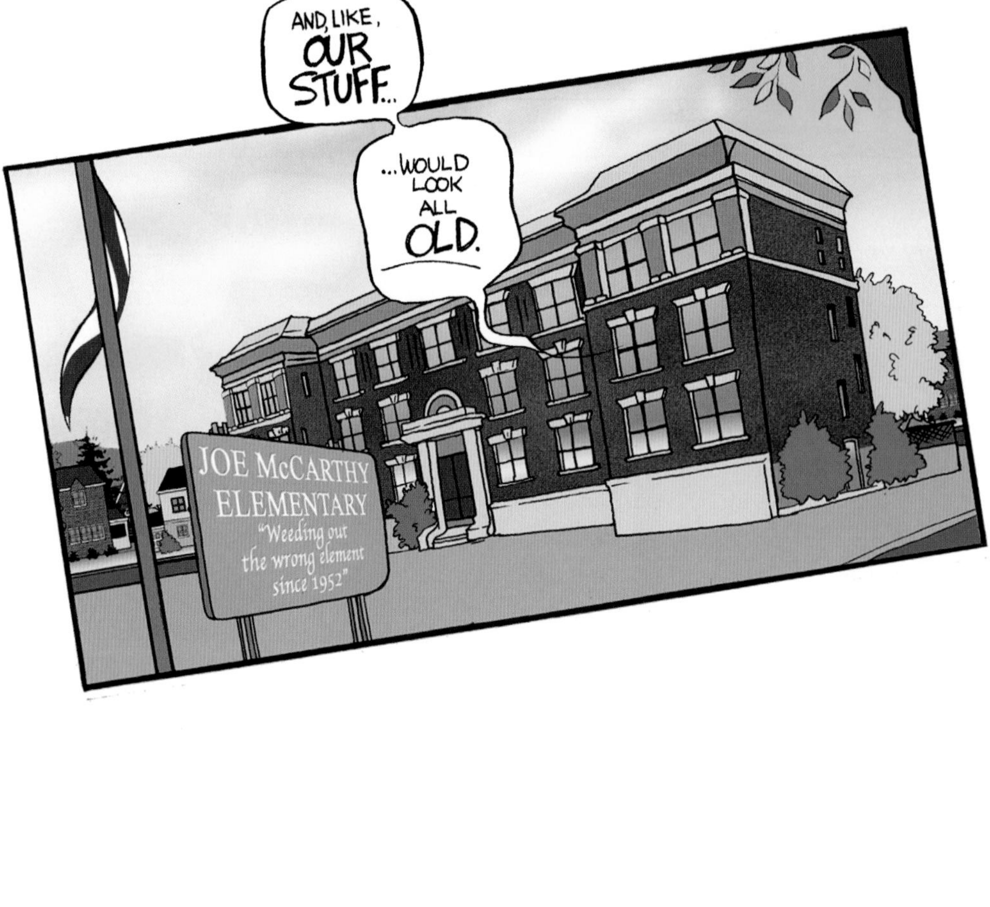
AND, LIKE, OUR STUFF...
...WOULD LOOK ALL OLD.
JOE McCARTHY ELEMENTARY
"Weeding out the wrong element since 1952"

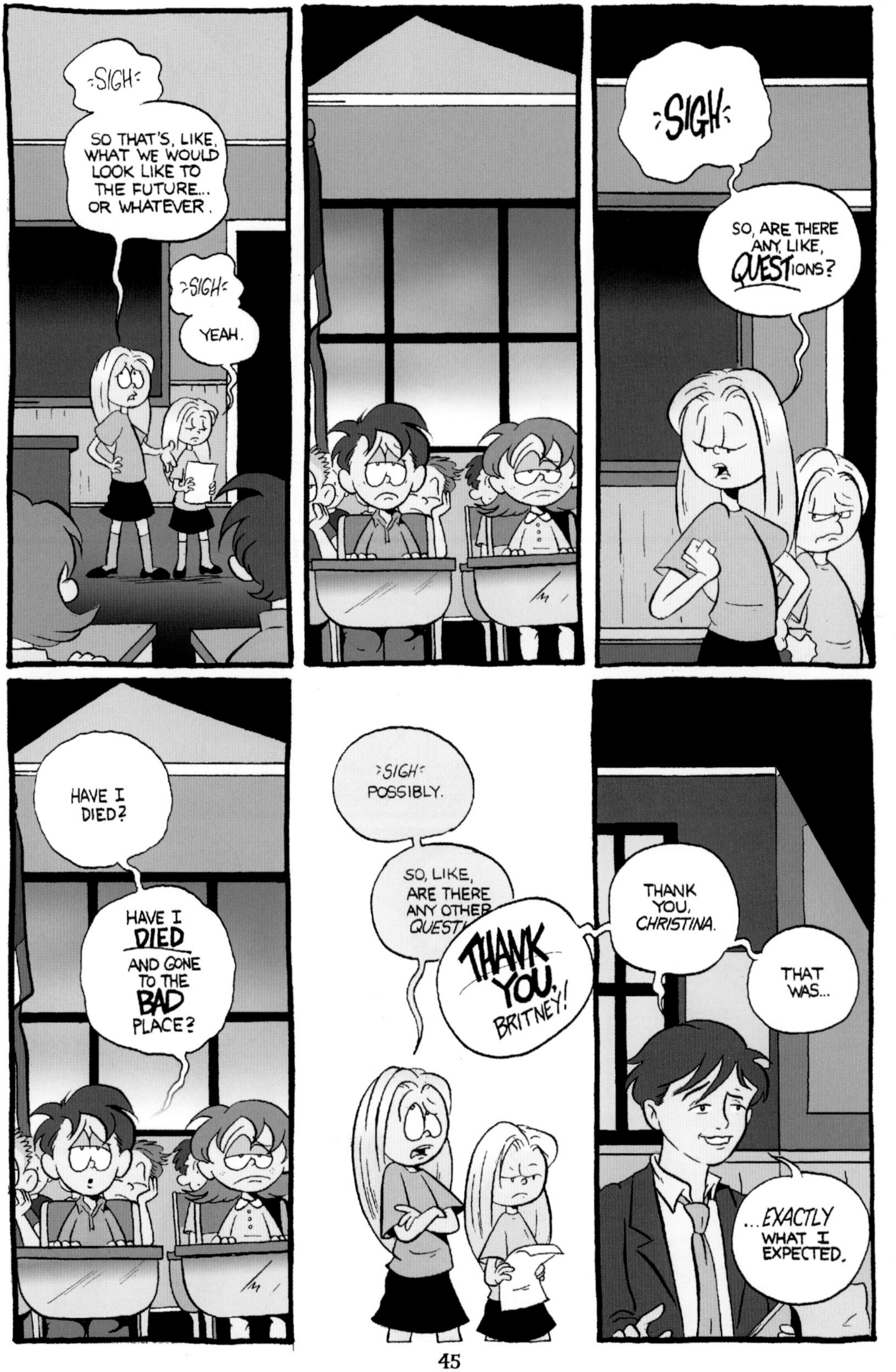
:SIGH:
SO THAT'S, LIKE, WHAT WE WOULD LOOK LIKE TO THE FUTURE... OR WHATEVER.
:SIGH:
YEAH.
:SIGH:
SO, ARE THERE ANY, LIKE, QUESTIONS?
HAVE I DIED?
HAVE I DIED AND GONE TO THE BAD PLACE?
:SIGH: POSSIBLY.
SO, LIKE, ARE THERE ANY OTHER QUEST
THANK YOU, BRITNEY!
THANK YOU, CHRISTINA.
THAT WAS...
...EXACTLY WHAT I EXPECTED.

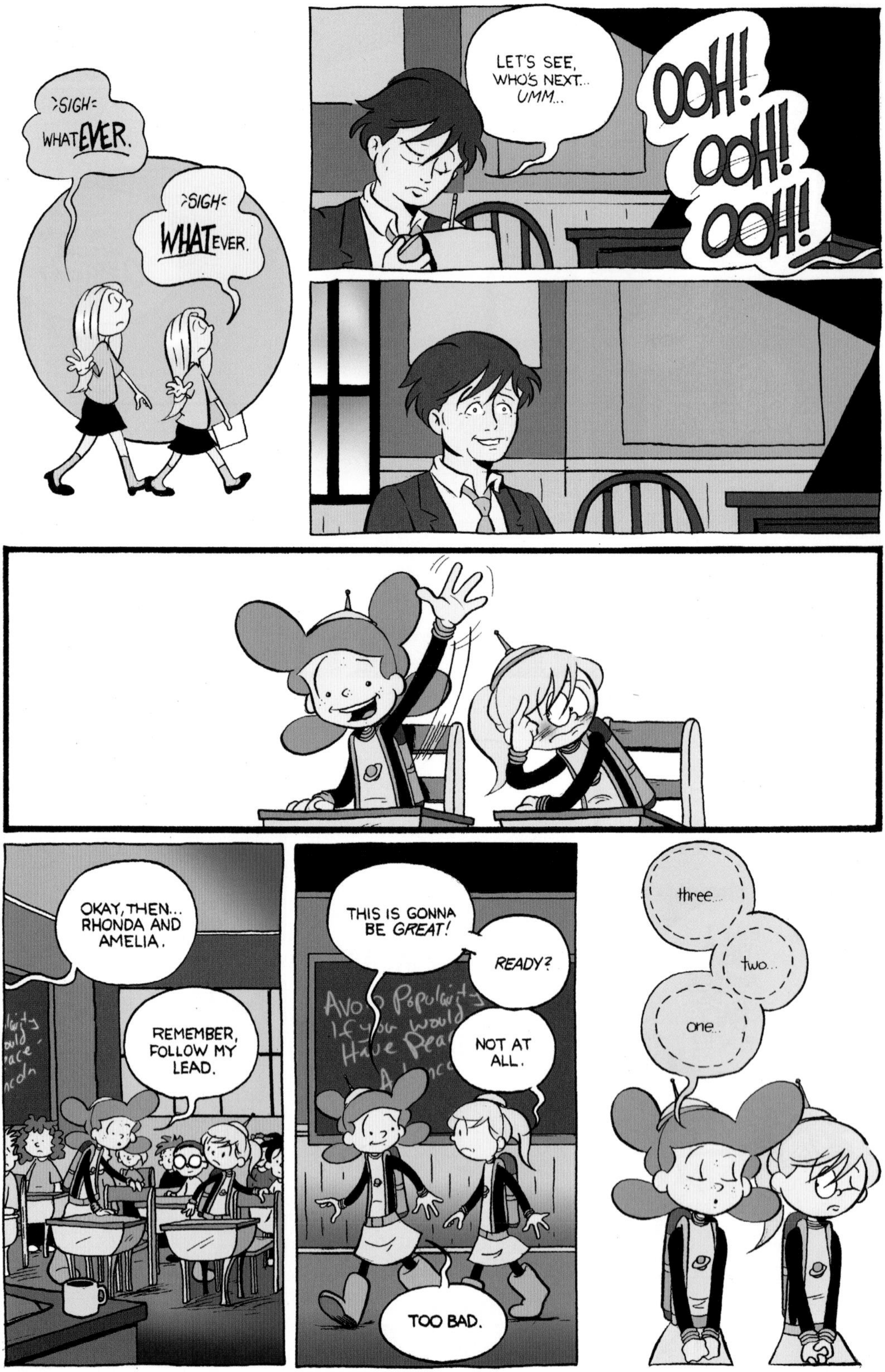

>SIGH<
WHATEVER.
>SIGH<
WHATEVER.
LET'S SEE, WHO'S NEXT... UMM...
OOH! OOH! OOH!
OKAY, THEN... RHONDA AND AMELIA.
REMEMBER, FOLLOW MY LEAD.
THIS IS GONNA BE GREAT!
READY?
NOT AT ALL.
TOO BAD.
three...
two...
one...

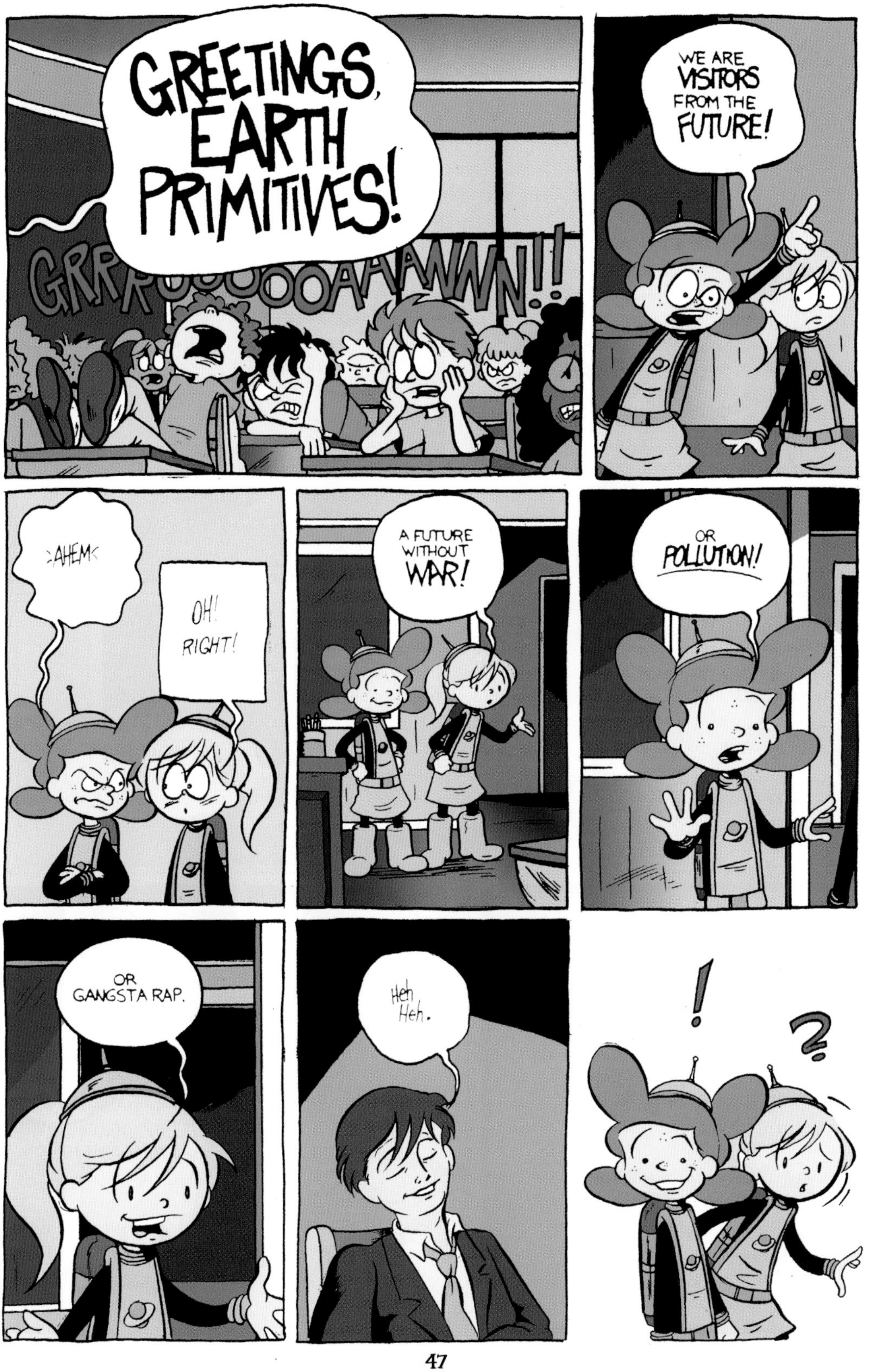
GREETINGS, EARTH PRIMITIVES!
GRRROOOOOOAAAWWWN!!
WE ARE VISITORS FROM THE FUTURE!
AHEM
OH! RIGHT!
A FUTURE WITHOUT WAR!
OR POLLUTION!
OR GANGSTA RAP.
Heh Heh.
!
?

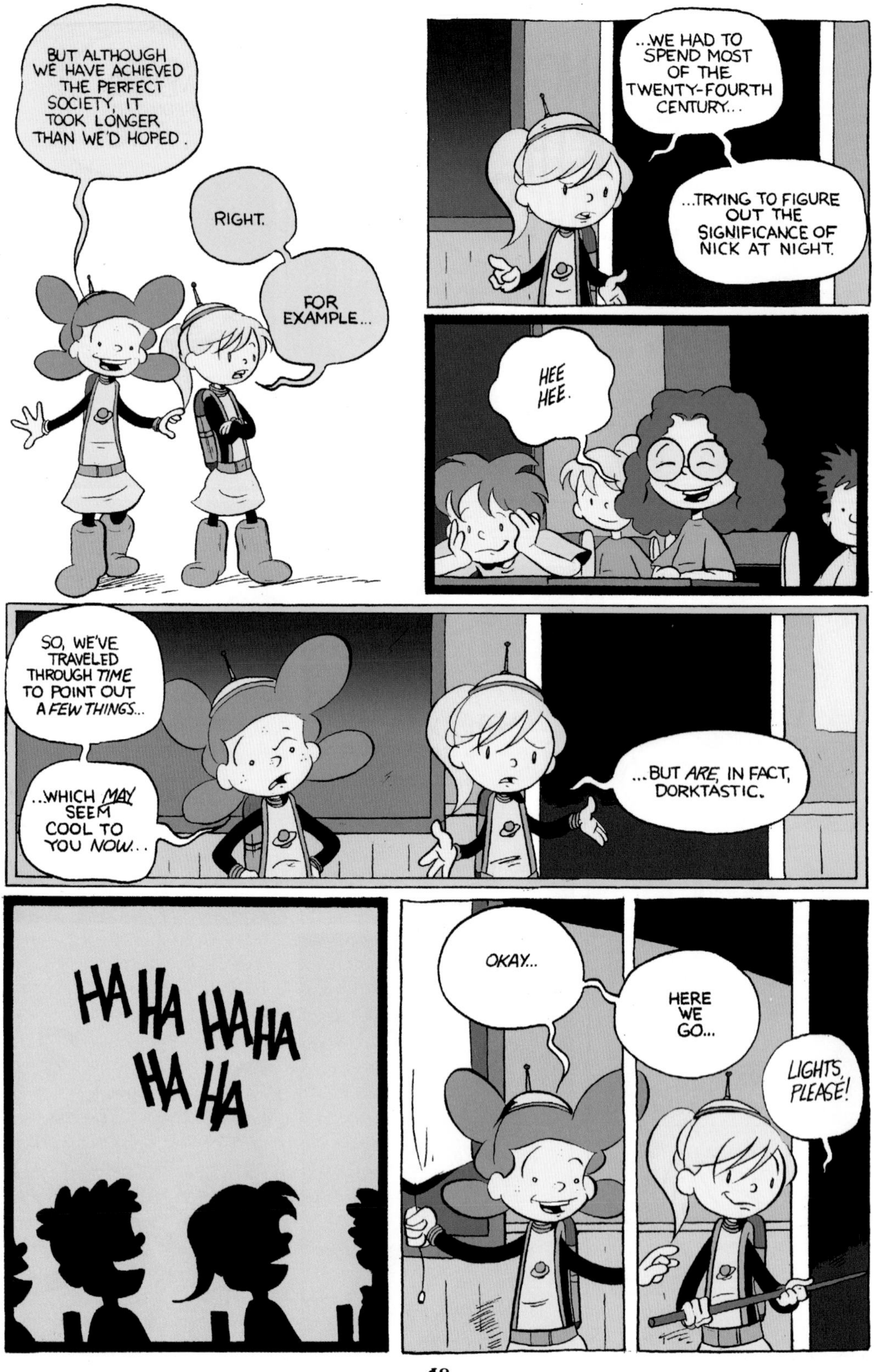

BUT ALTHOUGH WE HAVE ACHIEVED THE PERFECT SOCIETY, IT TOOK LONGER THAN WE'D HOPED.
RIGHT.
FOR EXAMPLE...
...WE HAD TO SPEND MOST OF THE TWENTY-FOURTH CENTURY...
...TRYING TO FIGURE OUT THE SIGNIFICANCE OF NICK AT NIGHT.
HEE HEE.
SO, WE'VE TRAVELED THROUGH TIME TO POINT OUT A FEW THINGS...
...WHICH MAY SEEM COOL TO YOU NOW...
...BUT ARE, IN FACT, DORKTASTIC.
HA HA HAHA HA HA HA
OKAY...
HERE WE GO...
LIGHTS, PLEASE!

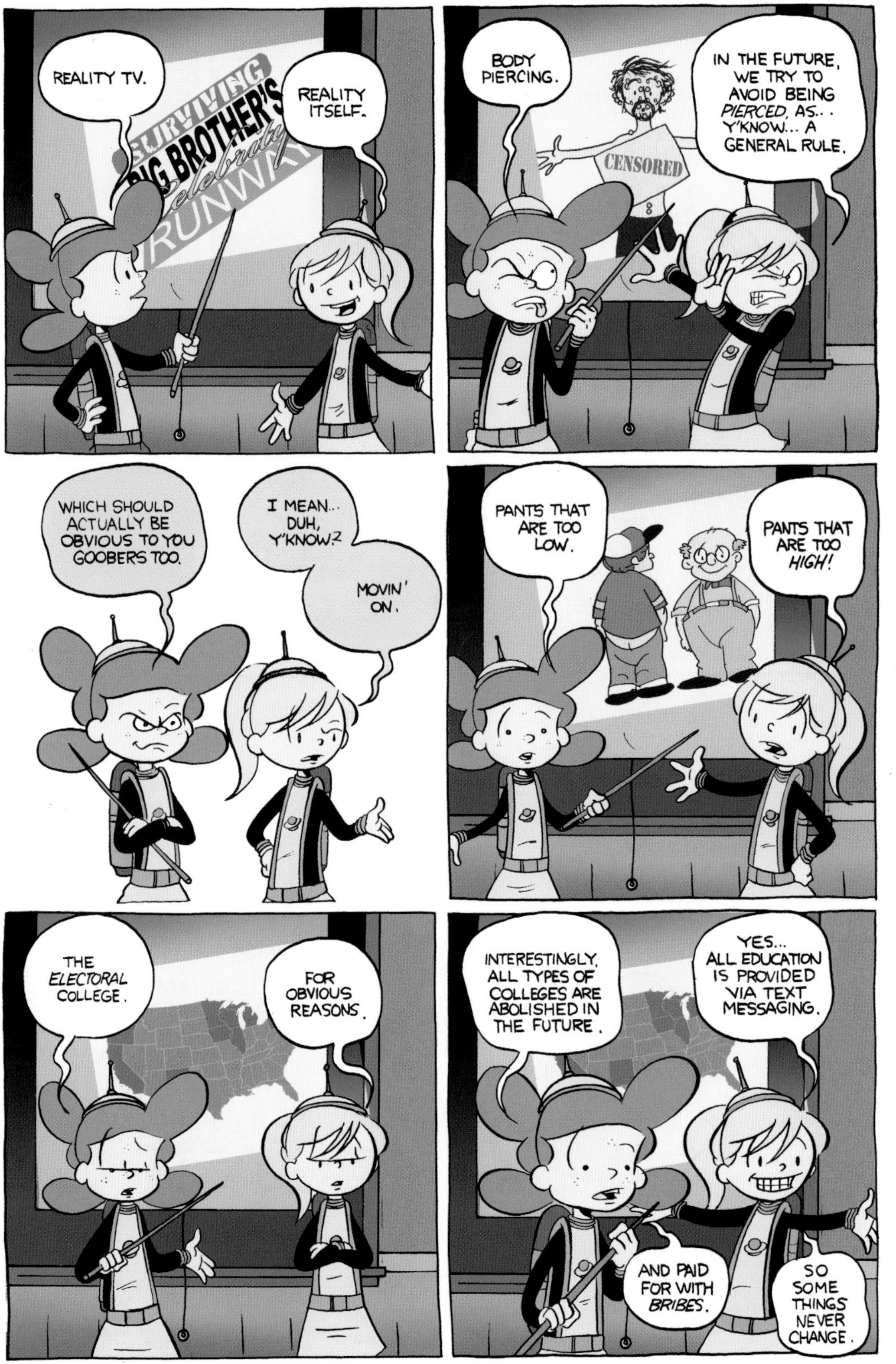
REALITY TV.
SURVIVING BIG BROTHER'S Celebrity RUNWAY
REALITY ITSELF.
BODY PIERCING.
CENSORED
IN THE FUTURE, WE TRY TO AVOID BEING *PIERCED*, AS... Y'KNOW... A GENERAL RULE.
WHICH SHOULD ACTUALLY BE OBVIOUS TO YOU GOOBERS TOO.
I MEAN... DUH, Y'KNOW?
MOVIN' ON.
PANTS THAT ARE TOO LOW.
PANTS THAT ARE TOO *HIGH!*
THE *ELECTORAL* COLLEGE.
FOR OBVIOUS REASONS.
INTERESTINGLY, ALL TYPES OF COLLEGES ARE ABOLISHED IN THE FUTURE.
YES... ALL EDUCATION IS PROVIDED VIA TEXT MESSAGING.
AND PAID FOR WITH *BRIBES*.
SO SOME THINGS NEVER CHANGE.

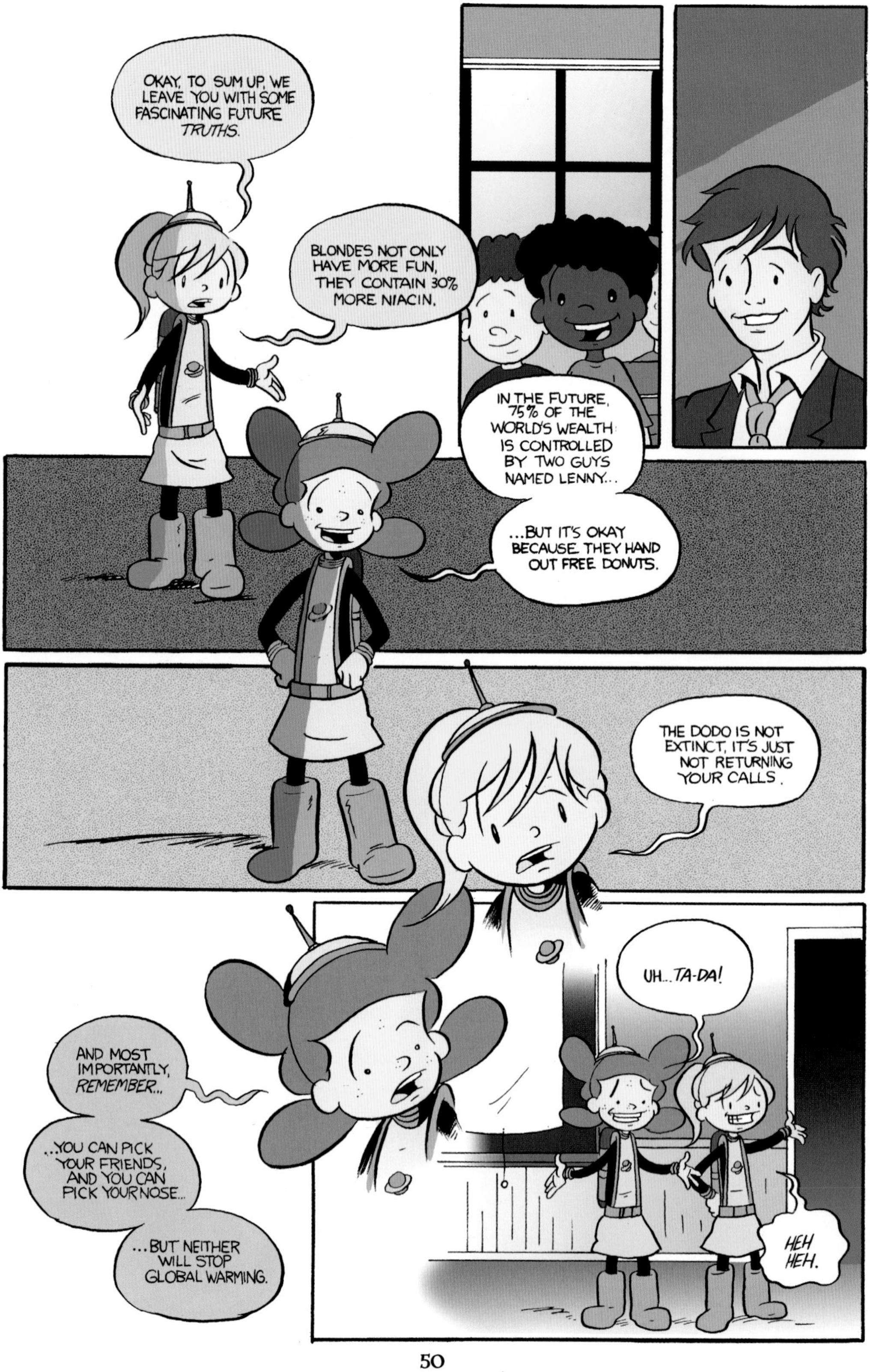
OKAY, TO SUM UP, WE LEAVE YOU WITH SOME FASCINATING FUTURE TRUTHS.
BLONDES NOT ONLY HAVE MORE FUN, THEY CONTAIN 30% MORE NIACIN.
IN THE FUTURE, 75% OF THE WORLD'S WEALTH IS CONTROLLED BY TWO GUYS NAMED LENNY...
...BUT IT'S OKAY BECAUSE THEY HAND OUT FREE DONUTS.
THE DODO IS NOT EXTINCT, IT'S JUST NOT RETURNING YOUR CALLS.
AND MOST IMPORTANTLY, REMEMBER...
...YOU CAN PICK YOUR FRIENDS, AND YOU CAN PICK YOUR NOSE...
...BUT NEITHER WILL STOP GLOBAL WARMING.
UH...TA-DA!
HEH HEH.

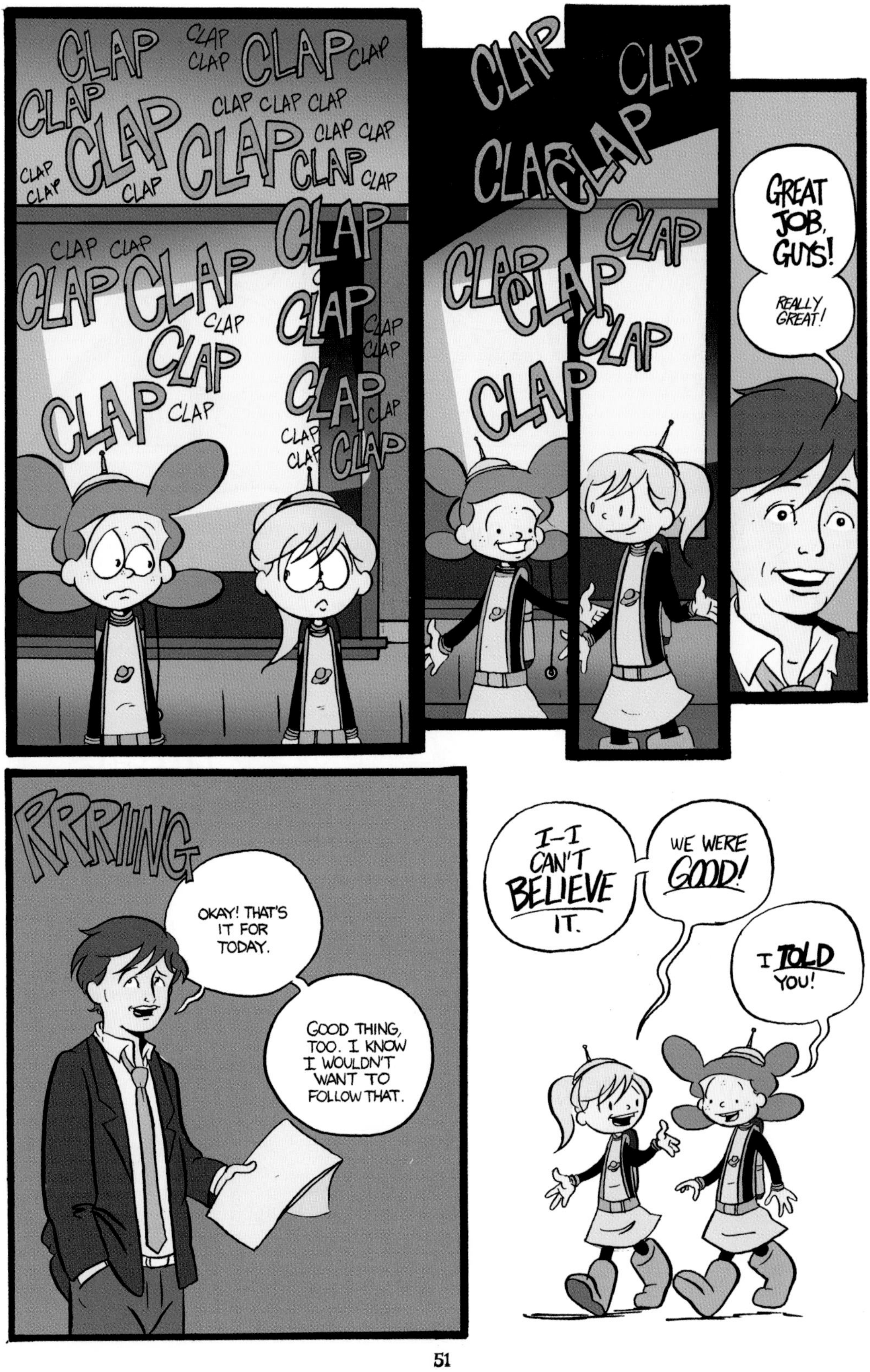
CLAP CLAP CLAP CLAP CLAP CLAP
CLAP CLAP CLAP CLAP
CLAP CLAP CLAP CLAP CLAP CLAP CLAP CLAP CLAP
CLAP CLAP CLAP CLAP CLAP CLAP CLAP CLAP CLAP CLAP CLAP CLAP CLAP CLAP CLAP CLAP CLAP
CLAP CLAP CLAP CLAP CLAP CLAP CLAP CLAP
GREAT JOB, GUYS!
REALLY GREAT!
RRRIING
OKAY! THAT'S IT FOR TODAY.
GOOD THING, TOO. I KNOW I WOULDN'T WANT TO FOLLOW THAT.
I–I CAN'T BELIEVE IT.
WE WERE GOOD!
I TOLD YOU!

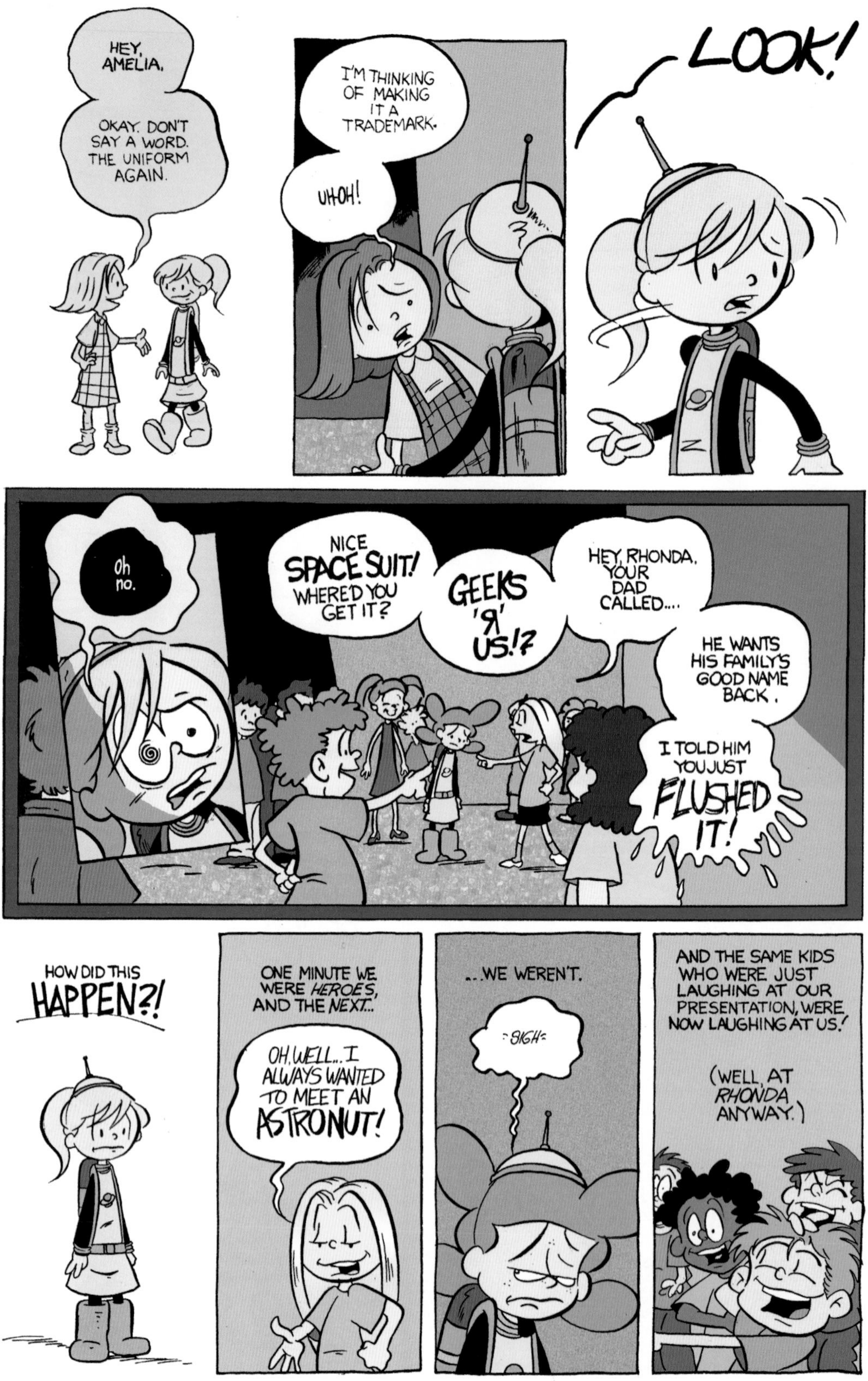
HEY, AMELIA.
OKAY. DON'T SAY A WORD. THE UNIFORM AGAIN.
I'M THINKING OF MAKING IT A TRADEMARK.
UH-OH!
LOOK!
Oh no.
NICE SPACE SUIT! WHERE'D YOU GET IT?
GEEKS 'Я' US!?
HEY, RHONDA, YOUR DAD CALLED....
HE WANTS HIS FAMILY'S GOOD NAME BACK.
I TOLD HIM YOU JUST FLUSHED IT!
HOW DID THIS HAPPEN?!
ONE MINUTE WE WERE HEROES, AND THE NEXT...
OH, WELL... I ALWAYS WANTED TO MEET AN ASTRONUT!
...WE WEREN'T.
SIGH
AND THE SAME KIDS WHO WERE JUST LAUGHING AT OUR PRESENTATION, WERE NOW LAUGHING AT US!
(WELL, AT RHONDA ANYWAY.)

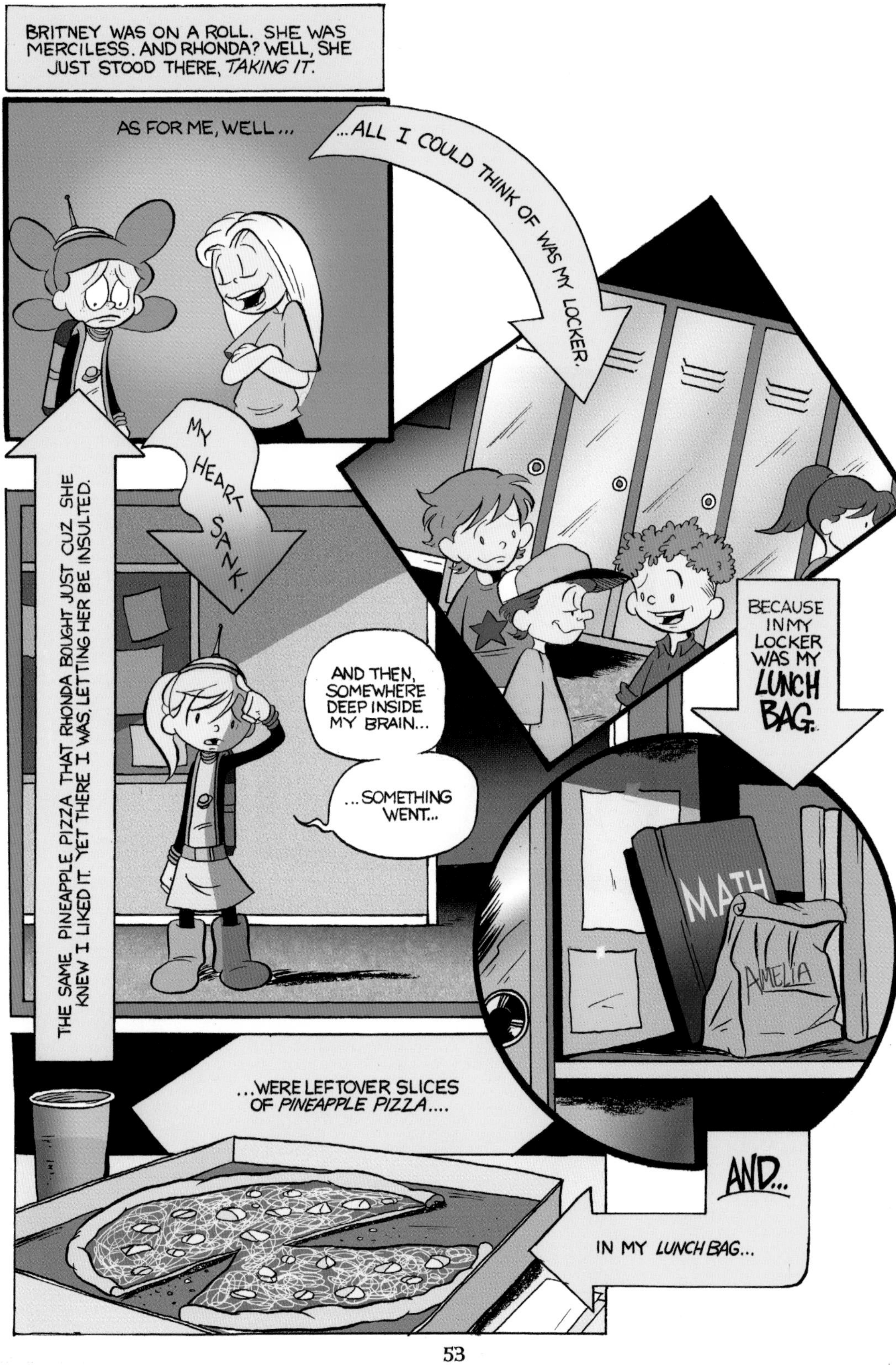
BRITNEY WAS ON A ROLL. SHE WAS MERCILESS. AND RHONDA? WELL, SHE JUST STOOD THERE, *TAKING IT*.
AS FOR ME, WELL...
...ALL I COULD THINK OF WAS MY LOCKER.
BECAUSE IN MY LOCKER WAS MY LUNCH BAG.
MATH
AMELIA
AND...
IN MY *LUNCH BAG*...
...WERE LEFTOVER SLICES OF *PINEAPPLE PIZZA*....
THE SAME PINEAPPLE PIZZA THAT RHONDA BOUGHT JUST CUZ SHE KNEW I LIKED IT. YET THERE I WAS, LETTING HER BE INSULTED.
MY HEART SANK.
AND THEN, SOMEWHERE DEEP INSIDE MY BRAIN...
...SOMETHING WENT...

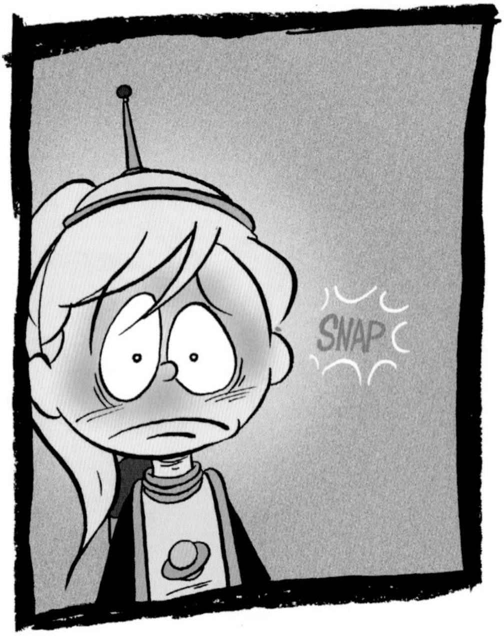
SNAP

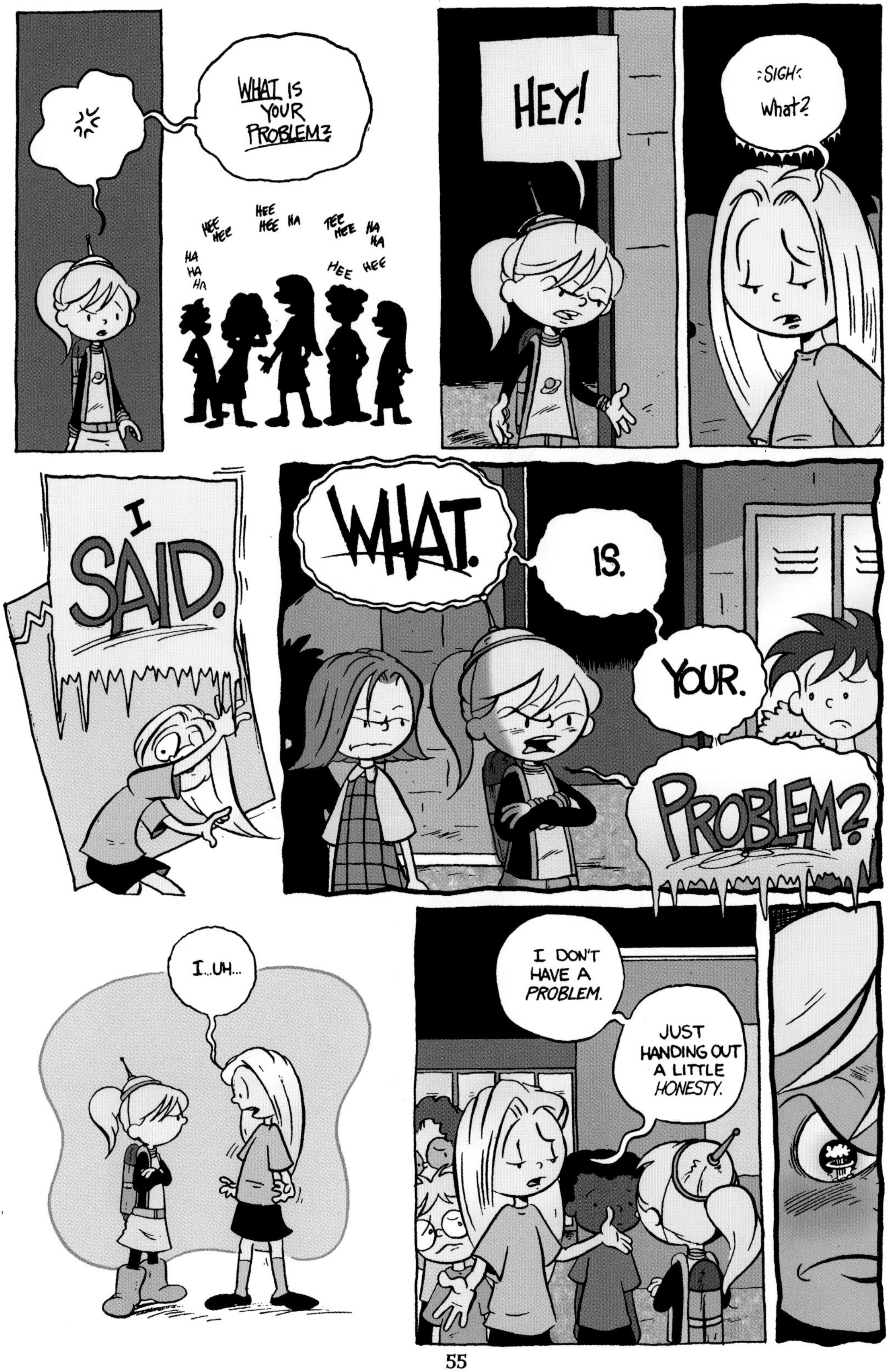
WHAT IS YOUR PROBLEM?
HEE HEE
HEE HEE HA
TEE HEE HA HA
HA HA HA
HEE HEE
HEY!
SIGH
What?
I SAID.
WHAT.
IS.
YOUR.
PROBLEM?
I...UH...
I DON'T HAVE A PROBLEM.
JUST HANDING OUT A LITTLE HONESTY.

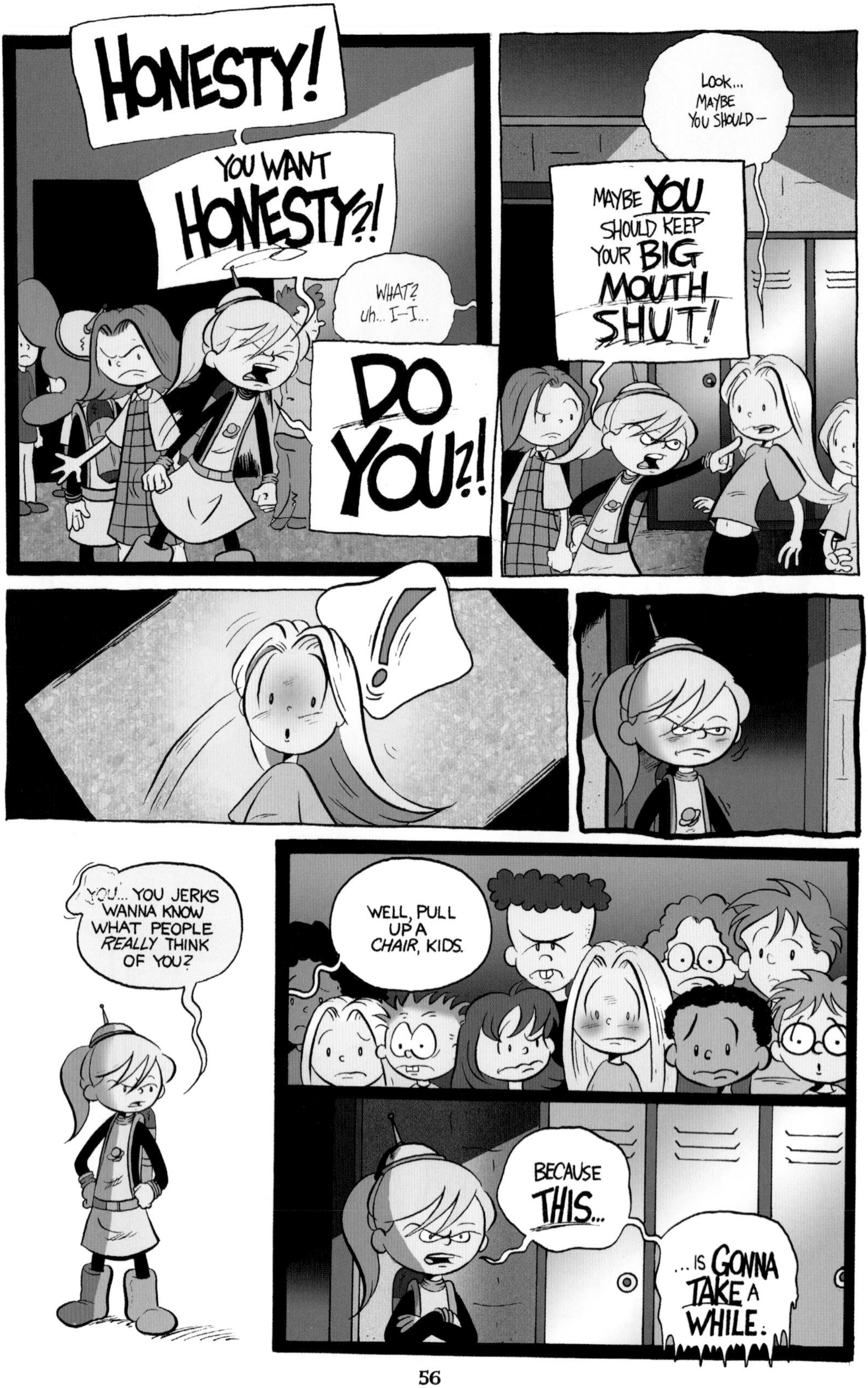
HONESTY!
YOU WANT HONESTY?!
WHAT? uh... I-I...
DO YOU?!
LOOK... MAYBE YOU SHOULD—
MAYBE YOU SHOULD KEEP YOUR BIG MOUTH SHUT!
!
YOU... YOU JERKS WANNA KNOW WHAT PEOPLE REALLY THINK OF YOU?
WELL, PULL UP A CHAIR, KIDS.
BECAUSE THIS...
...IS GONNA TAKE A WHILE.

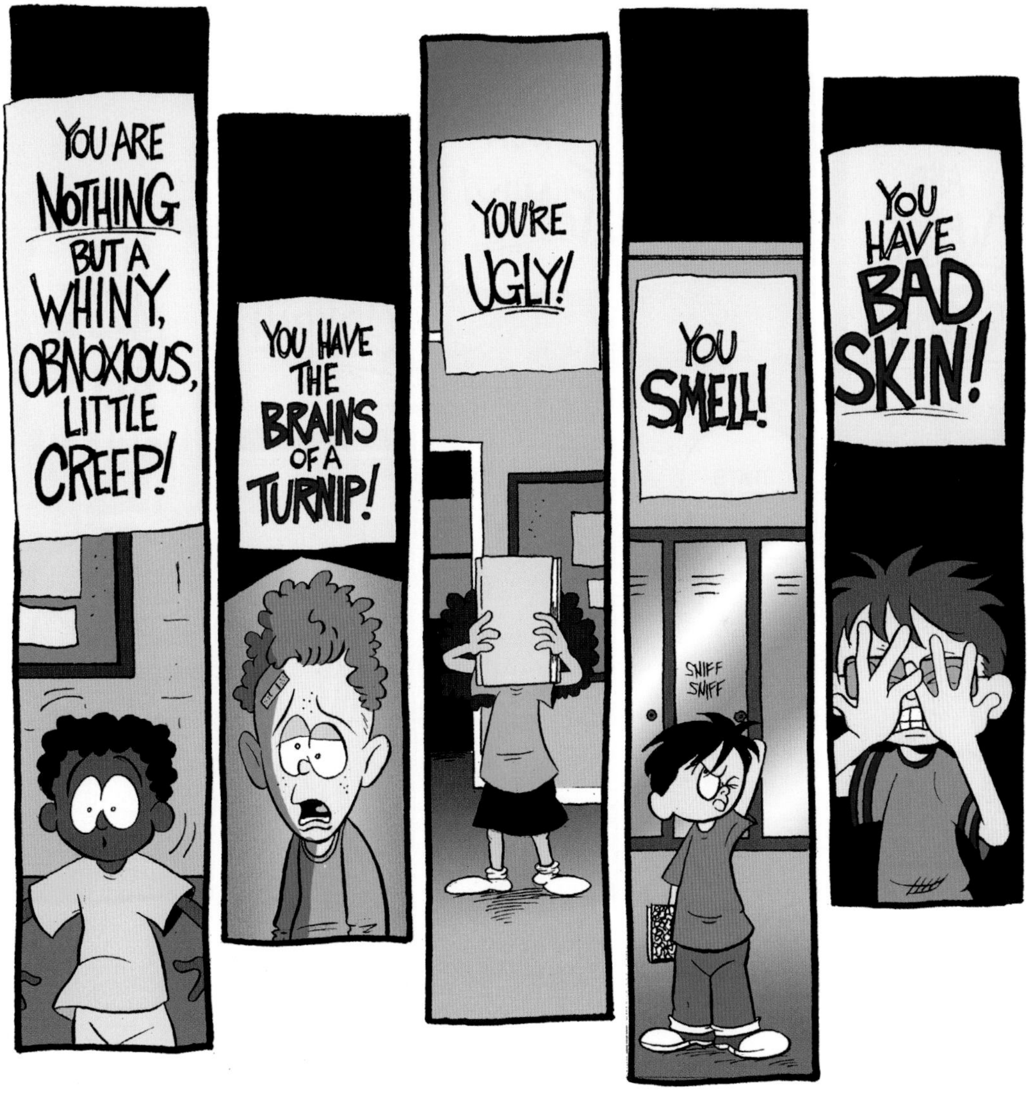
YOU ARE NOTHING BUT A WHINY, OBNOXIOUS, LITTLE CREEP!
YOU HAVE THE BRAINS OF A TURNIP!
YOU'RE UGLY!
YOU SMELL!
SNIFF SNIFF
YOU HAVE BAD SKIN!

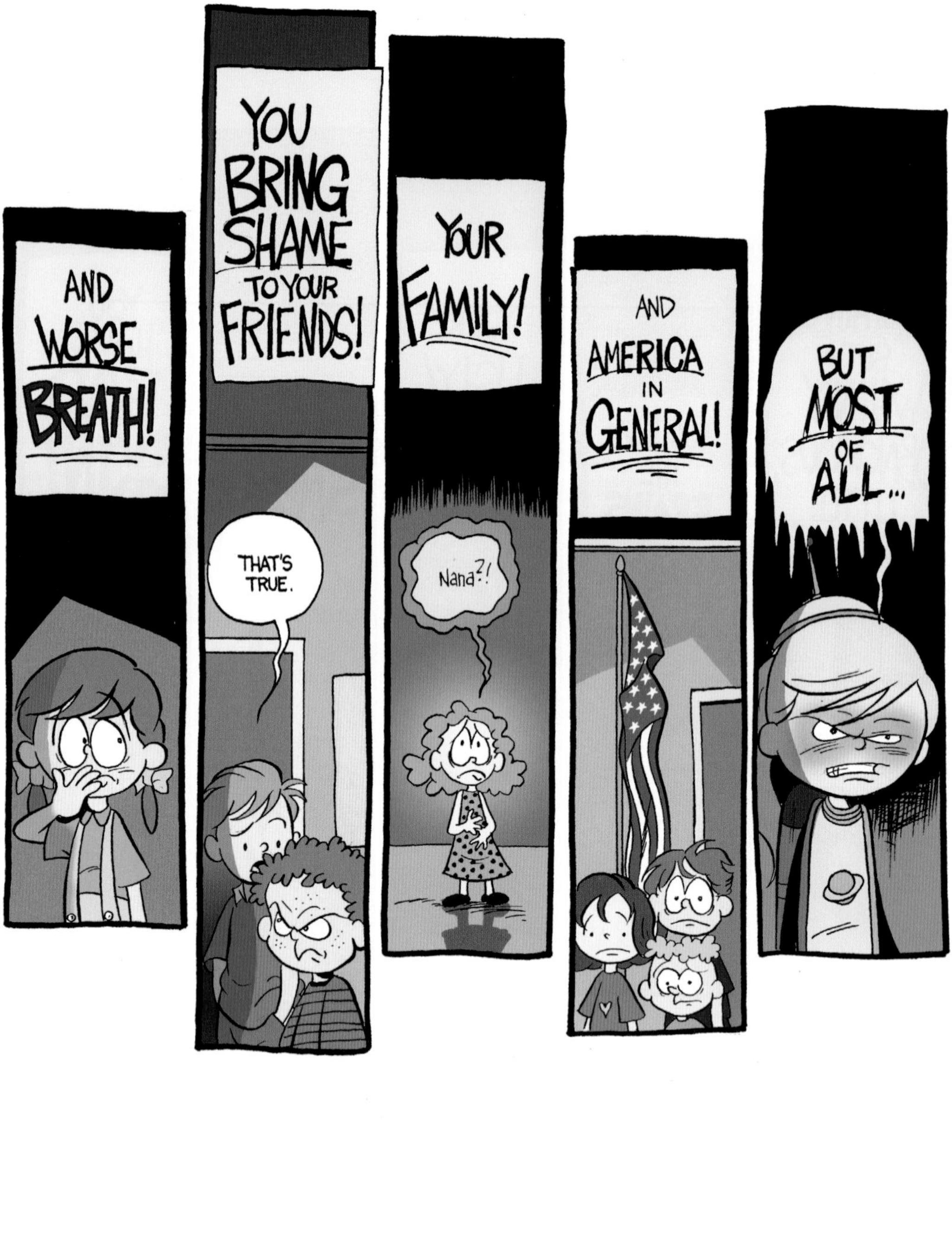
AND WORSE BREATH!
YOU BRING SHAME TO YOUR FRIENDS!
THAT'S TRUE.
YOUR FAMILY!
Nana?!
AND AMERICA IN GENERAL!
BUT MOST OF ALL...

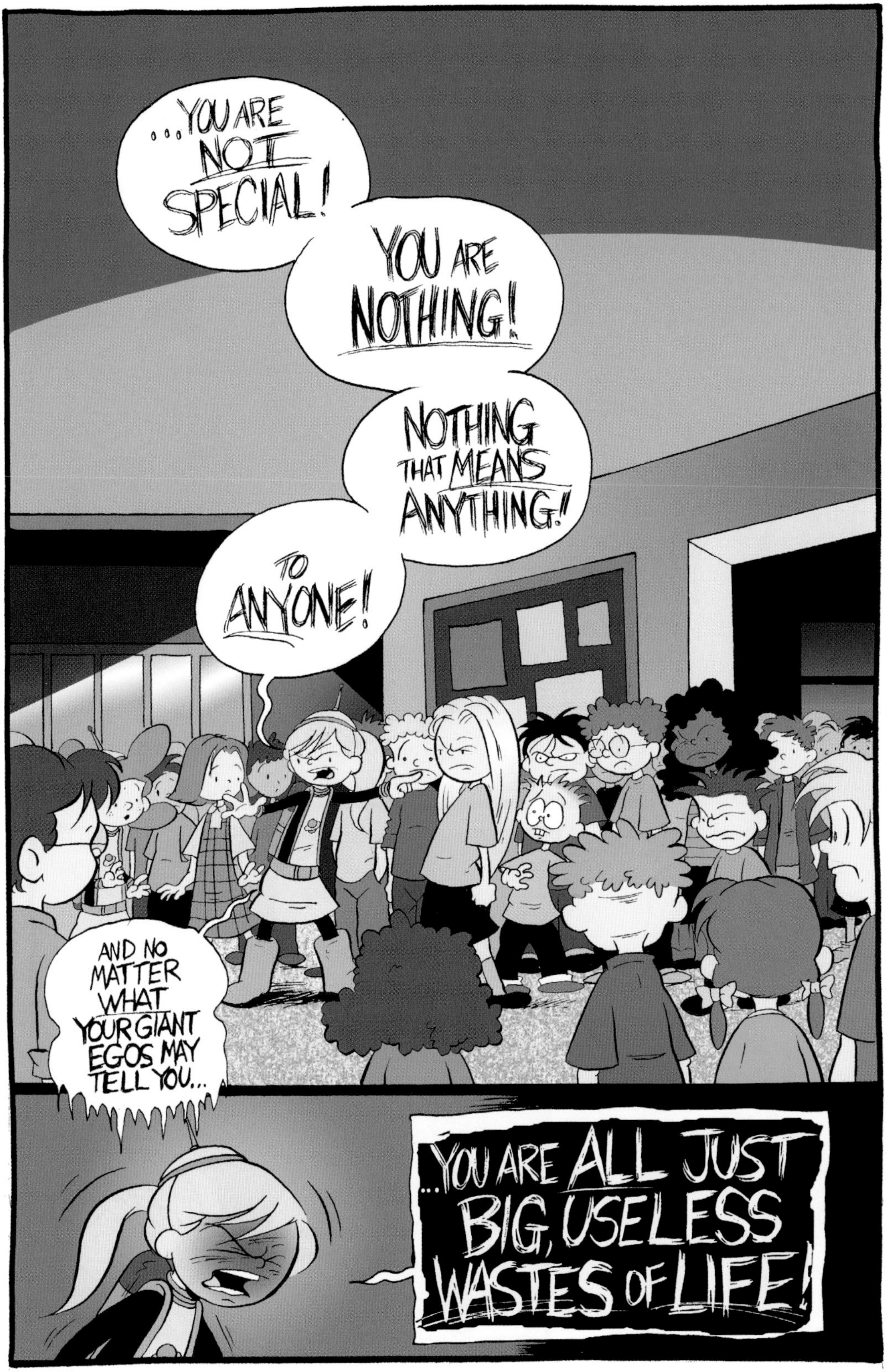
...YOU ARE NOT SPECIAL!
YOU ARE NOTHING!
NOTHING THAT MEANS ANYTHING!
TO ANYONE!
AND NO MATTER WHAT YOUR GIANT EGOS MAY TELL YOU...
...YOU ARE ALL JUST BIG, USELESS WASTES OF LIFE!

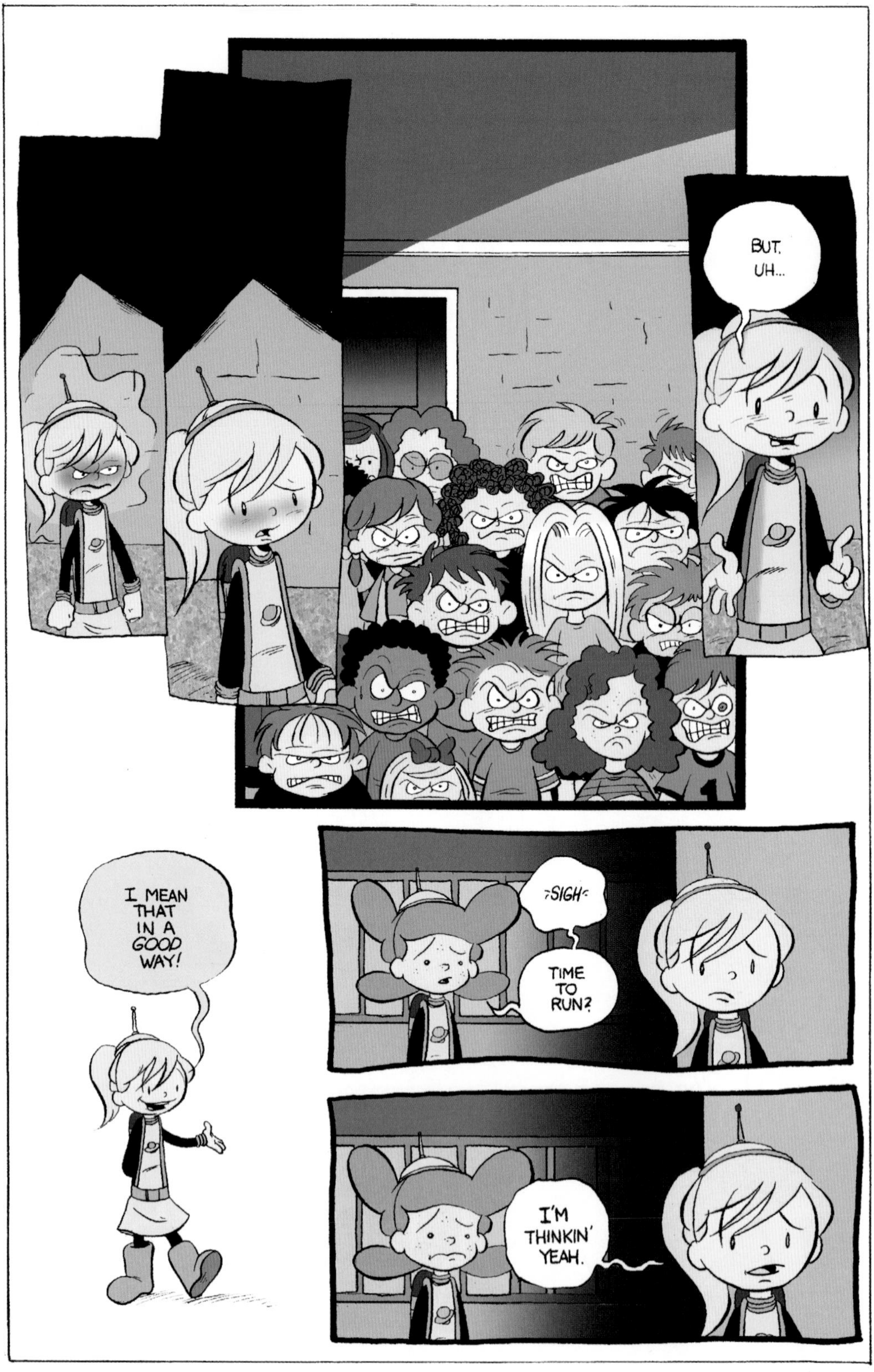
BUT, UH...
I MEAN THAT IN A GOOD WAY!
~SIGH~
TIME TO RUN?
I'M THINKIN' YEAH.

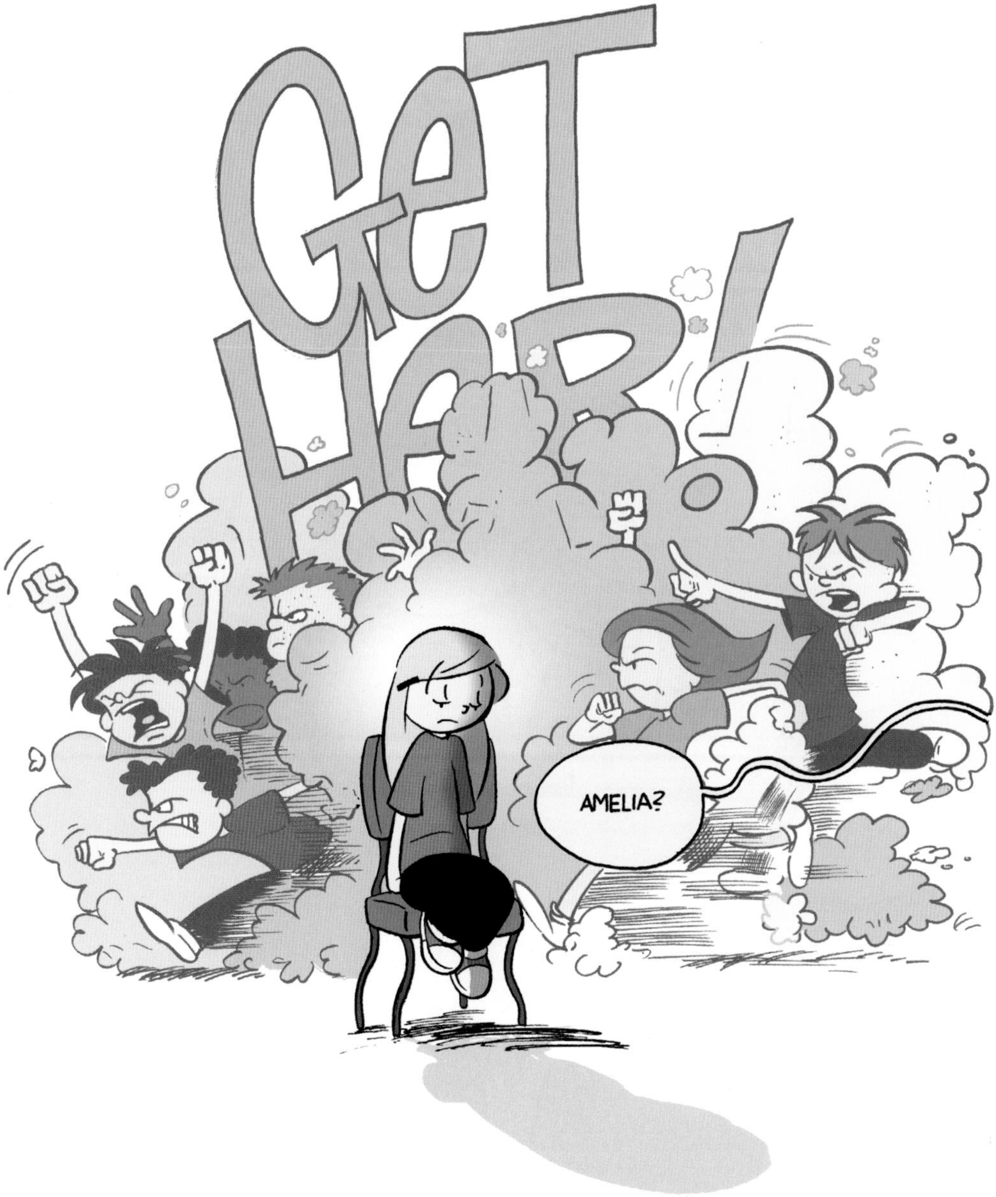
GET HER!
AMELIA?

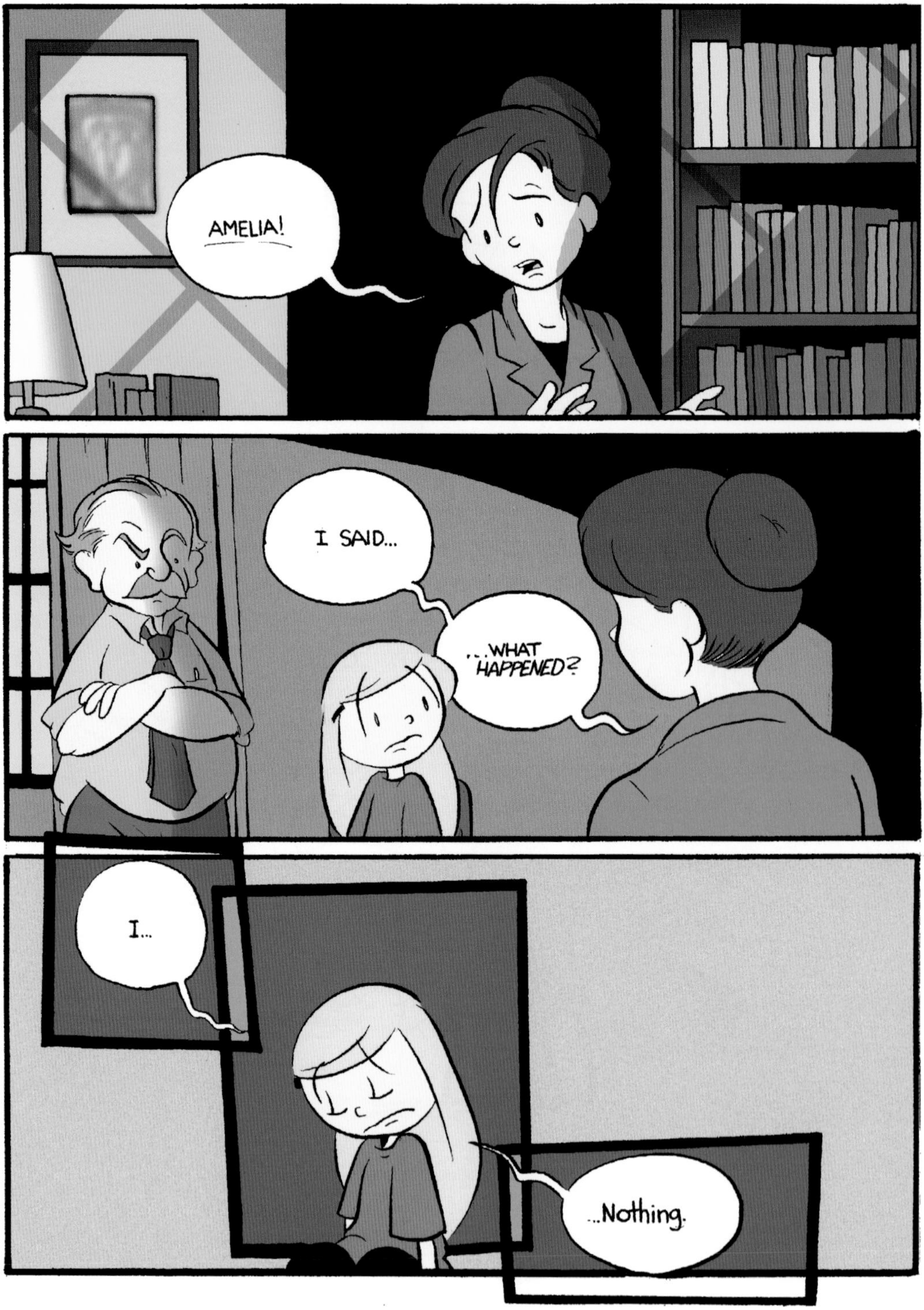
AMELIA!
I SAID...
...WHAT HAPPENED?
I...
...Nothing.

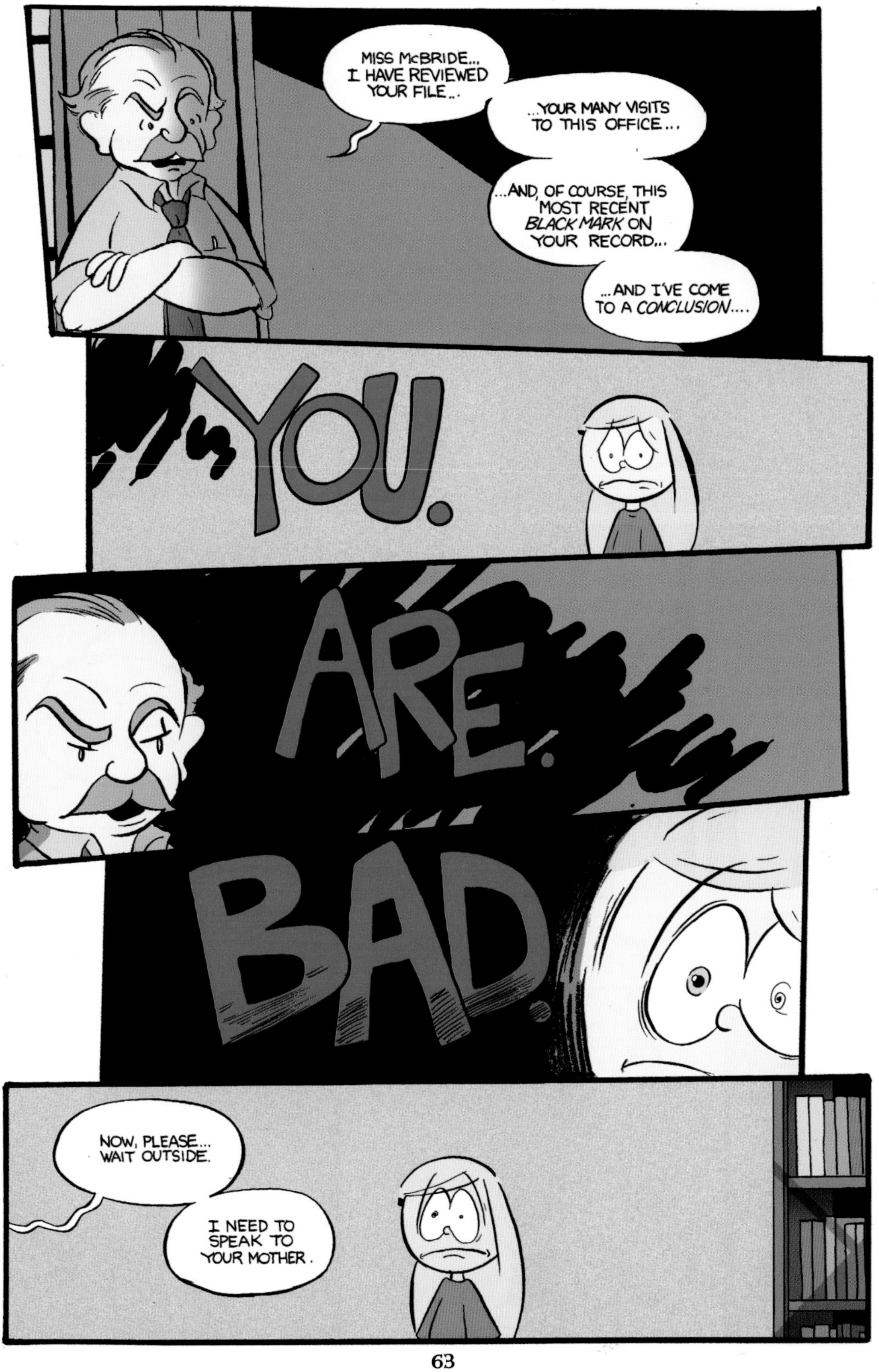
MISS McBRIDE... I HAVE REVIEWED YOUR FILE...
...YOUR MANY VISITS TO THIS OFFICE...
...AND, OF COURSE, THIS MOST RECENT *BLACK MARK* ON YOUR RECORD...
...AND I'VE COME TO A *CONCLUSION*....
YOU.
ARE.
BAD.
NOW, PLEASE... WAIT OUTSIDE.
I NEED TO SPEAK TO YOUR MOTHER.

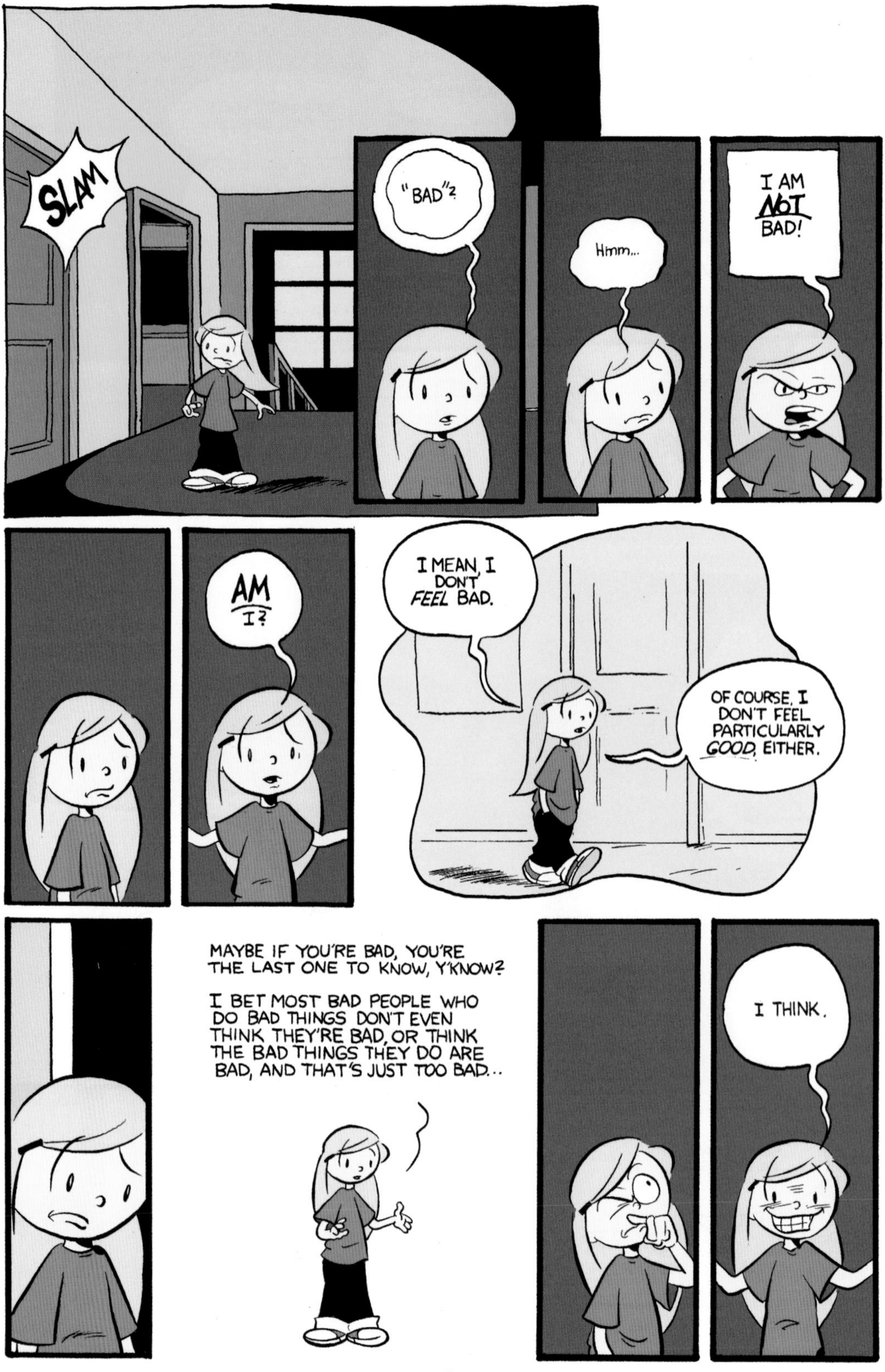
SLAM
"BAD"?
Hmm...
I AM NOT BAD!
AM I?
I MEAN, I DON'T FEEL BAD.
OF COURSE, I DON'T FEEL PARTICULARLY GOOD, EITHER.
MAYBE IF YOU'RE BAD, YOU'RE THE LAST ONE TO KNOW, Y'KNOW?
I BET MOST BAD PEOPLE WHO DO BAD THINGS DON'T EVEN THINK THEY'RE BAD, OR THINK THE BAD THINGS THEY DO ARE BAD, AND THAT'S JUST TOO BAD...
I THINK.

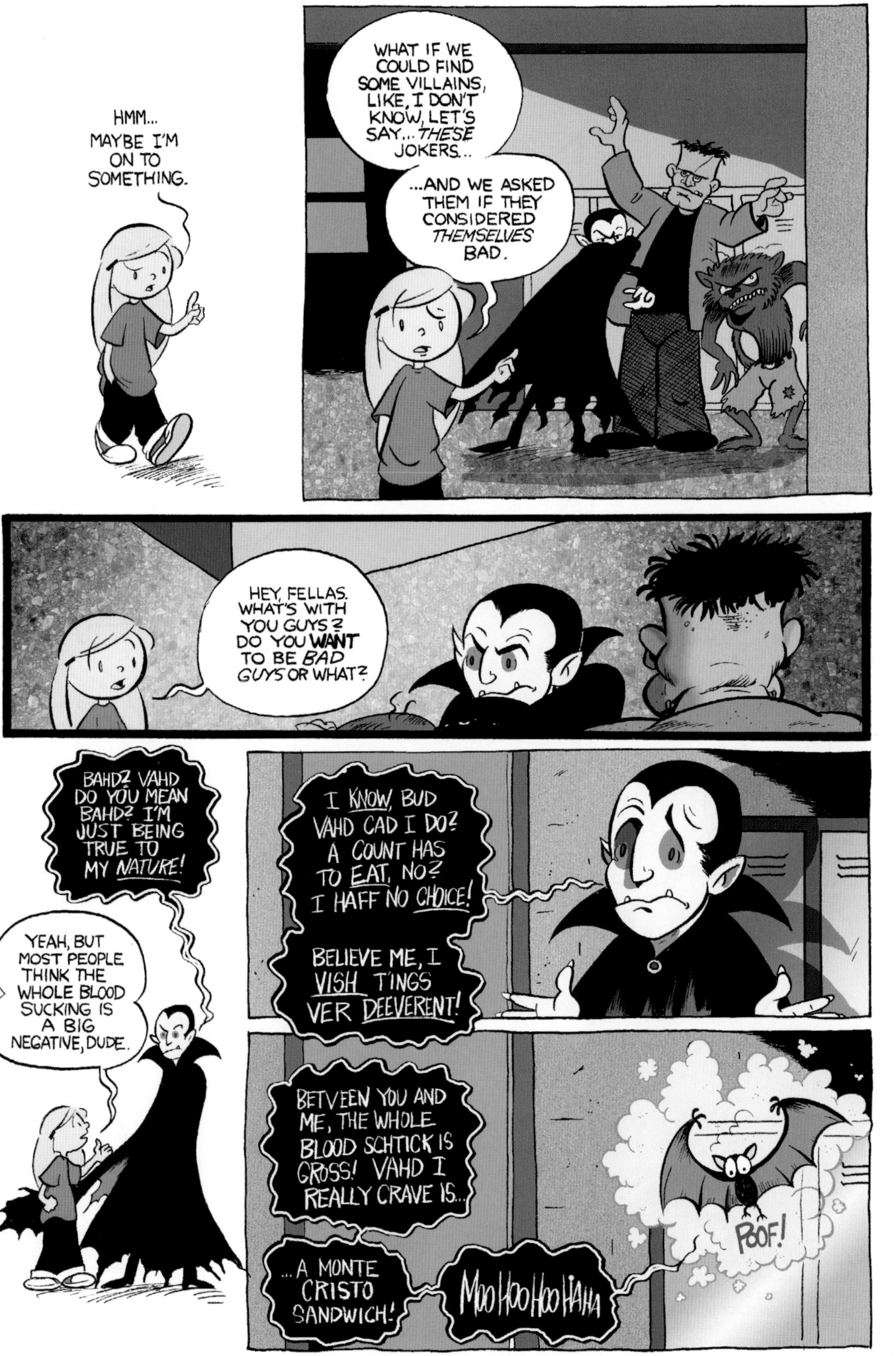
HMM... MAYBE I'M ON TO SOMETHING.
WHAT IF WE COULD FIND SOME VILLAINS, LIKE, I DON'T KNOW, LET'S SAY... THESE JOKERS...
...AND WE ASKED THEM IF THEY CONSIDERED THEMSELVES BAD.
HEY, FELLAS. WHAT'S WITH YOU GUYS? DO YOU WANT TO BE BAD GUYS OR WHAT?
BAHD? VAHD DO YOU MEAN BAHD? I'M JUST BEING TRUE TO MY NATURE!
YEAH, BUT MOST PEOPLE THINK THE WHOLE BLOOD SUCKING IS A BIG NEGATIVE, DUDE.
I KNOW, BUD VAHD CAD I DO? A COUNT HAS TO EAT, NO? I HAFF NO CHOICE!
BELIEVE ME, I VISH T'INGS VER DEEVERENT!
BETVEEN YOU AND ME, THE WHOLE BLOOD SCHTICK IS GROSS! VAHD I REALLY CRAVE IS...
...A MONTE CRISTO SANDWICH!
MOO HOO HOO HAHA
POOF!

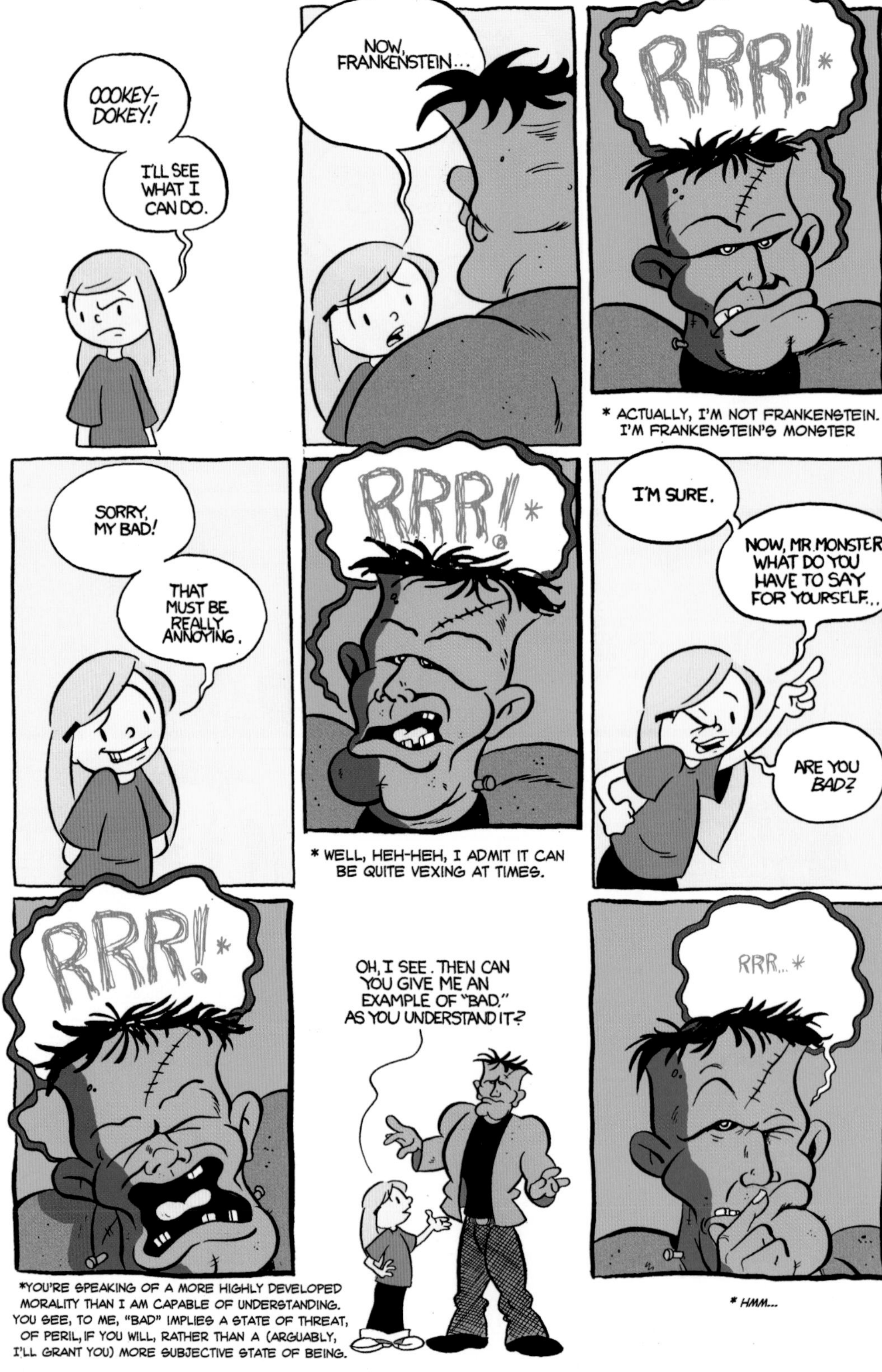
OOOKEY-DOKEY!
I'LL SEE WHAT I CAN DO.
NOW, FRANKENSTEIN...
RRR!*
* ACTUALLY, I'M NOT FRANKENSTEIN. I'M FRANKENSTEIN'S MONSTER
SORRY, MY BAD!
THAT MUST BE REALLY ANNOYING.
RRR!*
* WELL, HEH-HEH, I ADMIT IT CAN BE QUITE VEXING AT TIMES.
I'M SURE.
NOW, MR. MONSTER, WHAT DO YOU HAVE TO SAY FOR YOURSELF...
ARE YOU BAD?
RRR!*
*YOU'RE SPEAKING OF A MORE HIGHLY DEVELOPED MORALITY THAN I AM CAPABLE OF UNDERSTANDING. YOU SEE, TO ME, "BAD" IMPLIES A STATE OF THREAT, OF PERIL, IF YOU WILL, RATHER THAN A (ARGUABLY, I'LL GRANT YOU) MORE SUBJECTIVE STATE OF BEING.
OH, I SEE. THEN CAN YOU GIVE ME AN EXAMPLE OF "BAD," AS YOU UNDERSTAND IT?
RRR...*
* HMM...

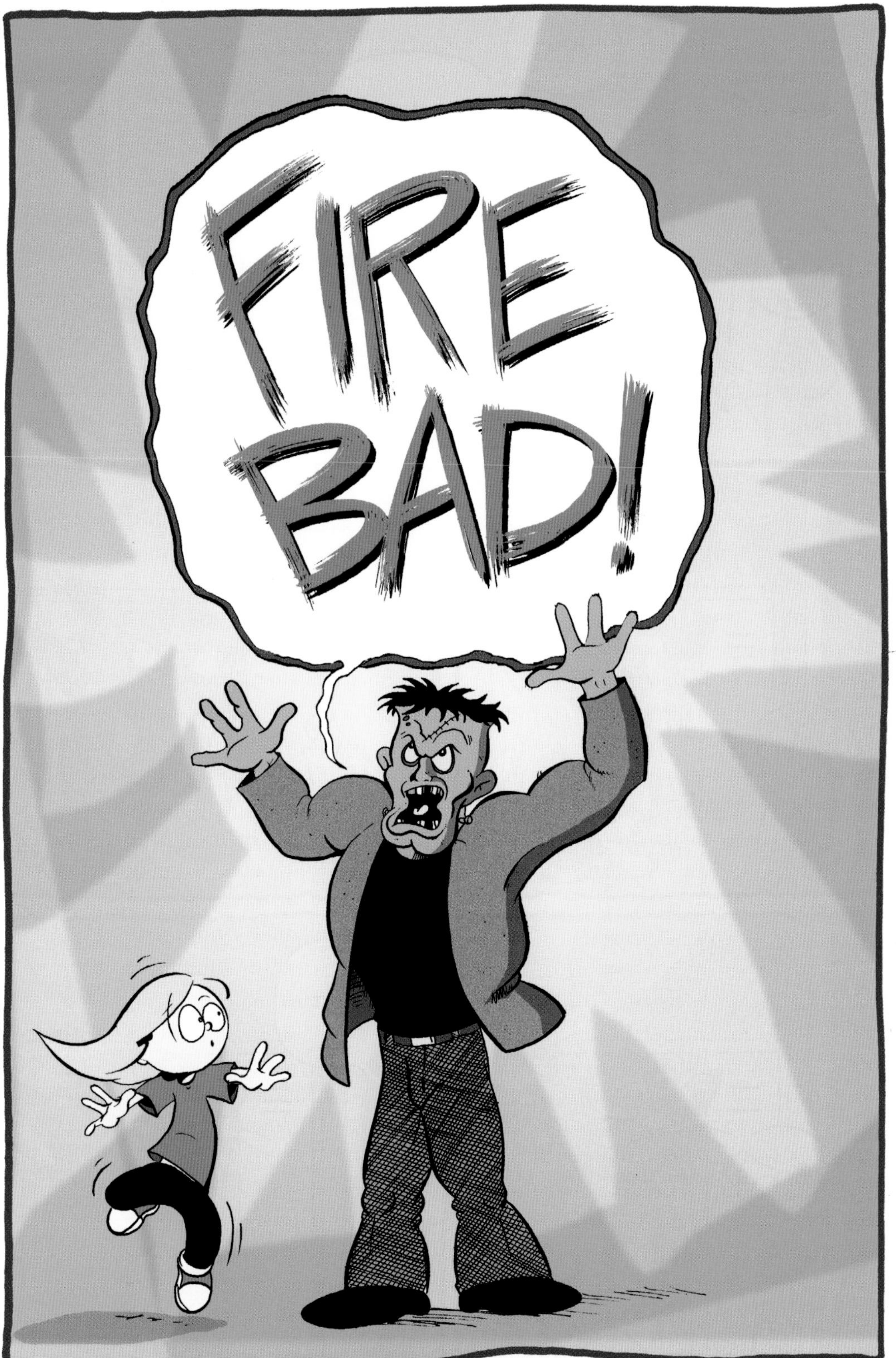
FIRE BAD!

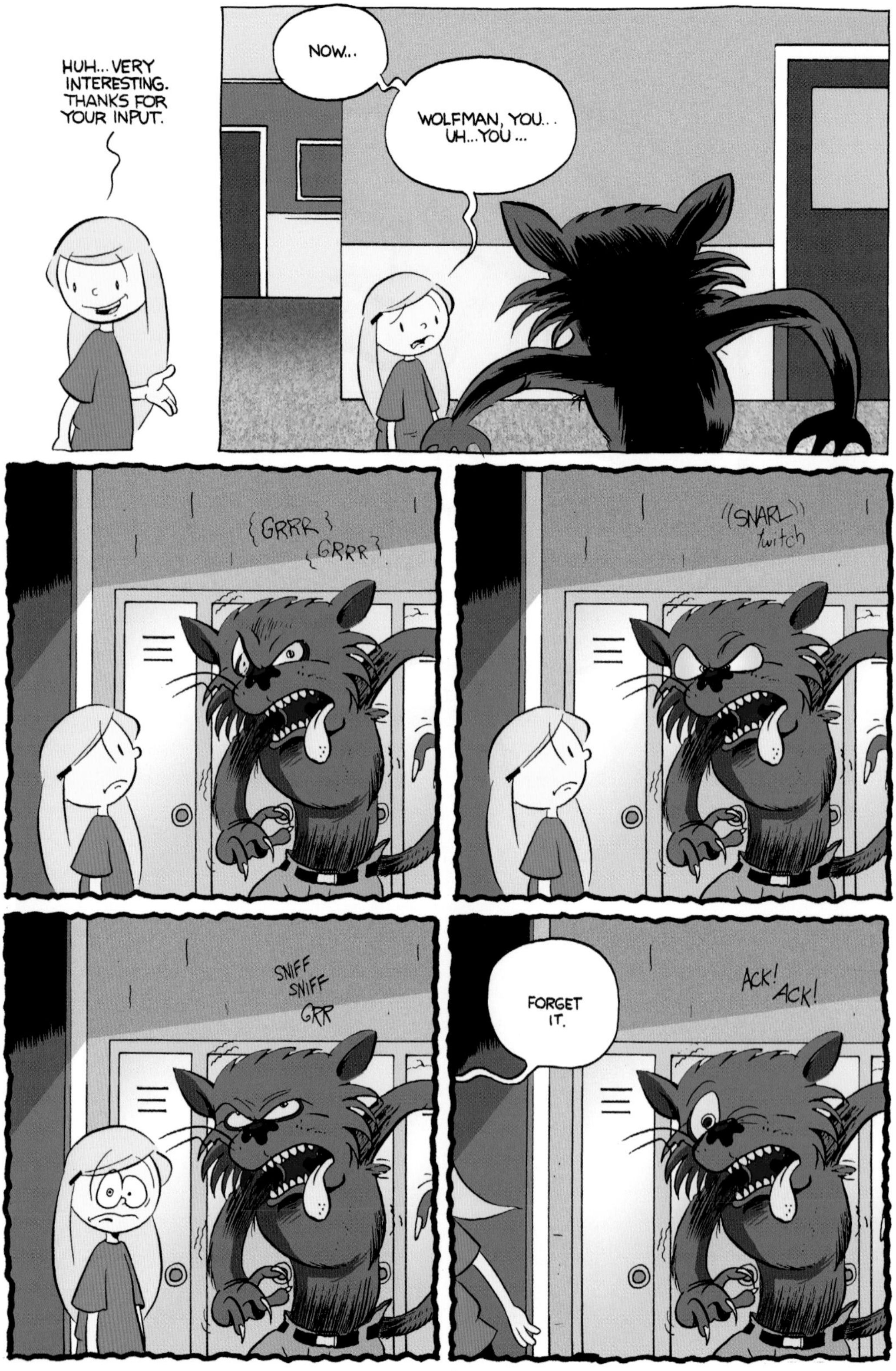
HUH... VERY INTERESTING. THANKS FOR YOUR INPUT.
NOW...
WOLFMAN, YOU... UH... YOU ...
{GRRR}
{GRRR}
((SNARL))
twitch
SNIFF
SNIFF
GRR
FORGET IT.
ACK!
ACK!

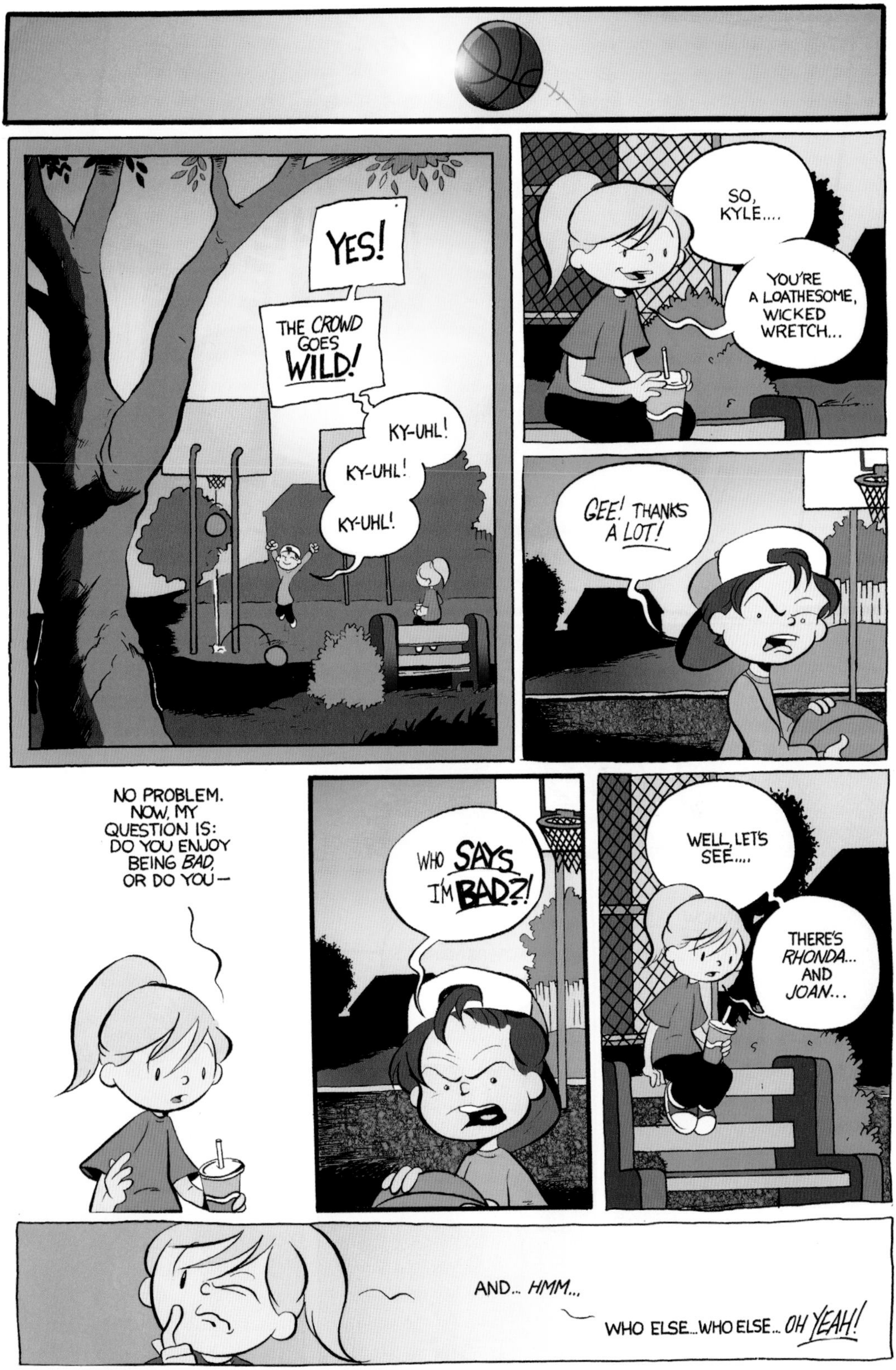

YES!
THE CROWD GOES WILD!
KY-UHL!
KY-UHL!
KY-UHL!
SO, KYLE....
YOU'RE A LOATHESOME, WICKED WRETCH...
GEE! THANKS A LOT!
NO PROBLEM. NOW, MY QUESTION IS: DO YOU ENJOY BEING BAD, OR DO YOU—
WHO SAYS I'M BAD?!
WELL, LET'S SEE....
THERE'S RHONDA... AND JOAN...
AND... HMM...
WHO ELSE...WHO ELSE... OH YEAH!

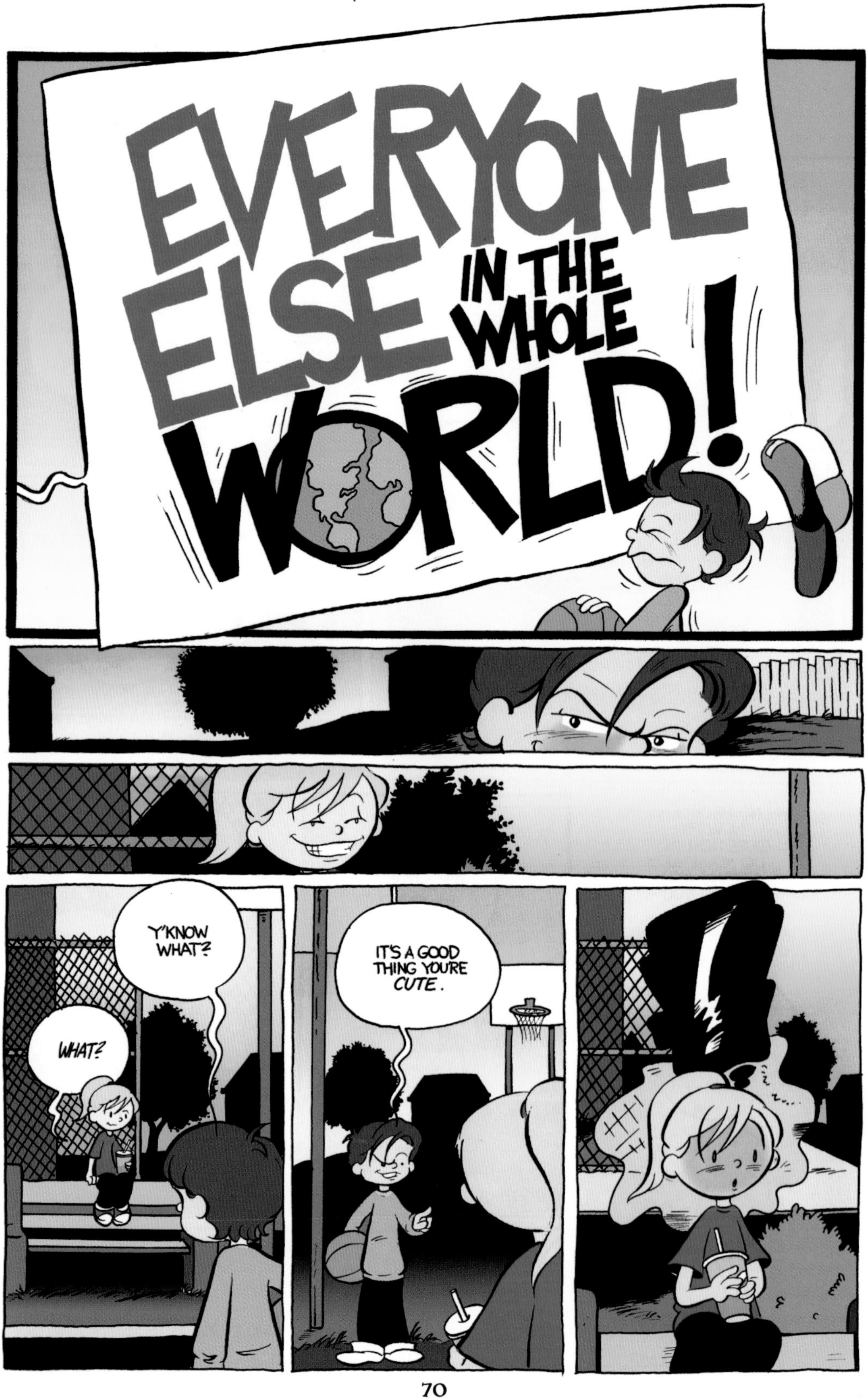
EVERYONE ELSE IN THE WHOLE WORLD!
Y'KNOW WHAT?
WHAT?
IT'S A GOOD THING YOU'RE CUTE.

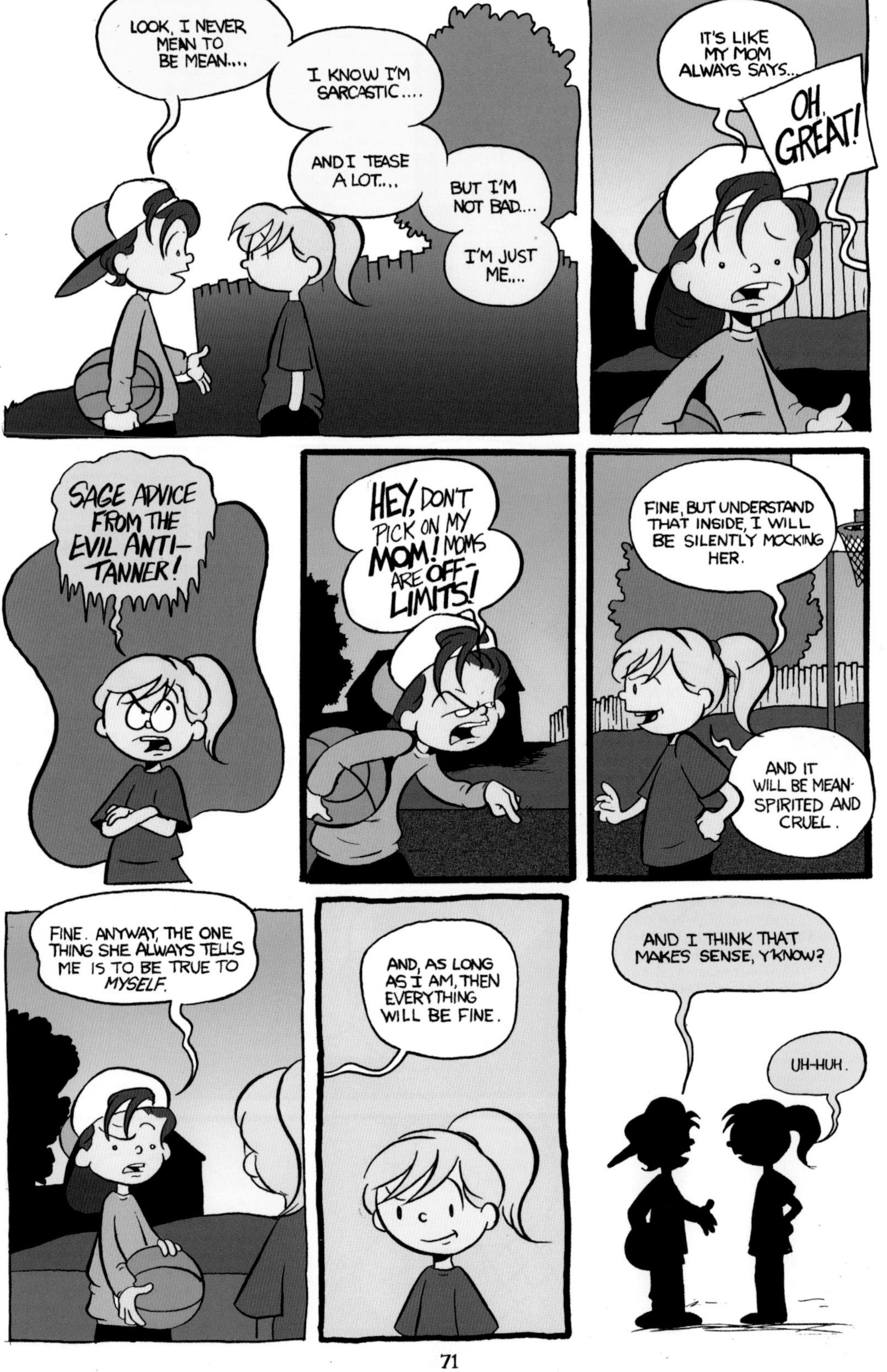
LOOK, I NEVER MEAN TO BE MEAN....
I KNOW I'M SARCASTIC....
AND I TEASE A LOT....
BUT I'M NOT BAD....
I'M JUST ME....
IT'S LIKE MY MOM ALWAYS SAYS...
OH, GREAT!
SAGE ADVICE FROM THE EVIL ANTI-TANNER!
HEY, DON'T PICK ON MY MOM! MOMS ARE OFF-LIMITS!
FINE, BUT UNDERSTAND THAT INSIDE, I WILL BE SILENTLY MOCKING HER.
AND IT WILL BE MEAN-SPIRITED AND CRUEL.
FINE. ANYWAY, THE ONE THING SHE ALWAYS TELLS ME IS TO BE TRUE TO MYSELF.
AND, AS LONG AS I AM, THEN EVERYTHING WILL BE FINE.
AND I THINK THAT MAKES SENSE, Y'KNOW?
UH-HUH.

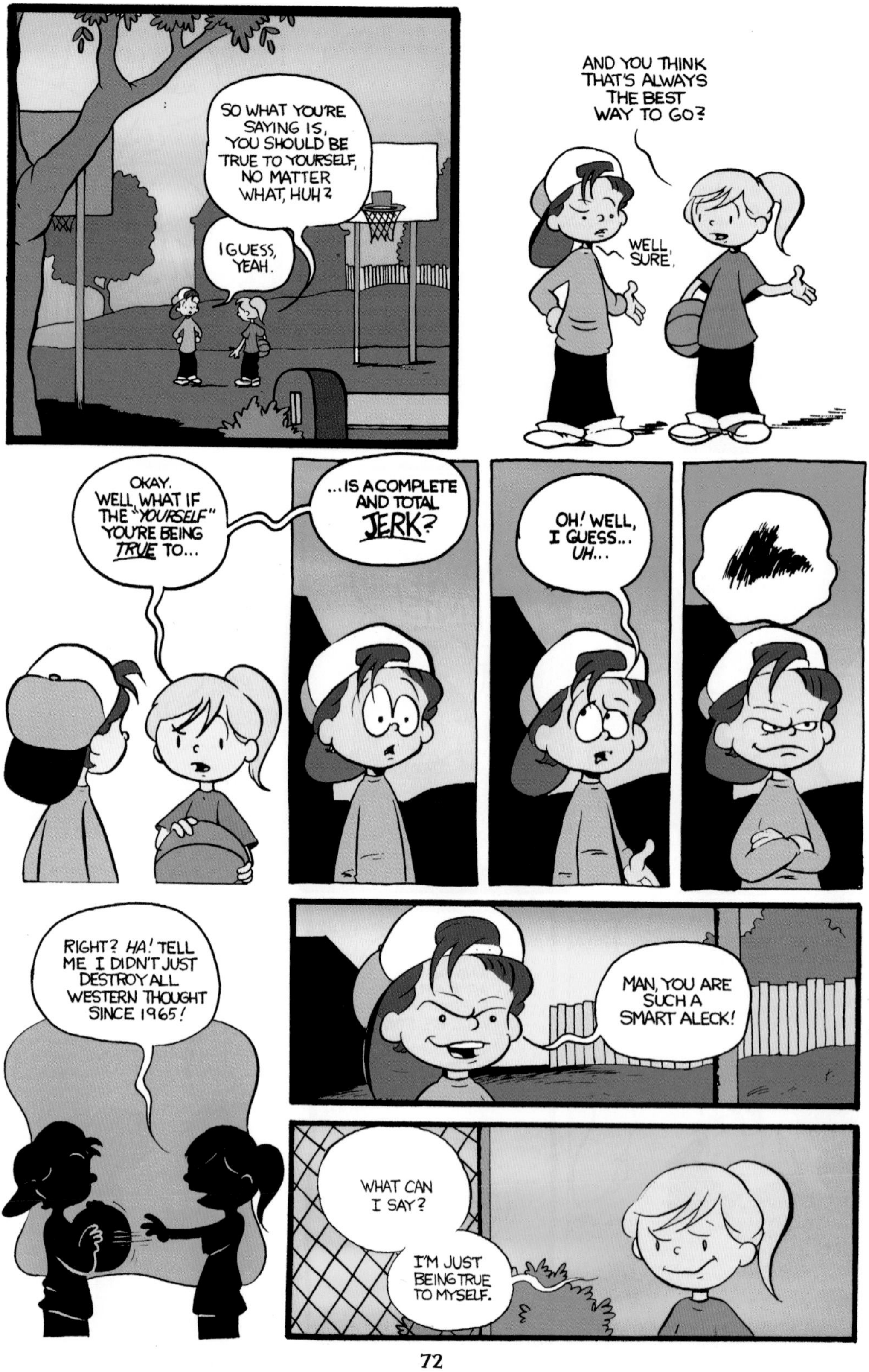
SO WHAT YOU'RE SAYING IS, YOU SHOULD BE TRUE TO YOURSELF, NO MATTER WHAT, HUH?
I GUESS, YEAH.
AND YOU THINK THAT'S ALWAYS THE BEST WAY TO GO?
WELL, SURE.
OKAY. WELL, WHAT IF THE "YOURSELF" YOU'RE BEING TRUE TO...
...IS A COMPLETE AND TOTAL JERK?
OH! WELL, I GUESS... UH...
RIGHT? HA! TELL ME I DIDN'T JUST DESTROY ALL WESTERN THOUGHT SINCE 1965!
MAN, YOU ARE SUCH A SMART ALECK!
WHAT CAN I SAY?
I'M JUST BEING TRUE TO MYSELF.

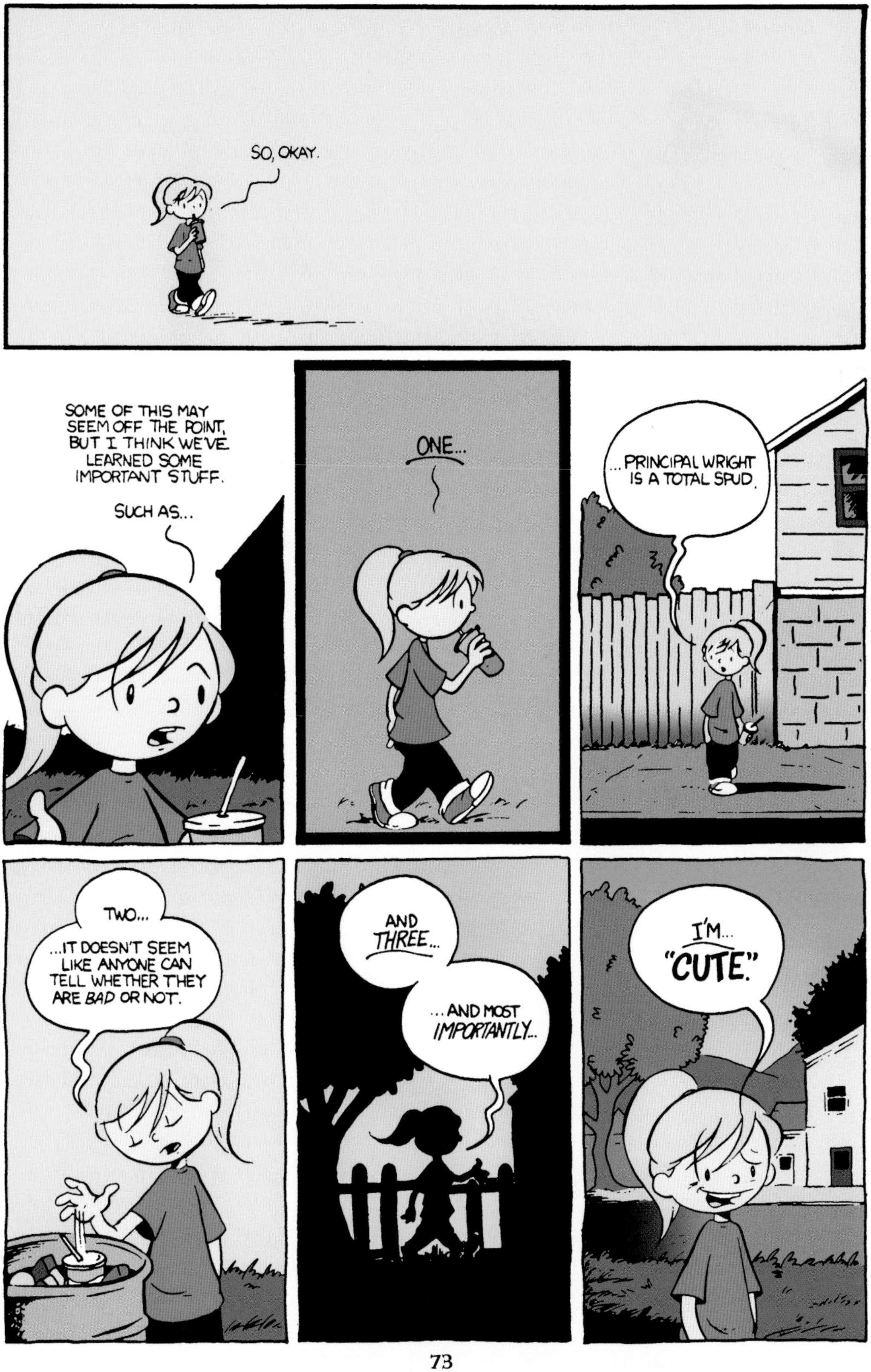
SO, OKAY.
SOME OF THIS MAY SEEM OFF THE POINT, BUT I THINK WE'VE LEARNED SOME IMPORTANT STUFF.
SUCH AS...
ONE...
...PRINCIPAL WRIGHT IS A TOTAL SPUD.
TWO...
...IT DOESN'T SEEM LIKE ANYONE CAN TELL WHETHER THEY ARE BAD OR NOT.
AND THREE...
...AND MOST IMPORTANTLY...
I'M... "CUTE."

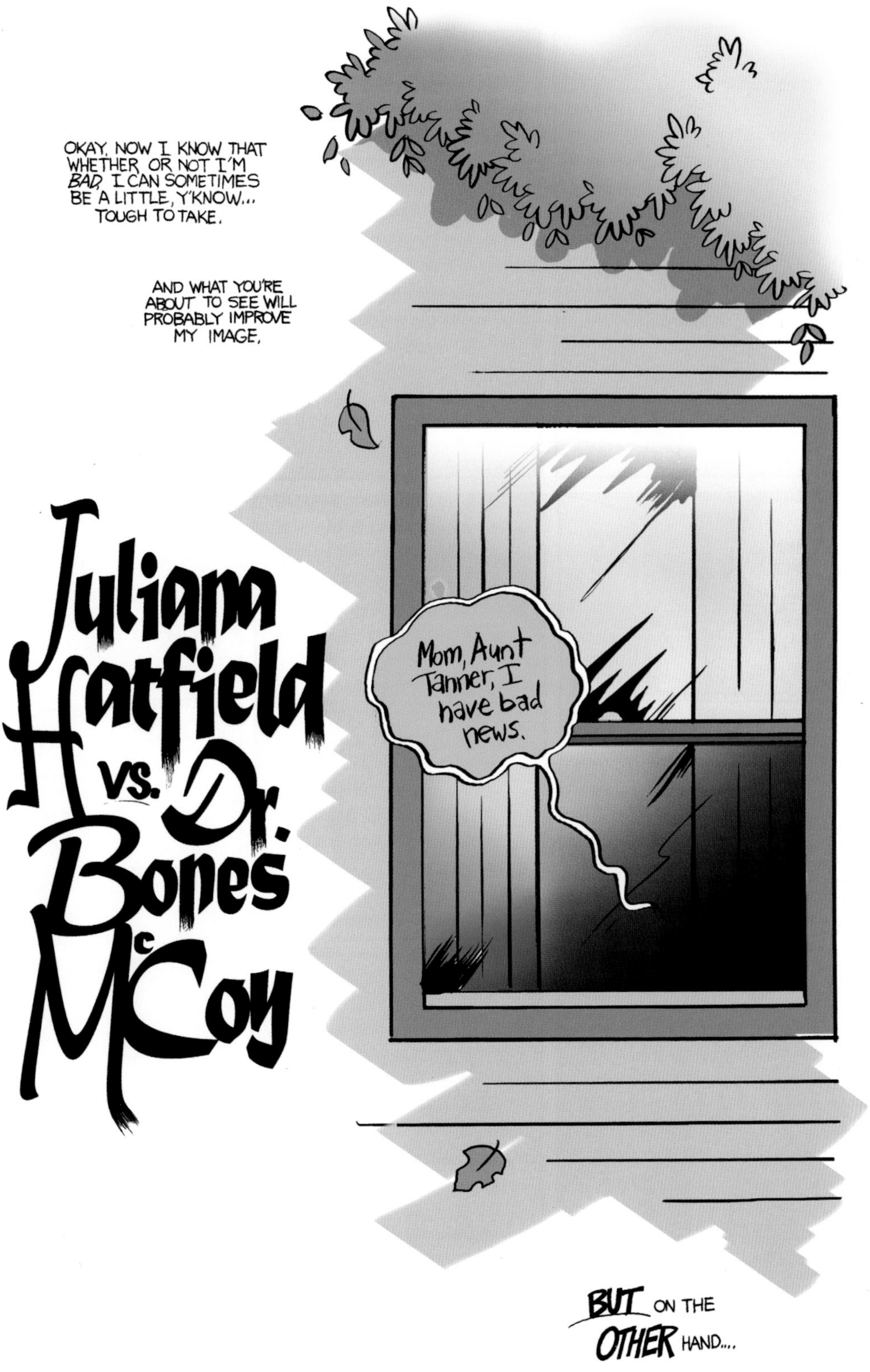
OKAY, NOW I KNOW THAT WHETHER OR NOT I'M *BAD*, I CAN SOMETIMES BE A LITTLE, Y'KNOW... TOUGH TO TAKE.
AND WHAT YOU'RE ABOUT TO SEE WILL PROBABLY IMPROVE MY IMAGE.
Juliana Hatfield vs. Dr. Bones McCoy
Mom, Aunt Tanner, I have bad news.
BUT ON THE OTHER HAND....

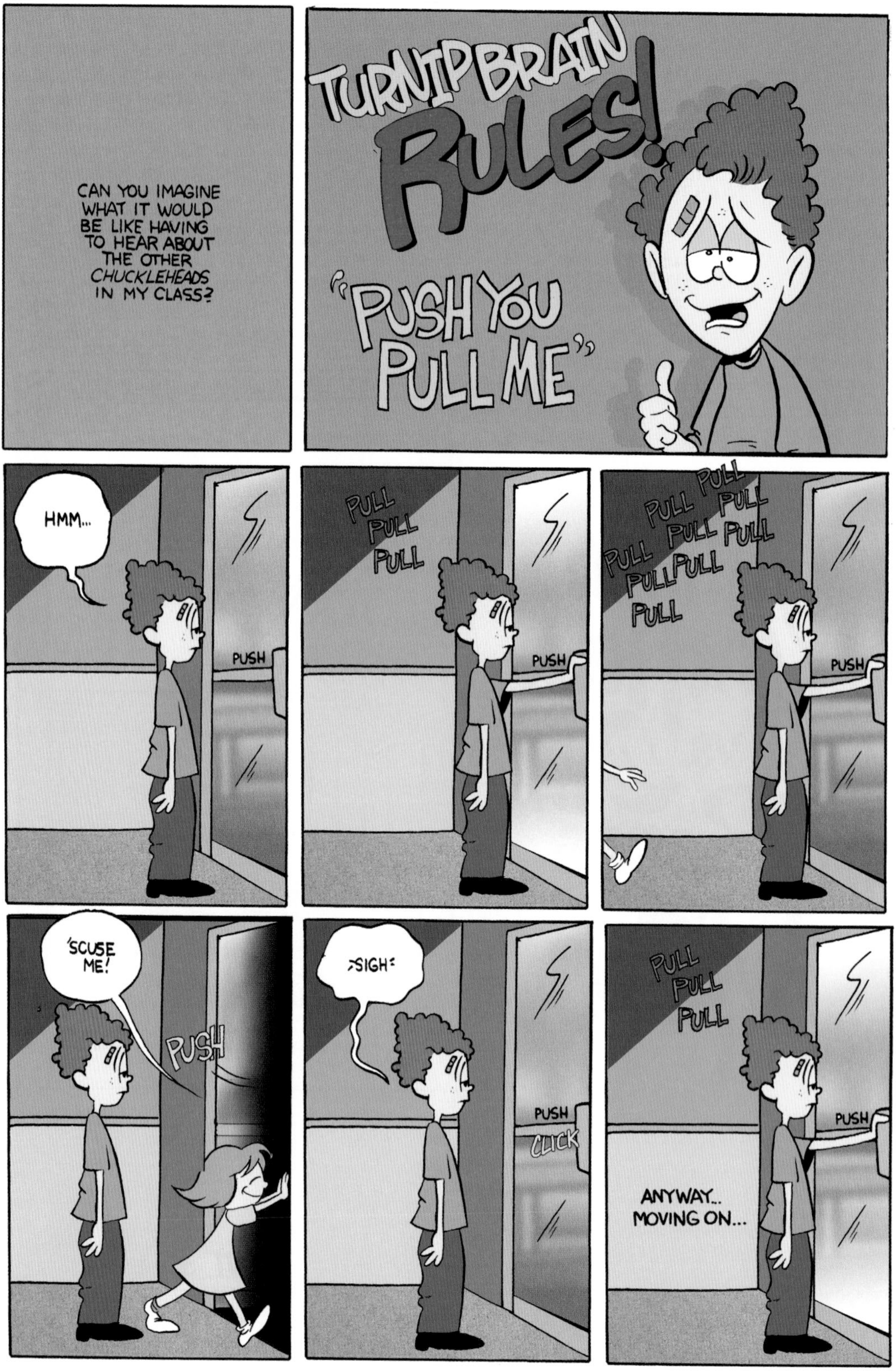
CAN YOU IMAGINE WHAT IT WOULD BE LIKE HAVING TO HEAR ABOUT THE OTHER *CHUCKLEHEADS* IN MY CLASS?
TURNIP BRAIN RULES!
"PUSH YOU PULL ME"
HMM...
PUSH
PULL
PULL
PULL
PUSH
PULL PULL PULL PULL PULL PULL PULL PULL PULL PULL
PUSH
'SCUSE ME!
PUSH
:SIGH:
PUSH
CLICK
PULL
PULL
PULL
PUSH
ANYWAY... MOVING ON...

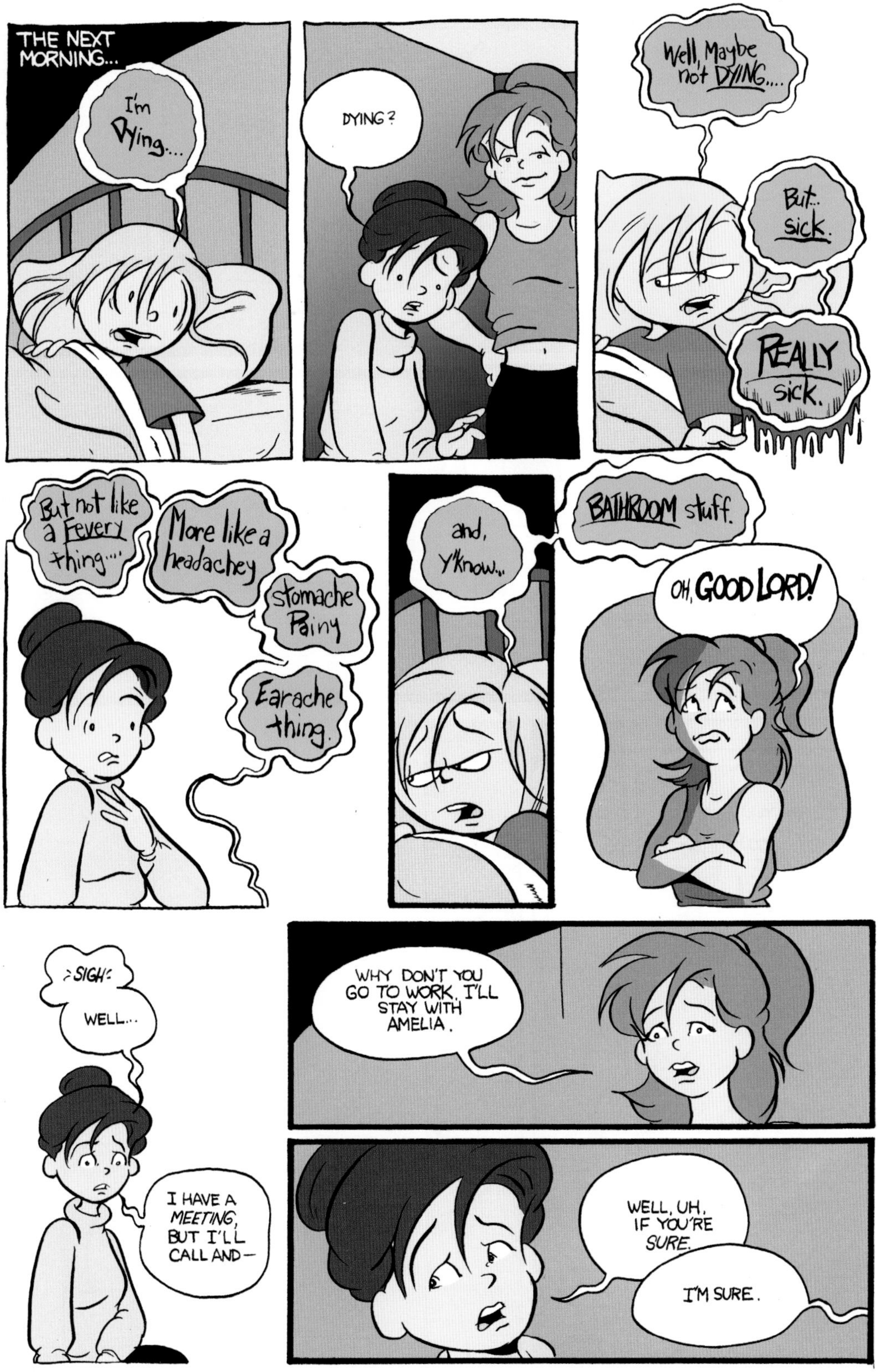
THE NEXT MORNING...
I'm Dying....
DYING?
Well, Maybe not DYING....
But.. sick.
REALLY sick.
But not like a Fevery thing....
More like a headachey
stomache Painy
Earache thing.
and, y'know...
BATHROOM stuff.
OH, GOOD LORD!
:SIGH:
WELL...
I HAVE A MEETING, BUT I'LL CALL AND—
WHY DON'T YOU GO TO WORK. I'LL STAY WITH AMELIA.
WELL, UH, IF YOU'RE SURE.
I'M SURE.

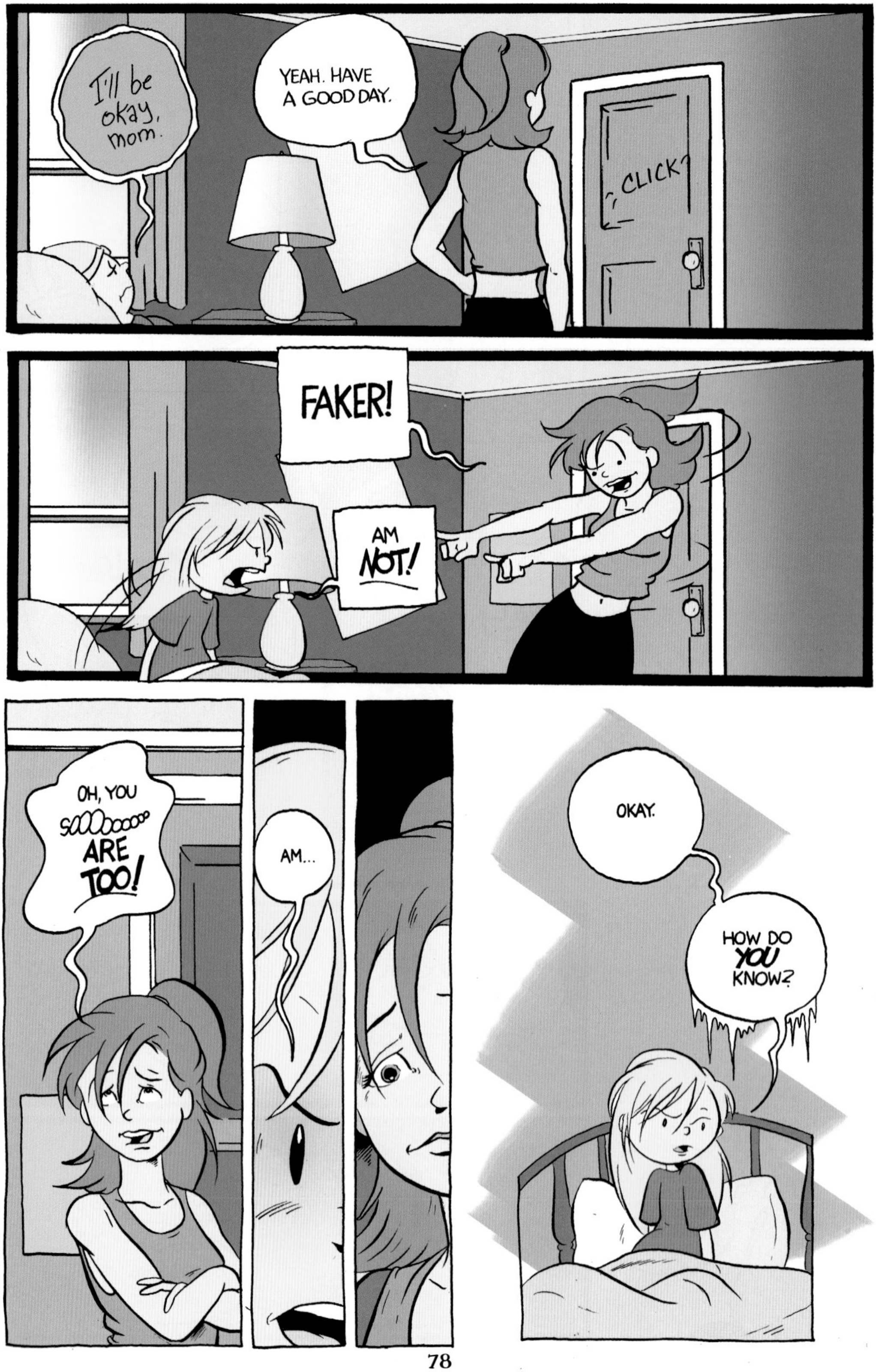
I'll be okay, mom.
YEAH. HAVE A GOOD DAY.
CLICK
FAKER!
AM NOT!
OH, YOU SOOOoooooo ARE TOO!
AM...
OKAY.
HOW DO YOU KNOW?

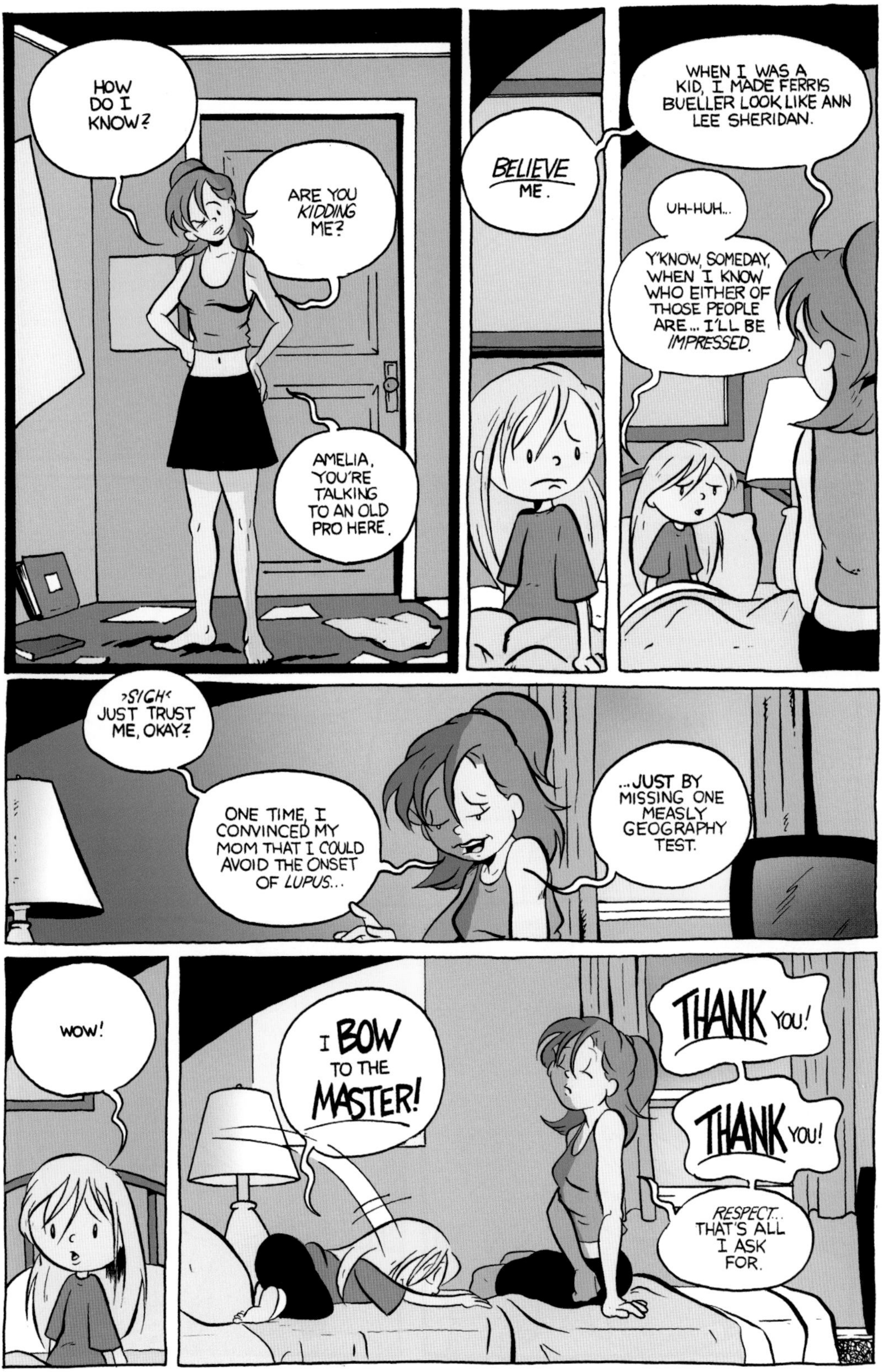
HOW DO I KNOW?
ARE YOU KIDDING ME?
AMELIA, YOU'RE TALKING TO AN OLD PRO HERE.
BELIEVE ME.
WHEN I WAS A KID, I MADE FERRIS BUELLER LOOK LIKE ANN LEE SHERIDAN.
UH-HUH...
Y'KNOW, SOMEDAY, WHEN I KNOW WHO EITHER OF THOSE PEOPLE ARE... I'LL BE IMPRESSED.
>SIGH< JUST TRUST ME, OKAY?
ONE TIME, I CONVINCED MY MOM THAT I COULD AVOID THE ONSET OF LUPUS...
...JUST BY MISSING ONE MEASLY GEOGRAPHY TEST.
WOW!
I BOW TO THE MASTER!
THANK YOU!
THANK YOU!
RESPECT... THAT'S ALL I ASK FOR.

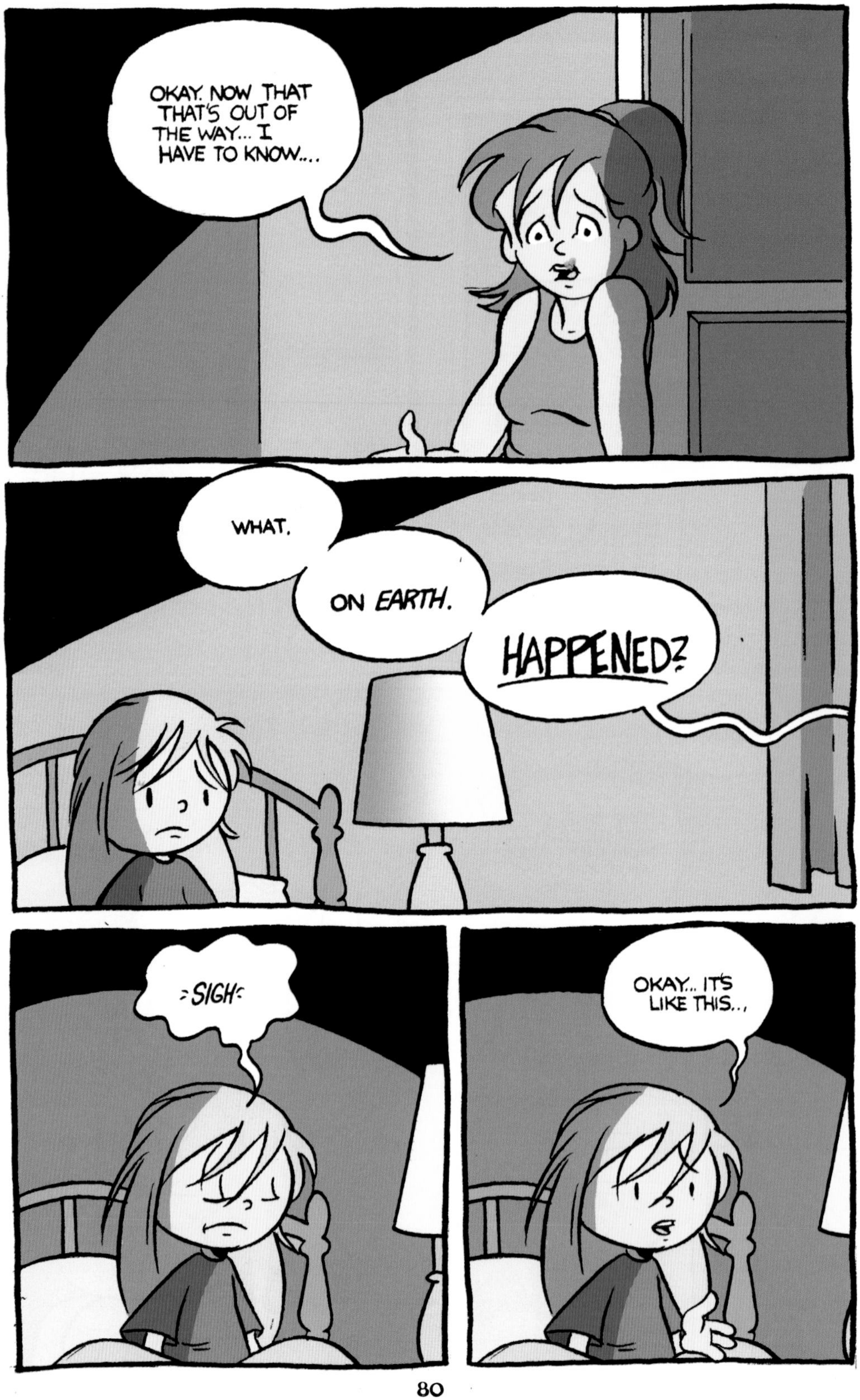
OKAY. NOW THAT THAT'S OUT OF THE WAY... I HAVE TO KNOW....
WHAT.
ON EARTH.
HAPPENED?
SIGH
OKAY... IT'S LIKE THIS...

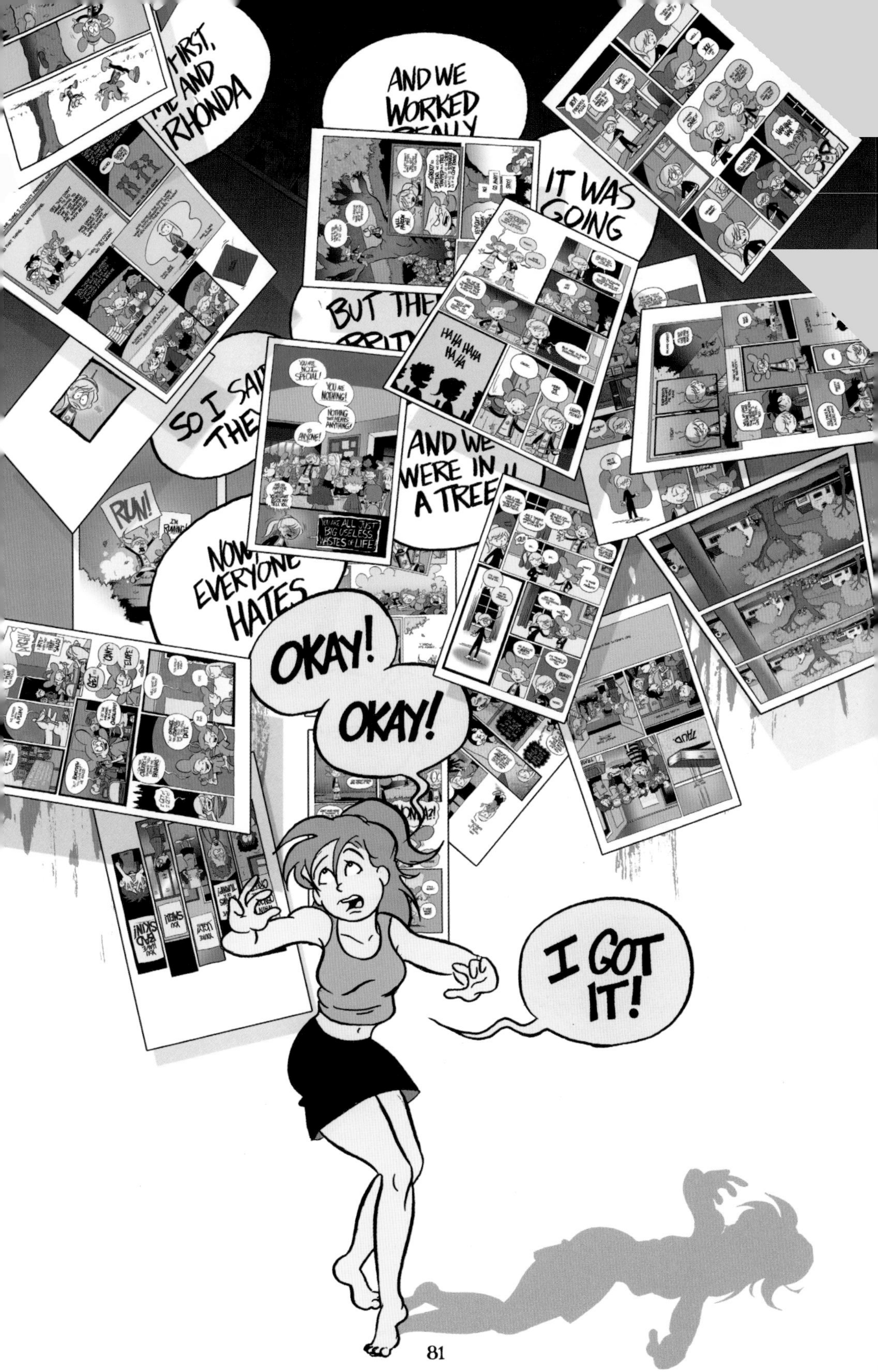
FIRST, ME AND RHONDA
AND WE WORKED
IT WAS GOING
BUT THE
SO I SAI
AND WE WERE IN A TREE
YOU ARE NOT SPECIAL!
YOU ARE NOTHING!
NOTHING THAT MEANS ANYTHING!
TO ANYONE!
YOU ARE ALL JUST BIG USELESS WASTES OF LIFE!
HA HA HAHA HA HA
RUN!
I'M RUNNING!
NOW EVERYONE HATES
OKAY!
OKAY!
I GOT IT!

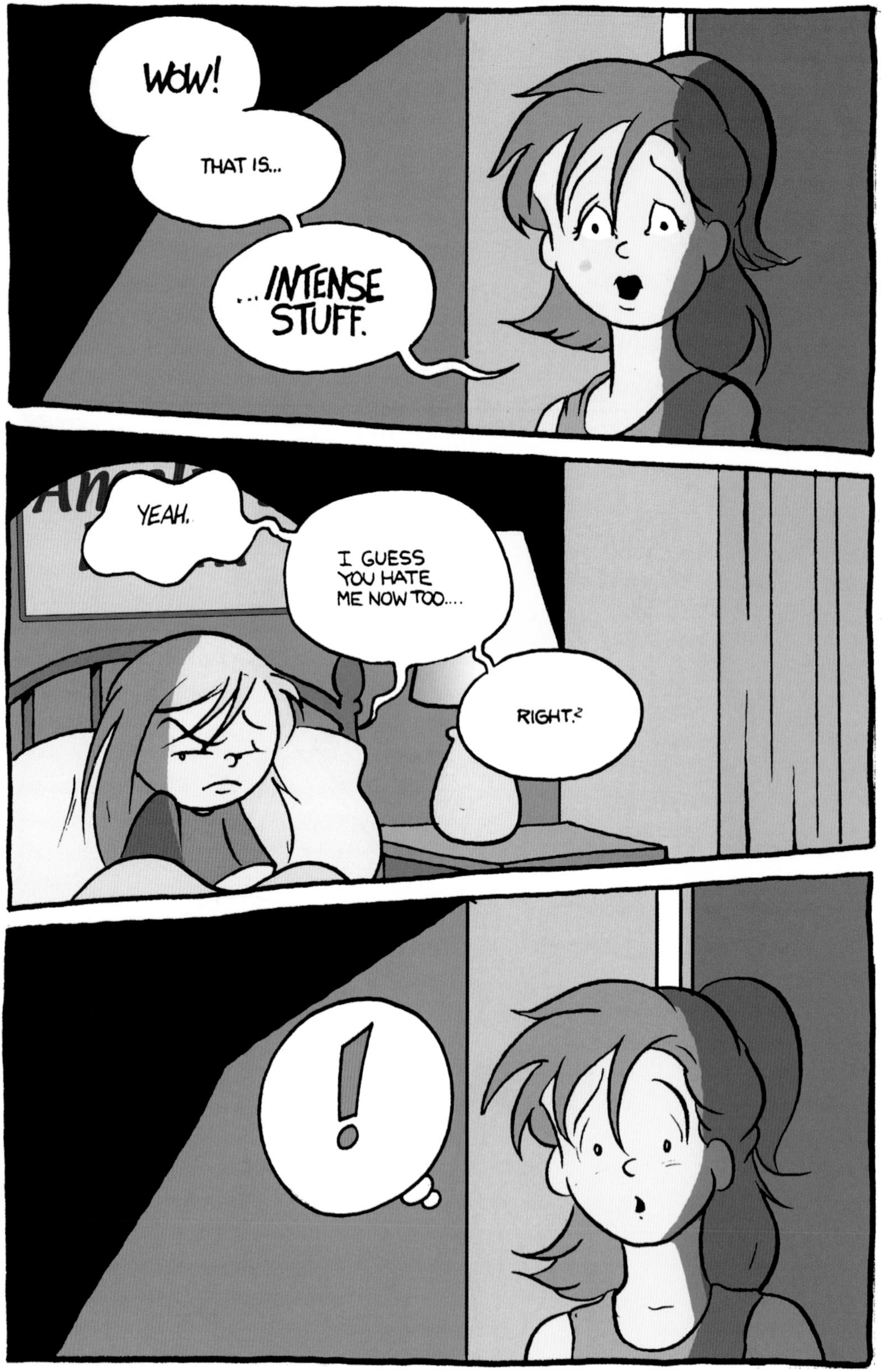
WOW!
THAT IS...
...INTENSE STUFF.
YEAH.
I GUESS YOU HATE ME NOW TOO....
RIGHT.?
!

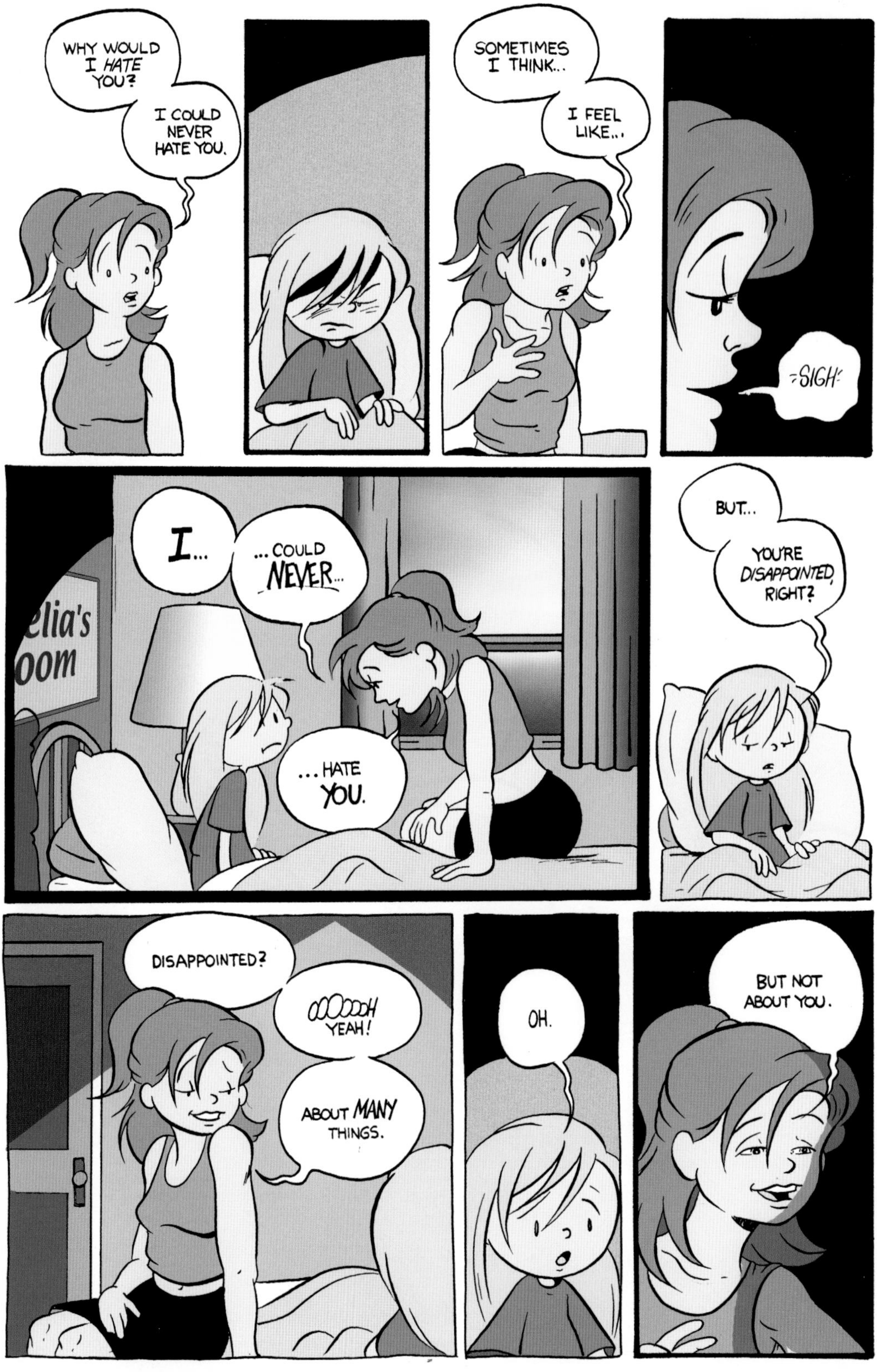
WHY WOULD I *HATE* YOU?
I COULD NEVER HATE YOU.
SOMETIMES I THINK...
I FEEL LIKE...
SIGH
I...
...COULD NEVER...
...HATE YOU.
elia's oom
BUT...
YOU'RE *DISAPPOINTED*, RIGHT?
DISAPPOINTED?
OOOOOOH YEAH!
ABOUT *MANY* THINGS.
OH.
BUT NOT ABOUT YOU.

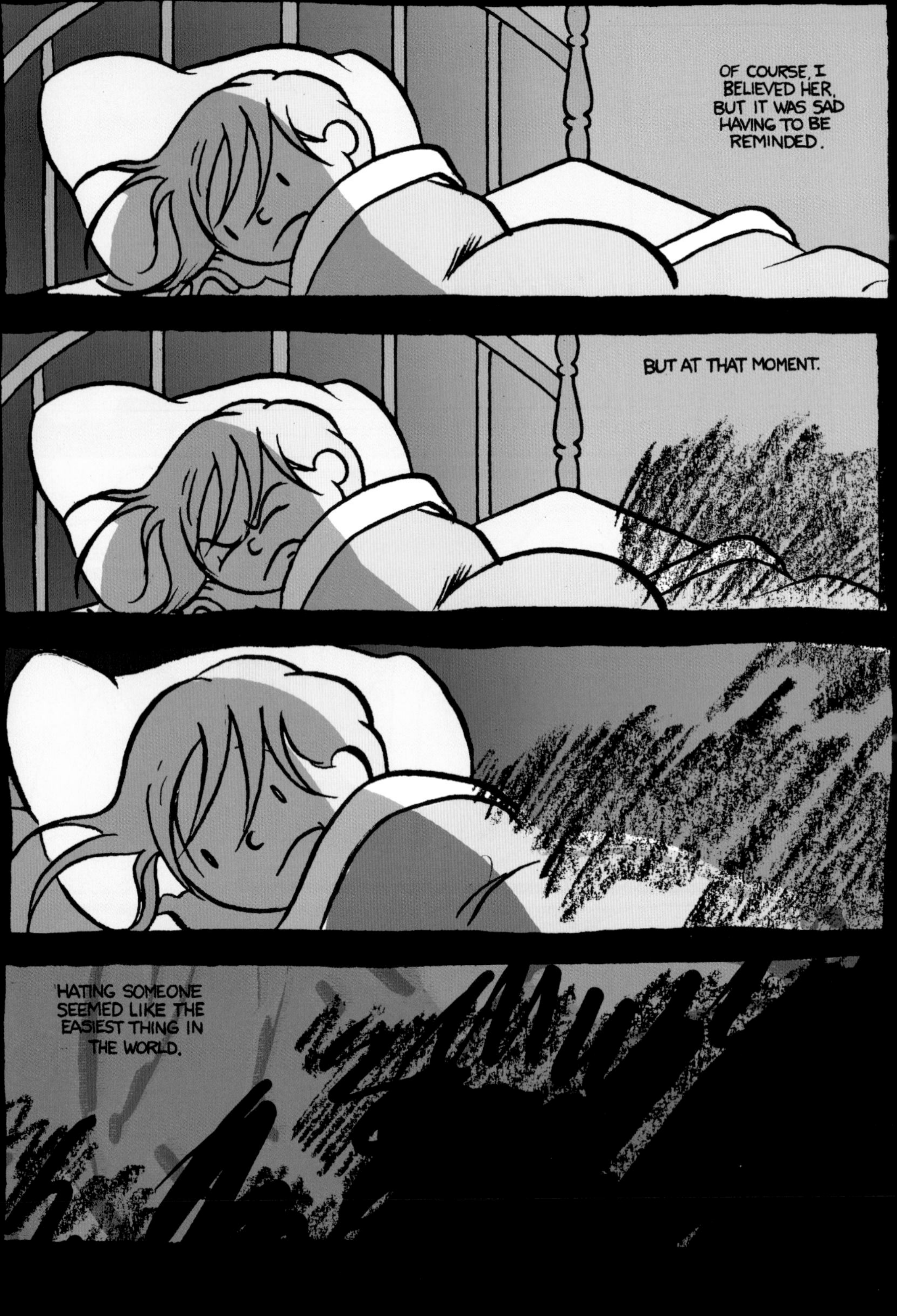
OF COURSE, I BELIEVED HER, BUT IT WAS SAD HAVING TO BE REMINDED.
BUT AT THAT MOMENT,
HATING SOMEONE SEEMED LIKE THE EASIEST THING IN THE WORLD.

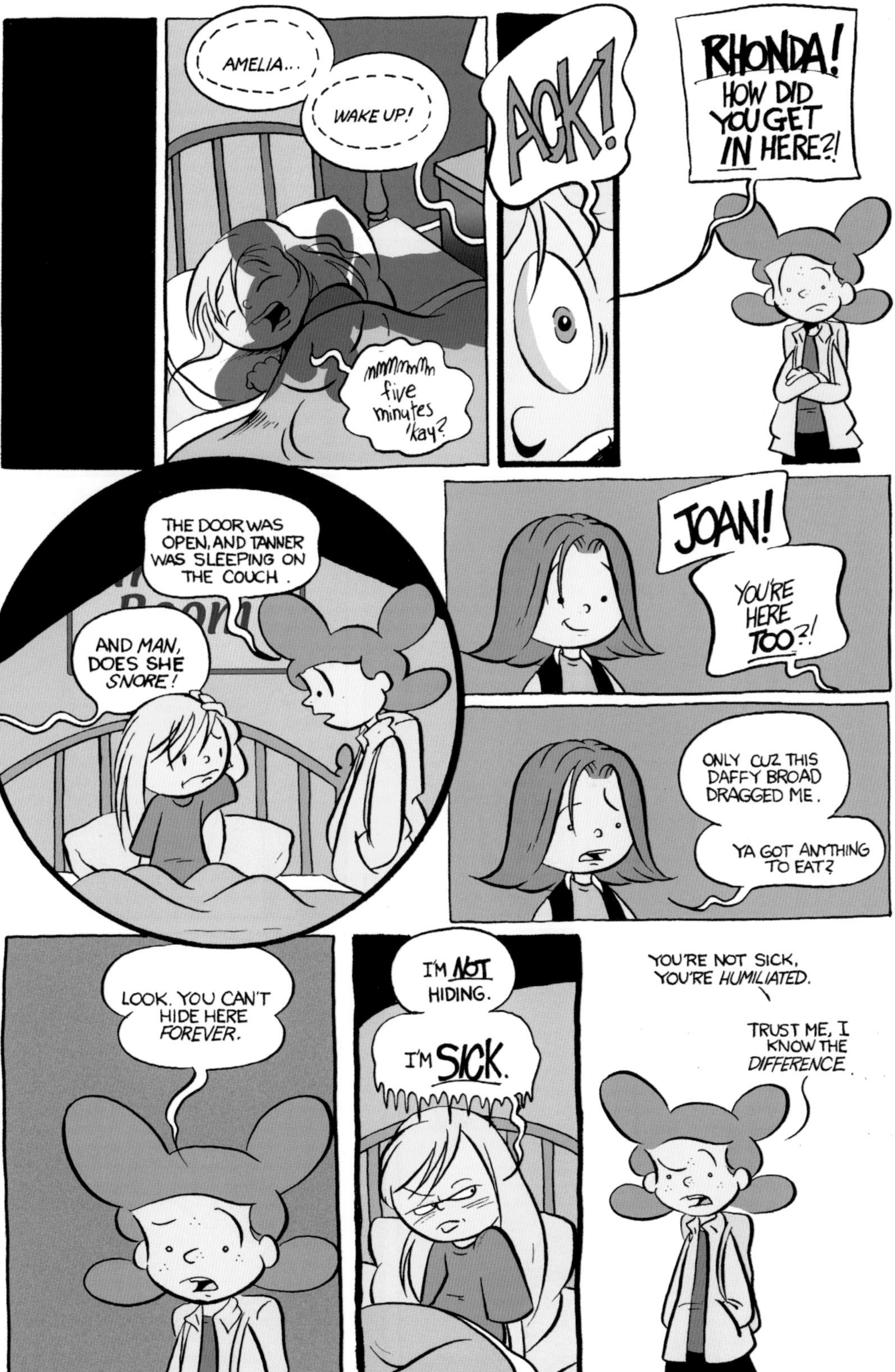
AMELIA...
WAKE UP!
mmmmmm five minutes 'kay?
ACK!
RHONDA! HOW DID YOU GET IN HERE?!
THE DOOR WAS OPEN, AND TANNER WAS SLEEPING ON THE COUCH.
AND MAN, DOES SHE SNORE!
JOAN!
YOU'RE HERE TOO?!
ONLY CUZ THIS DAFFY BROAD DRAGGED ME.
YA GOT ANYTHING TO EAT?
LOOK. YOU CAN'T HIDE HERE FOREVER.
I'M NOT HIDING.
I'M SICK.
YOU'RE NOT SICK, YOU'RE HUMILIATED.
TRUST ME, I KNOW THE DIFFERENCE.

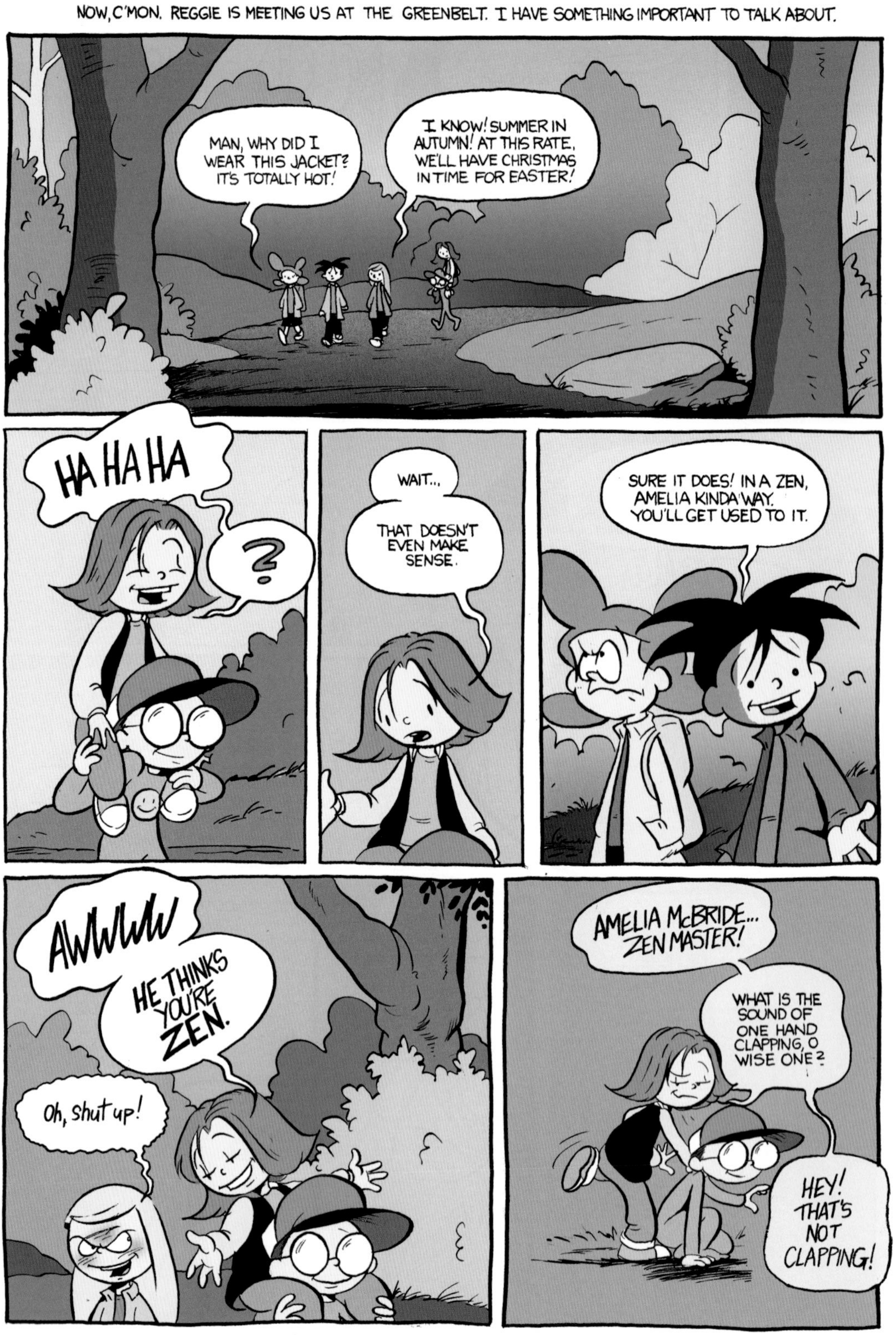
NOW, C'MON. REGGIE IS MEETING US AT THE GREENBELT. I HAVE SOMETHING IMPORTANT TO TALK ABOUT.
MAN, WHY DID I WEAR THIS JACKET? IT'S TOTALLY HOT!
I KNOW! SUMMER IN AUTUMN! AT THIS RATE, WE'LL HAVE CHRISTMAS IN TIME FOR EASTER!
HA HA HA
?
WAIT...
THAT DOESN'T EVEN MAKE SENSE.
SURE IT DOES! IN A ZEN, AMELIA KINDA WAY. YOU'LL GET USED TO IT.
AWWW
HE THINKS YOU'RE ZEN.
Oh, shut up!
AMELIA McBRIDE... ZEN MASTER!
WHAT IS THE SOUND OF ONE HAND CLAPPING, O WISE ONE?
HEY! THAT'S NOT CLAPPING!

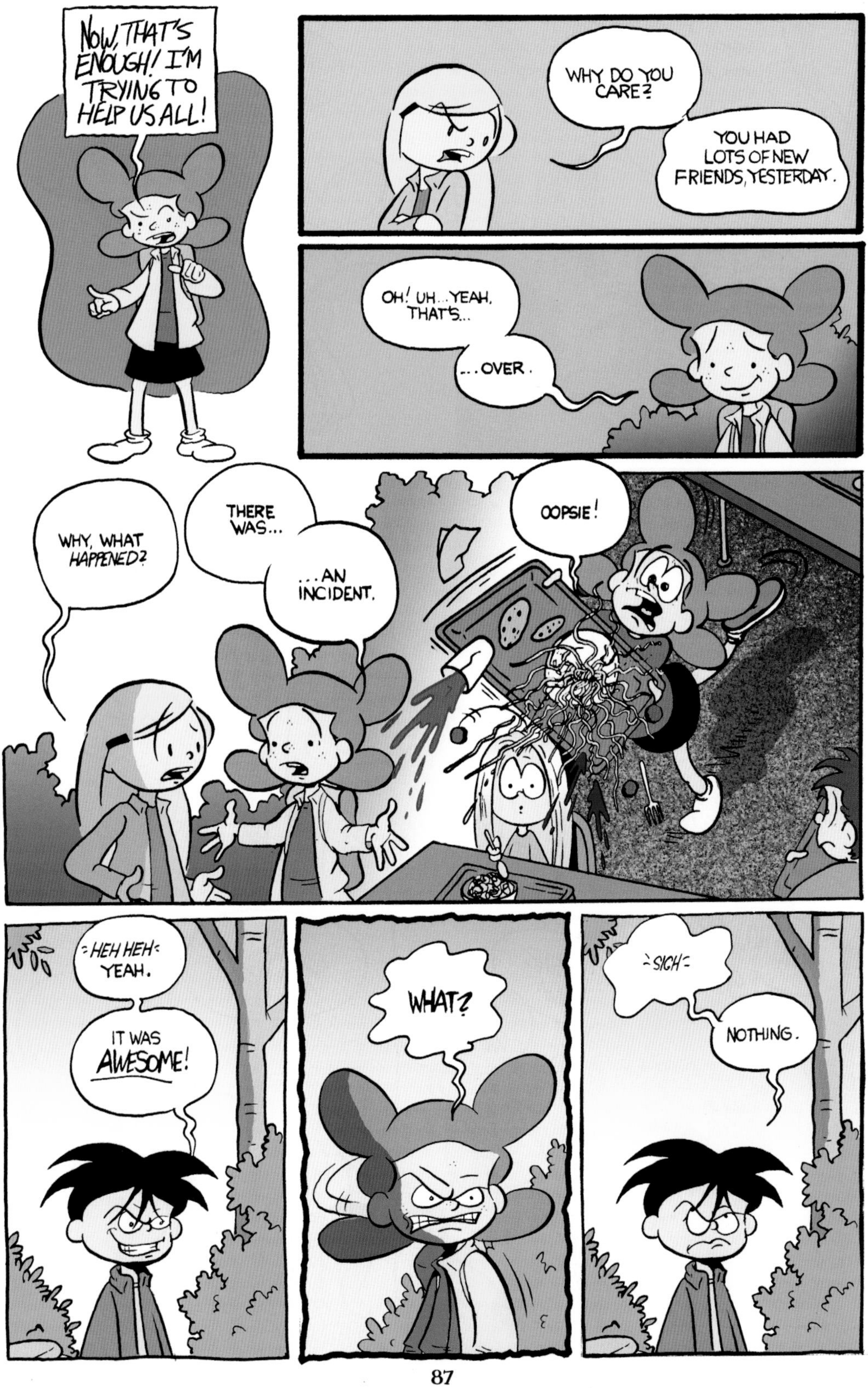
NOW, THAT'S ENOUGH! I'M TRYING TO HELP US ALL!
WHY DO YOU CARE?
YOU HAD LOTS OF NEW FRIENDS, YESTERDAY.
OH! UH... YEAH, THAT'S...
...OVER.
WHY, WHAT HAPPENED?
THERE WAS...
...AN INCIDENT.
OOPSIE!
HEH HEH YEAH.
IT WAS AWESOME!
WHAT?
SIGH
NOTHING.

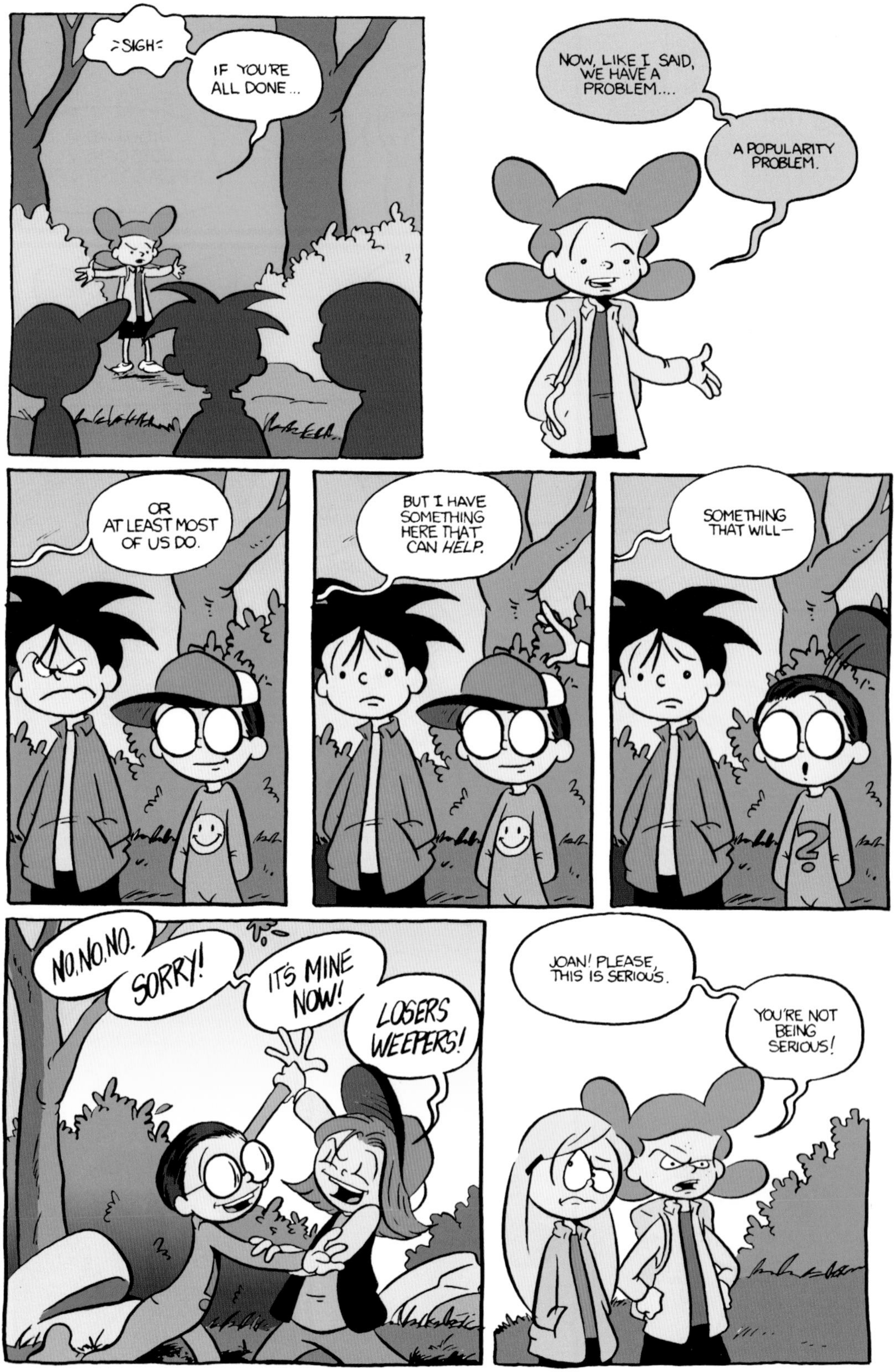
=SIGH=
IF YOU'RE ALL DONE...
NOW, LIKE I SAID, WE HAVE A PROBLEM....
A POPULARITY PROBLEM.
OR AT LEAST MOST OF US DO.
BUT I HAVE SOMETHING HERE THAT CAN *HELP.*
SOMETHING THAT WILL—
NO,NO,NO.
SORRY!
IT'S MINE NOW!
LOSERS WEEPERS!
JOAN! PLEASE, THIS IS SERIOUS.
YOU'RE NOT BEING SERIOUS!

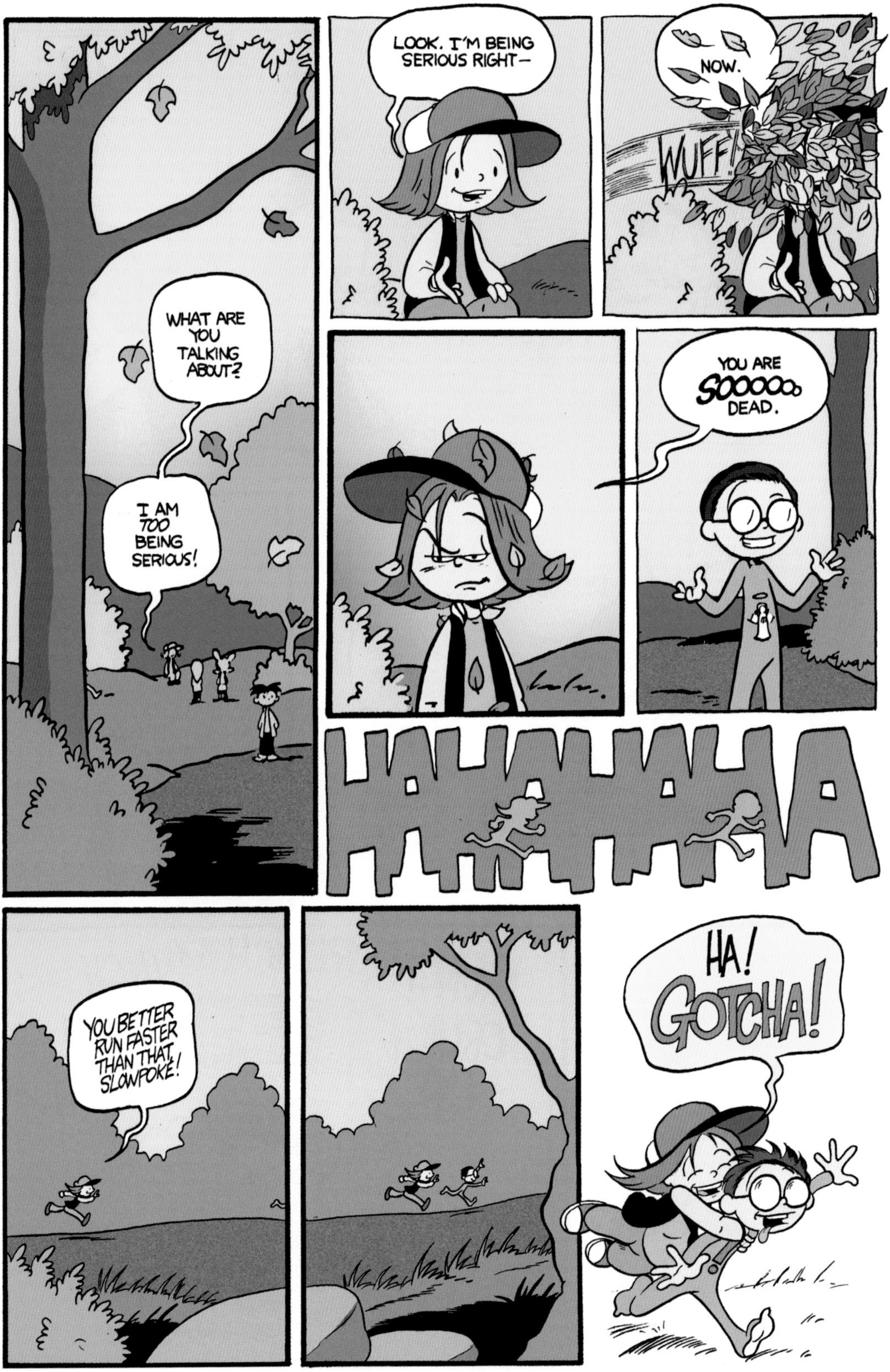
WHAT ARE YOU TALKING ABOUT?
I AM TOO BEING SERIOUS!
LOOK. I'M BEING SERIOUS RIGHT—
NOW.
WUFF!
YOU ARE SOOOOOo DEAD.
HAHAHAHA
YOU BETTER RUN FASTER THAN THAT, SLOWPOKE!
HA! GOTCHA!

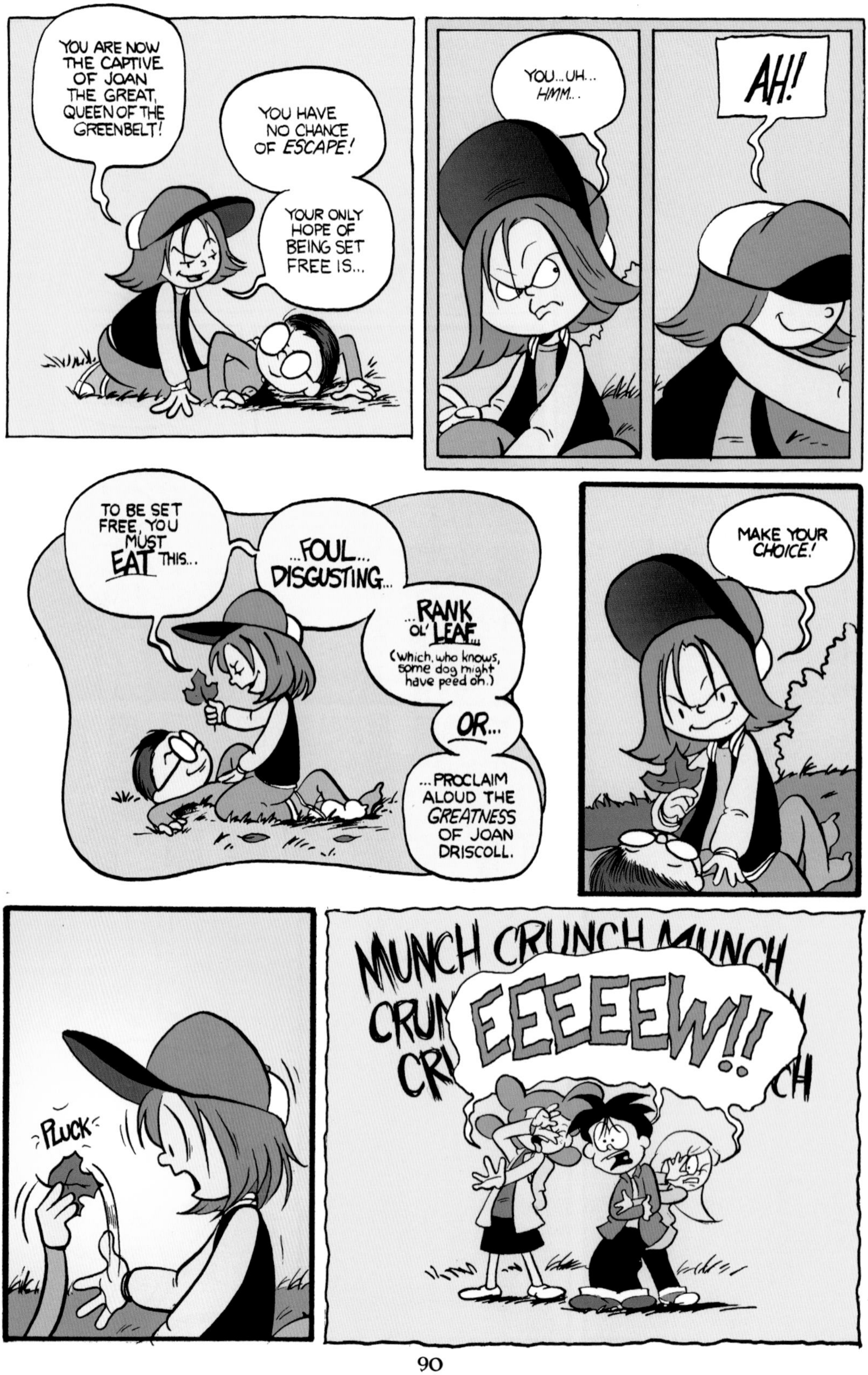
YOU ARE NOW THE CAPTIVE OF JOAN THE GREAT, QUEEN OF THE GREENBELT!
YOU HAVE NO CHANCE OF ESCAPE!
YOUR ONLY HOPE OF BEING SET FREE IS...
YOU... UH... HMM...
AH!
TO BE SET FREE, YOU MUST EAT THIS...
...FOUL... DISGUSTING...
...RANK OL' LEAF...
(which, who knows, some dog might have peed on.)
OR...
...PROCLAIM ALOUD THE GREATNESS OF JOAN DRISCOLL.
MAKE YOUR CHOICE!
PLUCK
MUNCH CRUNCH MUNCH
EEEEEW!!

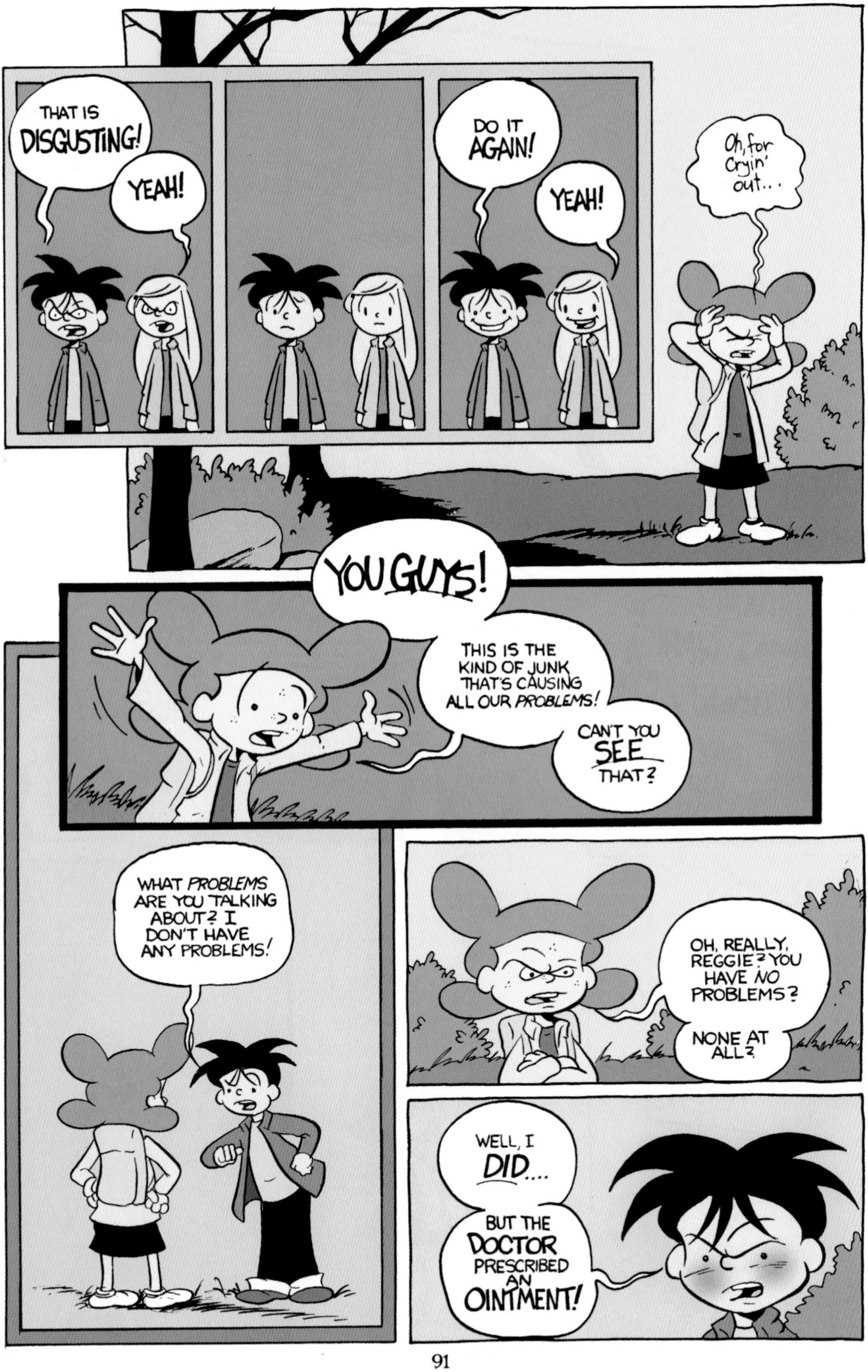

THAT IS DISGUSTING!
YEAH!
DO IT AGAIN!
YEAH!
Oh, for Cryin' out...
YOU GUYS!
THIS IS THE KIND OF JUNK THAT'S CAUSING ALL OUR PROBLEMS!
CAN'T YOU SEE THAT?
WHAT PROBLEMS ARE YOU TALKING ABOUT? I DON'T HAVE ANY PROBLEMS!
OH, REALLY, REGGIE? YOU HAVE NO PROBLEMS?
NONE AT ALL?
WELL, I DID....
BUT THE DOCTOR PRESCRIBED AN OINTMENT!

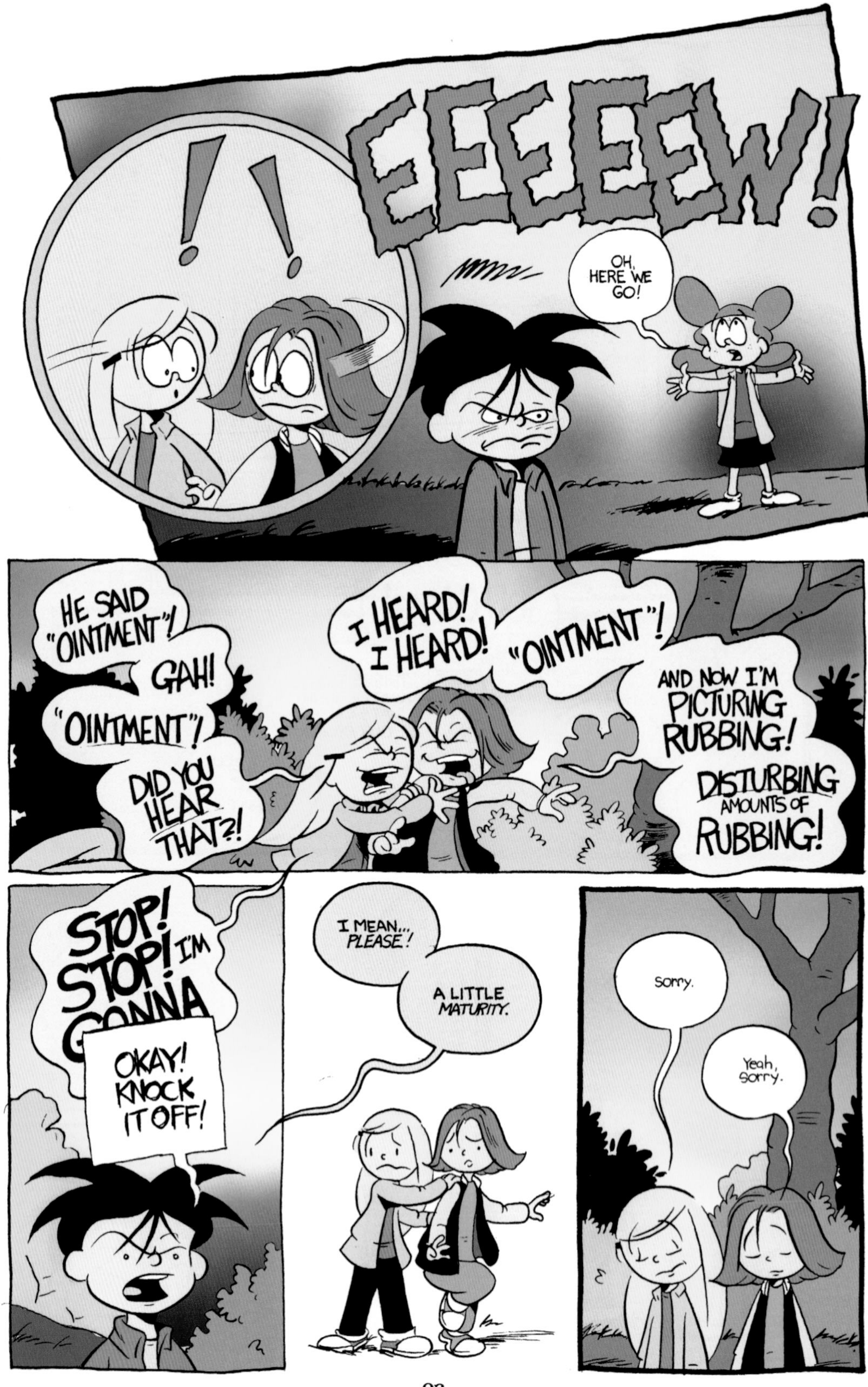
!!
EEEEEW!
OH, HERE WE GO!
HE SAID "OINTMENT"!
GAH!
"OINTMENT"!
DID YOU HEAR THAT?!
I HEARD! I HEARD!
"OINTMENT"!
AND NOW I'M PICTURING RUBBING!
DISTURBING AMOUNTS OF RUBBING!
STOP! STOP! I'M GONNA
OKAY! KNOCK IT OFF!
I MEAN... PLEASE!
A LITTLE MATURITY.
Sorry.
Yeah, sorry.

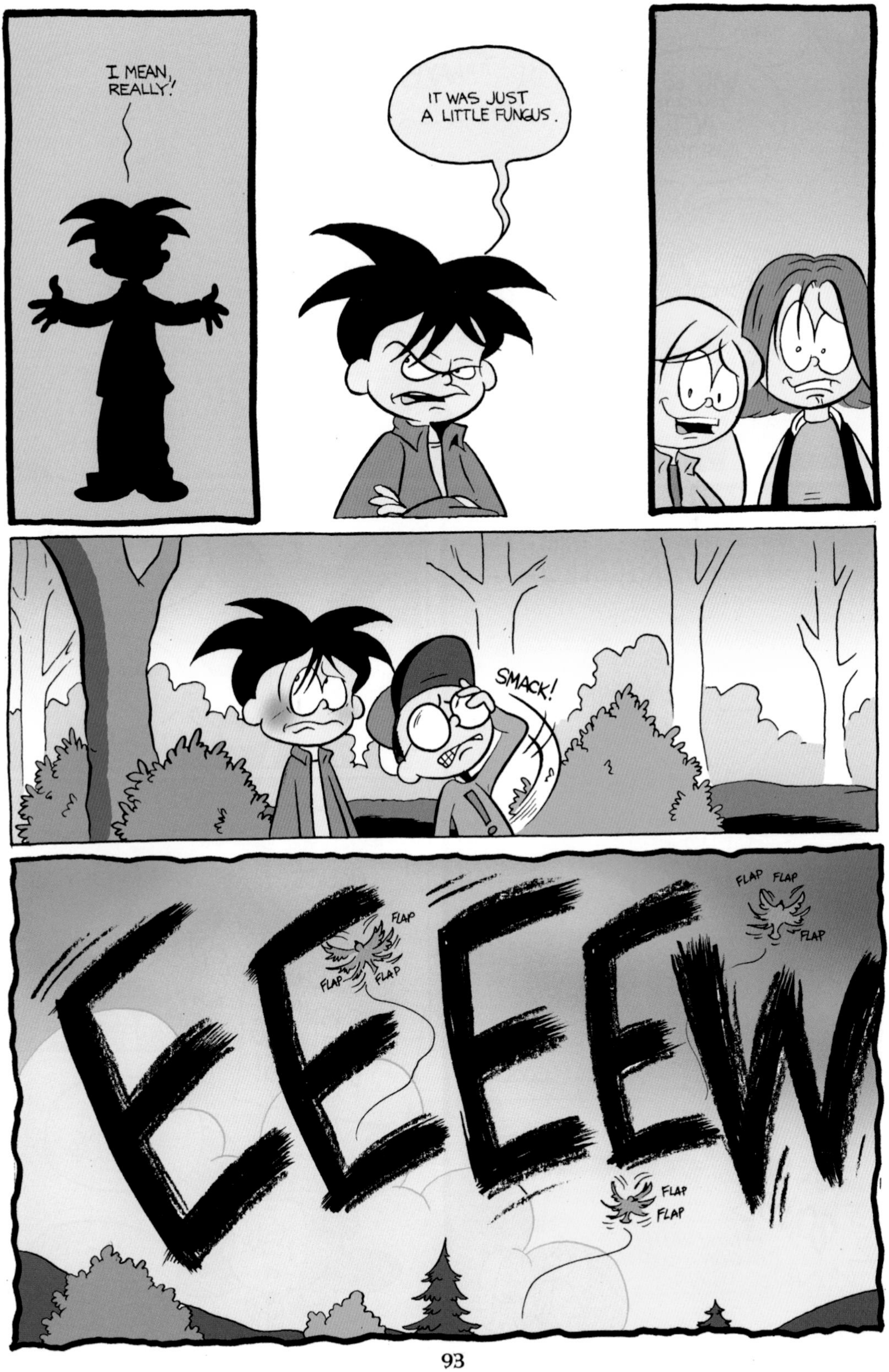
I MEAN, REALLY!
IT WAS JUST A LITTLE FUNGUS.
SMACK!
EEEEW
FLAP
FLAP FLAP
FLAP FLAP
FLAP
FLAP
FLAP

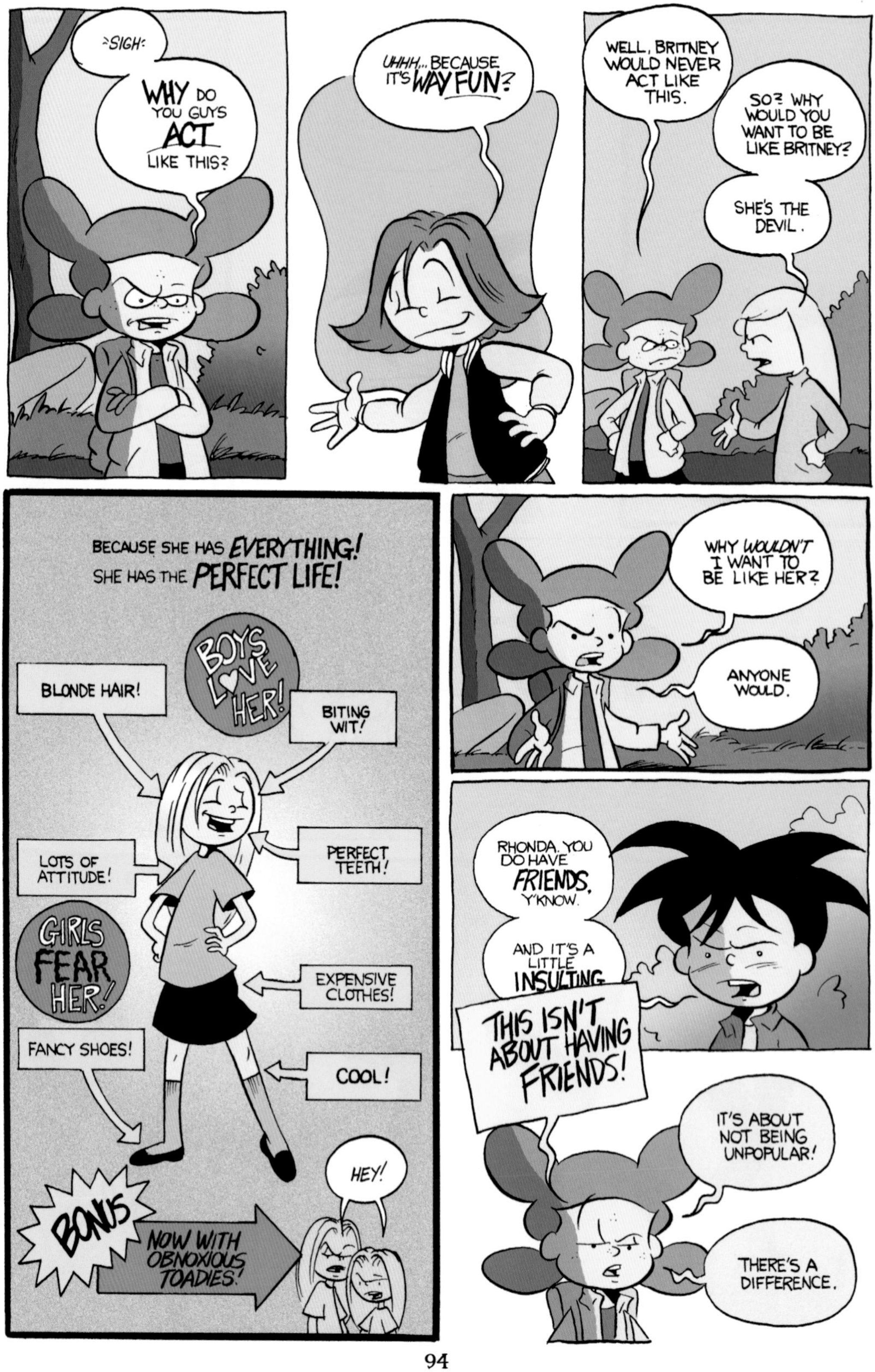

SIGH
WHY DO YOU GUYS ACT LIKE THIS?
UHHH... BECAUSE IT'S WAY FUN?
WELL, BRITNEY WOULD NEVER ACT LIKE THIS.
SO? WHY WOULD YOU WANT TO BE LIKE BRITNEY?
SHE'S THE DEVIL.
BECAUSE SHE HAS EVERYTHING! SHE HAS THE PERFECT LIFE!
BOYS LOVE HER!
BLONDE HAIR!
BITING WIT!
LOTS OF ATTITUDE!
PERFECT TEETH!
GIRLS FEAR HER!
EXPENSIVE CLOTHES!
FANCY SHOES!
COOL!
HEY!
BONUS
NOW WITH OBNOXIOUS TOADIES!
WHY WOULDN'T I WANT TO BE LIKE HER?
ANYONE WOULD.
RHONDA, YOU DO HAVE FRIENDS, Y'KNOW.
AND IT'S A LITTLE INSULTING
THIS ISN'T ABOUT HAVING FRIENDS!
IT'S ABOUT NOT BEING UNPOPULAR!
THERE'S A DIFFERENCE.

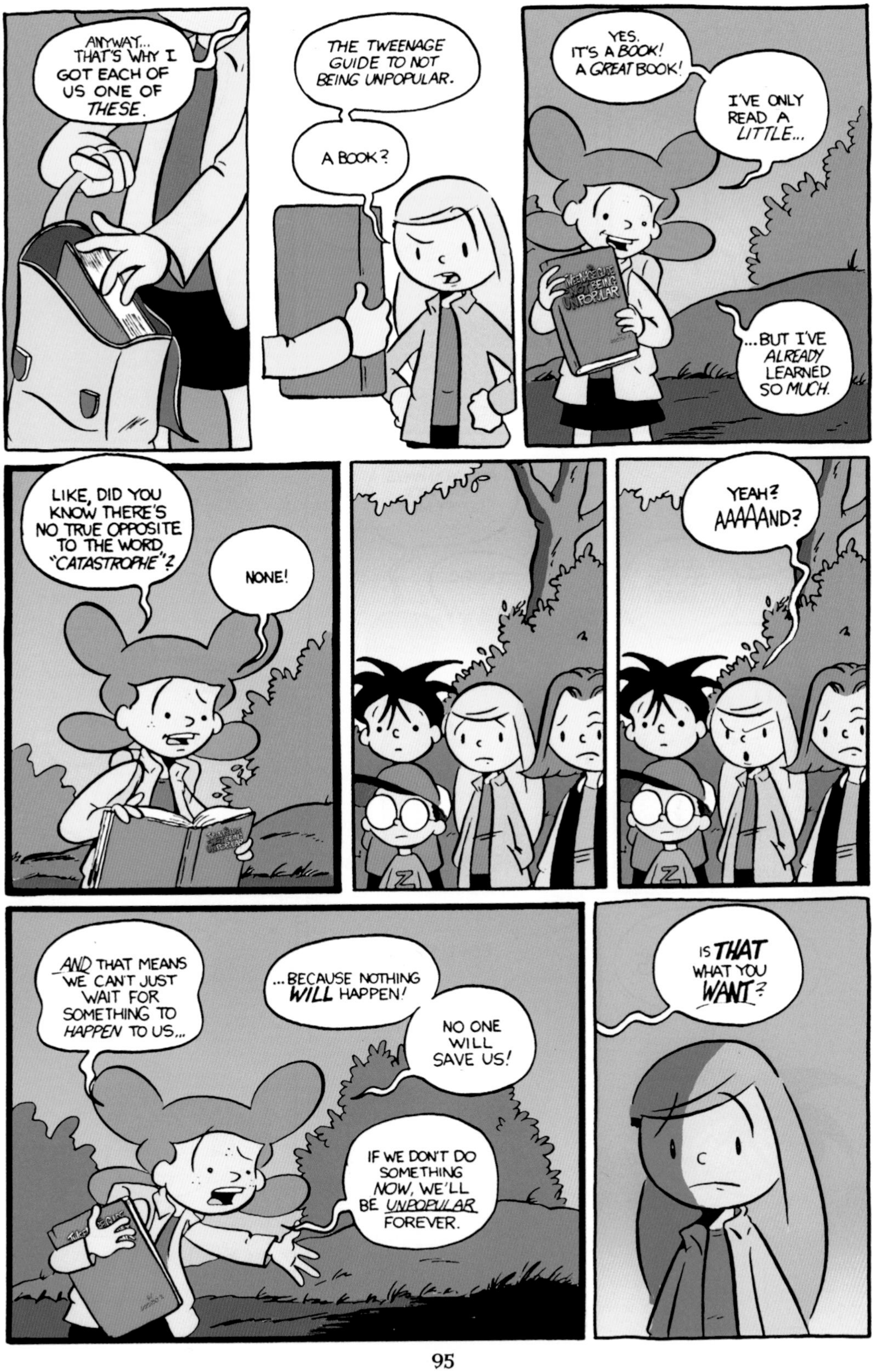

ANYWAY... THAT'S WHY I GOT EACH OF US ONE OF THESE.
THE TWEENAGE GUIDE TO NOT BEING UNPOPULAR.
A BOOK?
YES. IT'S A BOOK! A GREAT BOOK!
I'VE ONLY READ A LITTLE...
...BUT I'VE ALREADY LEARNED SO MUCH.
LIKE, DID YOU KNOW THERE'S NO TRUE OPPOSITE TO THE WORD "CATASTROPHE"?
NONE!
YEAH? AAAAAND?
AND THAT MEANS WE CAN'T JUST WAIT FOR SOMETHING TO HAPPEN TO US...
...BECAUSE NOTHING WILL HAPPEN!
NO ONE WILL SAVE US!
IF WE DON'T DO SOMETHING NOW, WE'LL BE UNPOPULAR FOREVER.
IS THAT WHAT YOU WANT?

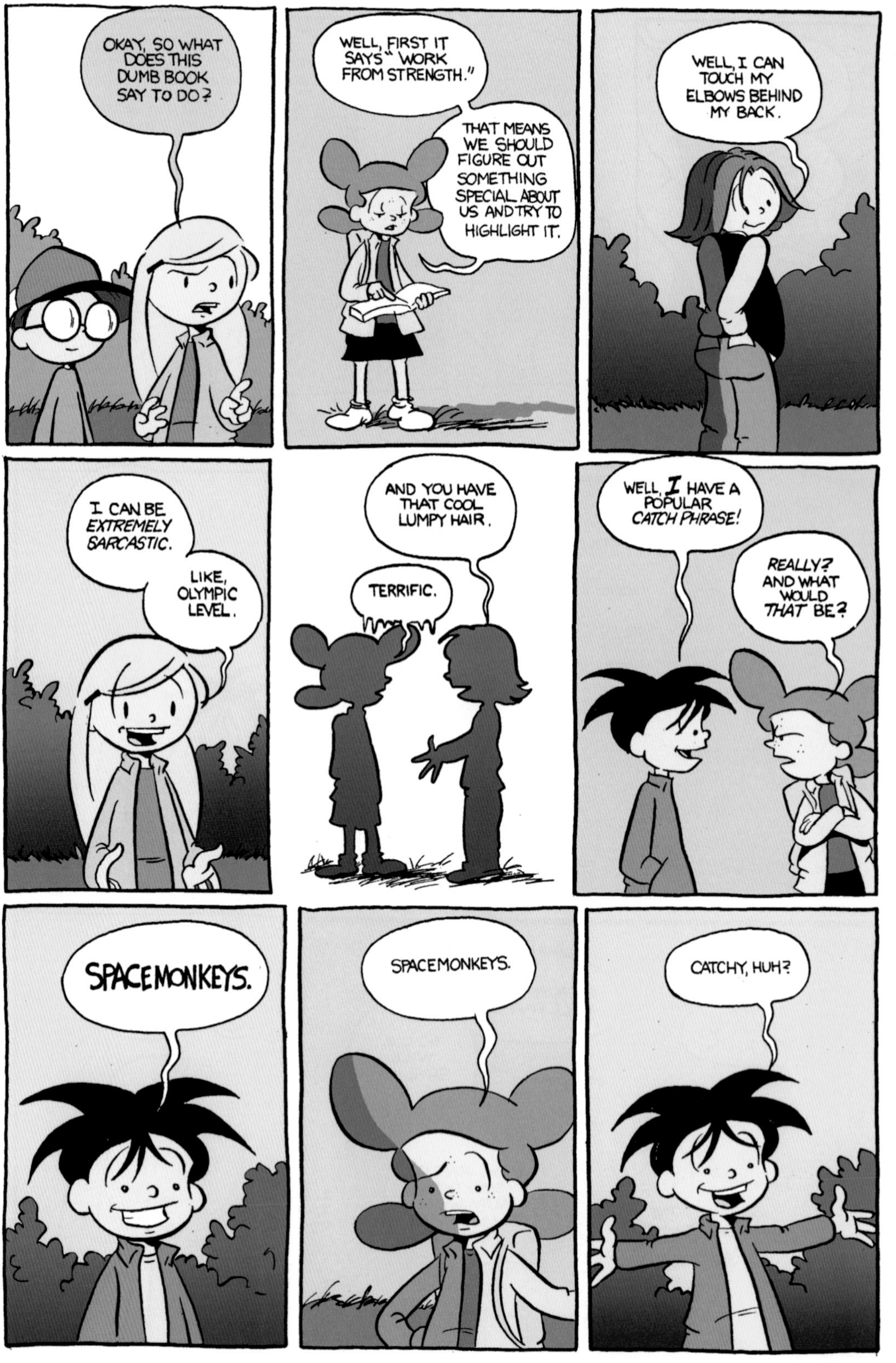
OKAY, SO WHAT DOES THIS DUMB BOOK SAY TO DO?
WELL, FIRST IT SAYS "WORK FROM STRENGTH."
THAT MEANS WE SHOULD FIGURE OUT SOMETHING SPECIAL ABOUT US AND TRY TO HIGHLIGHT IT.
WELL, I CAN TOUCH MY ELBOWS BEHIND MY BACK.
I CAN BE *EXTREMELY SARCASTIC*.
LIKE, OLYMPIC LEVEL.
AND YOU HAVE THAT COOL LUMPY HAIR.
TERRIFIC.
WELL, **I** HAVE A POPULAR *CATCH PHRASE!*
REALLY? AND WHAT WOULD *THAT* BE?
SPACEMONKEYS.
SPACEMONKEYS.
CATCHY, HUH?

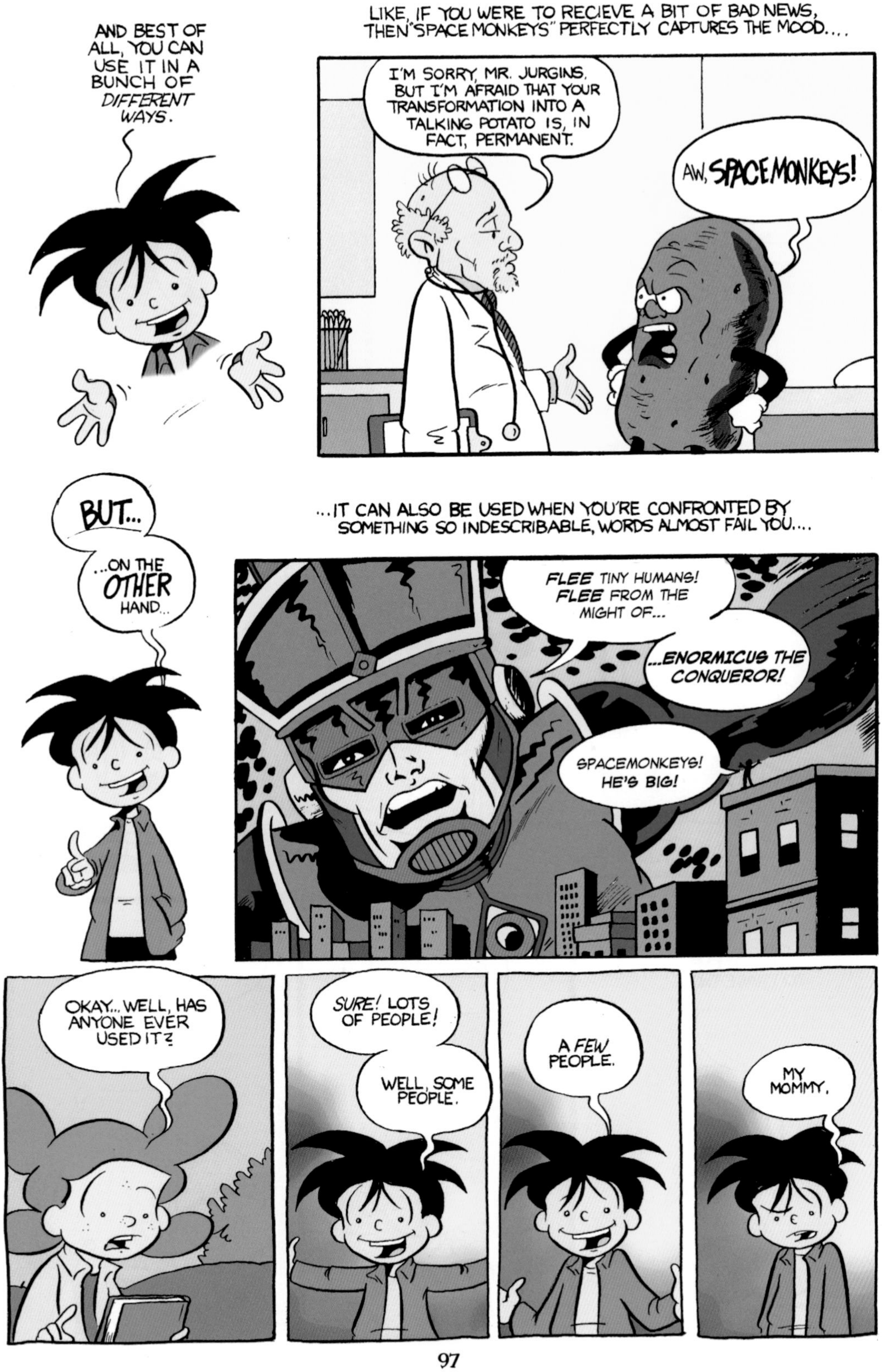
AND BEST OF ALL, YOU CAN USE IT IN A BUNCH OF DIFFERENT WAYS.
LIKE, IF YOU WERE TO RECIEVE A BIT OF BAD NEWS, THEN "SPACE MONKEYS" PERFECTLY CAPTURES THE MOOD....
I'M SORRY, MR. JURGINS, BUT I'M AFRAID THAT YOUR TRANSFORMATION INTO A TALKING POTATO IS, IN FACT, PERMANENT.
AW, SPACEMONKEYS!
BUT...
...ON THE OTHER HAND...
...IT CAN ALSO BE USED WHEN YOU'RE CONFRONTED BY SOMETHING SO INDESCRIBABLE, WORDS ALMOST FAIL YOU....
FLEE TINY HUMANS! FLEE FROM THE MIGHT OF...
...ENORMICUS THE CONQUEROR!
SPACEMONKEYS! HE'S BIG!
OKAY... WELL, HAS ANYONE EVER USED IT?
SURE! LOTS OF PEOPLE!
WELL, SOME PEOPLE.
A FEW PEOPLE.
MY MOMMY.

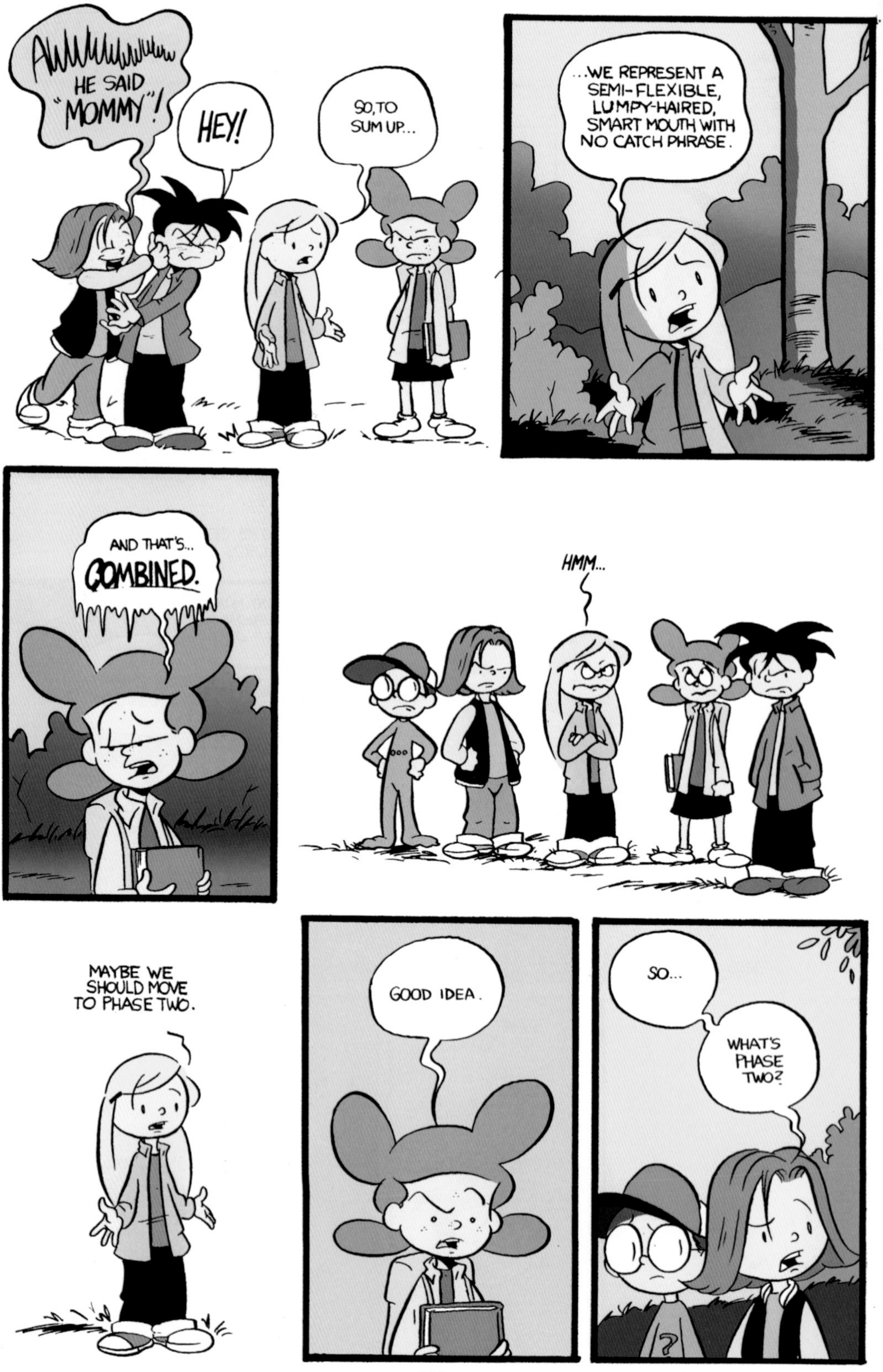
AWWWWWWWWW HE SAID "MOMMY"!
HEY!
SO, TO SUM UP...
...WE REPRESENT A SEMI-FLEXIBLE, LUMPY-HAIRED, SMART MOUTH WITH NO CATCH PHRASE.
AND THAT'S... COMBINED.
HMM...
MAYBE WE SHOULD MOVE TO PHASE TWO.
GOOD IDEA.
SO...
WHAT'S PHASE TWO?

PHASE TWO:
MAKEOVERS!

Face it. We live in a country where 83% of all citizens are obese and the other 17% have eating disorders. Now, I know I just made those statistics up, but that doesn't change the fact that unless you're 60% plastic, there's probably something wrong with the way you look.

Many people misunderstand the point of makeovers. Makeovers are not about making you look good, they are about making you look trendy. Also, they are about making you appear to be something you are not. This works to your advantage, though, as what you are must not be much, or you wouldn't be reading this book.

If you're still at a loss for where to start, my rule of thumb is to dress and act as age inappropriate as possible. The chart below should prove to be a useful makeover guide for the rest of your soon-to-be trend-obsessed life.

Ages 12–16—Dress like an 18–25-year-old, act like a 25–30-year-old.

Ages 17–21—Dress like a 25–30-year-old, act like a 12-year-old.

Ages 22–30—Dress like a 16-year-old, act like an old Madonna song.

Ages 31–45—Dress like a 50-year-old, read your old yearbook a lot.

Ages 46–up—Just try to stay indoors as much as possible.

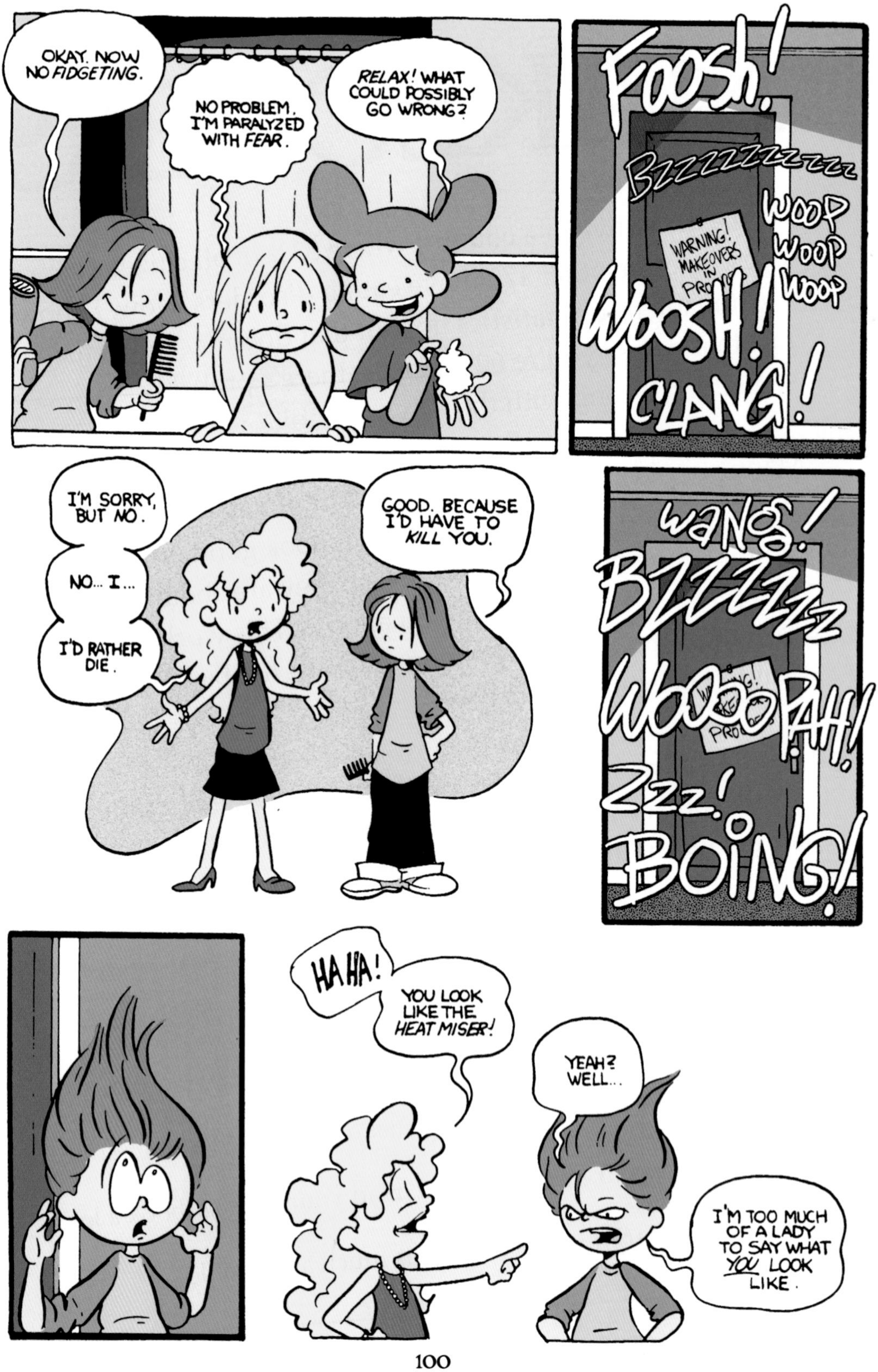
OKAY. NOW NO *FIDGETING*.
NO PROBLEM. I'M PARALYZED WITH *FEAR*.
RELAX! WHAT COULD POSSIBLY GO WRONG?
FOOSH!
BZZZZZZZZZZZ
WARNING! MAKEOVERS IN PROGRESS
WOOP WOOP WOOP
WOOSH!
CLANG!
I'M SORRY, BUT NO.
NO... I...
I'D RATHER DIE.
GOOD. BECAUSE I'D HAVE TO *KILL* YOU.
WANG!
BZZZZZZZ
WOOOOPAH!
ZZZ!
BOING!
HA HA!
YOU LOOK LIKE THE *HEAT MISER!*
YEAH? WELL...
I'M TOO MUCH OF A LADY TO SAY WHAT YOU LOOK LIKE.

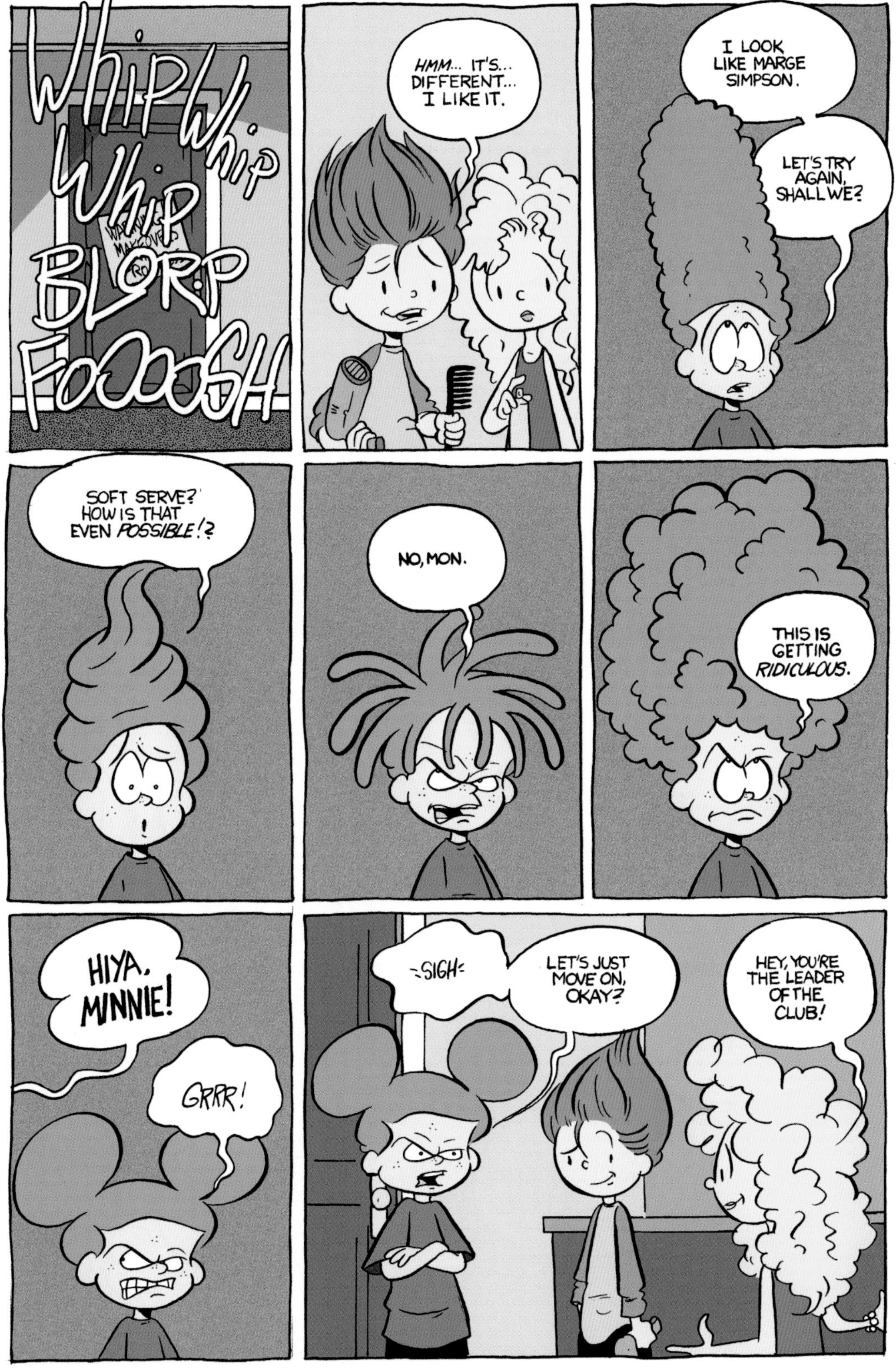
WHIP WHIP
WHIP
BLORP
FOOOOSH
HMM... IT'S... DIFFERENT... I LIKE IT.
I LOOK LIKE MARGE SIMPSON.
LET'S TRY AGAIN, SHALL WE?
SOFT SERVE? HOW IS THAT EVEN *POSSIBLE*!?
NO, MON.
THIS IS GETTING *RIDICULOUS*.
HIYA, MINNIE!
GRRR!
=SIGH=
LET'S JUST MOVE ON, OKAY?
HEY, YOU'RE THE LEADER OF THE CLUB!

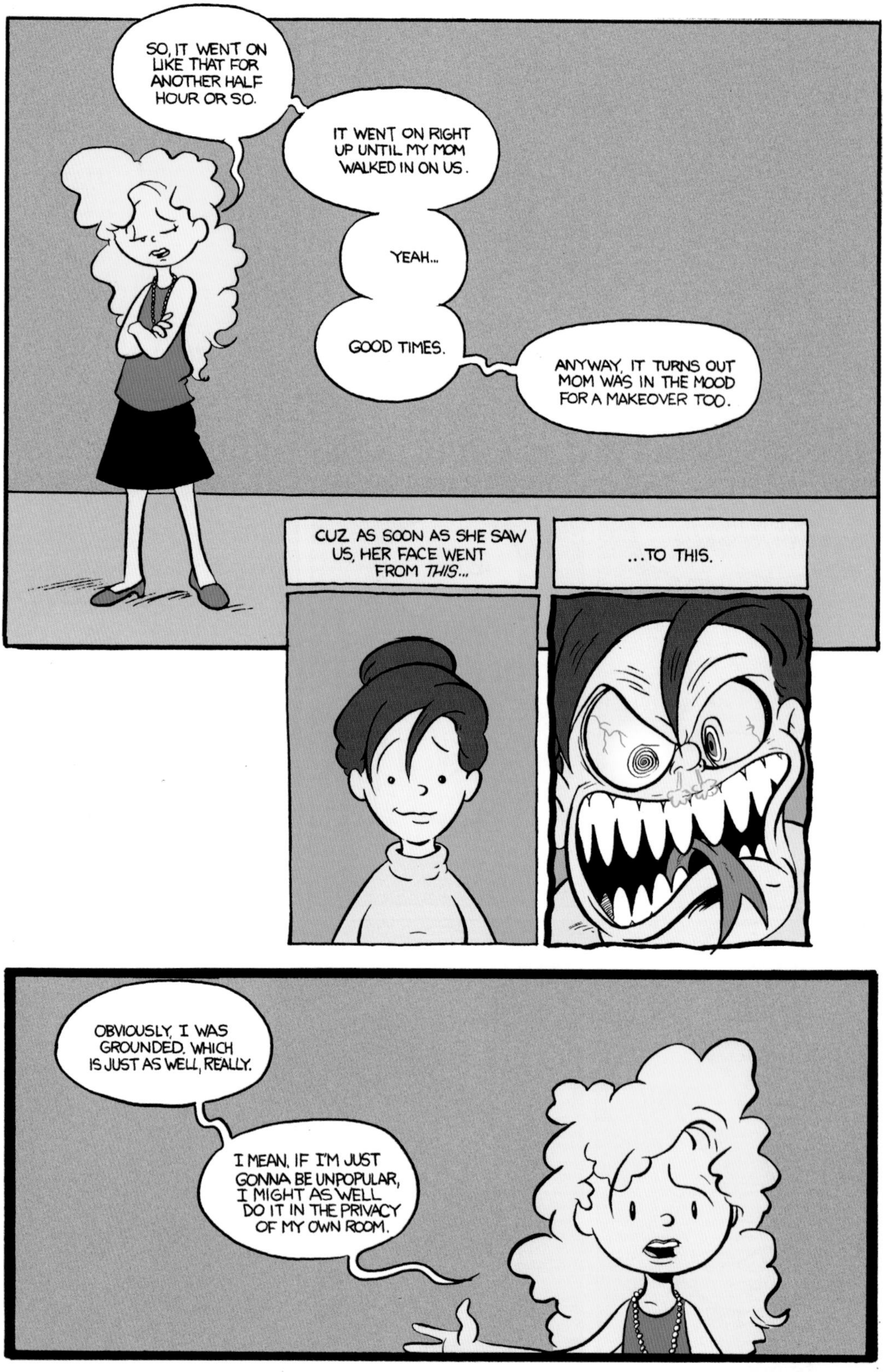
SO, IT WENT ON LIKE THAT FOR ANOTHER HALF HOUR OR SO.
IT WENT ON RIGHT UP UNTIL MY MOM WALKED IN ON US.
YEAH...
GOOD TIMES.
ANYWAY, IT TURNS OUT MOM WAS IN THE MOOD FOR A MAKEOVER TOO.
CUZ AS SOON AS SHE SAW US, HER FACE WENT FROM *THIS*...
...TO THIS.
OBVIOUSLY, I WAS GROUNDED. WHICH IS JUST AS WELL, REALLY.
I MEAN, IF I'M JUST GONNA BE UNPOPULAR, I MIGHT AS WELL DO IT IN THE PRIVACY OF MY OWN ROOM.

Dr. V. - On the Record

(cont. from p. 23)

book has been very controversial, especially among—
A: Opinionated loudmouths. (*laughs*)

Q: I was going to say "educators." How do you answer the charges that your book reinforces negative attitudes among children?
A: Well, those people have a right to be wrong (*laughs*), you know? (*sighs*) The way I see it, I'm just being realistic. People just don't enjoy hearing the truth. It makes them feel uncomfortable.

Q: And your book is the truth?
A: Absolutely. See, the problem is parents spend so much time telling their kids that they're special, right? That they can do anything. But that's not true. That's why very few parents encourage their kid to excel once the child is out of school.

Q: What do you mean?
A: Well, when a child is coming up through the ranks in school, he or she is encouraged to do well, to distinguish him- or herself, to strive for excellence. But as soon as he or she get a diploma and a degree, what do people tell them then? "Get a job with benefits, keep your head down, and wait to die."

Q: That's grim.
A: But it's true.

Q: So you say striving for excellence should be a life-long process?
A: (*laughs*) No, no. Just the opposite. My book is about dispelling the notions that each child is special. Most children are average by definition. Of course, do what you can to improve your standing, but be realistic. Accept your place in the pecking order early, and you'll have a lot less disappointment later in life. Don't expect miracles.

Q: And you think this is good advice?
A: My book has sold four million copies.

Did You Know?

1. Dr. V.'s books are translated into more than fourteen languages, including, French, Italian, Swahili, and Gullah.

2. When practicing for her driver's exam, the young Ms. V. ran over her own foot while practicing a three-point turn.

3. In high school she was voted student body president. Her first act was to disband the pep squad.

4. She has a twin brother. The two have not spoken in eleven years. This is due to what family insiders refer to as "hatred."

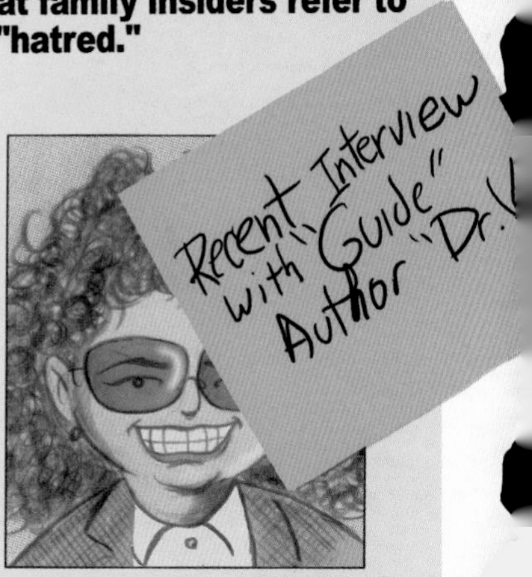
Recent Interview
with "Guide"
Author "Dr.

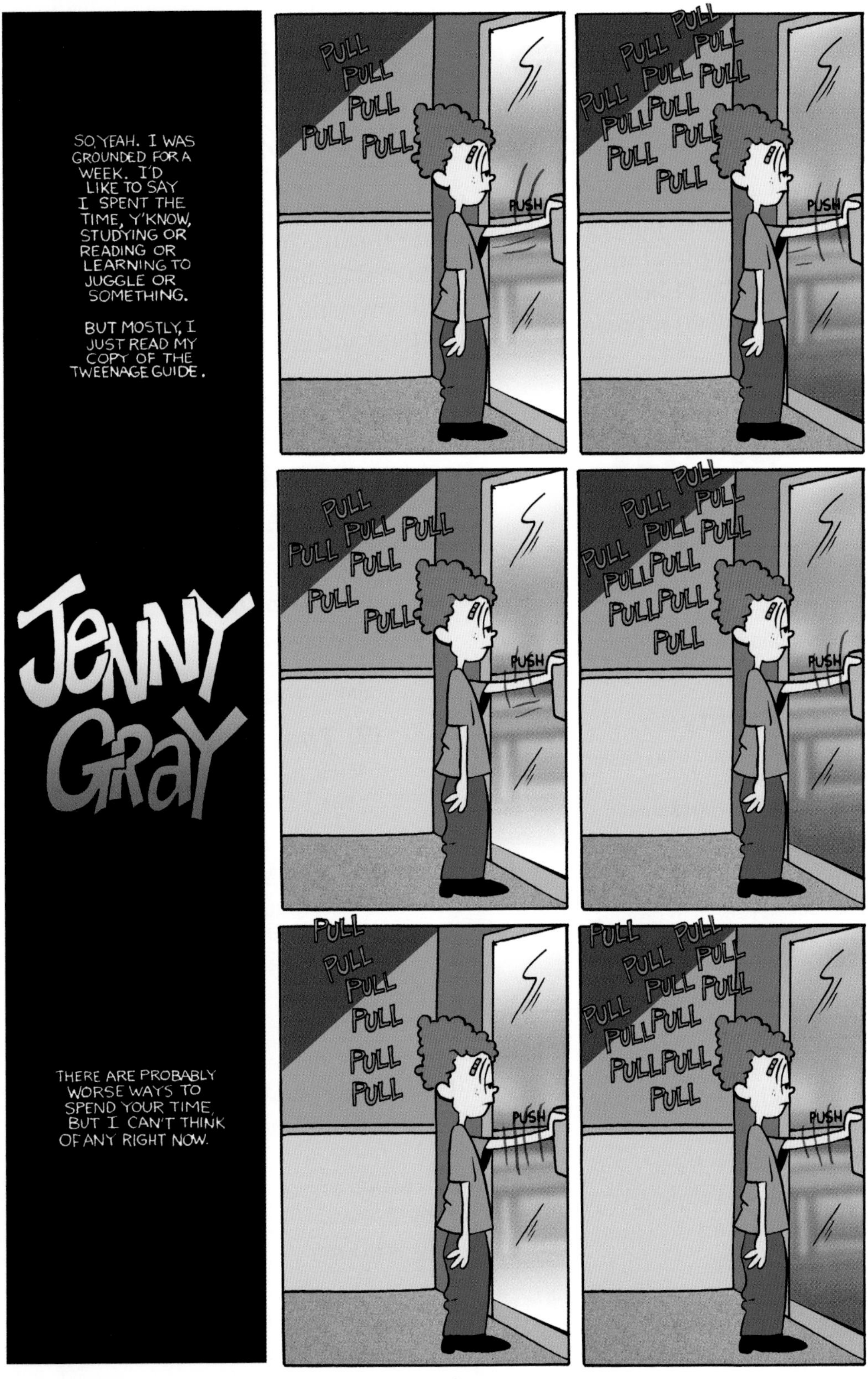

SO, YEAH. I WAS GROUNDED FOR A WEEK. I'D LIKE TO SAY I SPENT THE TIME, Y'KNOW, STUDYING OR READING OR LEARNING TO JUGGLE OR SOMETHING.
BUT MOSTLY, I JUST READ MY COPY OF THE TWEENAGE GUIDE.
JENNY GRAY
THERE ARE PROBABLY WORSE WAYS TO SPEND YOUR TIME, BUT I CAN'T THINK OF ANY RIGHT NOW.
PULL PULL PULL PULL PULL
PUSH
PULL PULL PULL PULL PULL PULL PULL PULL PULL PULL PULL PULL
PUSH
PULL PULL PULL PULL PULL PULL PULL
PUSH
PULL PULL PULL PULL PULL PULL PULL PULL PULL PULL PULL PULL
PUSH
PULL PULL PULL PULL PULL PULL
PUSH
PULL PULL PULL PULL PULL PULL PULL PULL PULL PULL PULL PULL
PUSH

CASE STUDY:

The Princess Effect

You can learn a lot from Snow White. Whether in the original Grimm's fairy tale, or any of the later theatrical versions, this chick is a great example of upwardly mobile social climbing! And hey, you can apply some of her techniques to your own life. But avoid the traps that the evil queen represents! Let's compare and contrast below.

SNOW WHITE

(1) Social Climbing
Scullery maid to princess with only a bad case of indigestion in between!

(2) Flexibility
Lose your spot at the castle? Slum it at the dwarfs'. Then ditch 'em when Mr. Right shows up.

(3) Ignorance Is Bliss
Other than pie making, knowing stuff doesn't seem to be one of SW's strengths. But who cares? She still wins.

EVIL QUEEN

(1) Knowledge
She knows chemistry, botany, and it appears a great deal more. What good did it do her?

(2) That Dumb Mirror
If you have something bad to say, save it for the Internet.

(3) Bad Makeover
Beauty queen to hag? No wonder she gets killed by an angry mob!

Who are your dwarfs? Is there a group on the next level up you can use for the time being? For example, if you're in the AV club, upgrade to the chess club, but be prepared to ditch them if the cheerleaders call.

Are you Prince Ready? Remember the lessons of our makeover chapter. Snow White always looked her best, even when she was dead. The least you can do is wear a nice skirt to school.

Can you bake a pie? It's always nice to have at least one semi-useful skill. Pick something fairly easy, but with a high show-off factor.

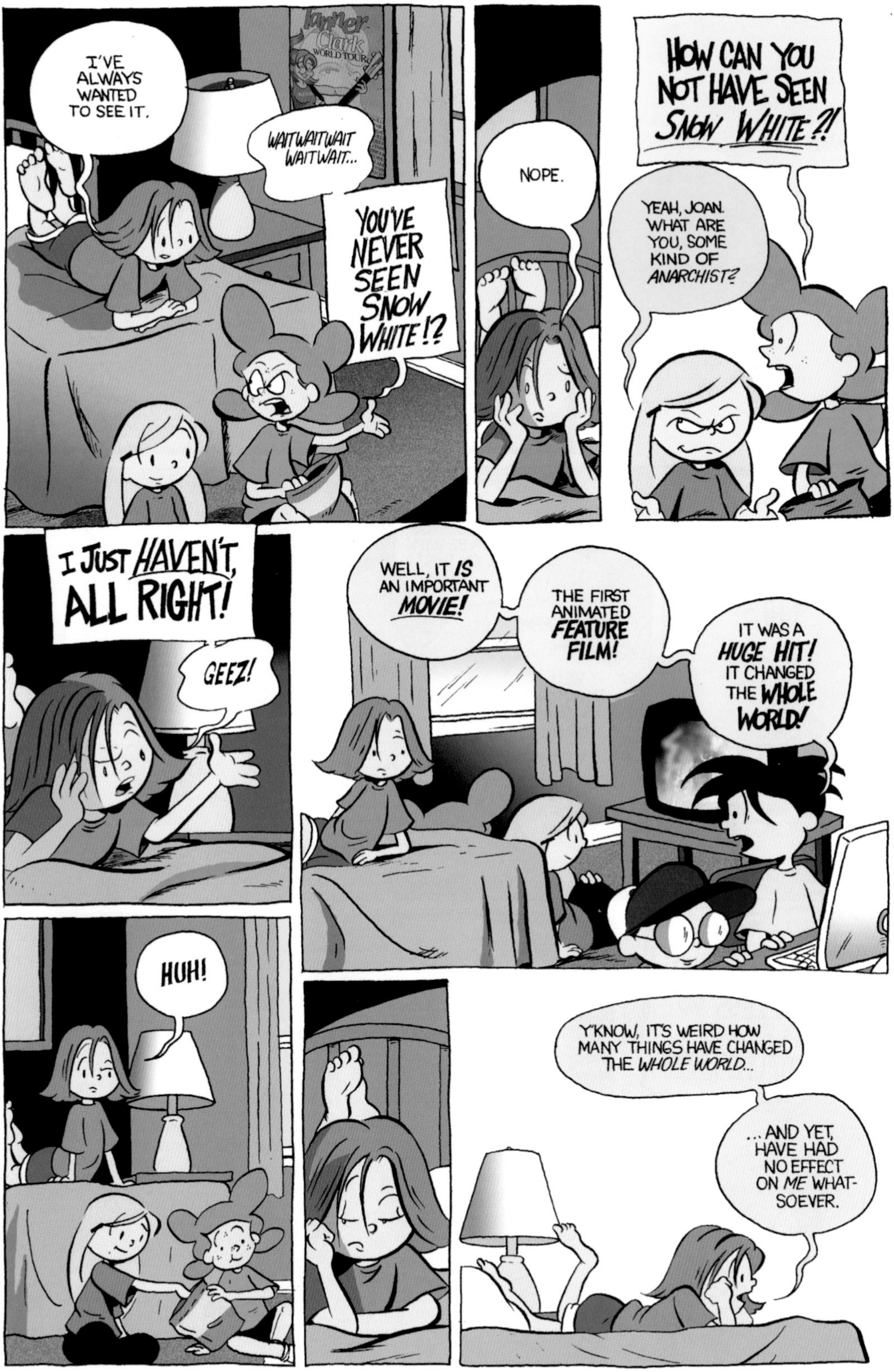

I'VE ALWAYS WANTED TO SEE IT.
WAITWAITWAIT WAITWAIT...
YOU'VE NEVER SEEN SNOW WHITE!?
NOPE.
HOW CAN YOU NOT HAVE SEEN SNOW WHITE?!
YEAH, JOAN. WHAT ARE YOU, SOME KIND OF ANARCHIST?
I JUST HAVEN'T, ALL RIGHT!
GEEZ!
WELL, IT IS AN IMPORTANT MOVIE!
THE FIRST ANIMATED FEATURE FILM!
IT WAS A HUGE HIT! IT CHANGED THE WHOLE WORLD!
HUH!
Y'KNOW, IT'S WEIRD HOW MANY THINGS HAVE CHANGED THE WHOLE WORLD...
...AND YET, HAVE HAD NO EFFECT ON ME WHATSOEVER.

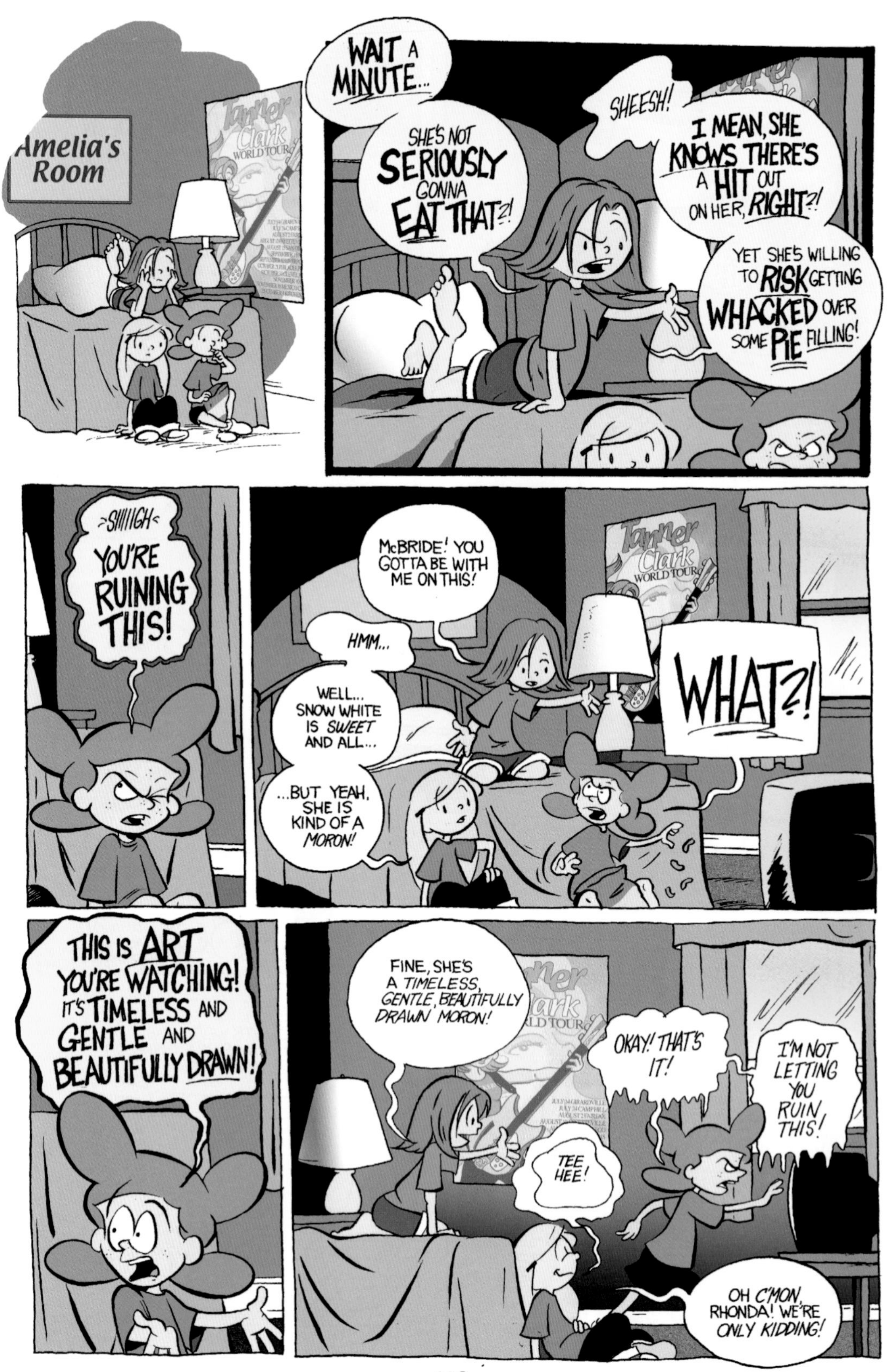
Amelia's Room
WAIT A MINUTE...
SHE'S NOT SERIOUSLY GONNA EAT THAT?!
SHEESH!
I MEAN, SHE KNOWS THERE'S A HIT OUT ON HER, RIGHT?!
YET SHE'S WILLING TO RISK GETTING WHACKED OVER SOME PIE FILLING!
SIIIIGH
YOU'RE RUINING THIS!
McBRIDE! YOU GOTTA BE WITH ME ON THIS!
HMM...
WELL... SNOW WHITE IS SWEET AND ALL...
...BUT YEAH, SHE IS KIND OF A MORON!
WHAT?!
THIS IS ART YOU'RE WATCHING! IT'S TIMELESS AND GENTLE AND BEAUTIFULLY DRAWN!
FINE, SHE'S A TIMELESS, GENTLE, BEAUTIFULLY DRAWN MORON!
OKAY! THAT'S IT!
I'M NOT LETTING YOU RUIN THIS!
TEE HEE!
OH C'MON, RHONDA! WE'RE ONLY KIDDING!

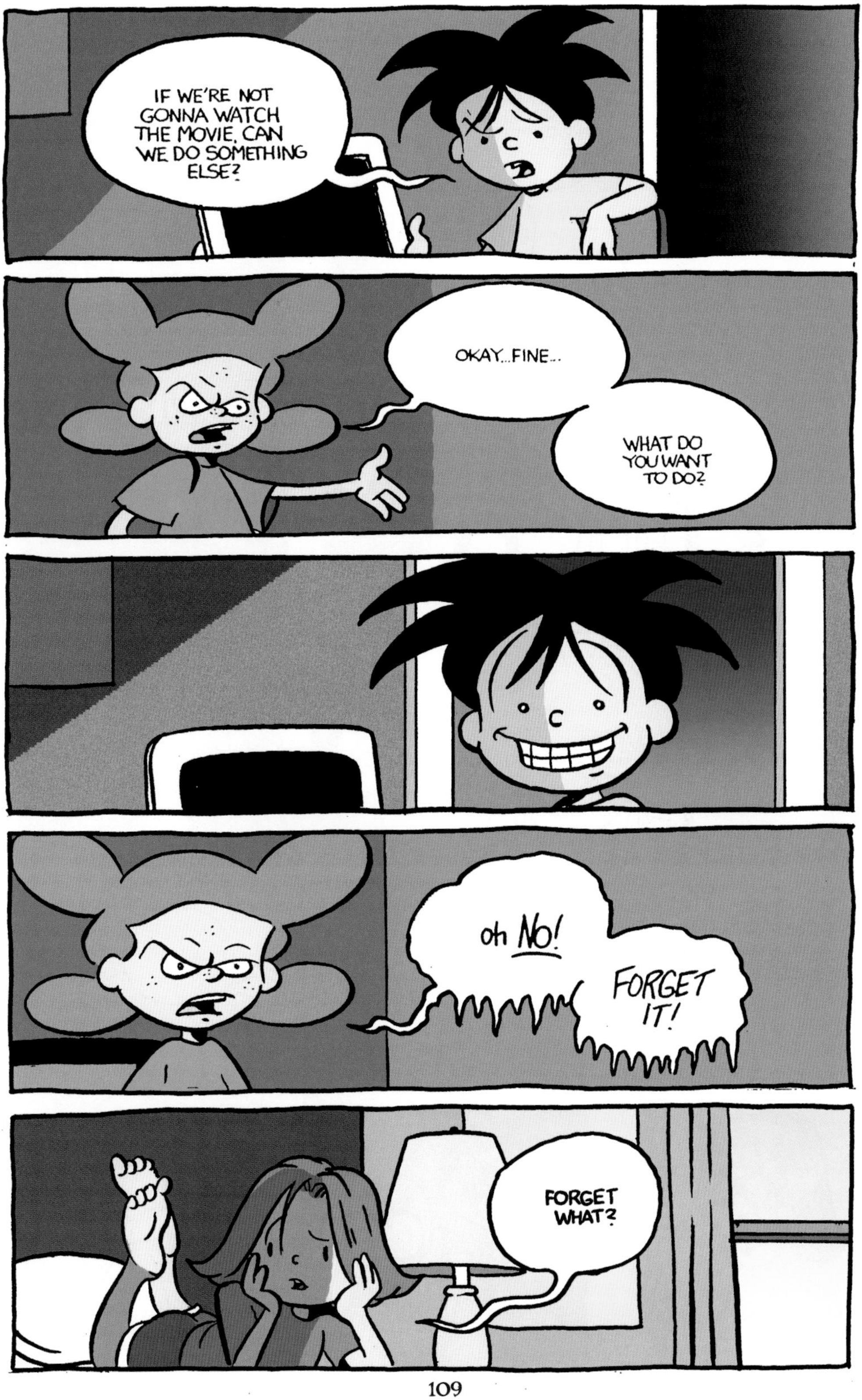
IF WE'RE NOT GONNA WATCH THE MOVIE, CAN WE DO SOMETHING ELSE?
OKAY...FINE...
WHAT DO YOU WANT TO DO?
oh NO!
FORGET IT!
FORGET WHAT?

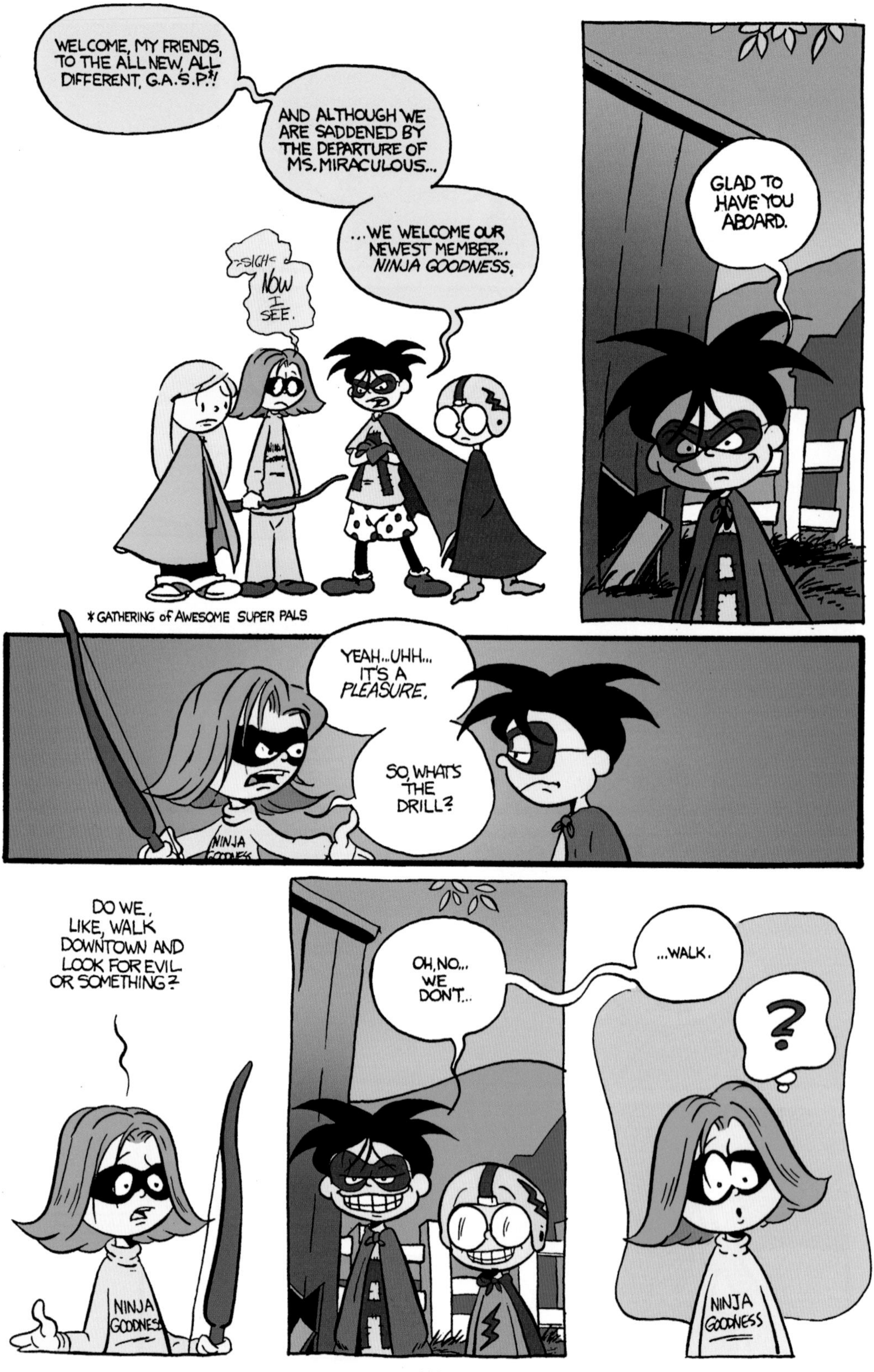
WELCOME, MY FRIENDS, TO THE ALL NEW, ALL DIFFERENT, G.A.S.P.*!
AND ALTHOUGH WE ARE SADDENED BY THE DEPARTURE OF MS. MIRACULOUS...
...WE WELCOME OUR NEWEST MEMBER... NINJA GOODNESS.
>SIGH< NOW I SEE.
* GATHERING of AWESOME SUPER PALS
GLAD TO HAVE YOU ABOARD.
YEAH...UHH... IT'S A PLEASURE.
SO, WHAT'S THE DRILL?
NINJA GOODNESS
DO WE, LIKE, WALK DOWNTOWN AND LOOK FOR EVIL OR SOMETHING?
NINJA GOODNESS
OH, NO... WE DON'T...
...WALK.
?
NINJA GOODNESS

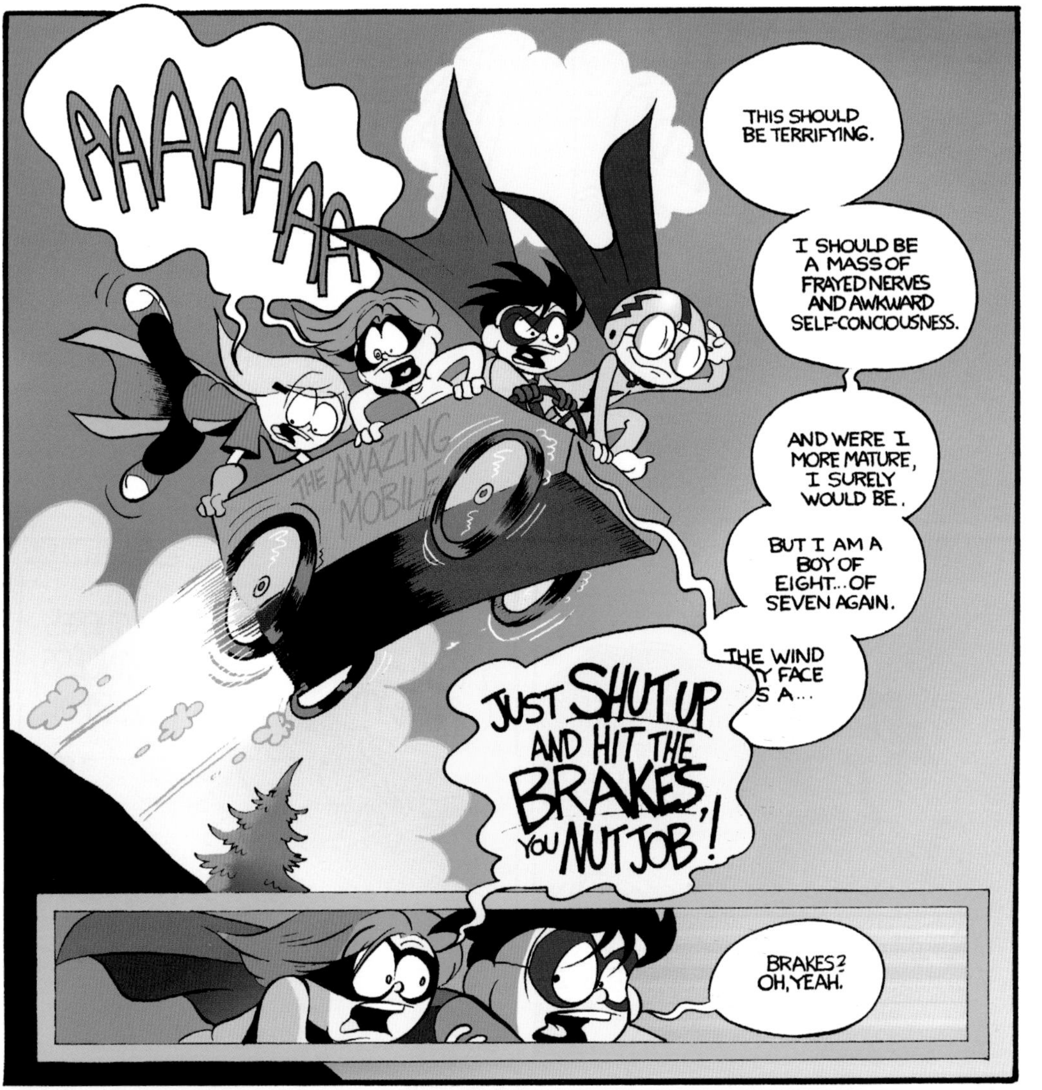
AAAAAAA
THIS SHOULD BE TERRIFYING.
I SHOULD BE A MASS OF FRAYED NERVES AND AWKWARD SELF-CONCIOUSNESS.
AND WERE I MORE MATURE, I SURELY WOULD BE.
BUT I AM A BOY OF EIGHT...OF SEVEN AGAIN.
THE AMAZING MOBILE
JUST SHUT UP AND HIT THE BRAKES, YOU NUT JOB!
BRAKES? OH, YEAH.

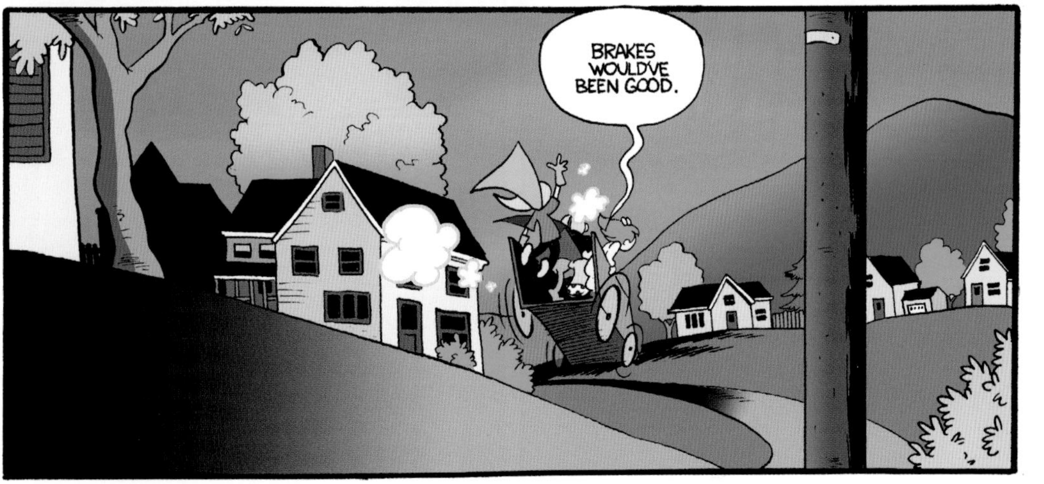
BRAKES WOULD'VE BEEN GOOD.

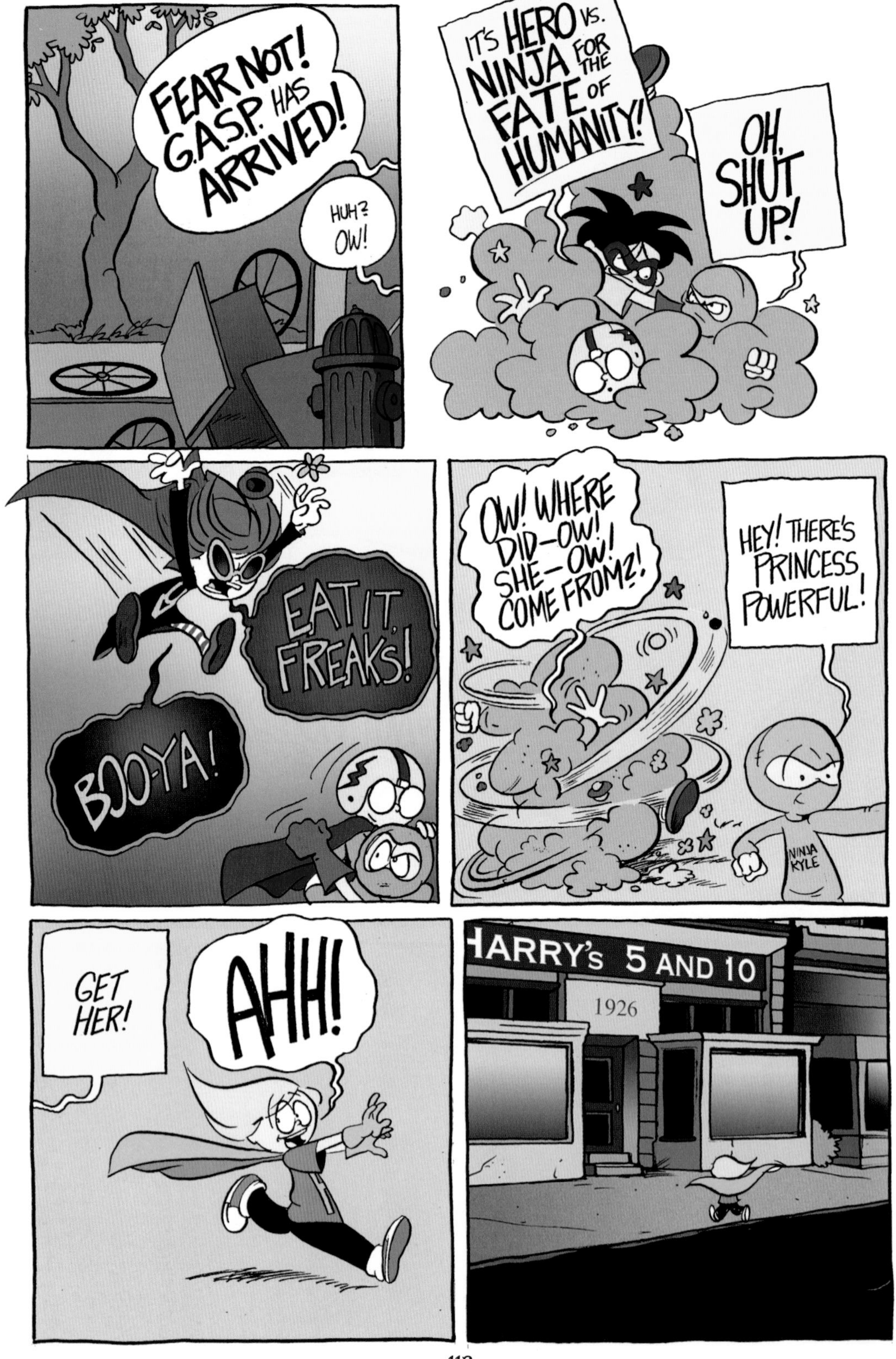
FEAR NOT! G.A.S.P. HAS ARRIVED!
HUH? OW!
IT'S HERO VS. NINJA FOR THE FATE OF HUMANITY!
OH, SHUT UP!
EAT IT, FREAKS!
BOO-YA!
OW! WHERE DID—OW! SHE—OW! COME FROM?!
HEY! THERE'S PRINCESS POWERFUL!
NINJA KYLE
GET HER!
AHH!
HARRY'S 5 AND 10
1926

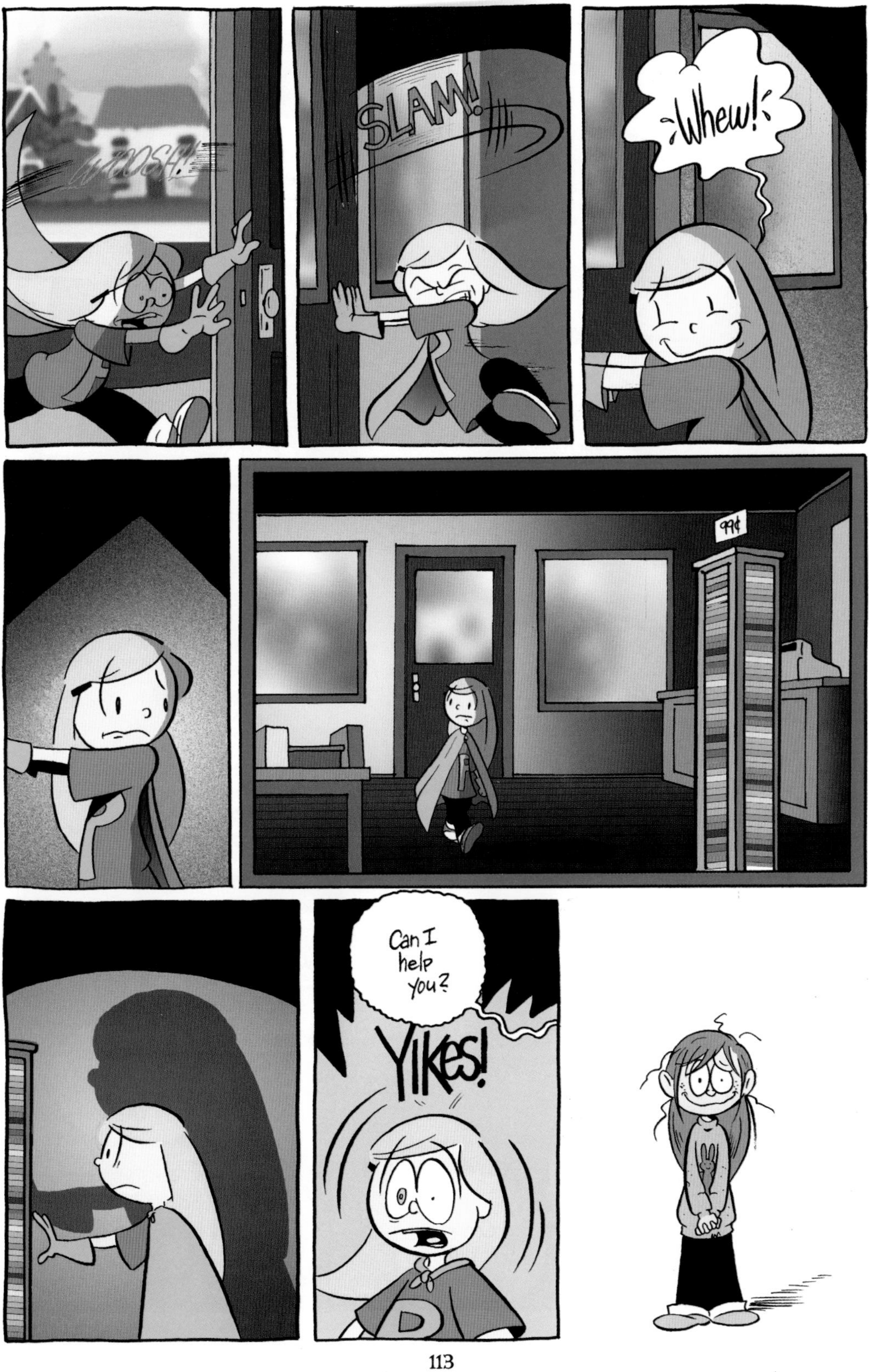
WHOOSH!!
SLAM!
Whew!
99¢
Can I help you?
YIKES!

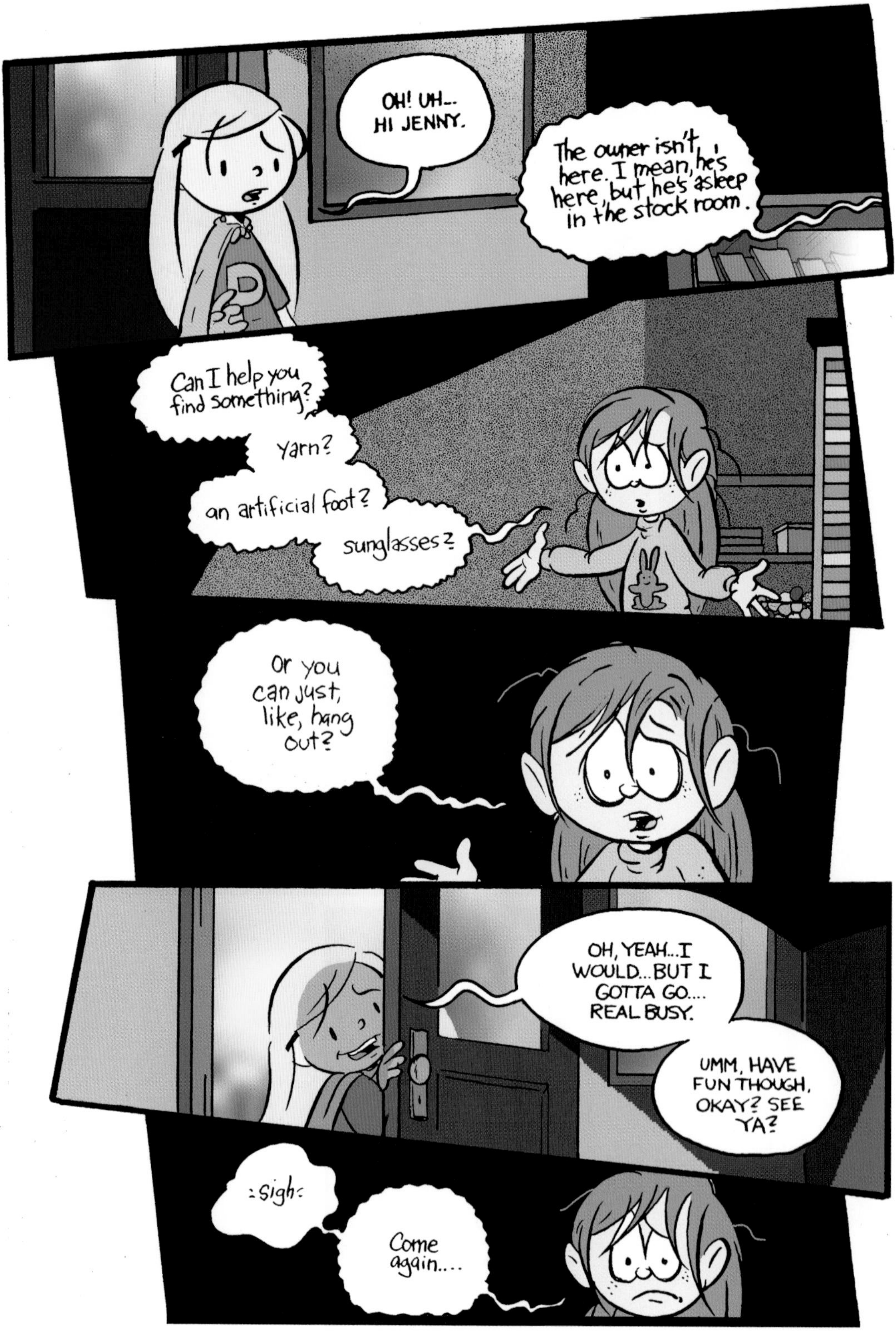
OH! UH..
HI JENNY.
The owner isn't here. I mean, he's here, but he's asleep in the stock room.
Can I help you find something?
Yarn?
an artificial foot?
sunglasses?
Or you can just, like, hang out?
OH, YEAH...I WOULD...BUT I GOTTA GO.... REAL BUSY.
UMM, HAVE FUN THOUGH, OKAY? SEE YA?
:sigh:
Come again....

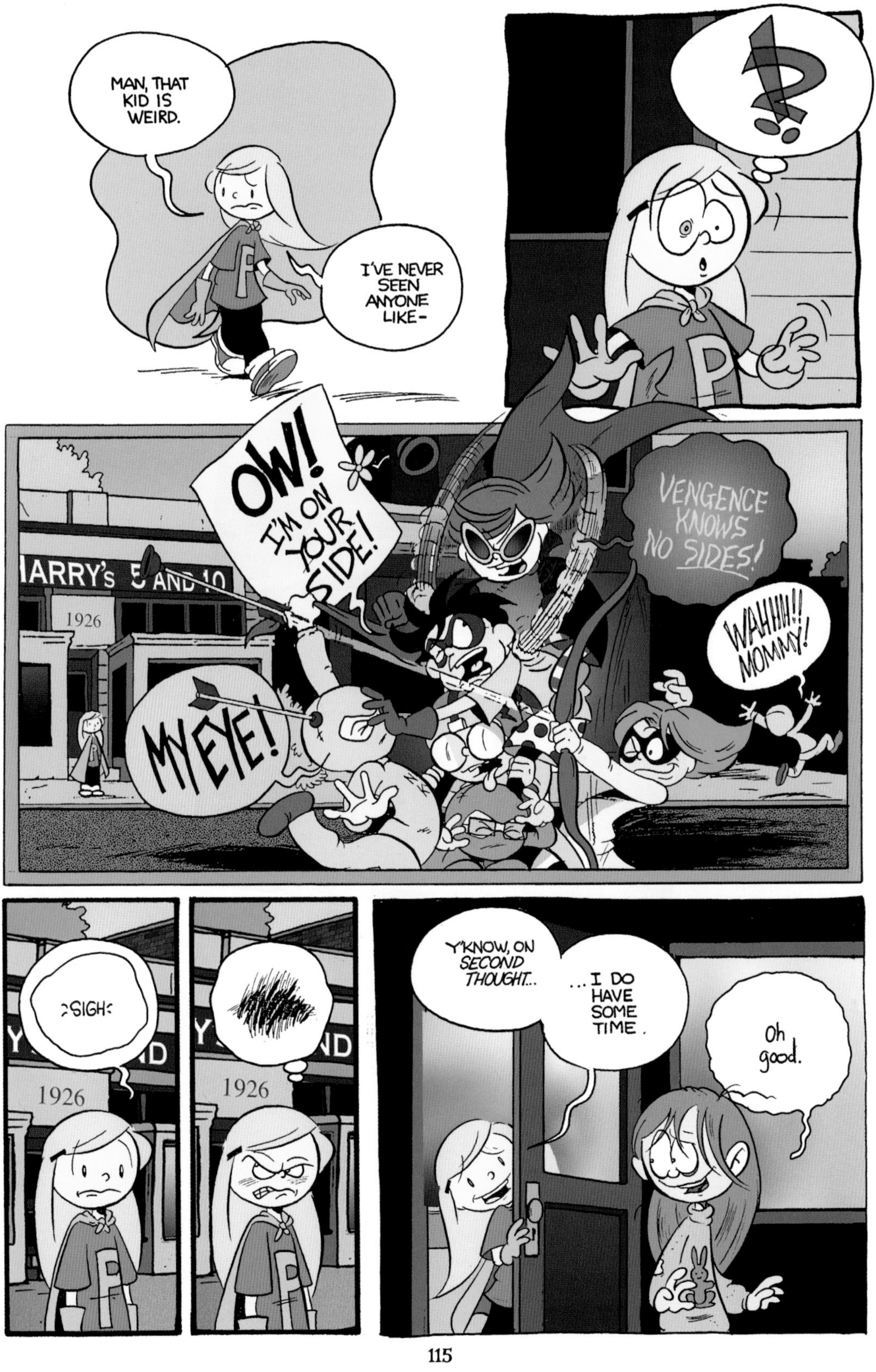

MAN, THAT KID IS WEIRD.
I'VE NEVER SEEN ANYONE LIKE-
OW! I'M ON YOUR SIDE!
HARRY's 5 AND 10
1926
VENGENCE KNOWS NO SIDES!
WAHHH!! MOMMY!
MY EYE!
:SIGH:
1926
1926
Y'KNOW, ON SECOND THOUGHT...
...I DO HAVE SOME TIME.
Oh good.

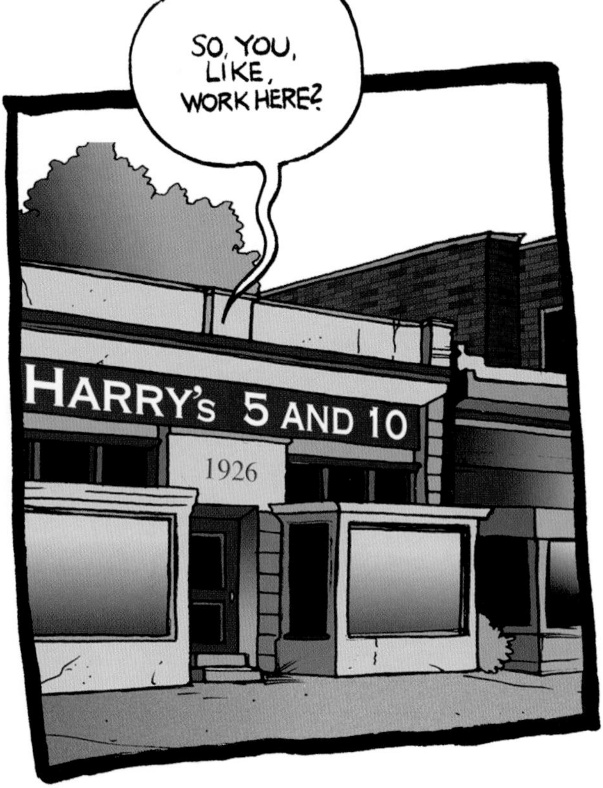
SO, YOU, LIKE, WORK HERE?
HARRY's 5 AND 10
1926

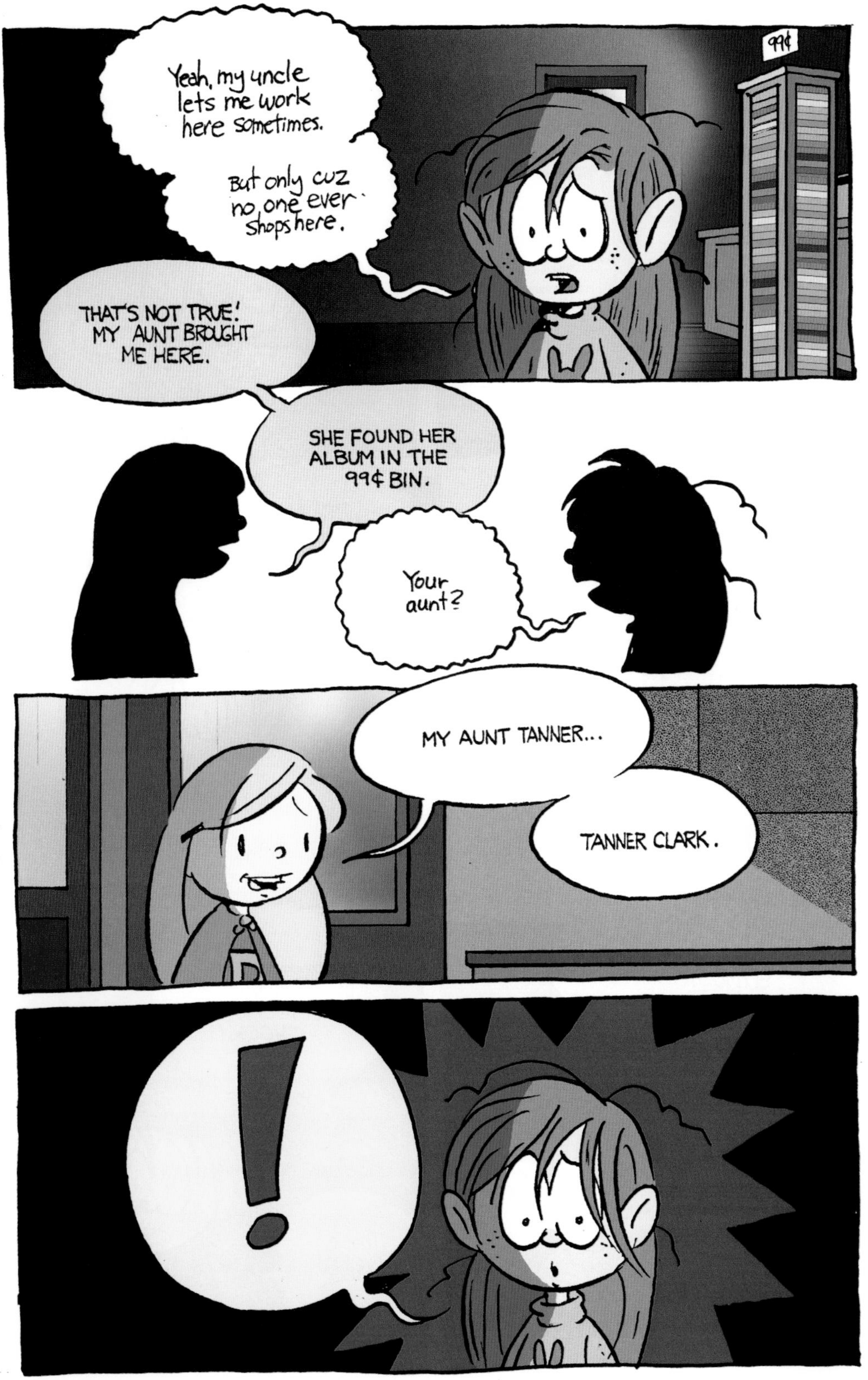
99¢
Yeah, my uncle lets me work here sometimes.
But only cuz no one ever shops here.
THAT'S NOT TRUE! MY AUNT BROUGHT ME HERE.
SHE FOUND HER ALBUM IN THE 99¢ BIN.
Your aunt?
MY AUNT TANNER...
TANNER CLARK.
!

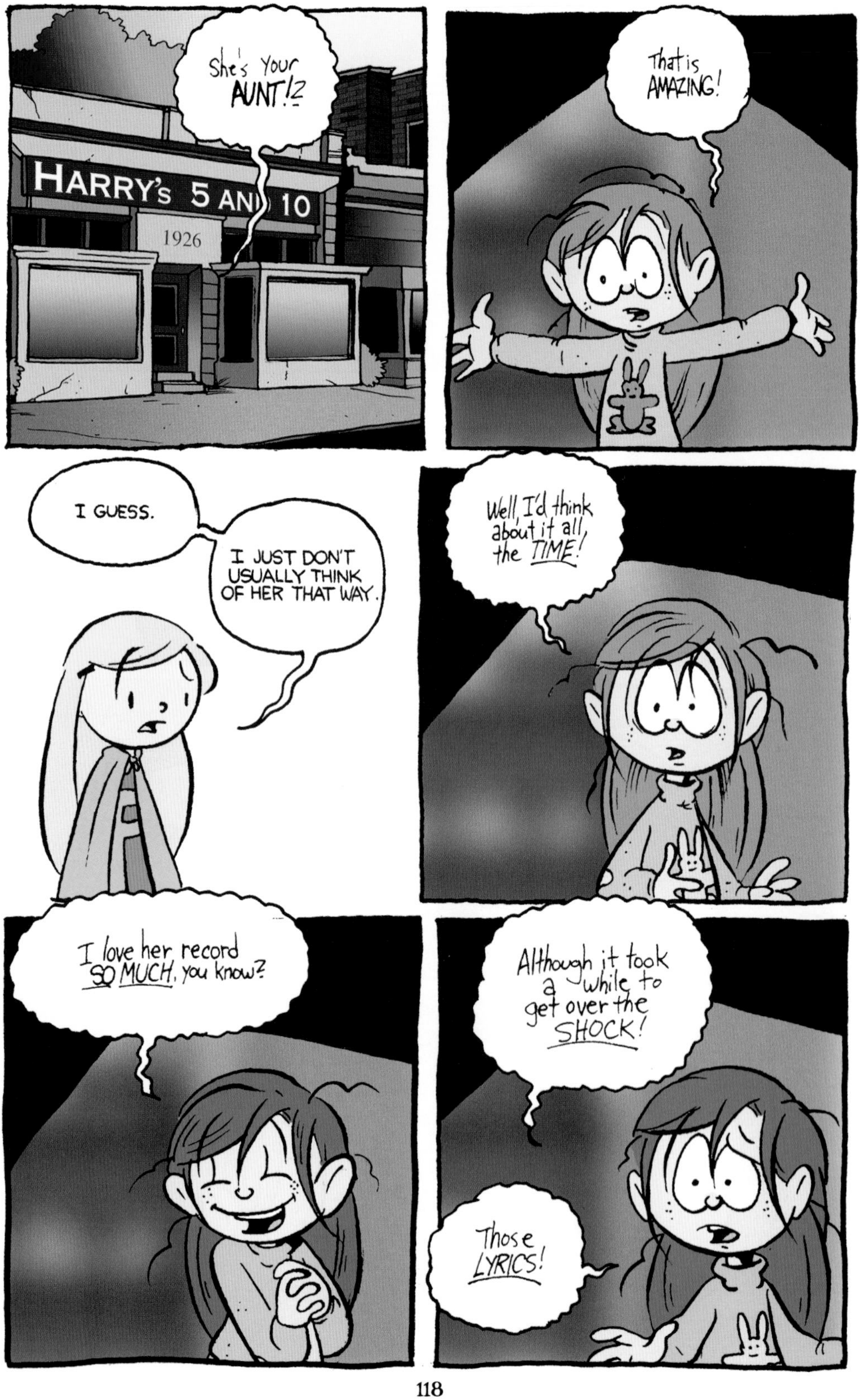

HARRY'S 5 AND 10
1926
She's Your AUNT!?
That is AMAZING!
I GUESS.
I JUST DON'T USUALLY THINK OF HER THAT WAY.
Well I'd think about it all the TIME!
I love her record SO MUCH, you know?
Although it took a while to get over the SHOCK!
Those LYRICS!

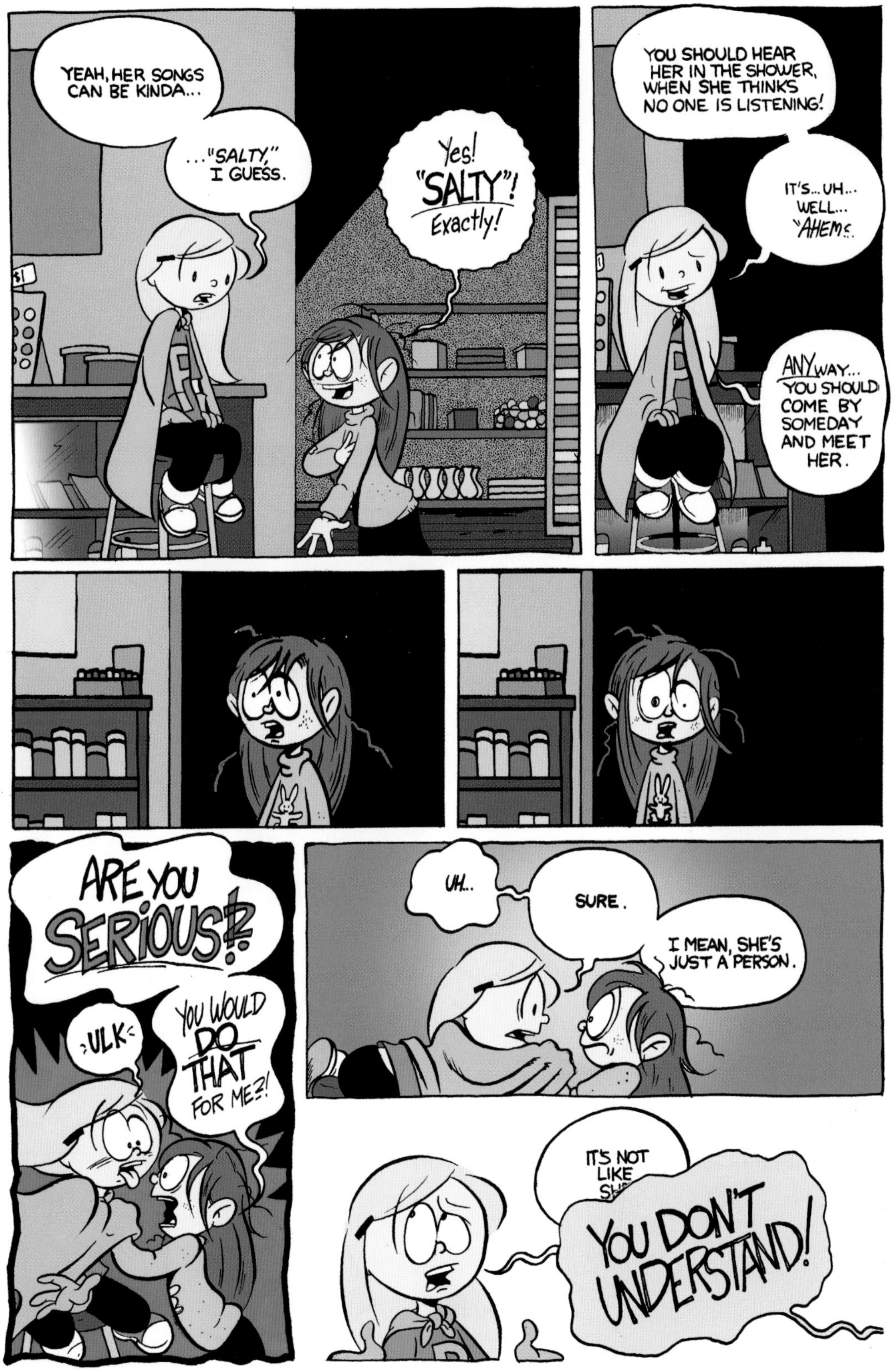

YEAH, HER SONGS CAN BE KINDA...
..."SALTY," I GUESS.
Yes! "SALTY"! Exactly!
YOU SHOULD HEAR HER IN THE SHOWER, WHEN SHE THINKS NO ONE IS LISTENING!
IT'S...UH... WELL... AHEM
ANYWAY... YOU SHOULD COME BY SOMEDAY AND MEET HER.
ARE YOU SERIOUS!?
ULK
YOU WOULD DO THAT FOR ME?!
UH...
SURE.
I MEAN, SHE'S JUST A PERSON.
IT'S NOT LIKE
YOU DON'T UNDERSTAND!

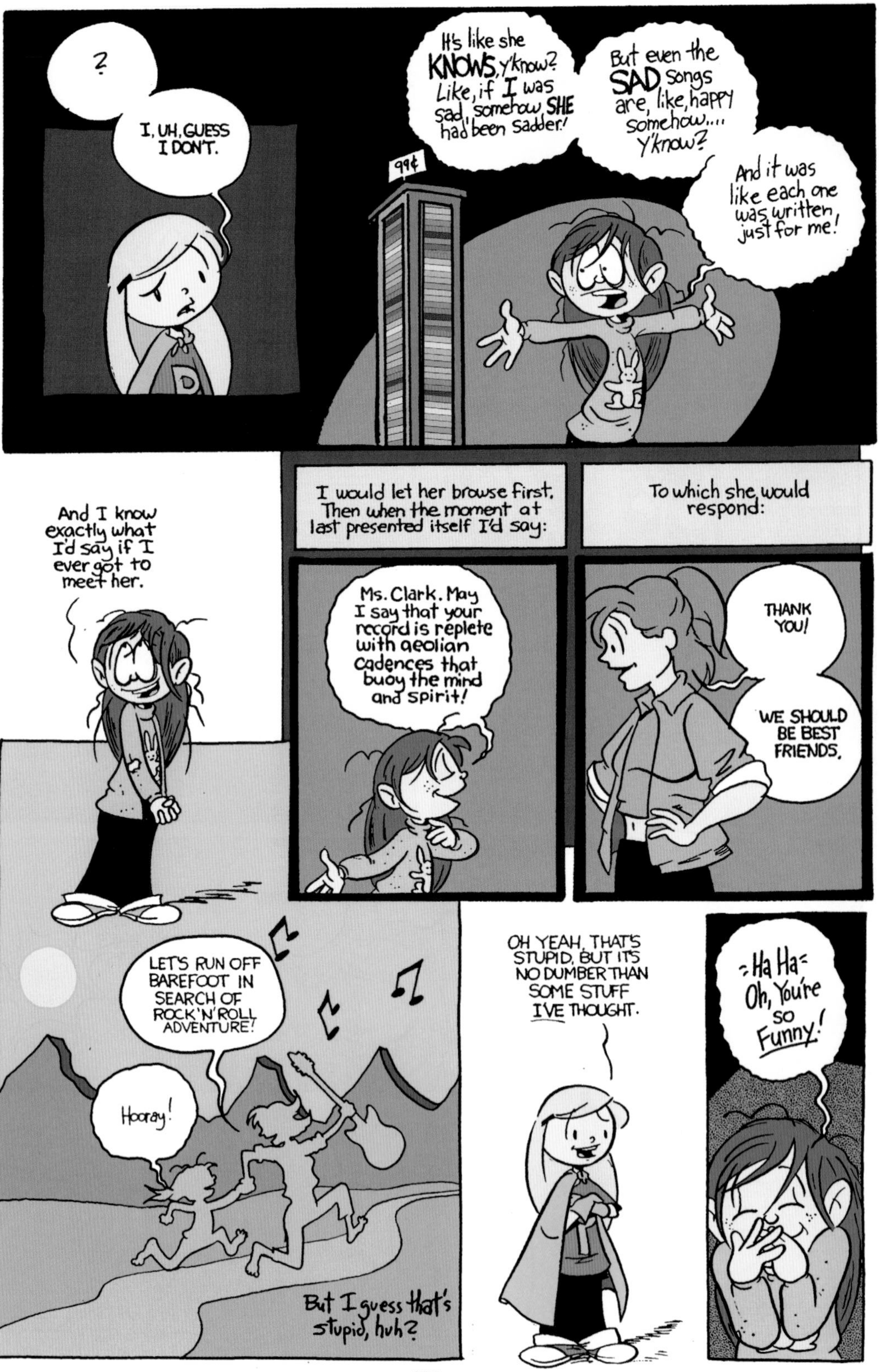
?
I, UH, GUESS I DON'T.
It's like she KNOWS, y'know? Like, if I was sad, somehow SHE had been sadder!
But even the SAD songs are, like, happy somehow.... y'know?
And it was like each one was written just for me!
99¢
And I know exactly what I'd say if I ever got to meet her.
I would let her browse first. Then when the moment at last presented itself I'd say:
To which she would respond:
Ms. Clark. May I say that your record is replete with aeolian cadences that buoy the mind and spirit!
THANK YOU!
WE SHOULD BE BEST FRIENDS.
LET'S RUN OFF BAREFOOT IN SEARCH OF ROCK'N'ROLL ADVENTURE!
Hooray!
But I guess that's stupid, huh?
OH YEAH, THAT'S STUPID, BUT IT'S NO DUMBER THAN SOME STUFF I'VE THOUGHT.
Ha Ha Oh, You're so Funny!

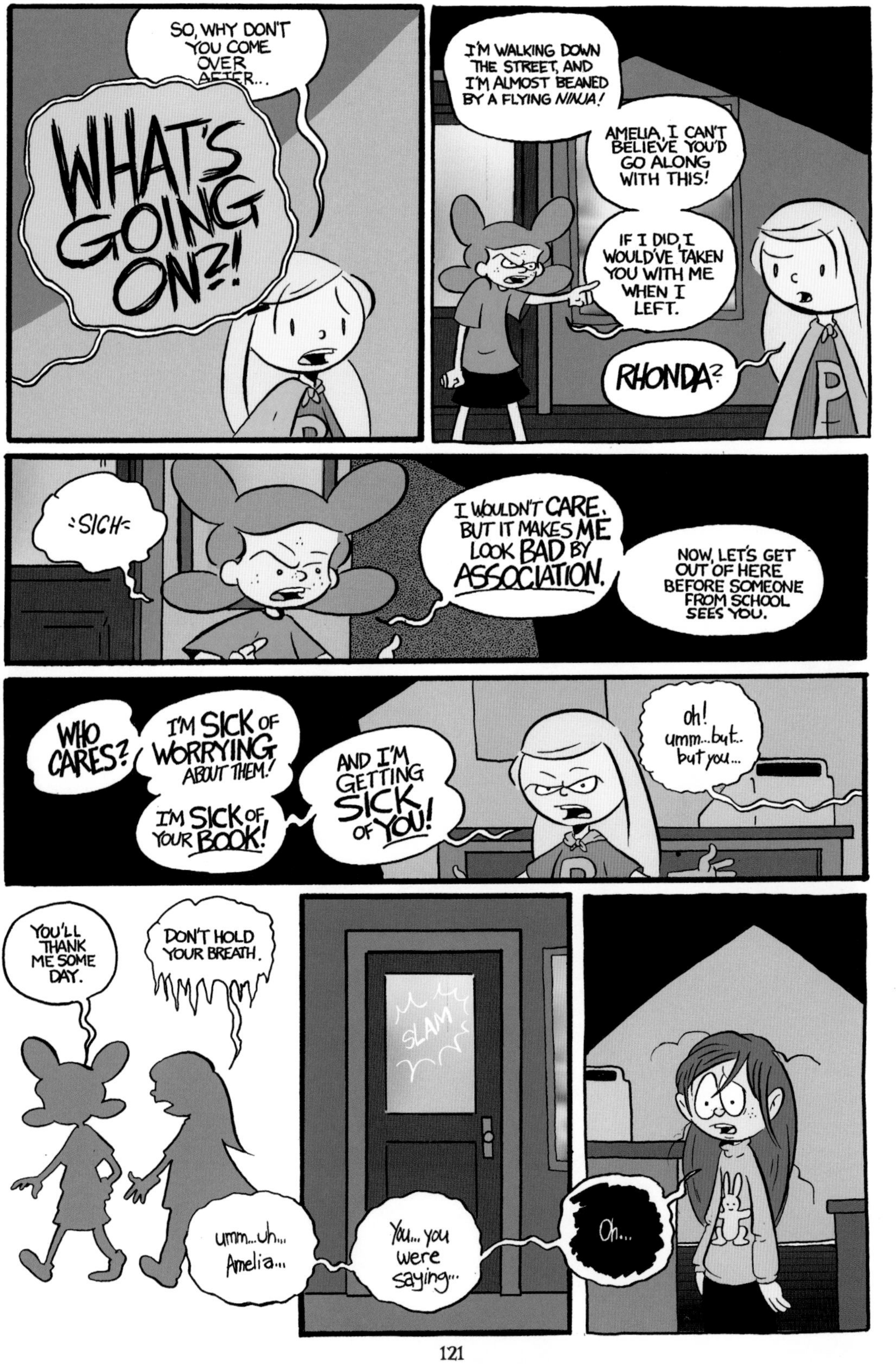
SO, WHY DON'T YOU COME OVER AFTER...
WHAT'S GOING ON?!
I'M WALKING DOWN THE STREET, AND I'M ALMOST BEANED BY A FLYING NINJA!
AMELIA, I CAN'T BELIEVE YOU'D GO ALONG WITH THIS!
IF I DID, I WOULD'VE TAKEN YOU WITH ME WHEN I LEFT.
RHONDA?
SIGH
I WOULDN'T CARE. BUT IT MAKES ME LOOK BAD BY ASSOCIATION.
NOW, LET'S GET OUT OF HERE BEFORE SOMEONE FROM SCHOOL SEES YOU.
WHO CARES?
I'M SICK OF WORRYING ABOUT THEM!
I'M SICK OF YOUR BOOK!
AND I'M GETTING SICK OF YOU!
oh! umm...but.. but you...
YOU'LL THANK ME SOME DAY.
DON'T HOLD YOUR BREATH.
SLAM
umm...uh... Amelia...
You... you were saying...
Oh...

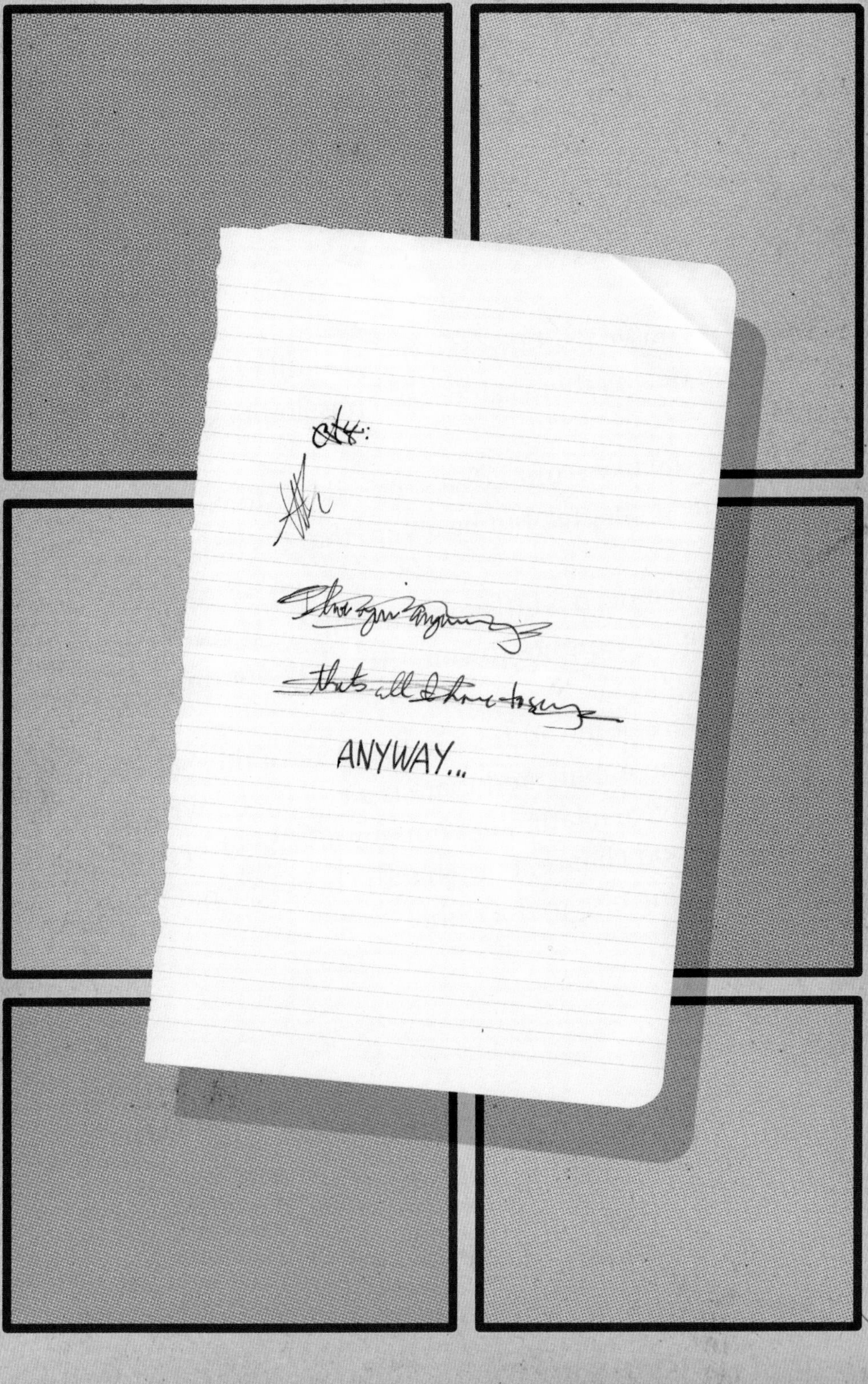
ANYWAY...

Getting Desperate?

Look, if you've read this far and are still not seeing the results you desire, there can be two possibilities:

(1) You may be like Aunt Edna's noodles. More on that in the next chapter, but be aware that it's not good.

(2) You may just need a little extra attention. If you think this second option applies to you, then why not drop me a line?

Write to me, care of the address in the front of this book; a real letter now, not an e-mail, and there is a chance I'll write back with custom advice relating to your specific needs. I mean, there's not a good chance, but what the heck, it's not like you have anything else to do, right?

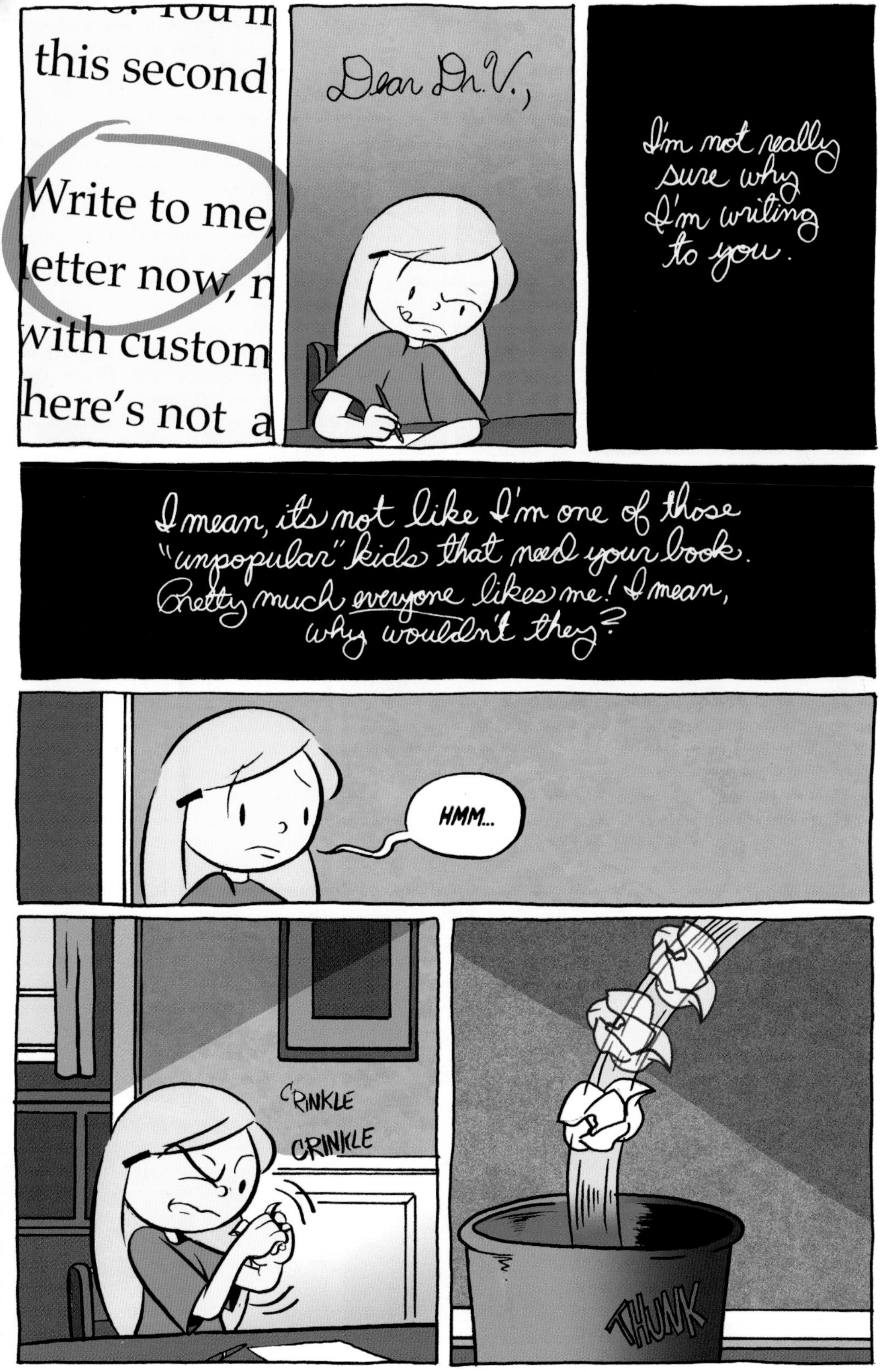

this second
Write to me,
letter now,
with custom
here's not a
Dear Dr. V.,
I'm not really sure why I'm writing to you.
I mean, it's not like I'm one of those "unpopular" kids that need your book. Pretty much everyone likes me! I mean, why wouldn't they?
HMM...
CRINKLE
CRINKLE
THUNK

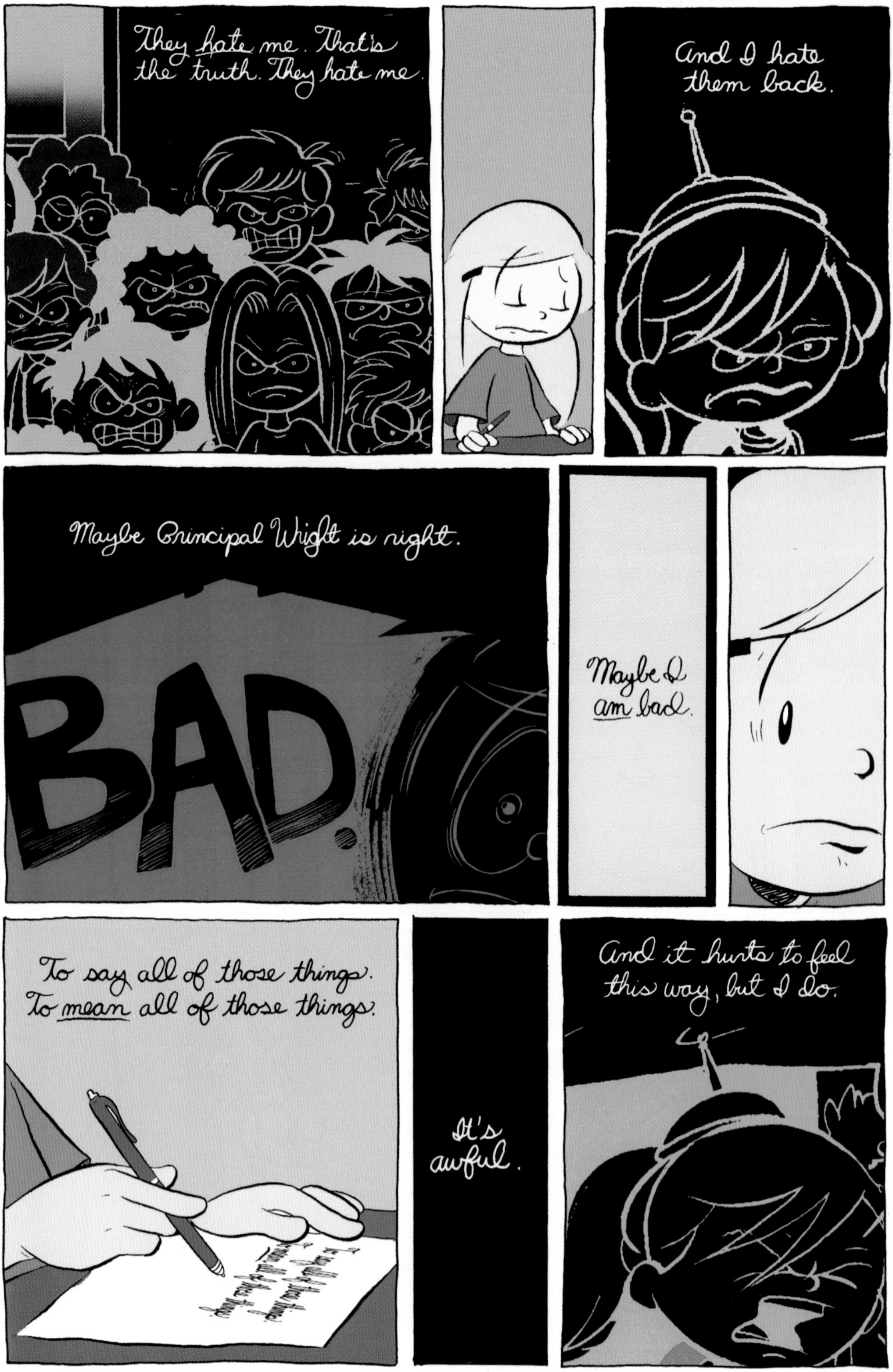
They hate me. That's the truth. They hate me.
And I hate them back.
Maybe Principal Wright is right.
BAD.
Maybe I am bad.
To say all of those things. To mean all of those things.
It's awful.
And it hurts to feel this way, but I do.

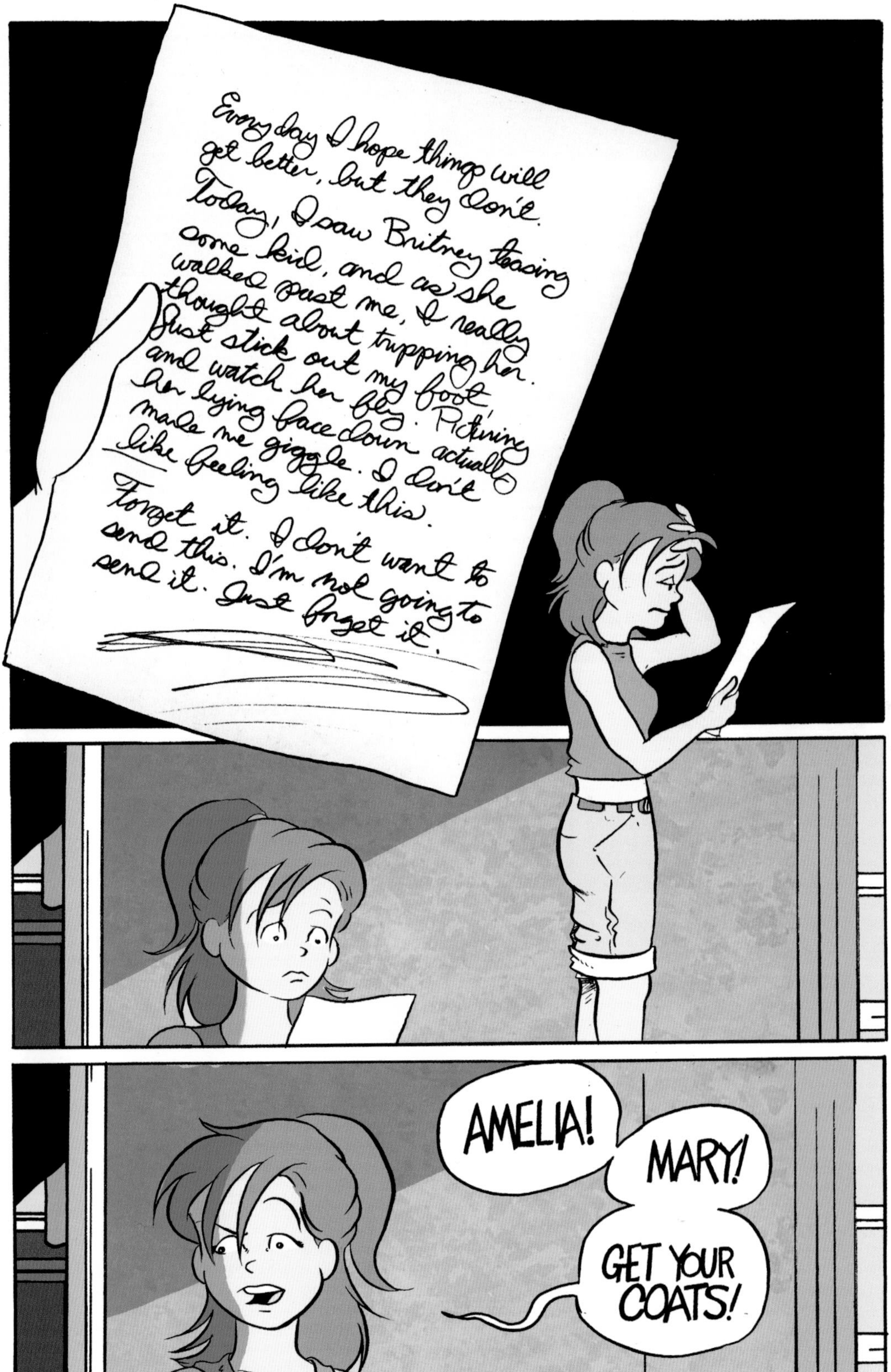
Every day I hope things will get better, but they don't. Today, I saw Britney teasing some kid, and as she walked past me, I really thought about tripping her. Just stick out my foot and watch her fly. Picturing her lying face down actually made me giggle. I don't like feeling like this.
Forget it. I don't want to send this. I'm not going to send it. Just forget it.
AMELIA!
MARY!
GET YOUR COATS!

WE'RE GOING FOR A WALK.

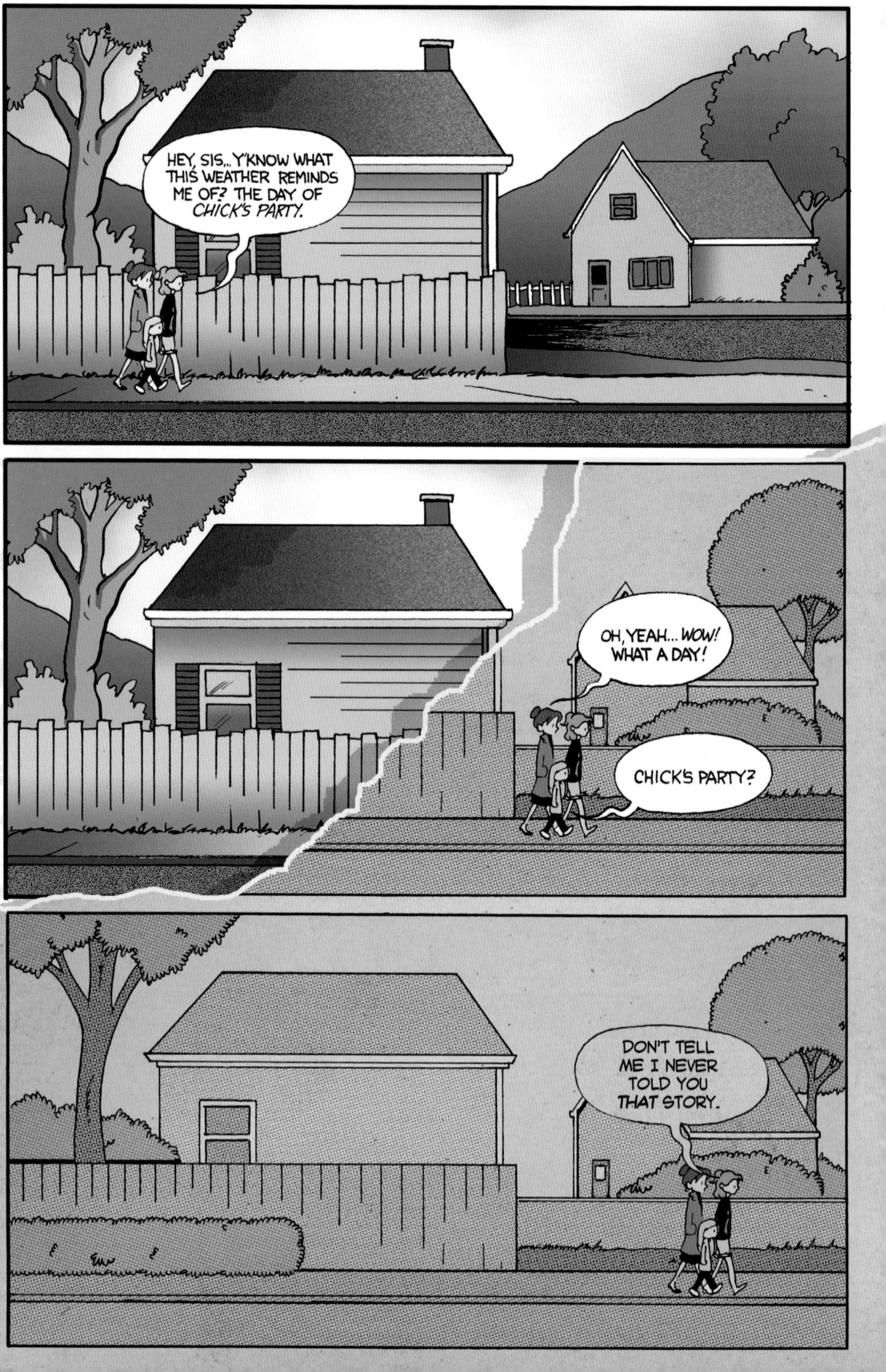
HEY, SIS... Y'KNOW WHAT THIS WEATHER REMINDS ME OF? THE DAY OF *CHICK'S PARTY.*
OH, YEAH... *WOW!* WHAT A DAY!
CHICK'S PARTY?
DON'T TELL ME I NEVER TOLD YOU *THAT* STORY.

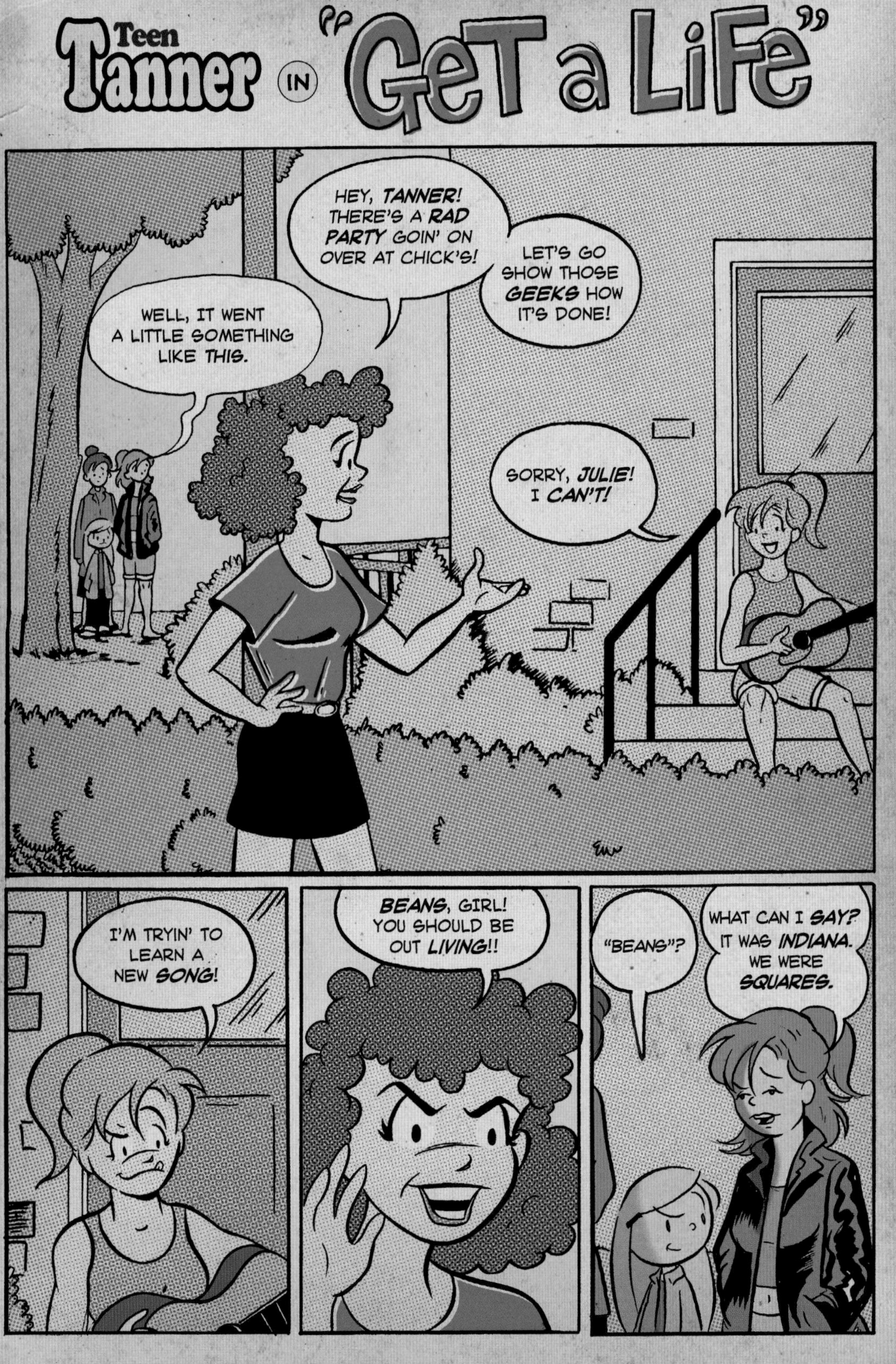
Teen Tanner IN "GeT a LiFe"
WELL, IT WENT A LITTLE SOMETHING LIKE THIS.
HEY, TANNER! THERE'S A RAD PARTY GOIN' ON OVER AT CHICK'S!
LET'S GO SHOW THOSE GEEKS HOW IT'S DONE!
SORRY, JULIE! I CAN'T!
I'M TRYIN' TO LEARN A NEW SONG!
BEANS, GIRL! YOU SHOULD BE OUT LIVING!!
"BEANS"?
WHAT CAN I SAY? IT WAS INDIANA. WE WERE SQUARES.

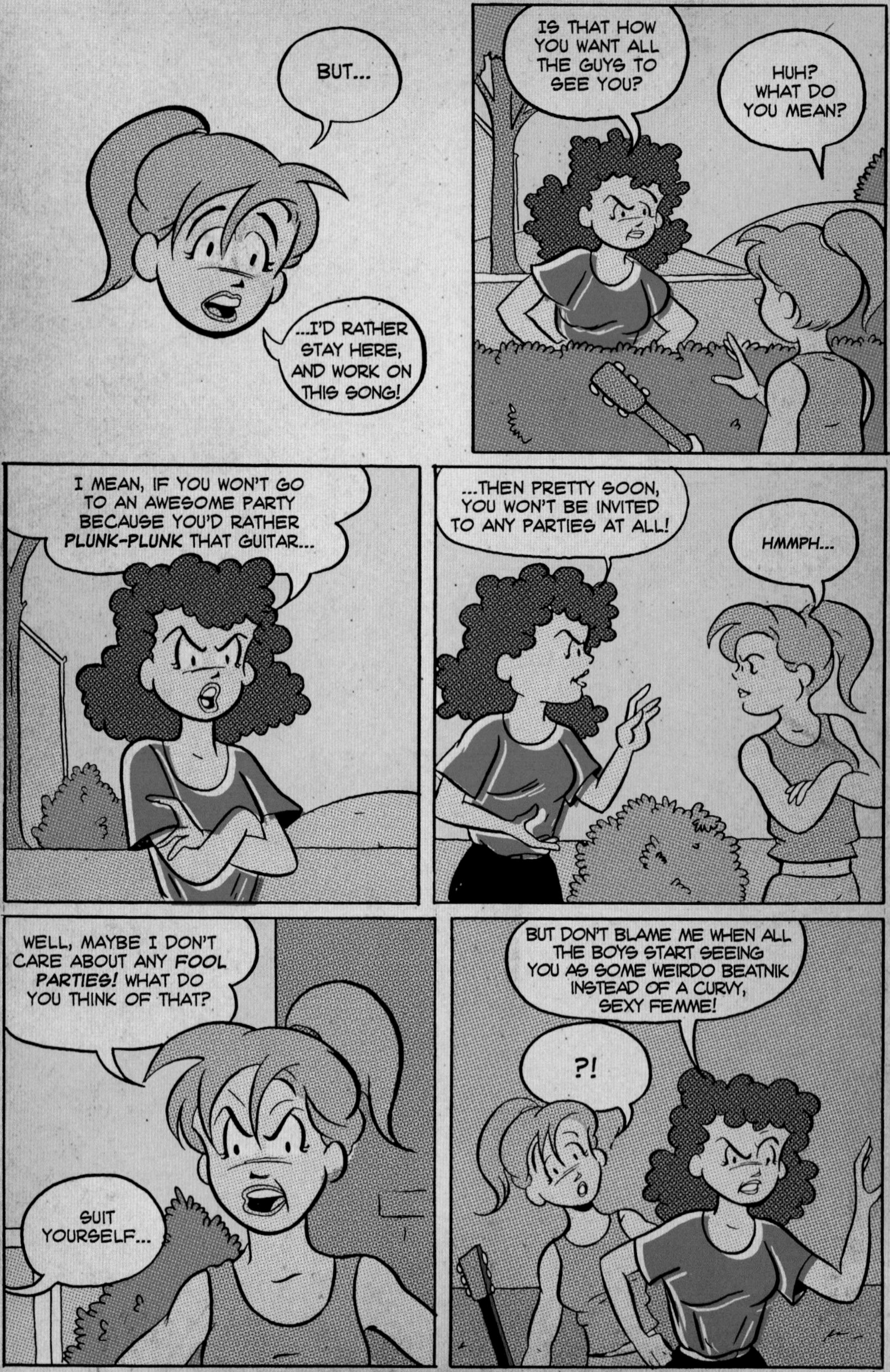
BUT...
...I'D RATHER STAY HERE, AND WORK ON THIS SONG!
IS THAT HOW YOU WANT ALL THE GUYS TO SEE YOU?
HUH? WHAT DO YOU MEAN?
I MEAN, IF YOU WON'T GO TO AN AWESOME PARTY BECAUSE YOU'D RATHER PLUNK-PLUNK THAT GUITAR...
...THEN PRETTY SOON, YOU WON'T BE INVITED TO ANY PARTIES AT ALL!
HMMPH...
WELL, MAYBE I DON'T CARE ABOUT ANY FOOL PARTIES! WHAT DO YOU THINK OF THAT?
SUIT YOURSELF...
BUT DON'T BLAME ME WHEN ALL THE BOYS START SEEING YOU AS SOME WEIRDO BEATNIK INSTEAD OF A CURVY, SEXY FEMME!
?!

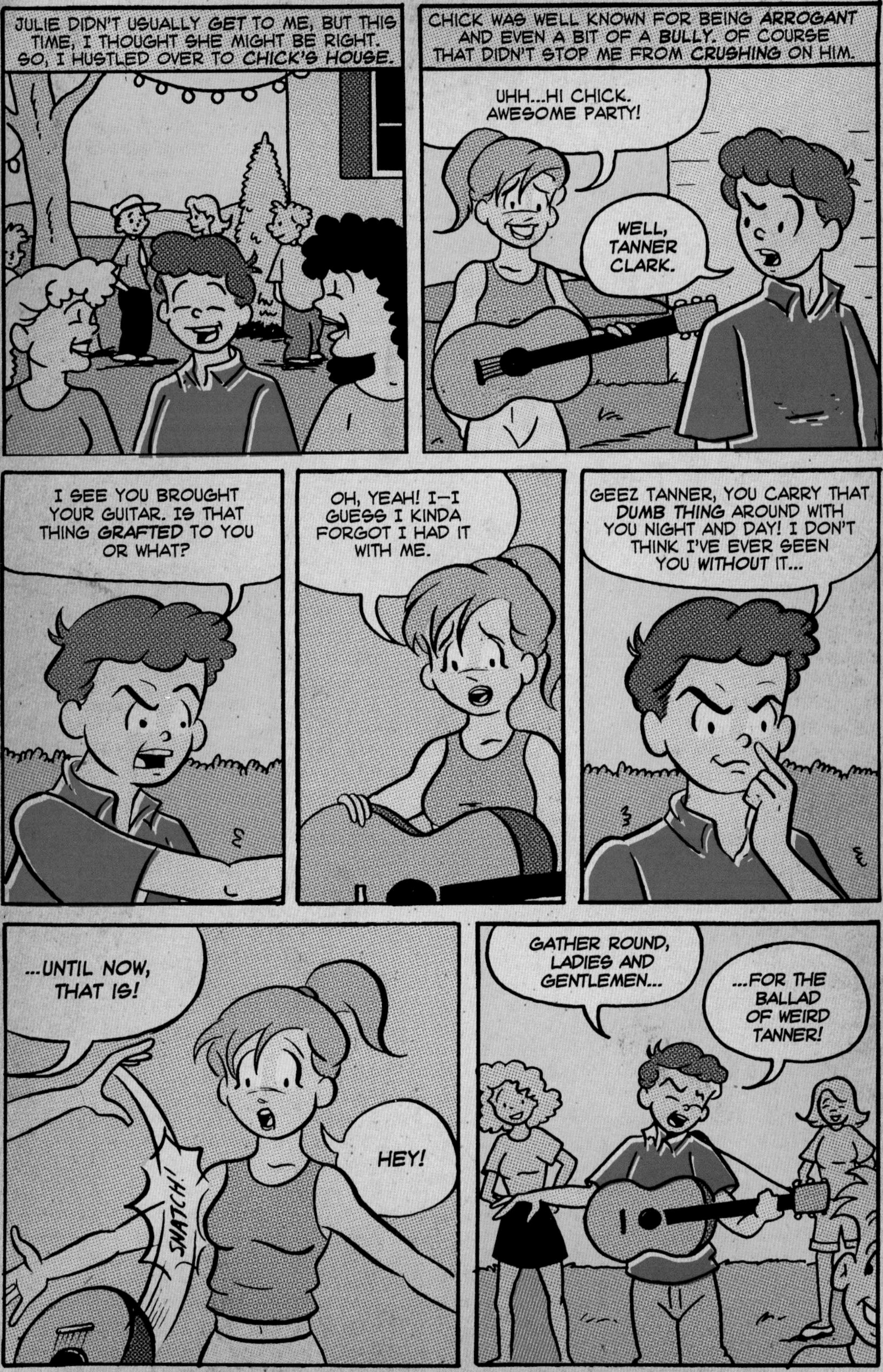
JULIE DIDN'T USUALLY GET TO ME, BUT THIS TIME, I THOUGHT SHE MIGHT BE RIGHT. SO, I HUSTLED OVER TO CHICK'S HOUSE.
CHICK WAS WELL KNOWN FOR BEING ARROGANT AND EVEN A BIT OF A BULLY. OF COURSE THAT DIDN'T STOP ME FROM CRUSHING ON HIM.
UHH...HI CHICK. AWESOME PARTY!
WELL, TANNER CLARK.
I SEE YOU BROUGHT YOUR GUITAR. IS THAT THING GRAFTED TO YOU OR WHAT?
OH, YEAH! I—I GUESS I KINDA FORGOT I HAD IT WITH ME.
GEEZ TANNER, YOU CARRY THAT DUMB THING AROUND WITH YOU NIGHT AND DAY! I DON'T THINK I'VE EVER SEEN YOU WITHOUT IT...
...UNTIL NOW, THAT IS!
SNATCH!
HEY!
GATHER ROUND, LADIES AND GENTLEMEN...
...FOR THE BALLAD OF WEIRD TANNER!

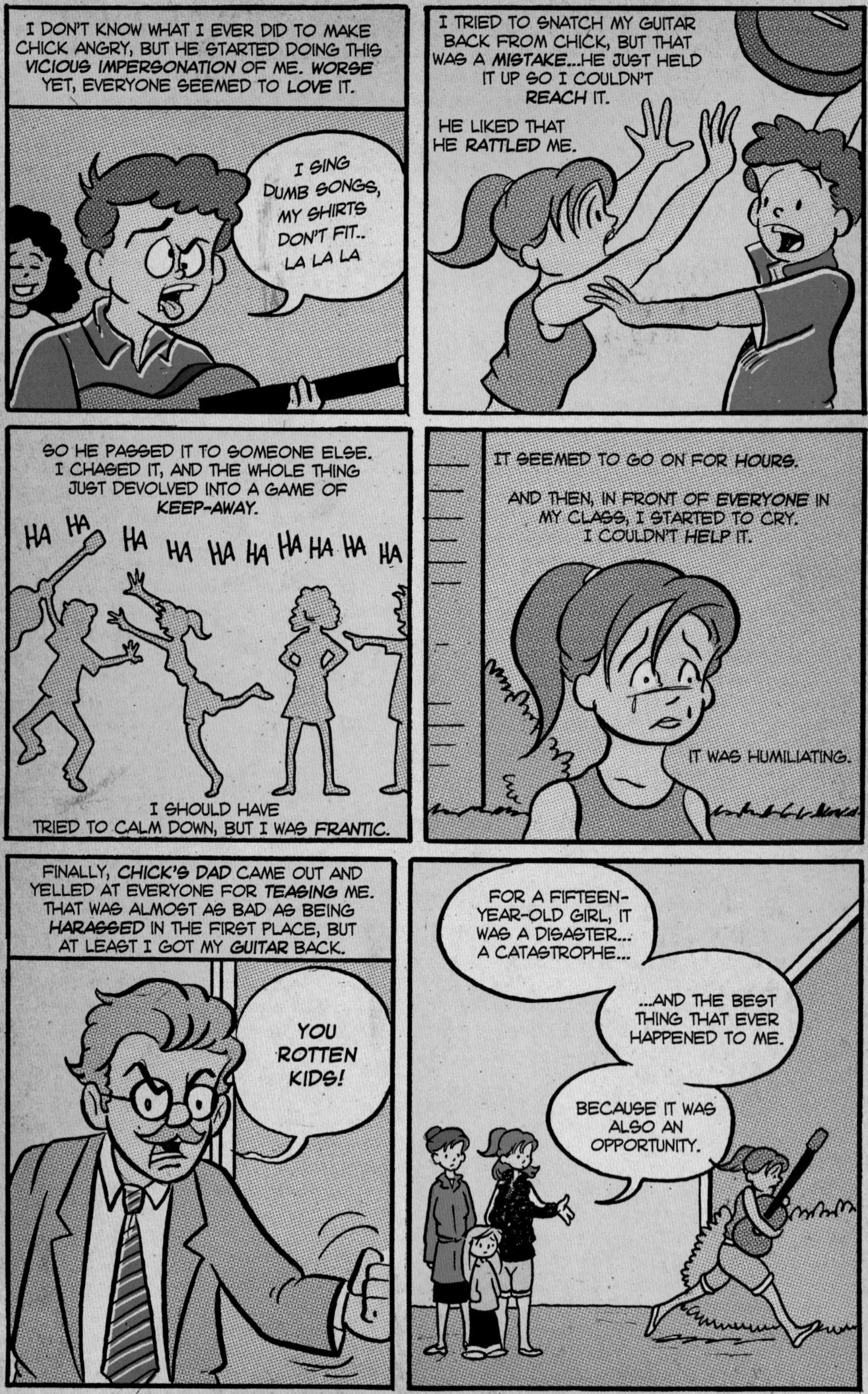
I DON'T KNOW WHAT I EVER DID TO MAKE CHICK ANGRY, BUT HE STARTED DOING THIS VICIOUS IMPERSONATION OF ME. WORSE YET, EVERYONE SEEMED TO LOVE IT.
I SING DUMB SONGS, MY SHIRTS DON'T FIT.. LA LA LA
I TRIED TO SNATCH MY GUITAR BACK FROM CHICK, BUT THAT WAS A MISTAKE...HE JUST HELD IT UP SO I COULDN'T REACH IT.
HE LIKED THAT HE RATTLED ME.
SO HE PASSED IT TO SOMEONE ELSE. I CHASED IT, AND THE WHOLE THING JUST DEVOLVED INTO A GAME OF KEEP-AWAY.
HA HA HA HA HA HA HA HA HA HA
I SHOULD HAVE TRIED TO CALM DOWN, BUT I WAS FRANTIC.
IT SEEMED TO GO ON FOR HOURS.
AND THEN, IN FRONT OF EVERYONE IN MY CLASS, I STARTED TO CRY. I COULDN'T HELP IT.
IT WAS HUMILIATING.
FINALLY, CHICK'S DAD CAME OUT AND YELLED AT EVERYONE FOR TEASING ME. THAT WAS ALMOST AS BAD AS BEING HARASSED IN THE FIRST PLACE, BUT AT LEAST I GOT MY GUITAR BACK.
YOU ROTTEN KIDS!
FOR A FIFTEEN-YEAR-OLD GIRL, IT WAS A DISASTER... A CATASTROPHE...
...AND THE BEST THING THAT EVER HAPPENED TO ME.
BECAUSE IT WAS ALSO AN OPPORTUNITY.

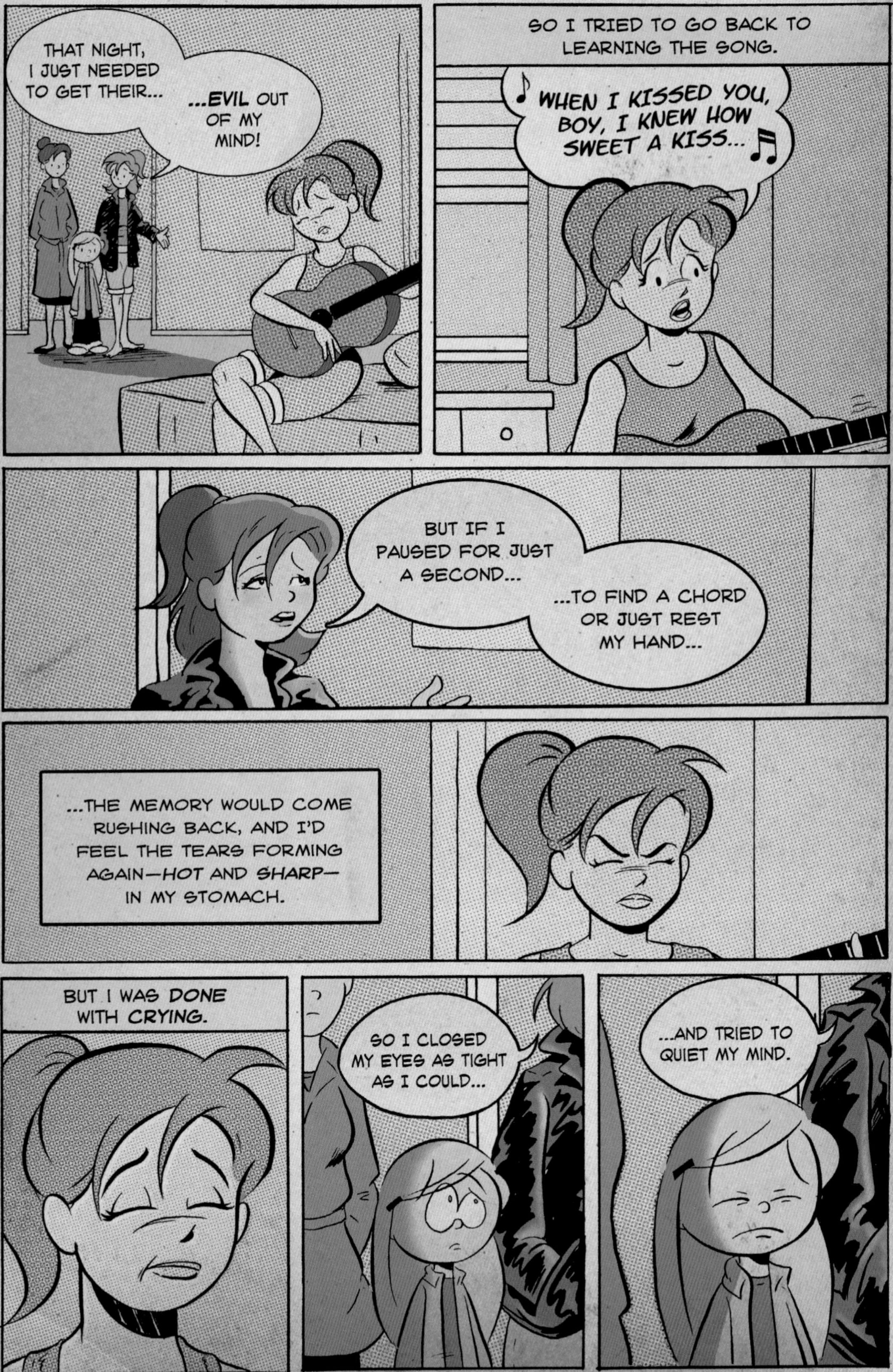
THAT NIGHT, I JUST NEEDED TO GET THEIR... ...EVIL OUT OF MY MIND!
SO I TRIED TO GO BACK TO LEARNING THE SONG.
♪ WHEN I KISSED YOU, BOY, I KNEW HOW SWEET A KISS... ♫
BUT IF I PAUSED FOR JUST A SECOND...
...TO FIND A CHORD OR JUST REST MY HAND...
...THE MEMORY WOULD COME RUSHING BACK, AND I'D FEEL THE TEARS FORMING AGAIN—HOT AND SHARP— IN MY STOMACH.
BUT I WAS DONE WITH CRYING.
SO I CLOSED MY EYES AS TIGHT AS I COULD...
...AND TRIED TO QUIET MY MIND.

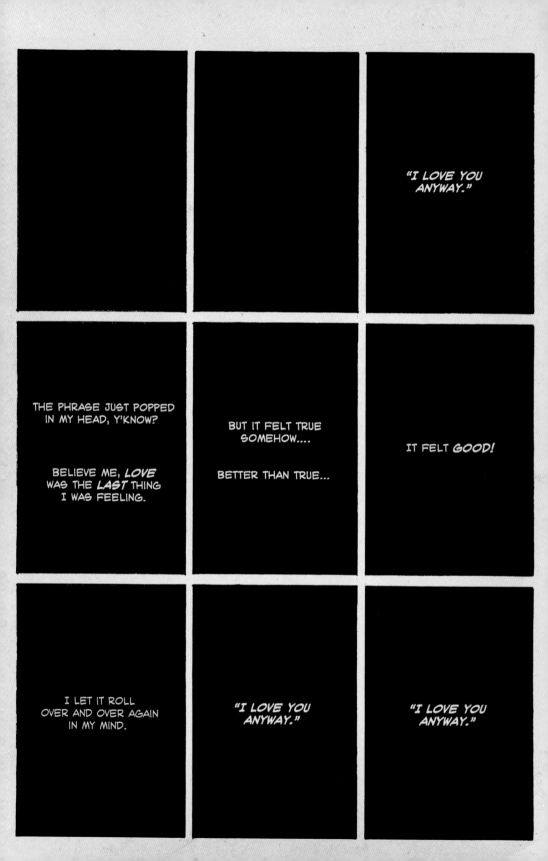

"I LOVE YOU ANYWAY."

THE PHRASE JUST POPPED IN MY HEAD, Y'KNOW?

BELIEVE ME, *LOVE* WAS THE *LAST* THING I WAS FEELING.

BUT IT FELT TRUE SOMEHOW....

BETTER THAN TRUE...

IT FELT *GOOD!*

I LET IT ROLL OVER AND OVER AGAIN IN MY MIND.

"I LOVE YOU ANYWAY."

"I LOVE YOU ANYWAY."

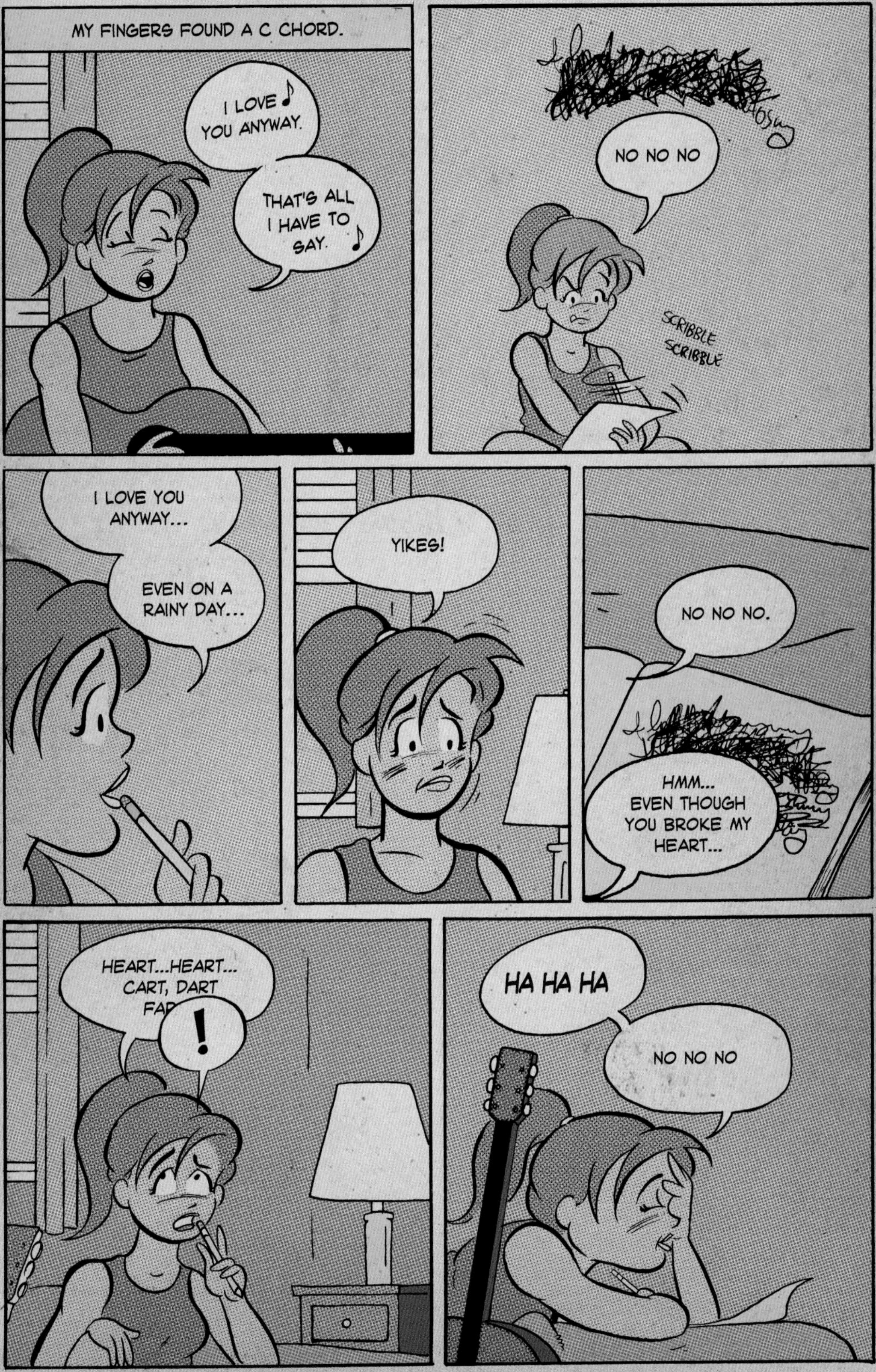
MY FINGERS FOUND A C CHORD.
I LOVE ♪ YOU ANYWAY.
THAT'S ALL I HAVE TO SAY. ♪
NO NO NO
SCRIBBLE SCRIBBLE
I LOVE YOU ANYWAY...
EVEN ON A RAINY DAY...
YIKES!
NO NO NO.
HMM... EVEN THOUGH YOU BROKE MY HEART...
HEART...HEART... CART, DART
!
HA HA HA
NO NO NO

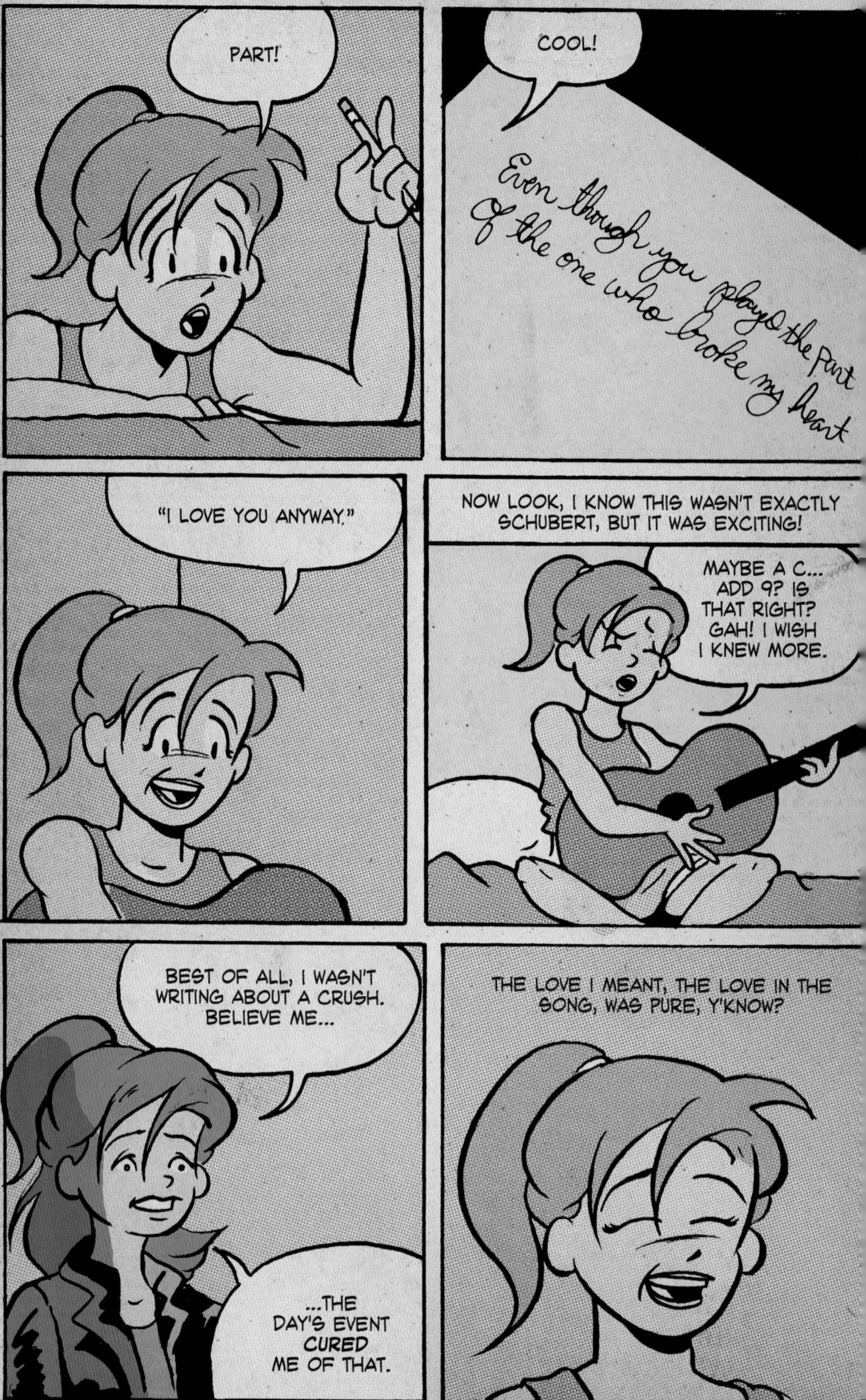
PART!
COOL!
Even though you played the part
of the one who broke my heart
"I LOVE YOU ANYWAY."
NOW LOOK, I KNOW THIS WASN'T EXACTLY SCHUBERT, BUT IT WAS EXCITING!
MAYBE A C... ADD 9? IS THAT RIGHT? GAH! I WISH I KNEW MORE.
BEST OF ALL, I WASN'T WRITING ABOUT A CRUSH. BELIEVE ME...
...THE DAY'S EVENT CURED ME OF THAT.
THE LOVE I MEANT, THE LOVE IN THE SONG, WAS PURE, Y'KNOW?

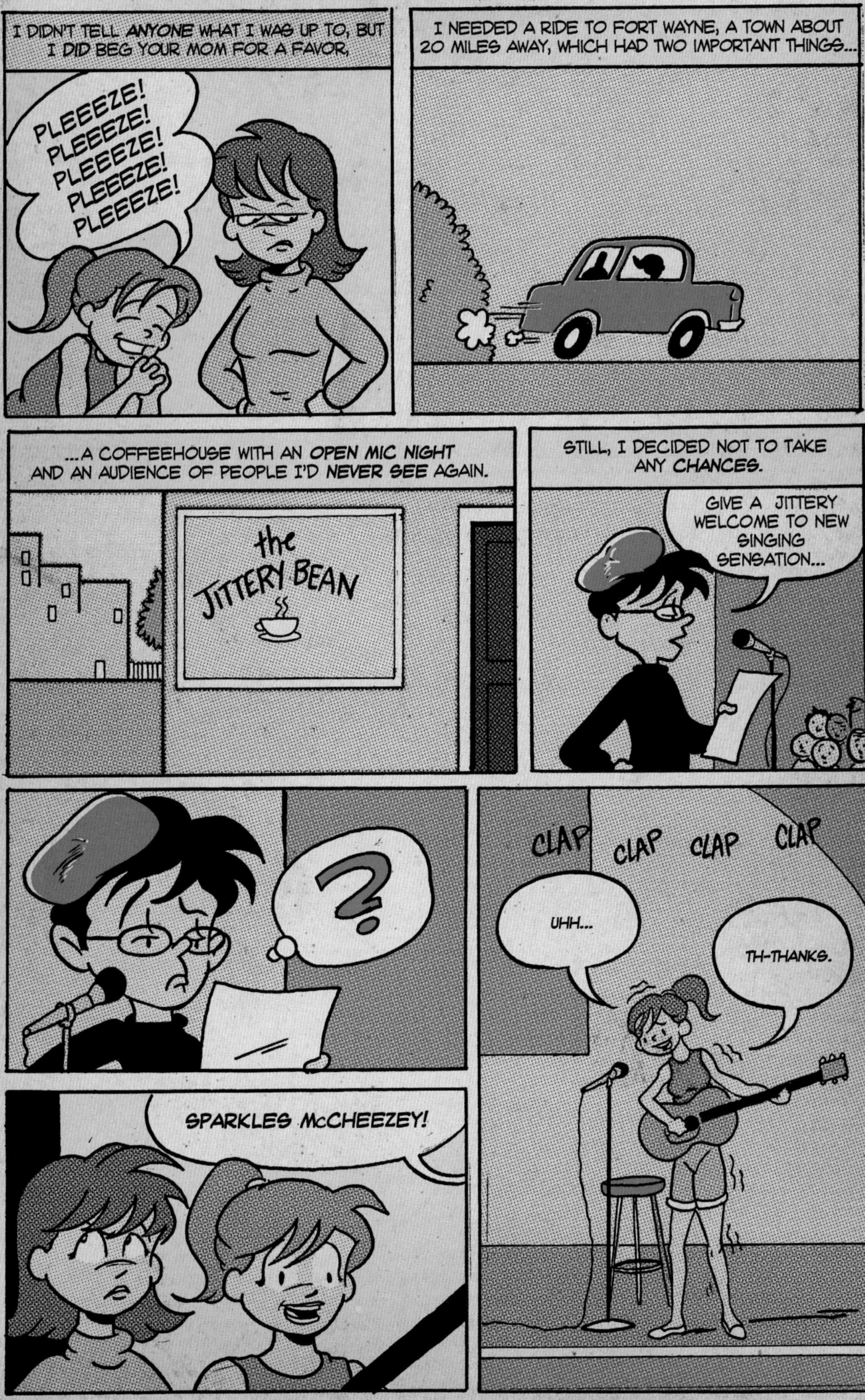

I DIDN'T TELL ANYONE WHAT I WAS UP TO, BUT I DID BEG YOUR MOM FOR A FAVOR,
PLEEEZE! PLEEEZE! PLEEEZE! PLEEEZE! PLEEEZE!
I NEEDED A RIDE TO FORT WAYNE, A TOWN ABOUT 20 MILES AWAY, WHICH HAD TWO IMPORTANT THINGS...
...A COFFEEHOUSE WITH AN OPEN MIC NIGHT AND AN AUDIENCE OF PEOPLE I'D NEVER SEE AGAIN.
the JITTERY BEAN
STILL, I DECIDED NOT TO TAKE ANY CHANCES.
GIVE A JITTERY WELCOME TO NEW SINGING SENSATION...
?
SPARKLES McCHEEZEY!
CLAP CLAP CLAP CLAP
UHH...
TH-THANKS.

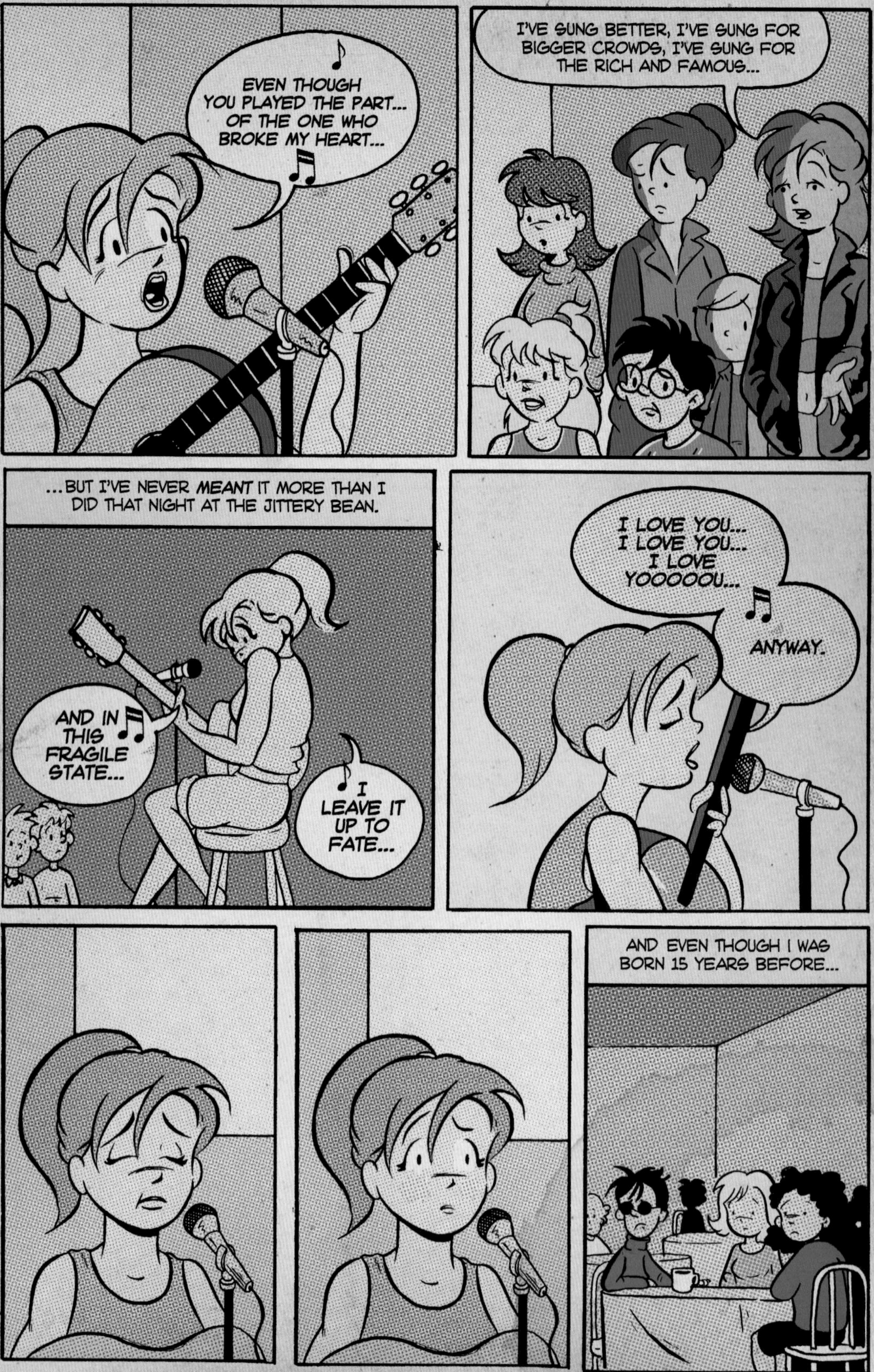
EVEN THOUGH YOU PLAYED THE PART... OF THE ONE WHO BROKE MY HEART...
I'VE SUNG BETTER, I'VE SUNG FOR BIGGER CROWDS, I'VE SUNG FOR THE RICH AND FAMOUS...
...BUT I'VE NEVER MEANT IT MORE THAN I DID THAT NIGHT AT THE JITTERY BEAN.
AND IN THIS FRAGILE STATE...
I LEAVE IT UP TO FATE...
I LOVE YOU... I LOVE YOU... I LOVE YOOOOOU...
ANYWAY.
AND EVEN THOUGH I WAS BORN 15 YEARS BEFORE...

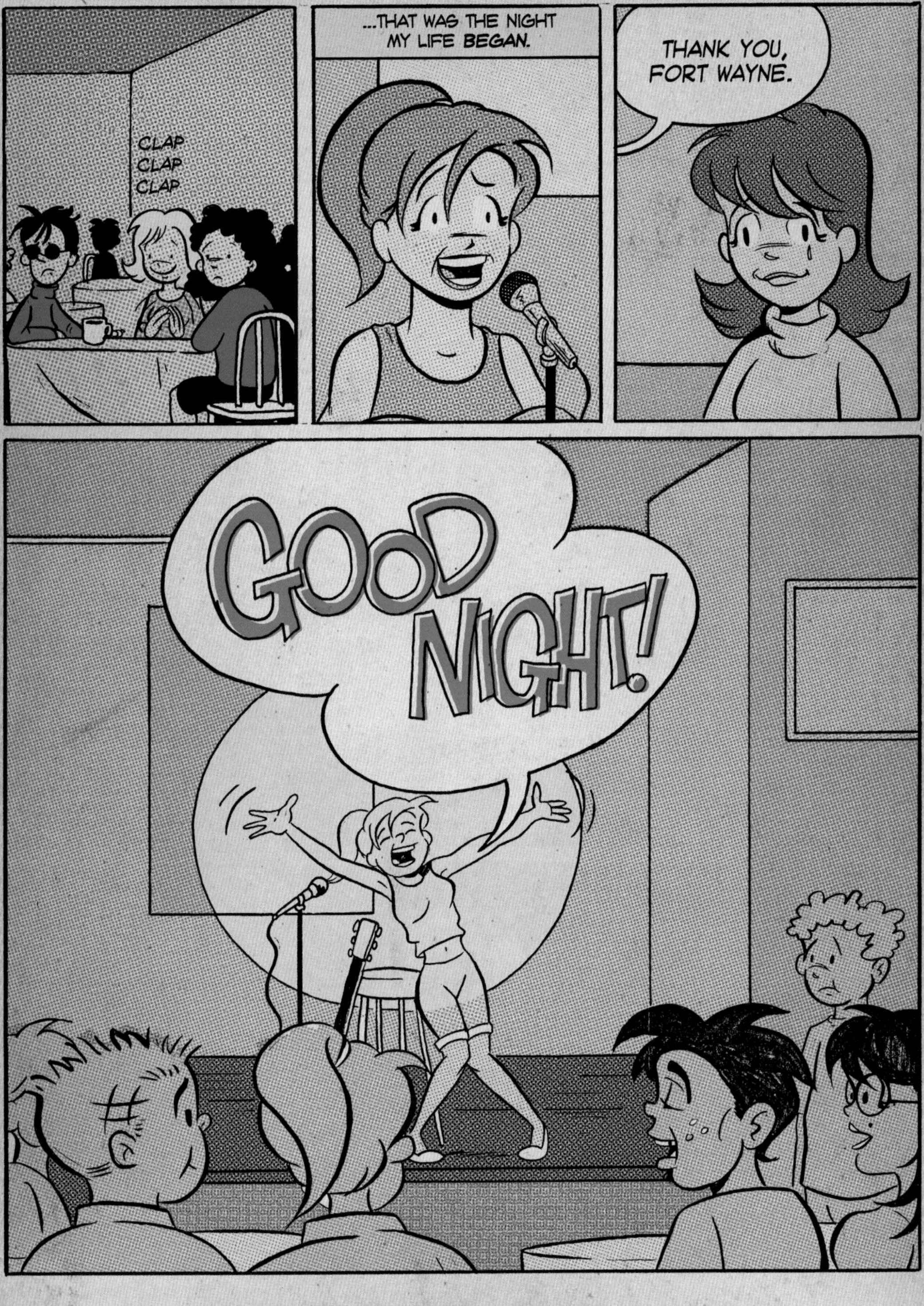
CLAP
CLAP
CLAP
...THAT WAS THE NIGHT MY LIFE BEGAN.
THANK YOU, FORT WAYNE.
GOOD NIGHT!

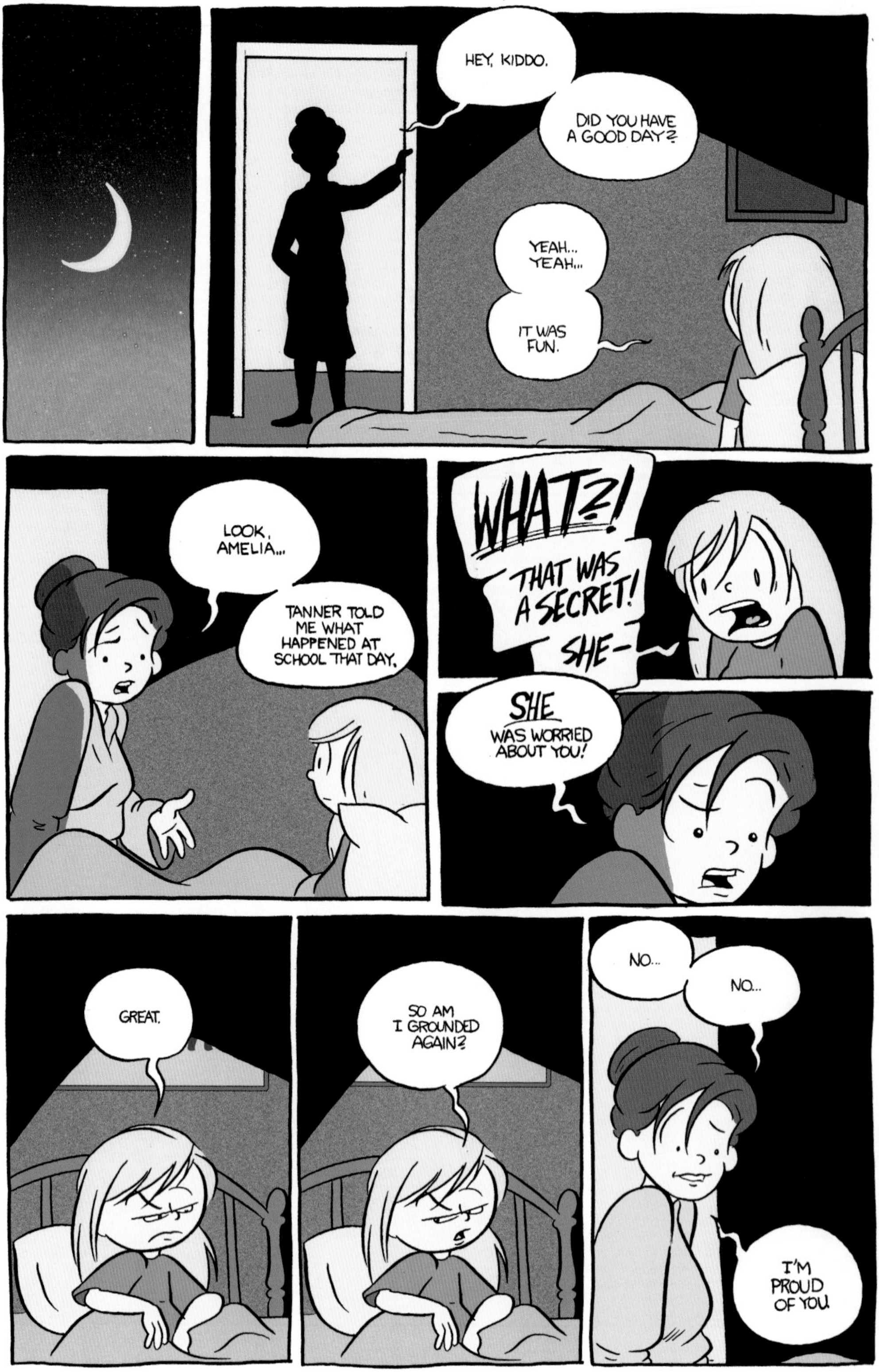
HEY, KIDDO.
DID YOU HAVE A GOOD DAY?
YEAH... YEAH...
IT WAS FUN.
LOOK, AMELIA...
TANNER TOLD ME WHAT HAPPENED AT SCHOOL THAT DAY.
WHAT?!
THAT WAS A SECRET!
SHE—
SHE WAS WORRIED ABOUT YOU!
GREAT.
SO AM I GROUNDED AGAIN?
NO...
NO...
I'M PROUD OF YOU.

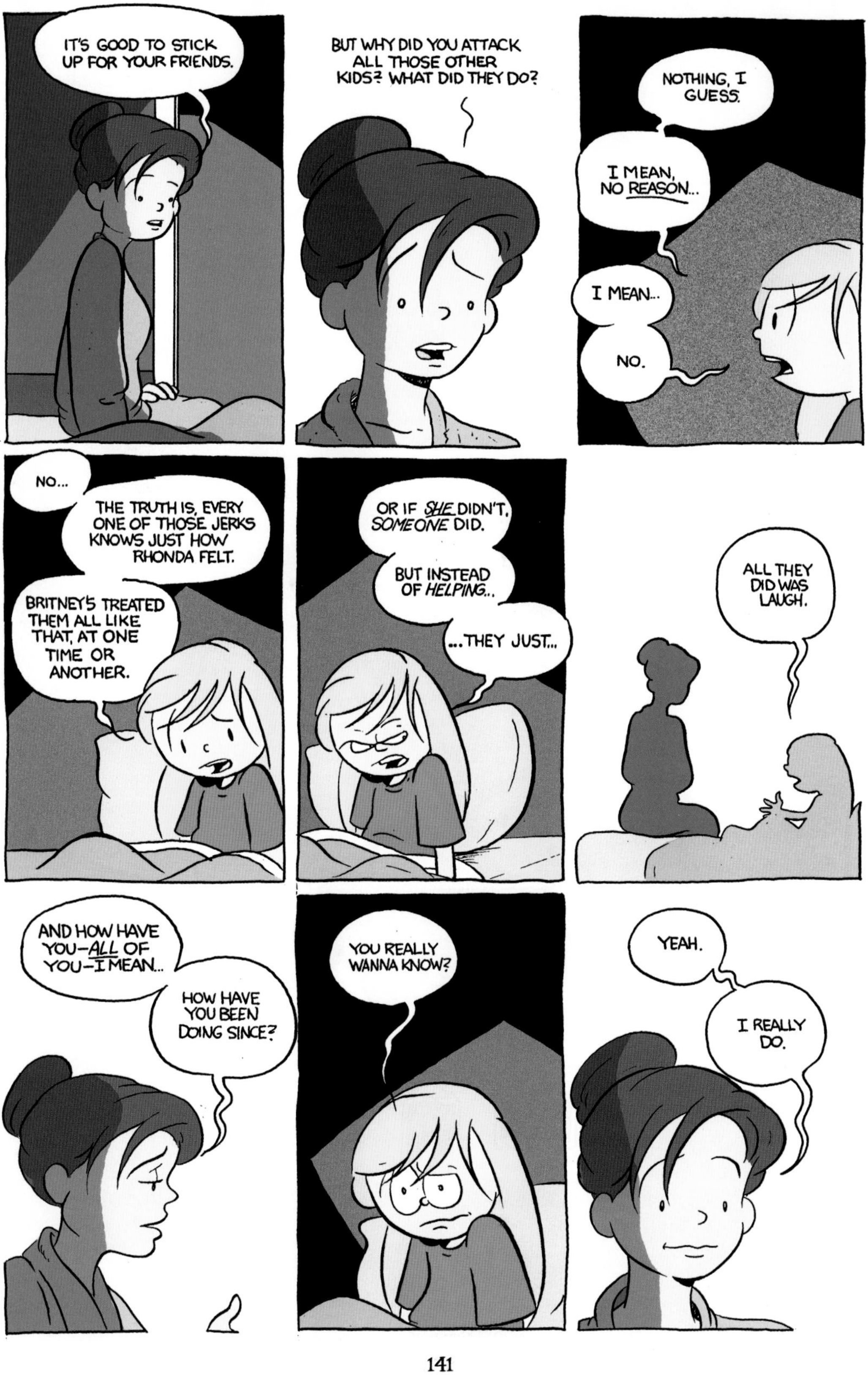
IT'S GOOD TO STICK UP FOR YOUR FRIENDS.
BUT WHY DID YOU ATTACK ALL THOSE OTHER KIDS? WHAT DID THEY DO?
NOTHING, I GUESS.
I MEAN, NO REASON...
I MEAN...
NO.
NO...
THE TRUTH IS, EVERY ONE OF THOSE JERKS KNOWS JUST HOW RHONDA FELT.
BRITNEY'S TREATED THEM ALL LIKE THAT, AT ONE TIME OR ANOTHER.
OR IF *SHE* DIDN'T, *SOMEONE* DID.
BUT INSTEAD OF *HELPING*...
...THEY JUST...
ALL THEY DID WAS LAUGH.
AND HOW HAVE YOU—*ALL* OF YOU—I MEAN...
HOW HAVE YOU BEEN DOING SINCE?
YOU REALLY WANNA KNOW?
YEAH.
I REALLY DO.

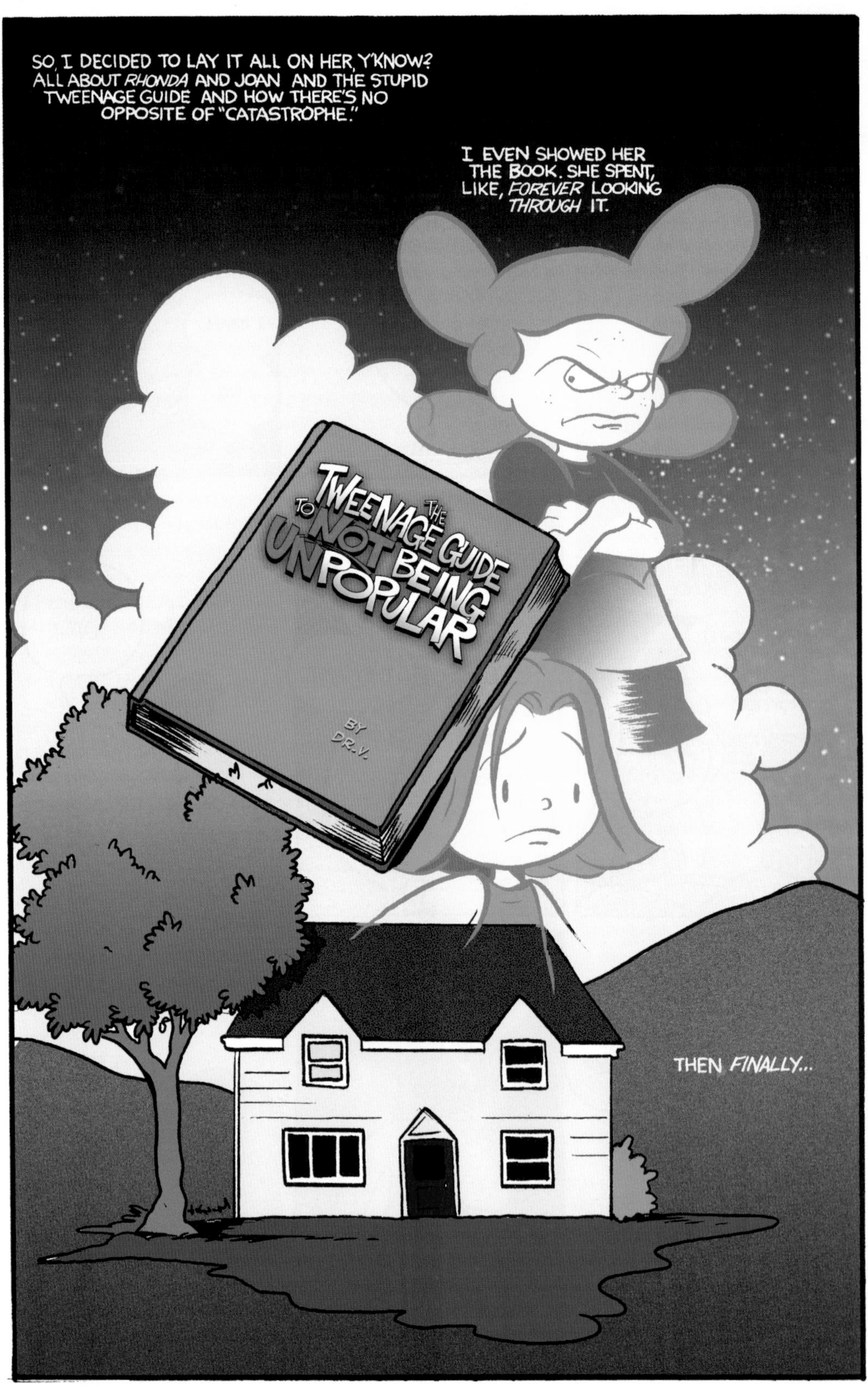
SO, I DECIDED TO LAY IT ALL ON HER, Y'KNOW? ALL ABOUT *RHONDA* AND JOAN AND THE STUPID TWEENAGE GUIDE AND HOW THERE'S NO OPPOSITE OF "CATASTROPHE."
I EVEN SHOWED HER THE BOOK. SHE SPENT, LIKE, *FOREVER* LOOKING *THROUGH* IT.
THE TWEENAGE GUIDE TO NOT BEING UNPOPULAR
BY DR. V.
THEN *FINALLY*...

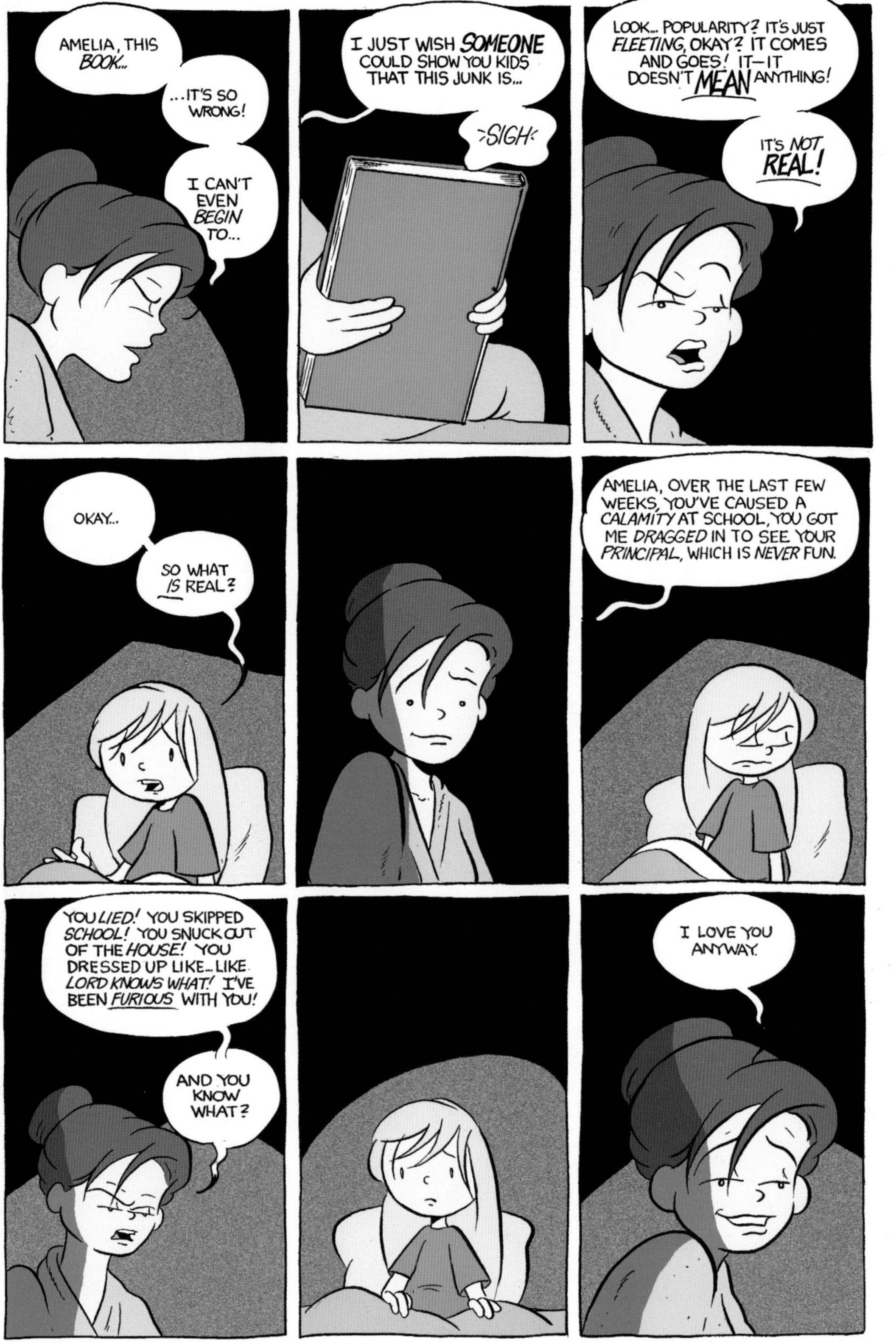
AMELIA, THIS BOOK...
...IT'S SO WRONG!
I CAN'T EVEN BEGIN TO...
I JUST WISH SOMEONE COULD SHOW YOU KIDS THAT THIS JUNK IS...
>SIGH<
LOOK... POPULARITY? IT'S JUST FLEETING, OKAY? IT COMES AND GOES! IT—IT DOESN'T MEAN ANYTHING!
IT'S NOT REAL!
OKAY...
SO WHAT IS REAL?
AMELIA, OVER THE LAST FEW WEEKS, YOU'VE CAUSED A CALAMITY AT SCHOOL, YOU GOT ME DRAGGED IN TO SEE YOUR PRINCIPAL, WHICH IS NEVER FUN.
YOU LIED! YOU SKIPPED SCHOOL! YOU SNUCK OUT OF THE HOUSE! YOU DRESSED UP LIKE... LIKE LORD KNOWS WHAT! I'VE BEEN FURIOUS WITH YOU!
AND YOU KNOW WHAT?
I LOVE YOU ANYWAY.

SNOW WHITE

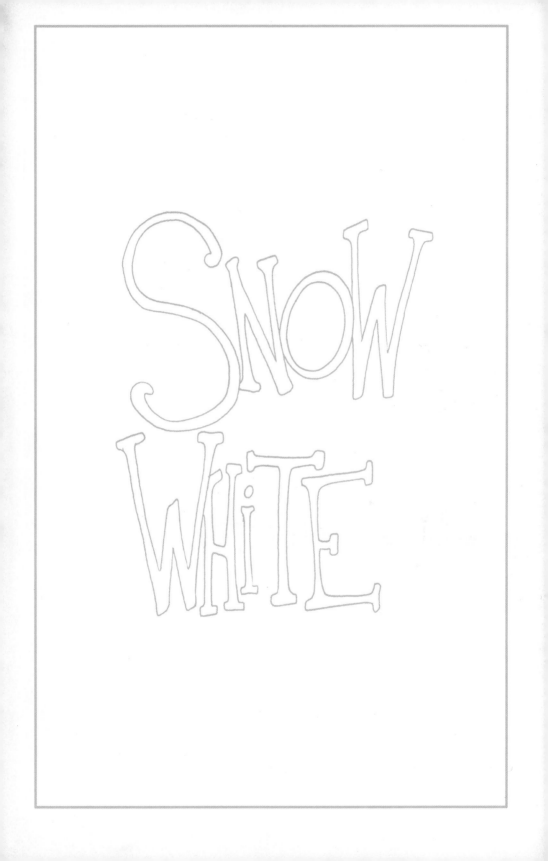

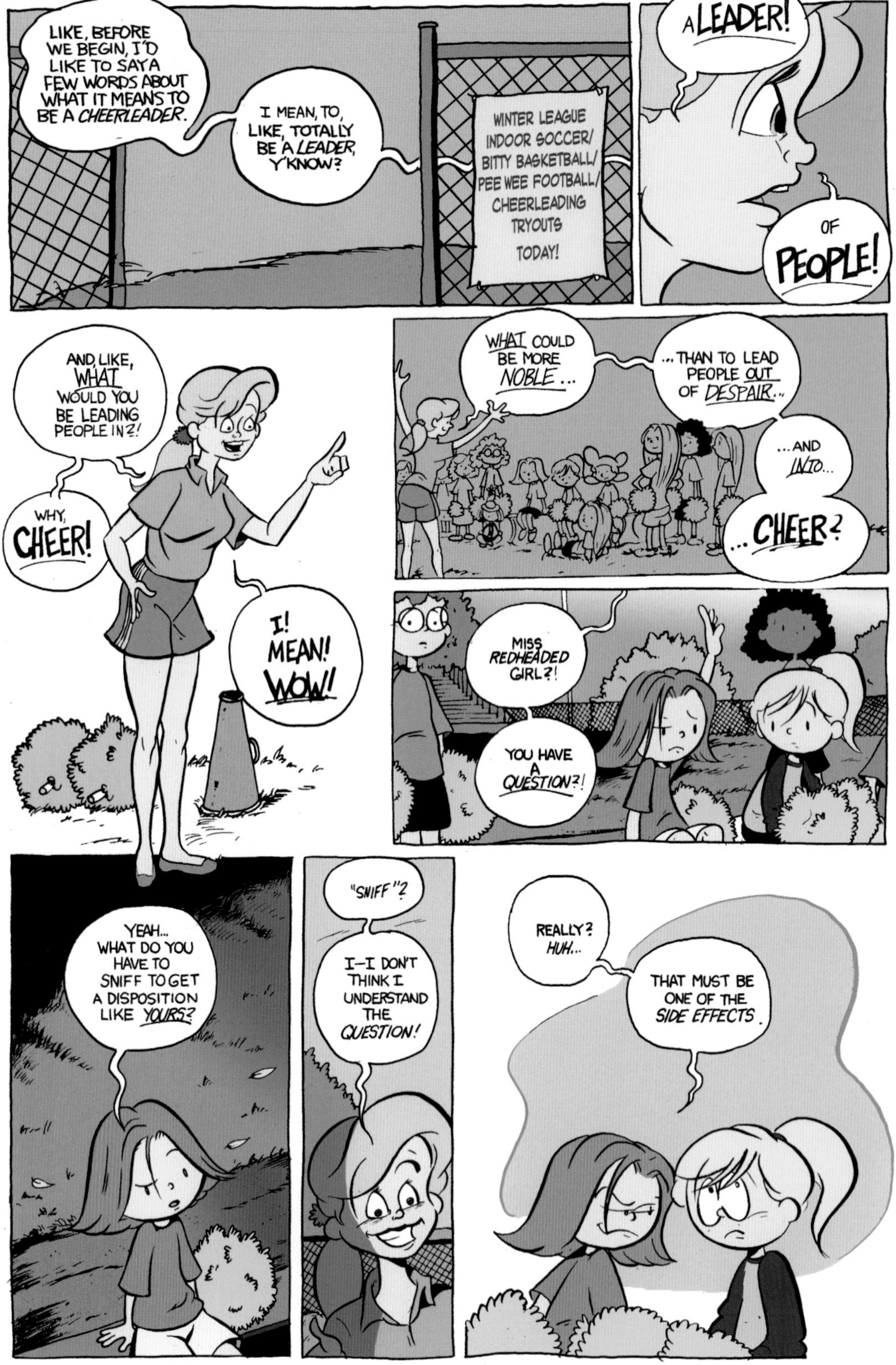
LIKE, BEFORE WE BEGIN, I'D LIKE TO SAY A FEW WORDS ABOUT WHAT IT MEANS TO BE A CHEERLEADER.
I MEAN, TO, LIKE, TOTALLY BE A LEADER, Y'KNOW?
WINTER LEAGUE INDOOR SOCCER/ BITTY BASKETBALL/ PEE WEE FOOTBALL/ CHEERLEADING TRYOUTS TODAY!
A LEADER!
OF PEOPLE!
AND, LIKE, WHAT WOULD YOU BE LEADING PEOPLE IN?!
WHY, CHEER!
I! MEAN! WOW!
WHAT COULD BE MORE NOBLE...
...THAN TO LEAD PEOPLE OUT OF DESPAIR...
...AND INTO...
...CHEER?
MISS REDHEADED GIRL?!
YOU HAVE A QUESTION?!
YEAH... WHAT DO YOU HAVE TO SNIFF TO GET A DISPOSITION LIKE YOURS?
"SNIFF"?
I-I DON'T THINK I UNDERSTAND THE QUESTION!
REALLY? HUH...
THAT MUST BE ONE OF THE SIDE EFFECTS.

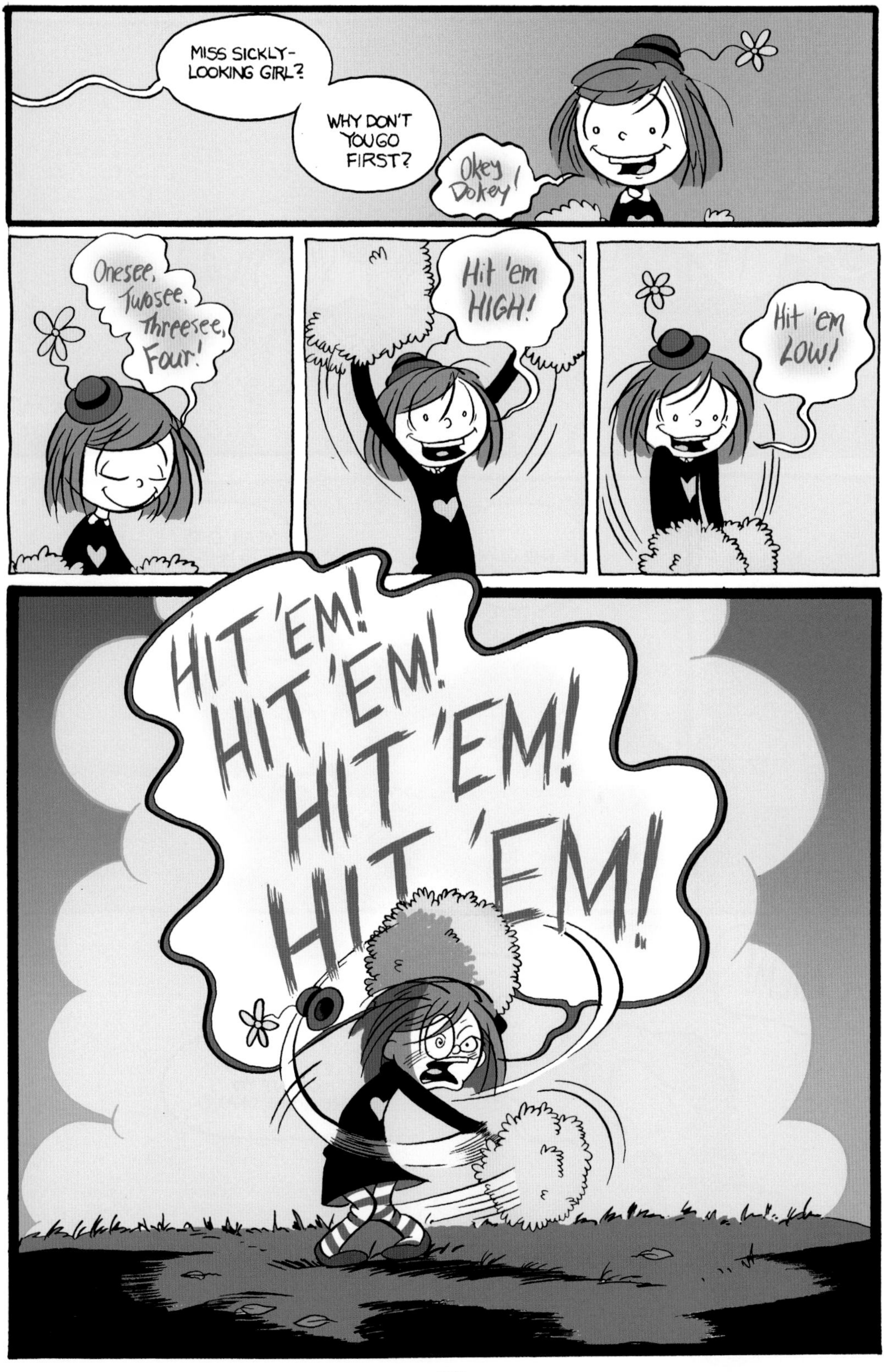

MISS SICKLY-LOOKING GIRL?
WHY DON'T YOU GO FIRST?
Okey Dokey!
Onesee, Twosee, Threesee, Four!
Hit 'em HIGH!
Hit 'em LOW!
HIT 'EM! HIT 'EM! HIT 'EM! HIT 'EM!

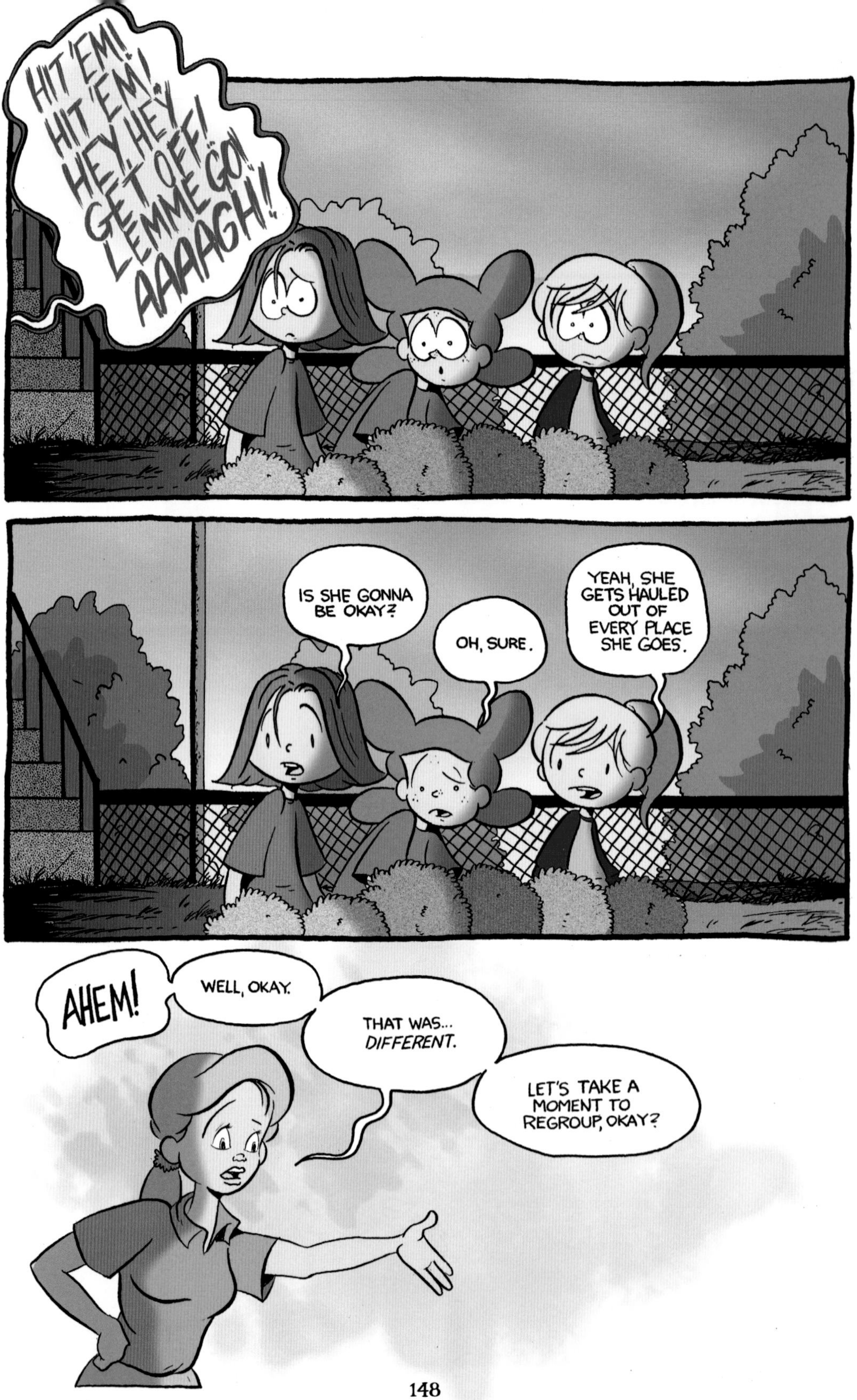
HIT 'EM! HIT 'EM! HEY, HEY! GET OFF! LEMME GO! AAAAGH!
IS SHE GONNA BE OKAY?
OH, SURE.
YEAH, SHE GETS HAULED OUT OF EVERY PLACE SHE GOES.
AHEM!
WELL, OKAY.
THAT WAS... *DIFFERENT*.
LET'S TAKE A MOMENT TO REGROUP, OKAY?

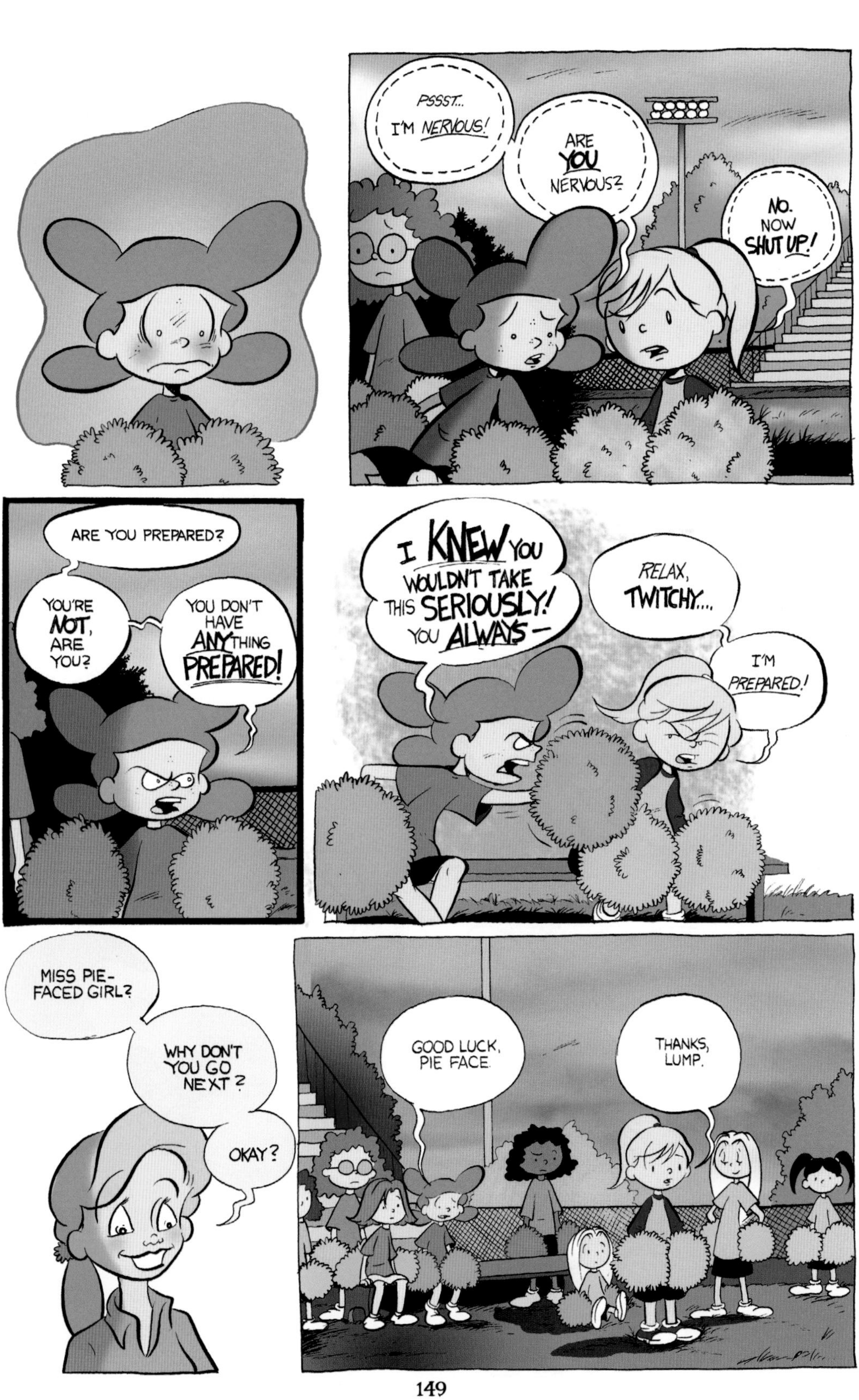

PSSST...
I'M NERVOUS!
ARE YOU NERVOUS?
NO. NOW SHUT UP!
ARE YOU PREPARED?
YOU'RE NOT, ARE YOU?
YOU DON'T HAVE ANYTHING PREPARED!
I KNEW YOU WOULDN'T TAKE THIS SERIOUSLY! YOU ALWAYS—
RELAX, TWITCHY....
I'M PREPARED!
MISS PIE-FACED GIRL?
WHY DON'T YOU GO NEXT?
OKAY?
GOOD LUCK, PIE FACE.
THANKS, LUMP.

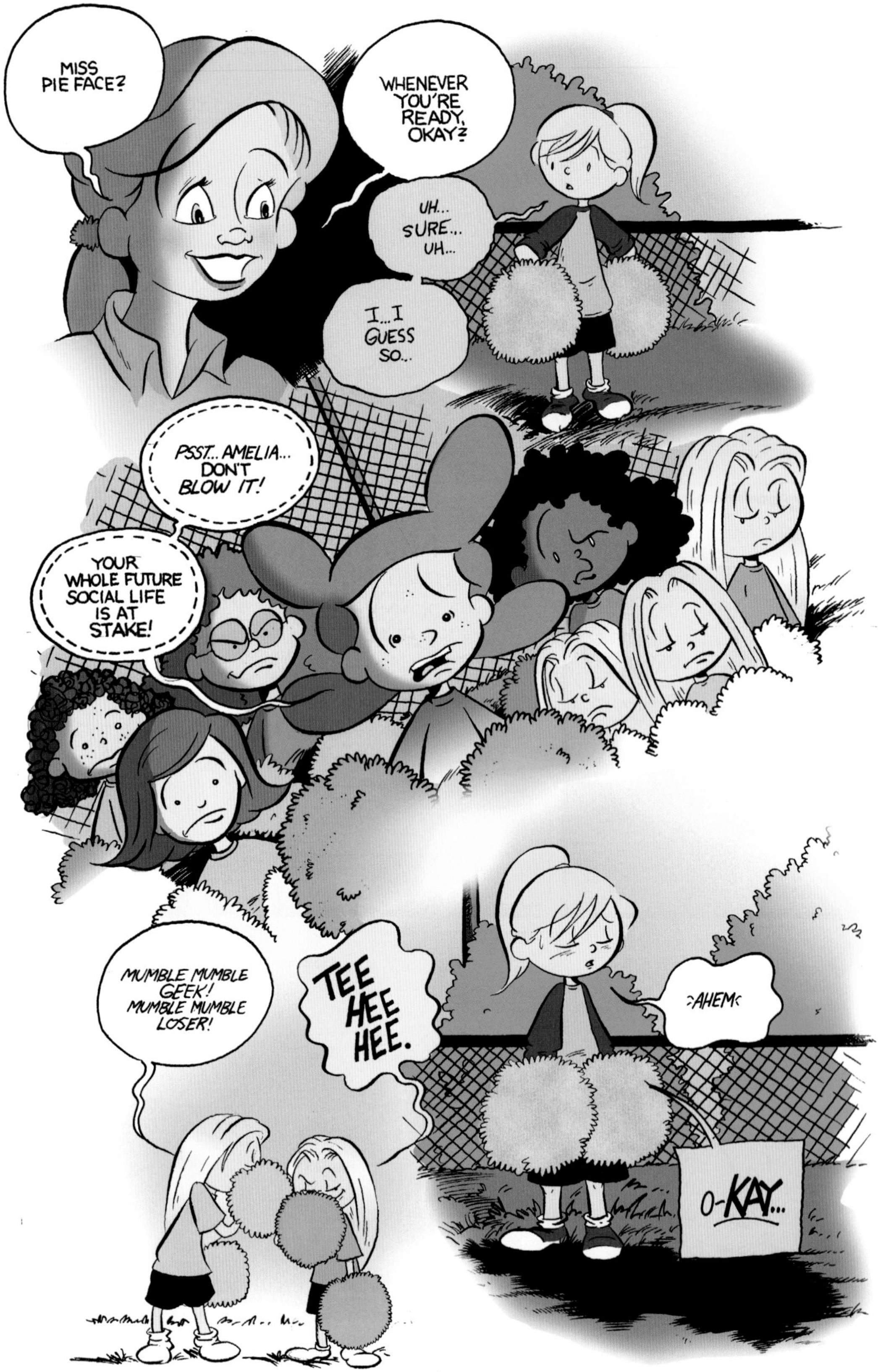
MISS PIE FACE?
WHENEVER YOU'RE READY, OKAY?
UH... SURE... UH...
I...I GUESS SO...
PSST... AMELIA... DON'T BLOW IT!
YOUR WHOLE FUTURE SOCIAL LIFE IS AT STAKE!
MUMBLE MUMBLE GEEK! MUMBLE MUMBLE LOSER!
TEE HEE HEE.
AHEM
O-KAY...

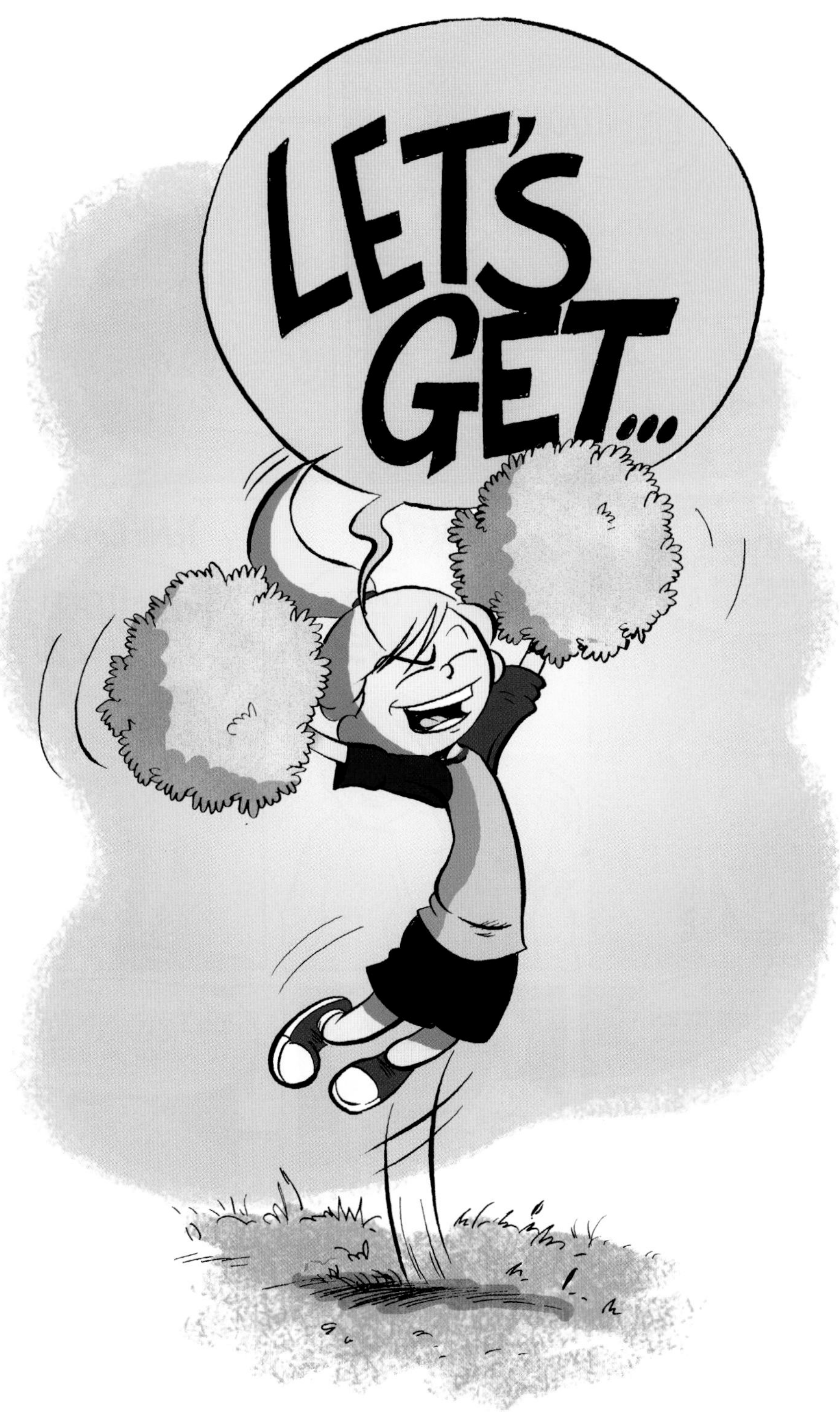
LET'S GET...

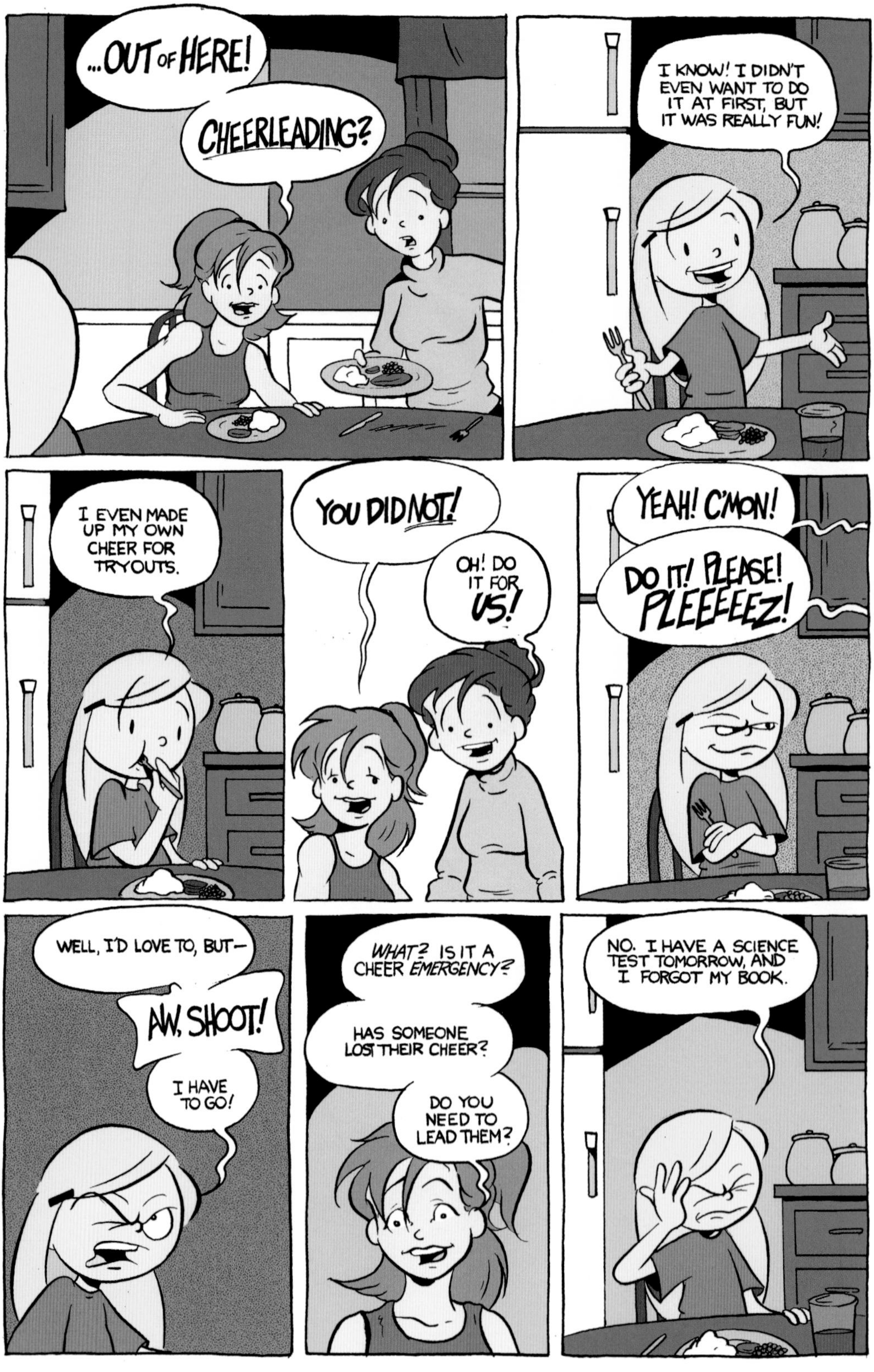
...OUT OF HERE!
CHEERLEADING?
I KNOW! I DIDN'T EVEN WANT TO DO IT AT FIRST, BUT IT WAS REALLY FUN!
I EVEN MADE UP MY OWN CHEER FOR TRYOUTS.
YOU DID NOT!
OH! DO IT FOR US!
YEAH! C'MON!
DO IT! PLEASE! PLEEEEEZ!
WELL, I'D LOVE TO, BUT—
AW, SHOOT!
I HAVE TO GO!
WHAT? IS IT A CHEER EMERGENCY?
HAS SOMEONE LOST THEIR CHEER?
DO YOU NEED TO LEAD THEM?
NO. I HAVE A SCIENCE TEST TOMORROW, AND I FORGOT MY BOOK.

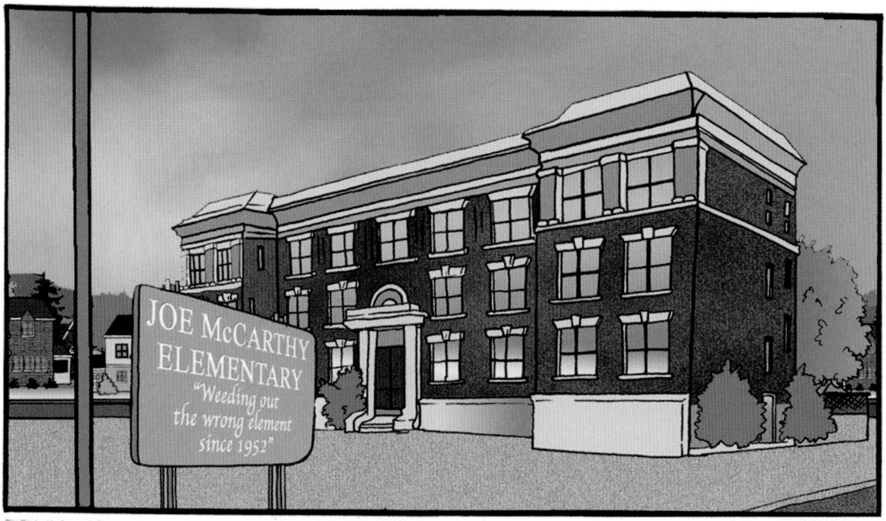
JOE McCARTHY
ELEMENTARY
"Weeding out
the wrong element
since 1952"

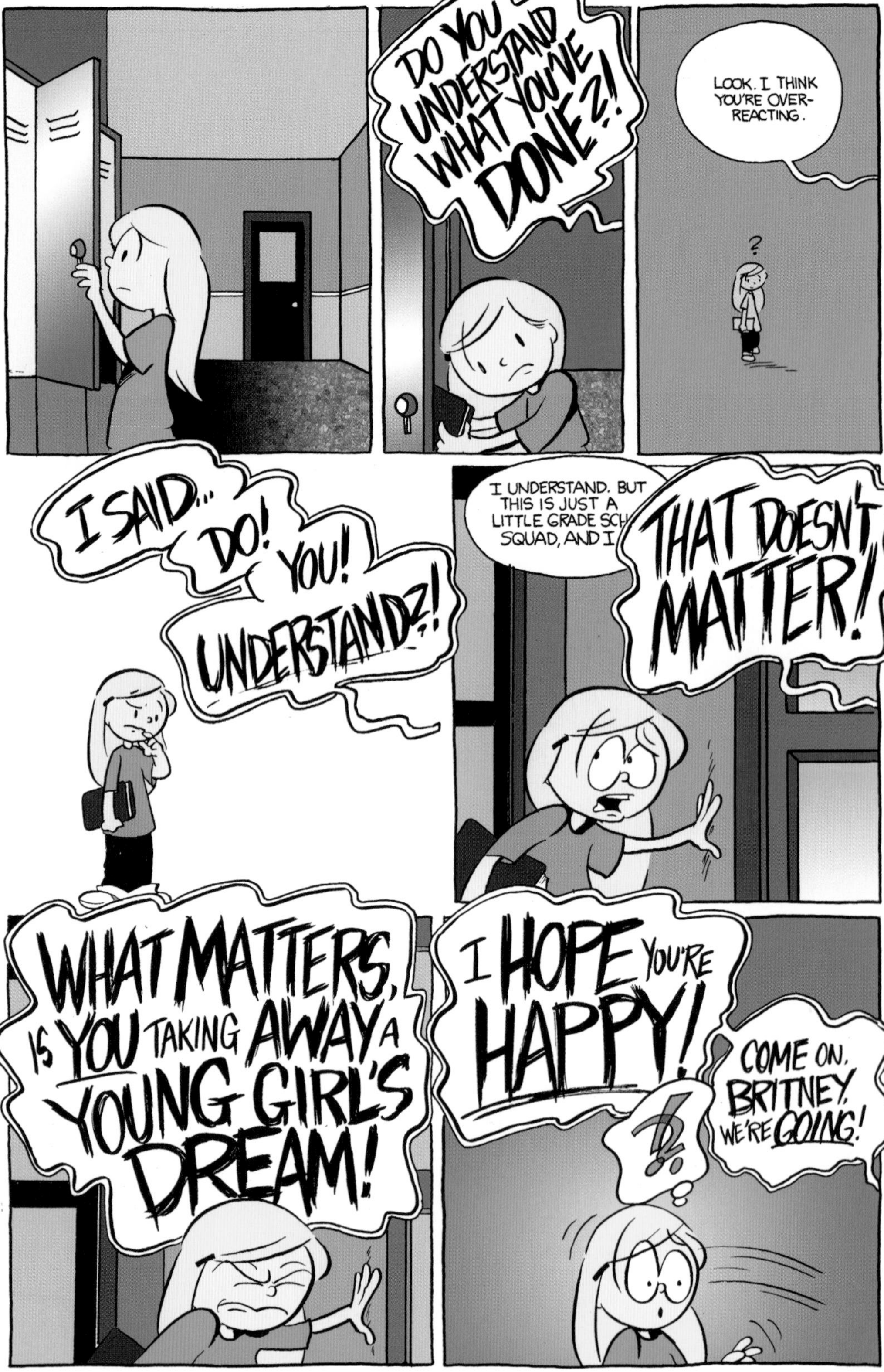
DO YOU UNDERSTAND WHAT YOU'VE DONE?!
LOOK. I THINK YOU'RE OVER-REACTING.
I SAID... DO! YOU! UNDERSTAND?!
I UNDERSTAND. BUT THIS IS JUST A LITTLE GRADE SCH SQUAD, AND I
THAT DOESN'T MATTER!
WHAT MATTERS, IS YOU TAKING AWAY A YOUNG GIRL'S DREAM!
I HOPE YOU'RE HAPPY!
COME ON, BRITNEY, WE'RE GOING!

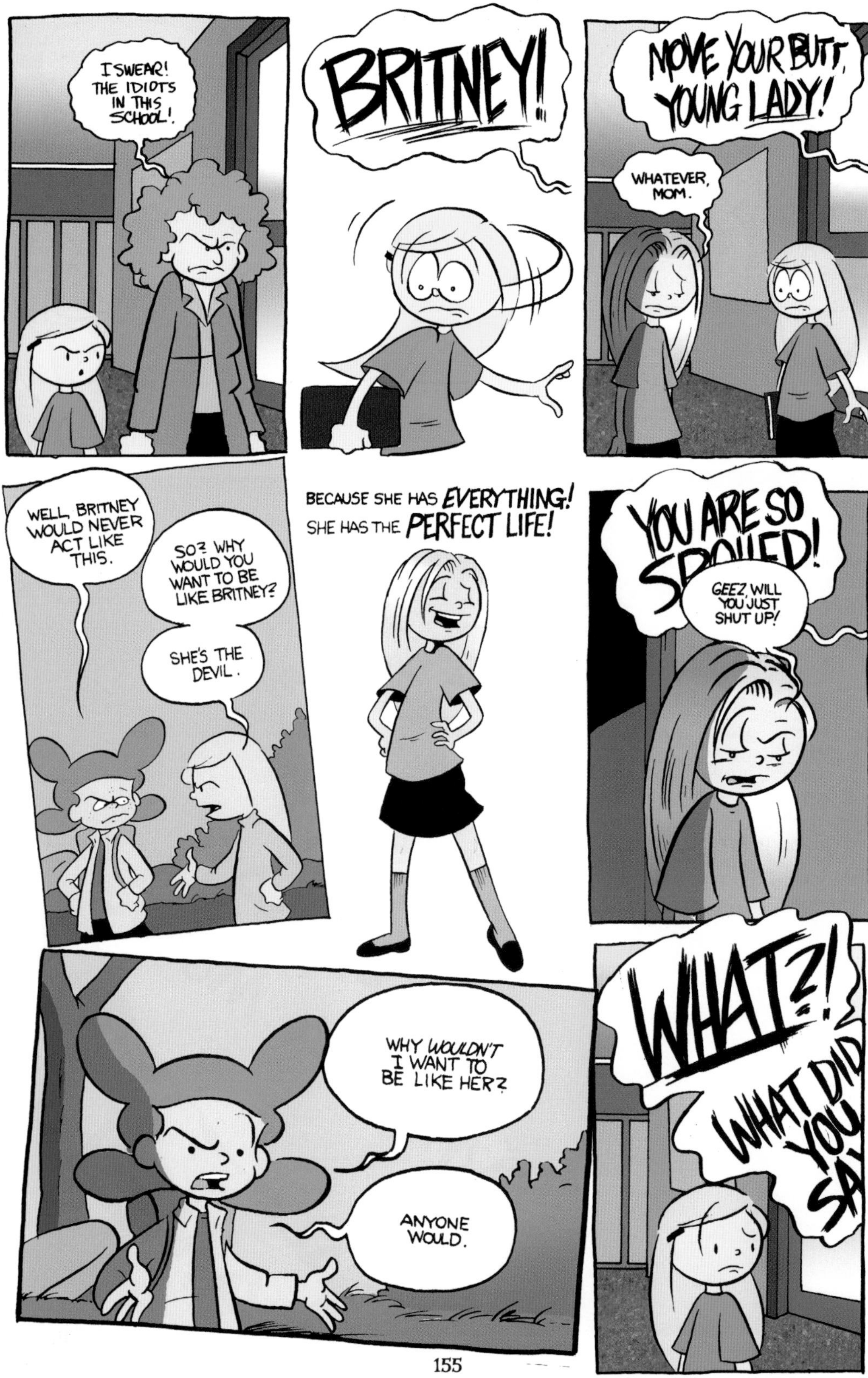
I SWEAR! THE IDIOTS IN THIS SCHOOL!
BRITNEY!
MOVE YOUR BUTT, YOUNG LADY!
WHATEVER, MOM.
WELL, BRITNEY WOULD NEVER ACT LIKE THIS.
SO? WHY WOULD YOU WANT TO BE LIKE BRITNEY?
SHE'S THE DEVIL.
BECAUSE SHE HAS EVERYTHING! SHE HAS THE PERFECT LIFE!
YOU ARE SO SPOILED!
GEEZ, WILL YOU JUST SHUT UP!
WHY WOULDN'T I WANT TO BE LIKE HER?
ANYONE WOULD.
WHAT?!
WHAT DID YOU

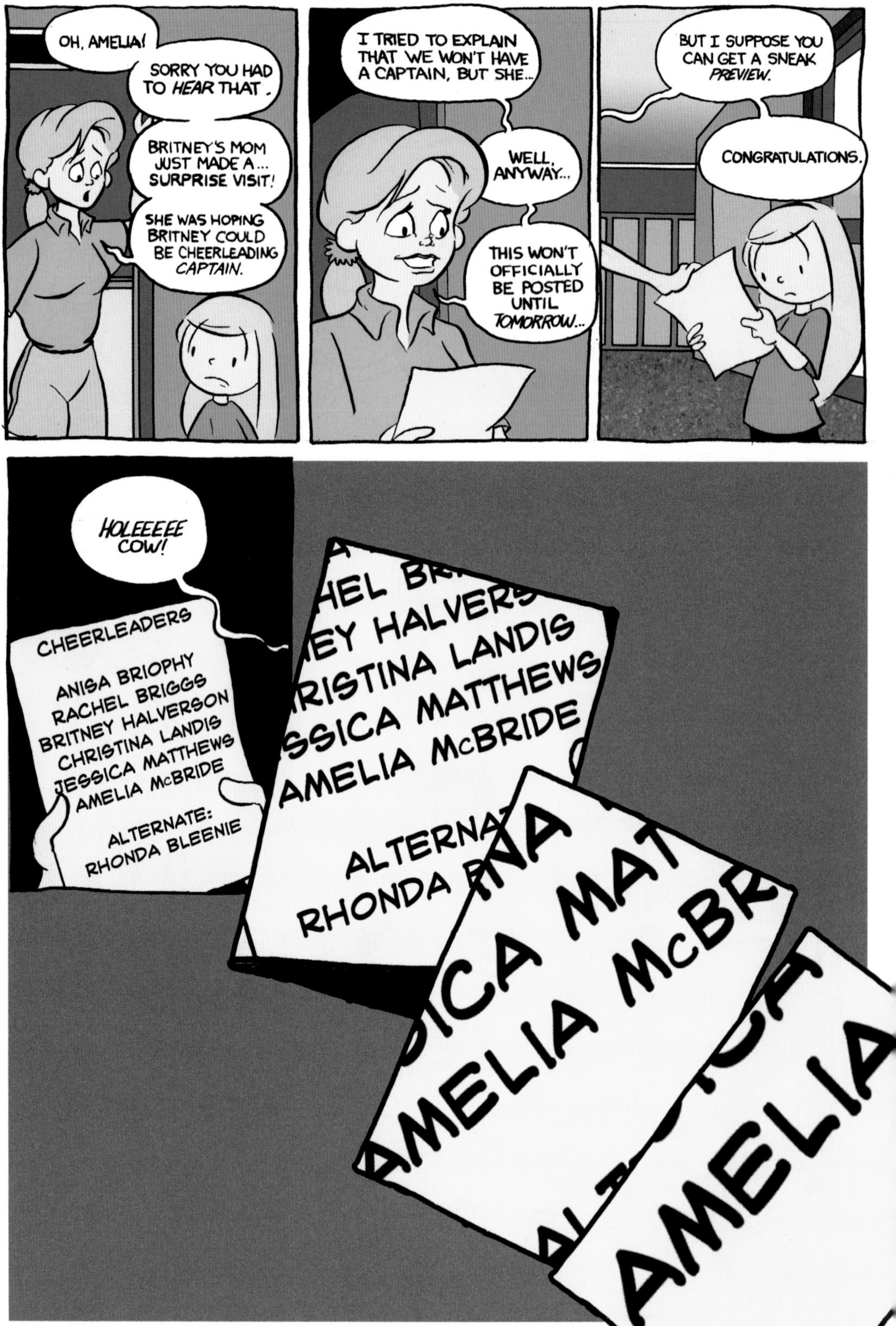
OH, AMELIA!
SORRY YOU HAD TO HEAR THAT.
BRITNEY'S MOM JUST MADE A... SURPRISE VISIT!
SHE WAS HOPING BRITNEY COULD BE CHEERLEADING CAPTAIN.
I TRIED TO EXPLAIN THAT WE WON'T HAVE A CAPTAIN, BUT SHE...
WELL, ANYWAY...
THIS WON'T OFFICIALLY BE POSTED UNTIL TOMORROW...
BUT I SUPPOSE YOU CAN GET A SNEAK PREVIEW.
CONGRATULATIONS.
HOLEEEEE COW!
CHEERLEADERS
ANISA BRIOPHY
RACHEL BRIGGS
BRITNEY HALVERSON
CHRISTINA LANDIS
JESSICA MATTHEWS
AMELIA McBRIDE
ALTERNATE:
RHONDA BLEENIE

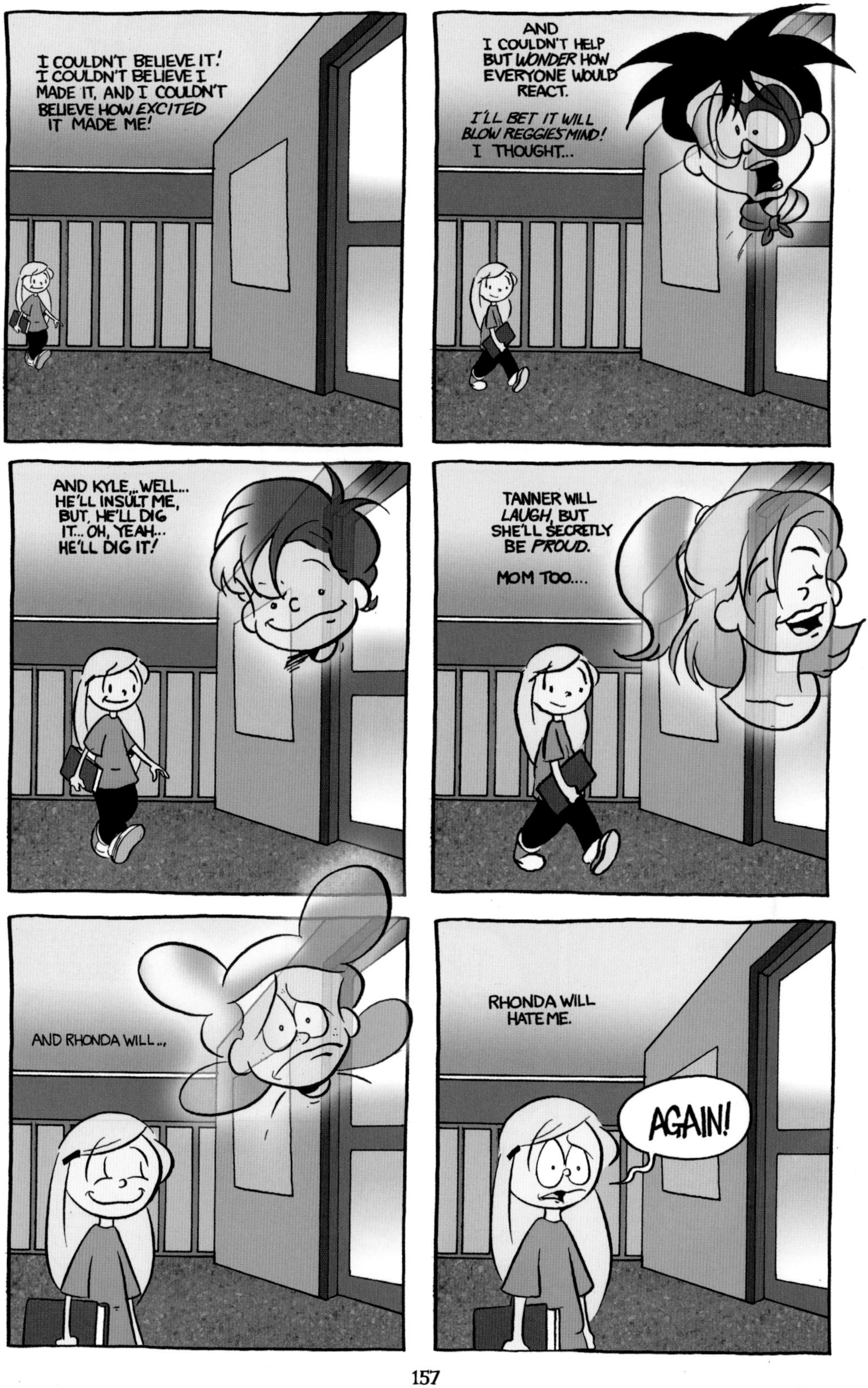
I COULDN'T BELIEVE IT! I COULDN'T BELIEVE I MADE IT, AND I COULDN'T BELIEVE HOW EXCITED IT MADE ME!
AND I COULDN'T HELP BUT WONDER HOW EVERYONE WOULD REACT.
I'LL BET IT WILL BLOW REGGIE'S MIND! I THOUGHT...
AND KYLE... WELL... HE'LL INSULT ME, BUT, HE'LL DIG IT... OH, YEAH... HE'LL DIG IT!
TANNER WILL LAUGH, BUT SHE'LL SECRETLY BE PROUD.
MOM TOO....
AND RHONDA WILL...,
RHONDA WILL HATE ME.
AGAIN!

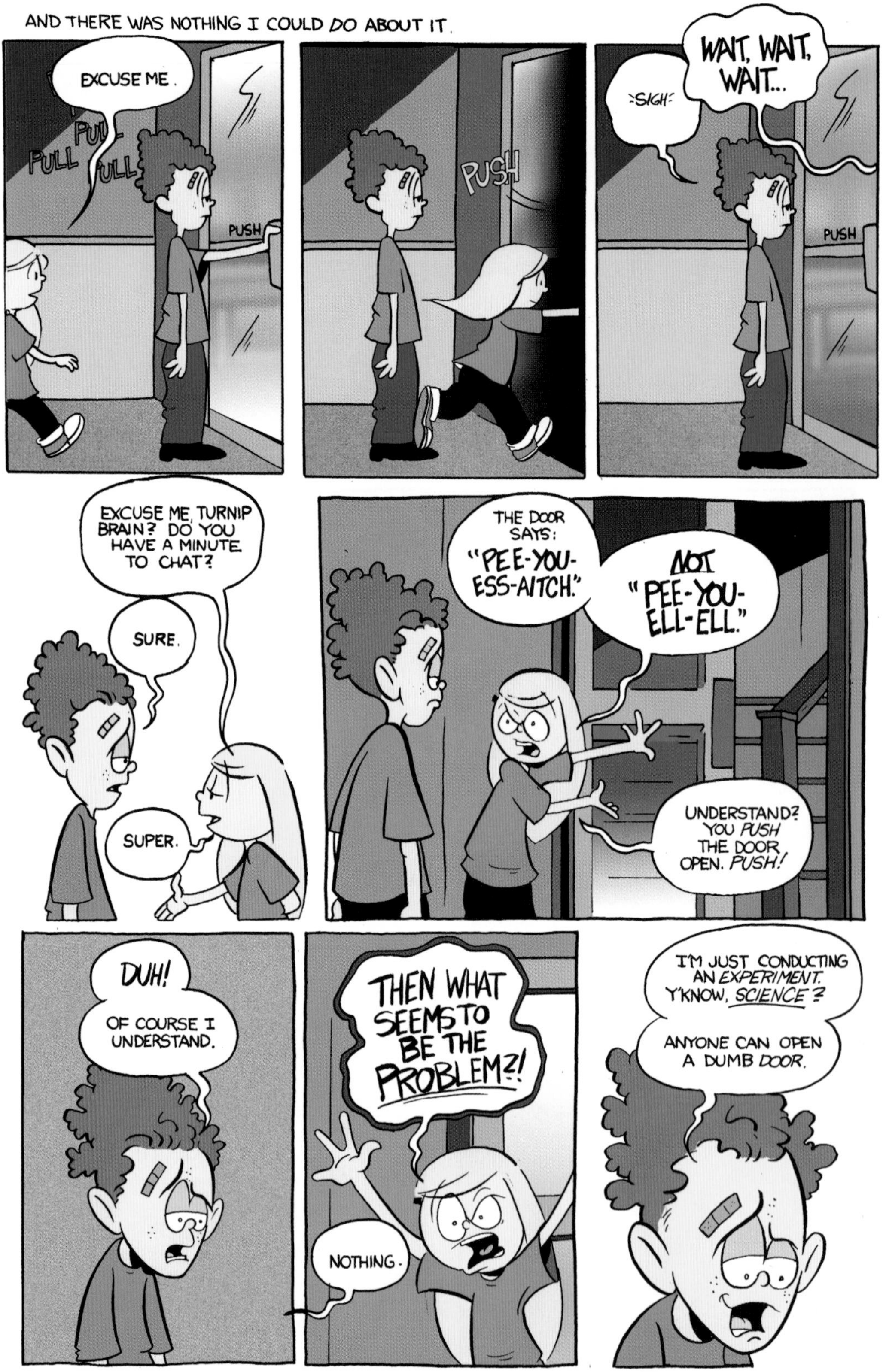
AND THERE WAS NOTHING I COULD *DO* ABOUT IT.
EXCUSE ME.
PULL PULL PULL
PUSH
PUSH
SIGH
WAIT, WAIT, WAIT...
PUSH
EXCUSE ME, TURNIP BRAIN? DO YOU HAVE A MINUTE TO CHAT?
SURE.
SUPER.
THE DOOR SAYS: "PEE-YOU-ESS-AITCH."
NOT "PEE-YOU-ELL-ELL."
UNDERSTAND? YOU *PUSH* THE DOOR OPEN. *PUSH!*
DUH!
OF COURSE I UNDERSTAND.
THEN WHAT SEEMS TO BE THE PROBLEM?!
NOTHING.
I'M JUST CONDUCTING AN *EXPERIMENT*. Y'KNOW, SCIENCE?
ANYONE CAN OPEN A DUMB *DOOR*.

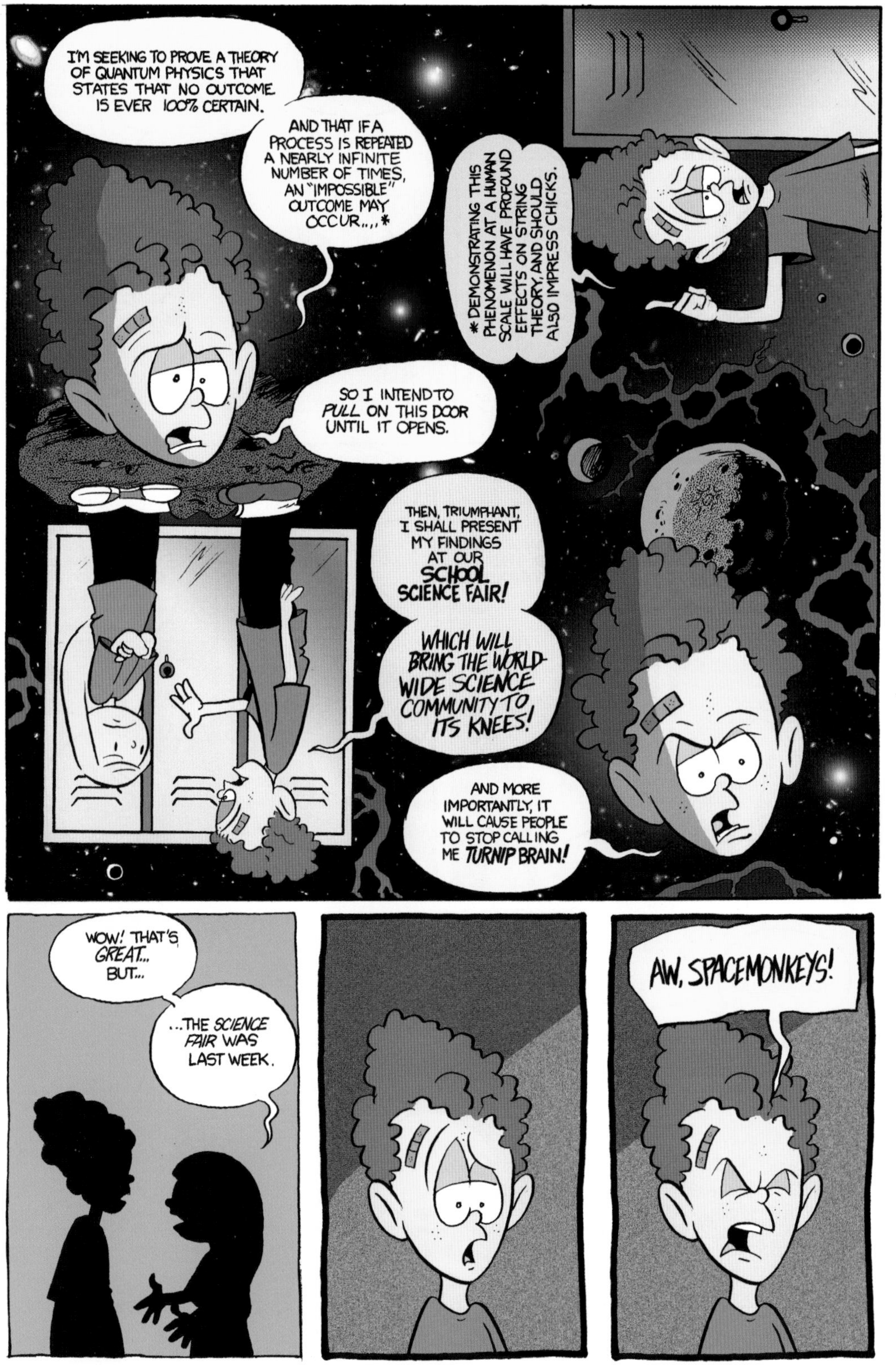
I'M SEEKING TO PROVE A THEORY OF QUANTUM PHYSICS THAT STATES THAT NO OUTCOME IS EVER 100% CERTAIN.
AND THAT IF A PROCESS IS REPEATED A NEARLY INFINITE NUMBER OF TIMES, AN "IMPOSSIBLE" OUTCOME MAY OCCUR...,*
* DEMONSTRATING THIS PHENOMENON AT A HUMAN SCALE WILL HAVE PROFOUND EFFECTS ON STRING THEORY, AND SHOULD ALSO IMPRESS CHICKS.
SO I INTEND TO PULL ON THIS DOOR UNTIL IT OPENS.
THEN, TRIUMPHANT, I SHALL PRESENT MY FINDINGS AT OUR SCHOOL SCIENCE FAIR!
WHICH WILL BRING THE WORLD WIDE SCIENCE COMMUNITY TO ITS KNEES!
AND MORE IMPORTANTLY, IT WILL CAUSE PEOPLE TO STOP CALLING ME TURNIP BRAIN!
WOW! THAT'S GREAT... BUT...
...THE SCIENCE FAIR WAS LAST WEEK.
AW, SPACEMONKEYS!

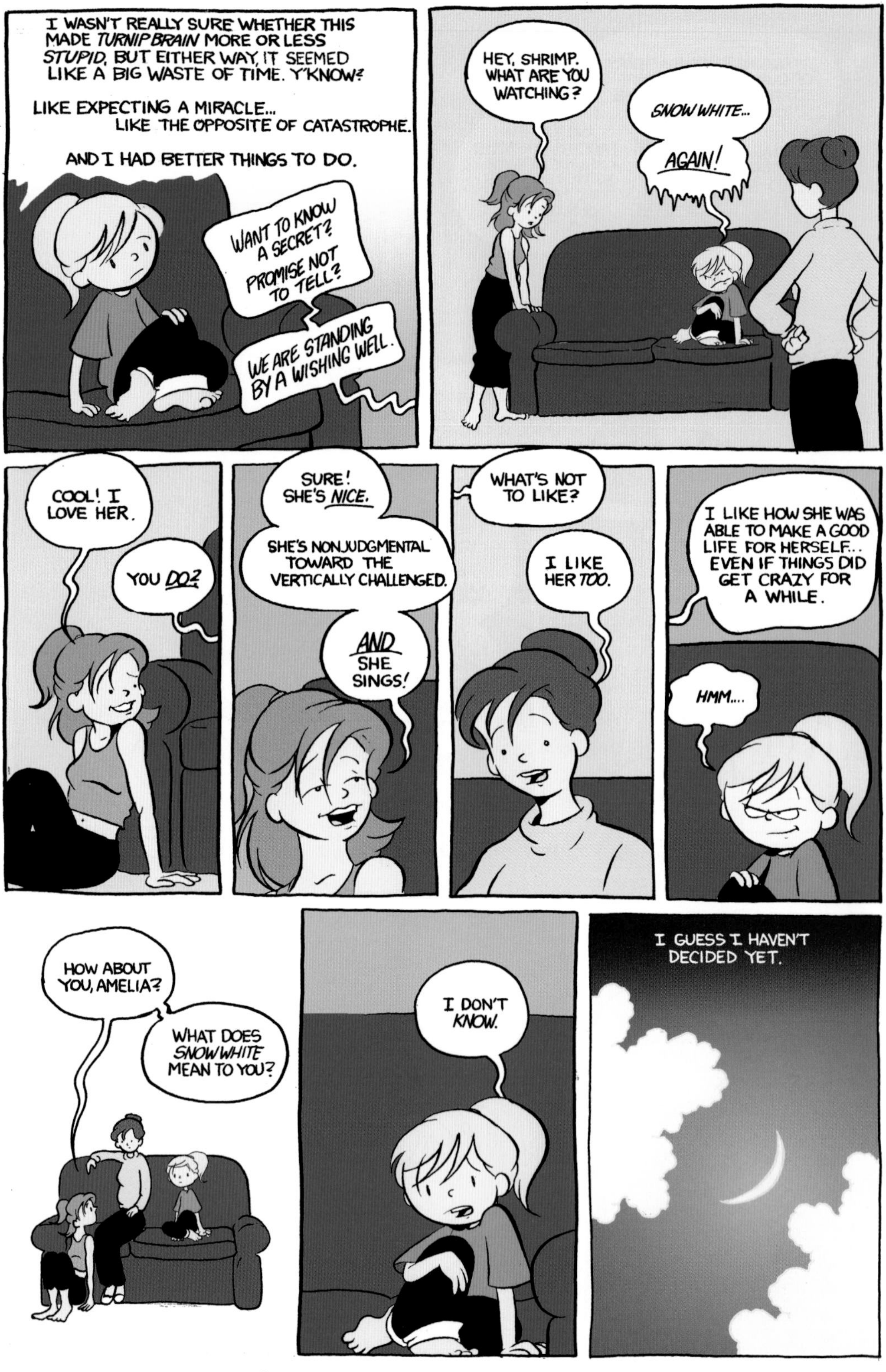
I WASN'T REALLY SURE WHETHER THIS MADE TURNIP BRAIN MORE OR LESS STUPID, BUT EITHER WAY, IT SEEMED LIKE A BIG WASTE OF TIME. Y'KNOW?
LIKE EXPECTING A MIRACLE... LIKE THE OPPOSITE OF CATASTROPHE.
AND I HAD BETTER THINGS TO DO.
WANT TO KNOW A SECRET? PROMISE NOT TO TELL?
WE ARE STANDING BY A WISHING WELL.
HEY, SHRIMP. WHAT ARE YOU WATCHING?
SNOW WHITE...
AGAIN!
COOL! I LOVE HER.
YOU DO?
SURE! SHE'S NICE.
SHE'S NONJUDGMENTAL TOWARD THE VERTICALLY CHALLENGED.
AND SHE SINGS!
WHAT'S NOT TO LIKE?
I LIKE HER TOO.
I LIKE HOW SHE WAS ABLE TO MAKE A GOOD LIFE FOR HERSELF... EVEN IF THINGS DID GET CRAZY FOR A WHILE.
HMM....
HOW ABOUT YOU, AMELIA?
WHAT DOES SNOW WHITE MEAN TO YOU?
I DON'T KNOW.
I GUESS I HAVEN'T DECIDED YET.

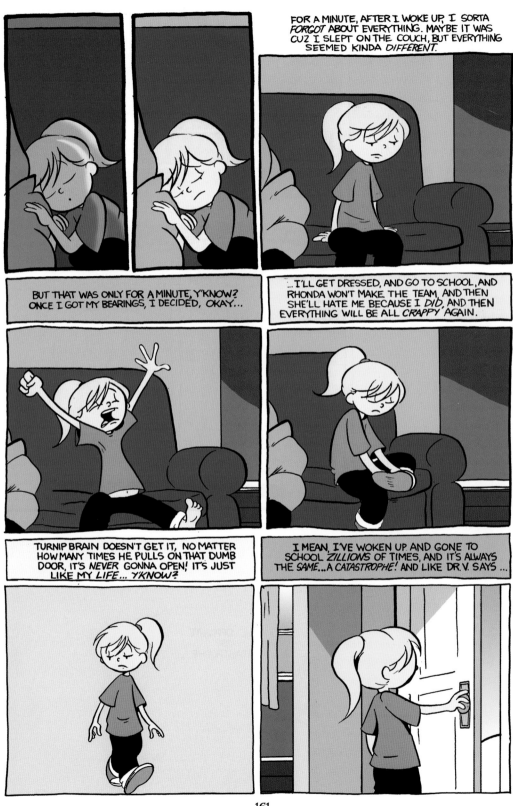

FOR A MINUTE, AFTER I WOKE UP, I SORTA *FORGOT* ABOUT EVERYTHING. MAYBE IT WAS CUZ I SLEPT ON THE COUCH, BUT EVERYTHING SEEMED KINDA *DIFFERENT.*

BUT THAT WAS ONLY FOR A MINUTE, Y'KNOW? ONCE I GOT MY BEARINGS, I DECIDED, OKAY...

...I'LL GET DRESSED, AND GO TO SCHOOL, AND RHONDA WON'T MAKE THE TEAM, AND THEN SHE'LL HATE ME BECAUSE I *DID*, AND THEN EVERYTHING WILL BE ALL *CRAPPY* AGAIN.

TURNIP BRAIN DOESN'T GET IT, NO MATTER HOW MANY TIMES HE PULLS ON THAT DUMB DOOR, IT'S *NEVER* GONNA OPEN! IT'S JUST LIKE MY *LIFE*... Y'KNOW?

I MEAN, I'VE WOKEN UP AND GONE TO SCHOOL *ZILLIONS* OF TIMES, AND IT'S ALWAYS THE *SAME*...A *CATASTROPHE!* AND LIKE DR. V. SAYS ...

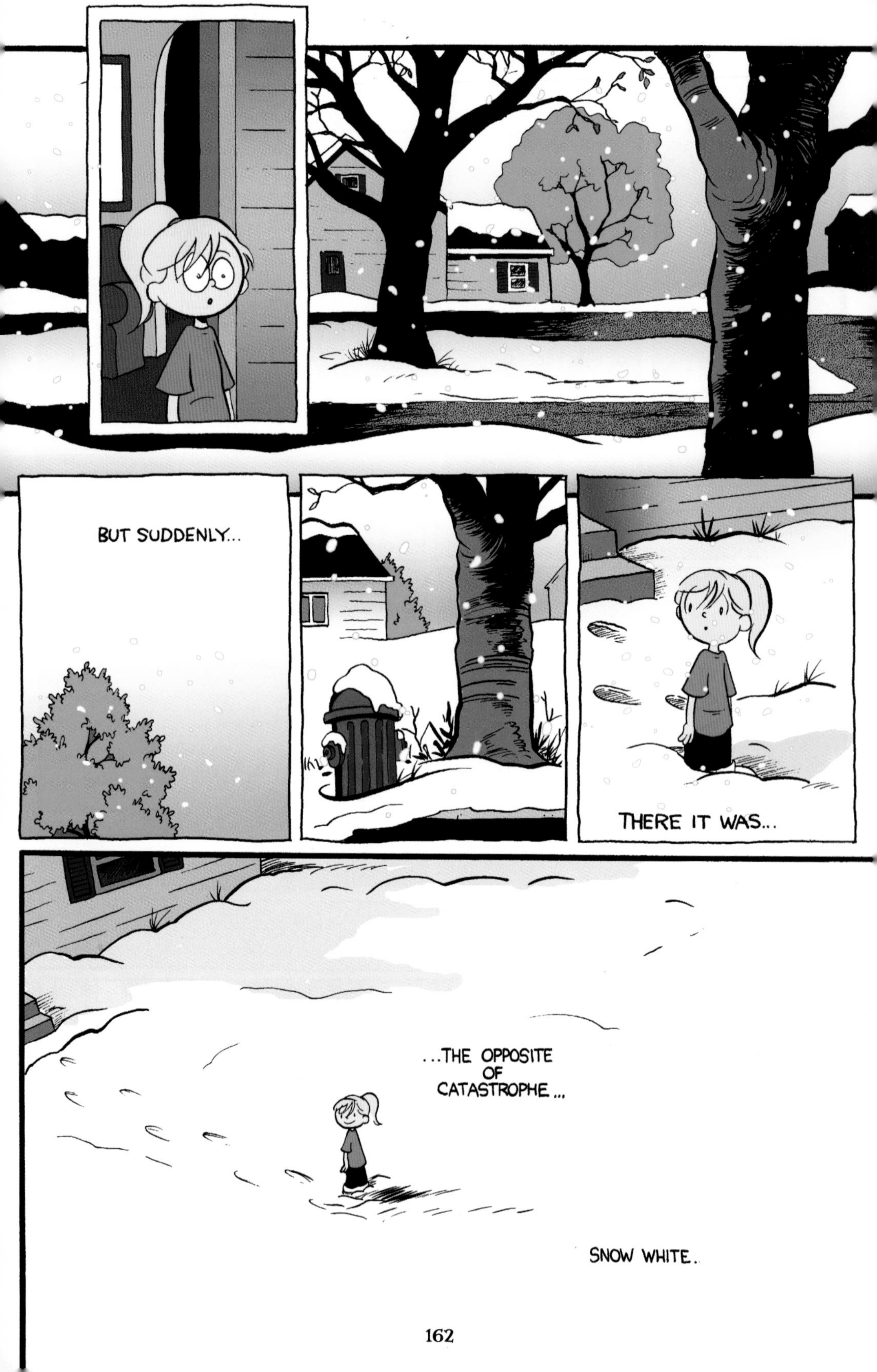
BUT SUDDENLY...
THERE IT WAS...
...THE OPPOSITE OF CATASTROPHE...
SNOW WHITE.

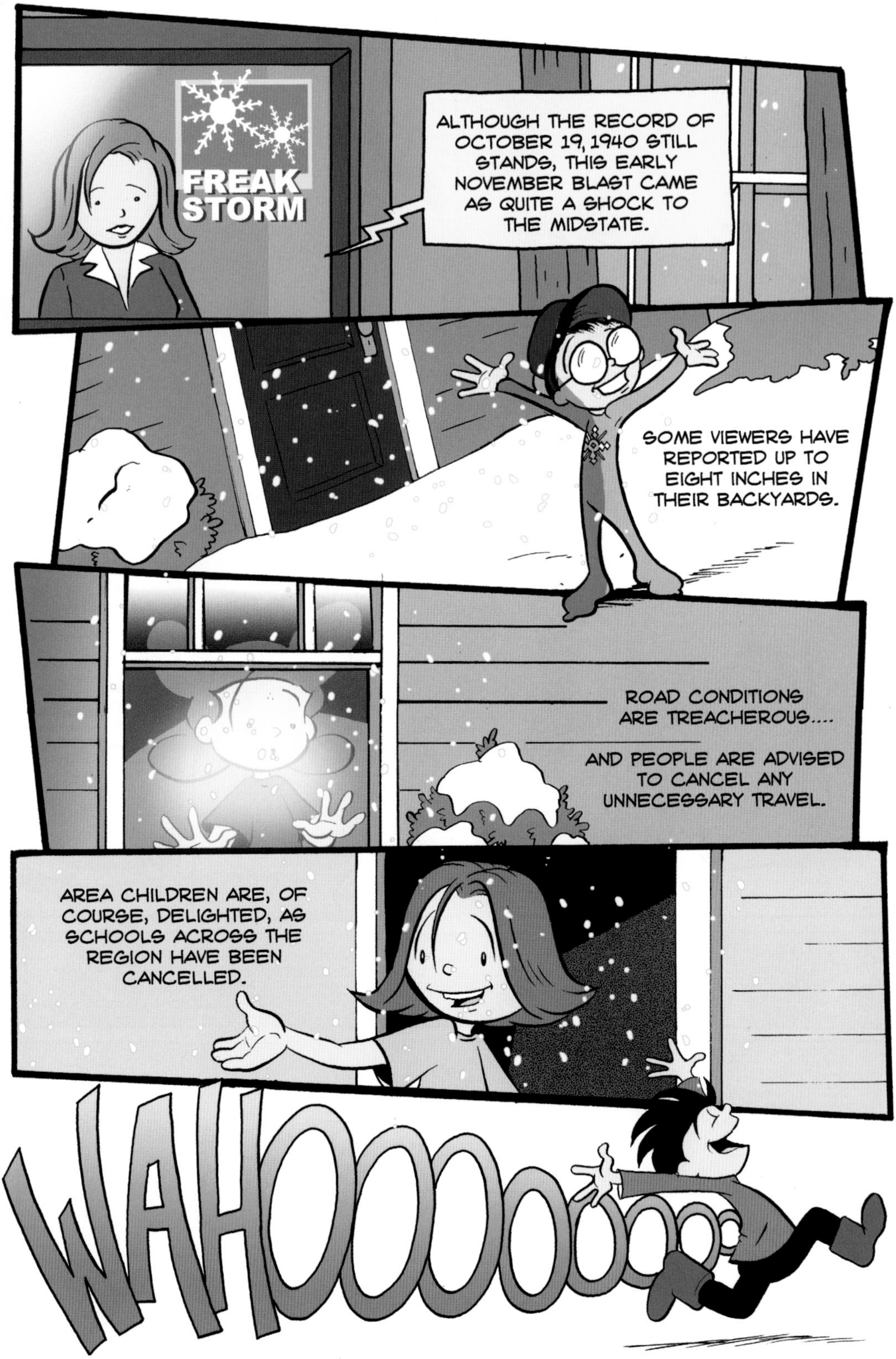
FREAK STORM
ALTHOUGH THE RECORD OF OCTOBER 19, 1940 STILL STANDS, THIS EARLY NOVEMBER BLAST CAME AS QUITE A SHOCK TO THE MIDSTATE.
SOME VIEWERS HAVE REPORTED UP TO EIGHT INCHES IN THEIR BACKYARDS.
ROAD CONDITIONS ARE TREACHEROUS....
AND PEOPLE ARE ADVISED TO CANCEL ANY UNNECESSARY TRAVEL.
AREA CHILDREN ARE, OF COURSE, DELIGHTED, AS SCHOOLS ACROSS THE REGION HAVE BEEN CANCELLED.
WAHOOOOOOOOO

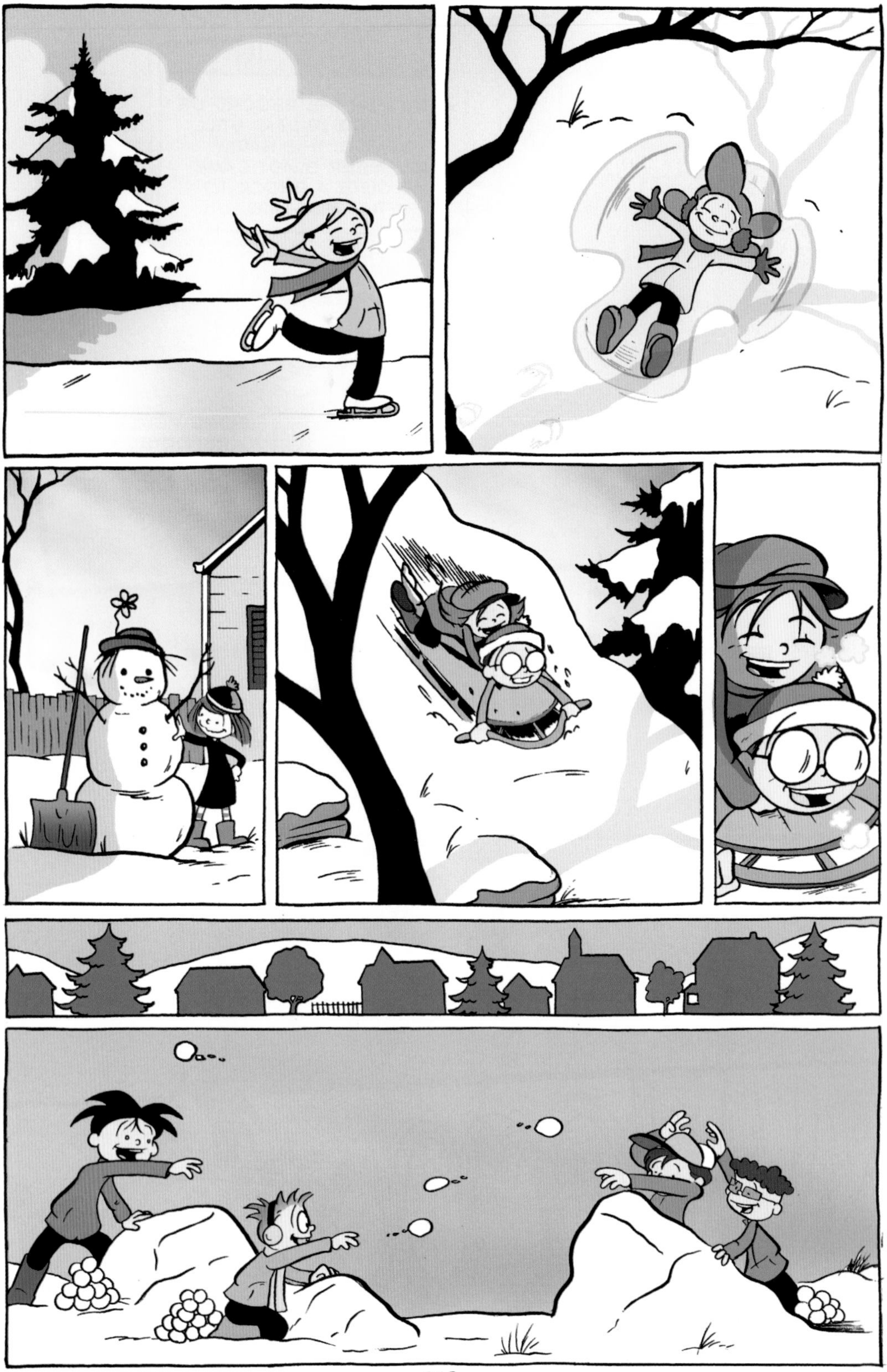

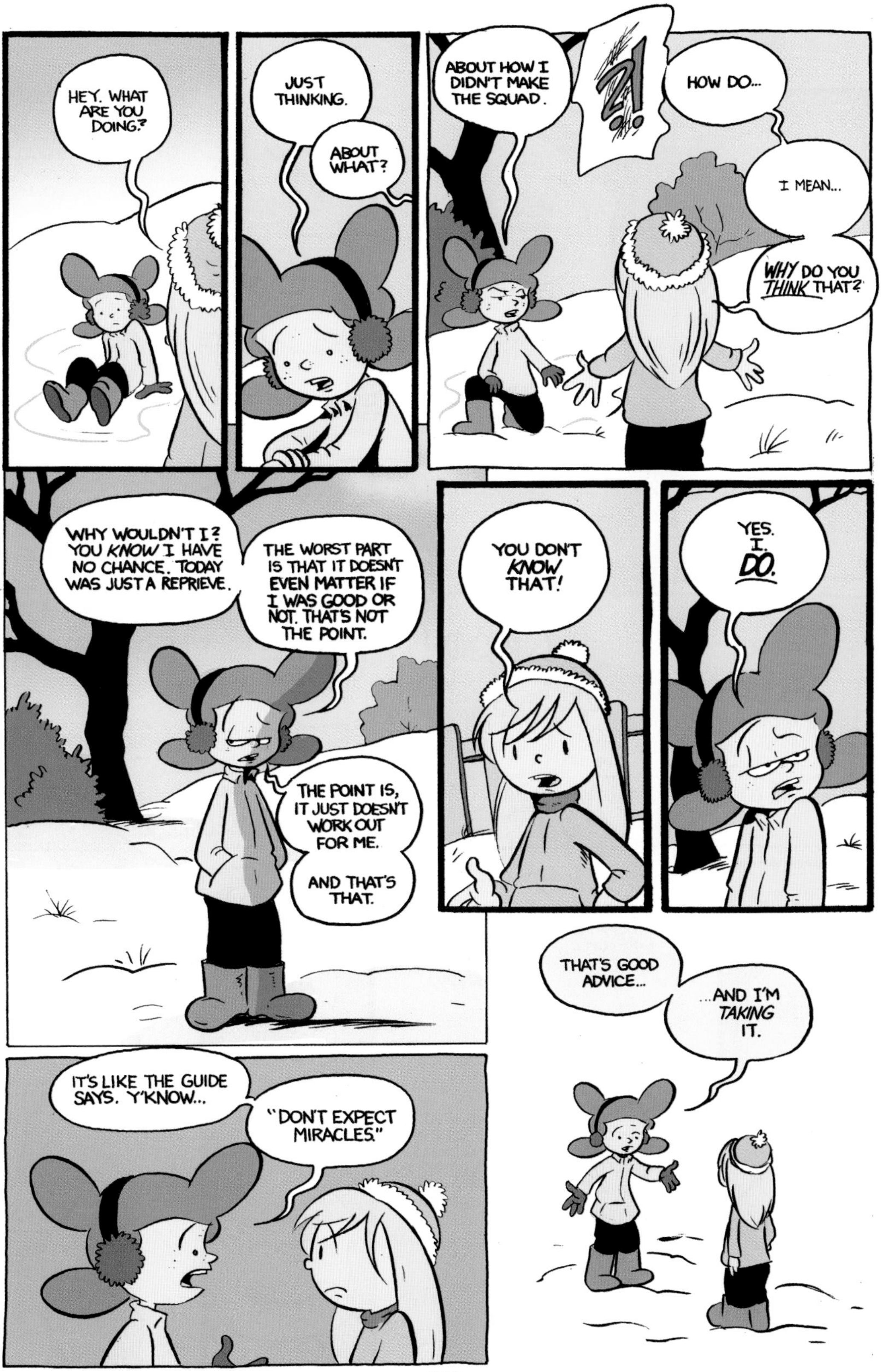
HEY. WHAT ARE YOU DOING?
JUST THINKING.
ABOUT WHAT?
ABOUT HOW I DIDN'T MAKE THE SQUAD.
?!
HOW DO...
I MEAN...
WHY DO YOU THINK THAT?
WHY WOULDN'T I? YOU KNOW I HAVE NO CHANCE. TODAY WAS JUST A REPRIEVE.
THE WORST PART IS THAT IT DOESN'T EVEN MATTER IF I WAS GOOD OR NOT. THAT'S NOT THE POINT.
THE POINT IS, IT JUST DOESN'T WORK OUT FOR ME.
AND THAT'S THAT.
YOU DON'T KNOW THAT!
YES. I. DO.
IT'S LIKE THE GUIDE SAYS. Y'KNOW...
"DON'T EXPECT MIRACLES."
THAT'S GOOD ADVICE...
...AND I'M TAKING IT.

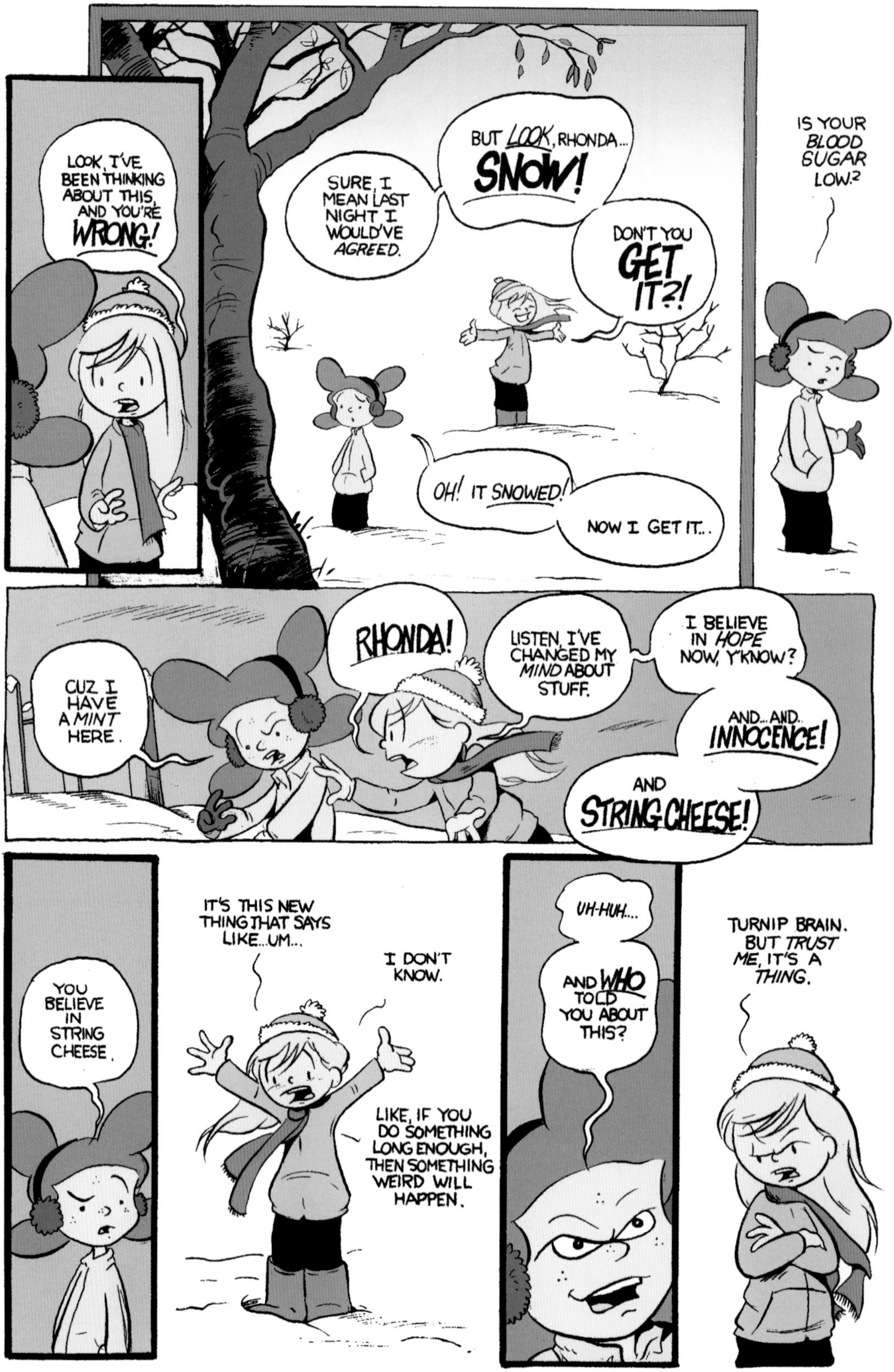
LOOK, I'VE BEEN THINKING ABOUT THIS, AND YOU'RE WRONG!
SURE, I MEAN LAST NIGHT I WOULD'VE AGREED.
BUT LOOK, RHONDA... SNOW!
DON'T YOU GET IT?!
OH! IT SNOWED!
NOW I GET IT...
IS YOUR BLOOD SUGAR LOW?
CUZ I HAVE A MINT HERE.
RHONDA!
LISTEN, I'VE CHANGED MY MIND ABOUT STUFF.
I BELIEVE IN HOPE NOW, Y'KNOW?
AND...AND.. INNOCENCE!
AND STRING CHEESE!
YOU BELIEVE IN STRING CHEESE.
IT'S THIS NEW THING THAT SAYS LIKE...UM...
I DON'T KNOW.
LIKE, IF YOU DO SOMETHING LONG ENOUGH, THEN SOMETHING WEIRD WILL HAPPEN.
UH-HUH...
AND WHO TOLD YOU ABOUT THIS?
TURNIP BRAIN. BUT TRUST ME, IT'S A THING.

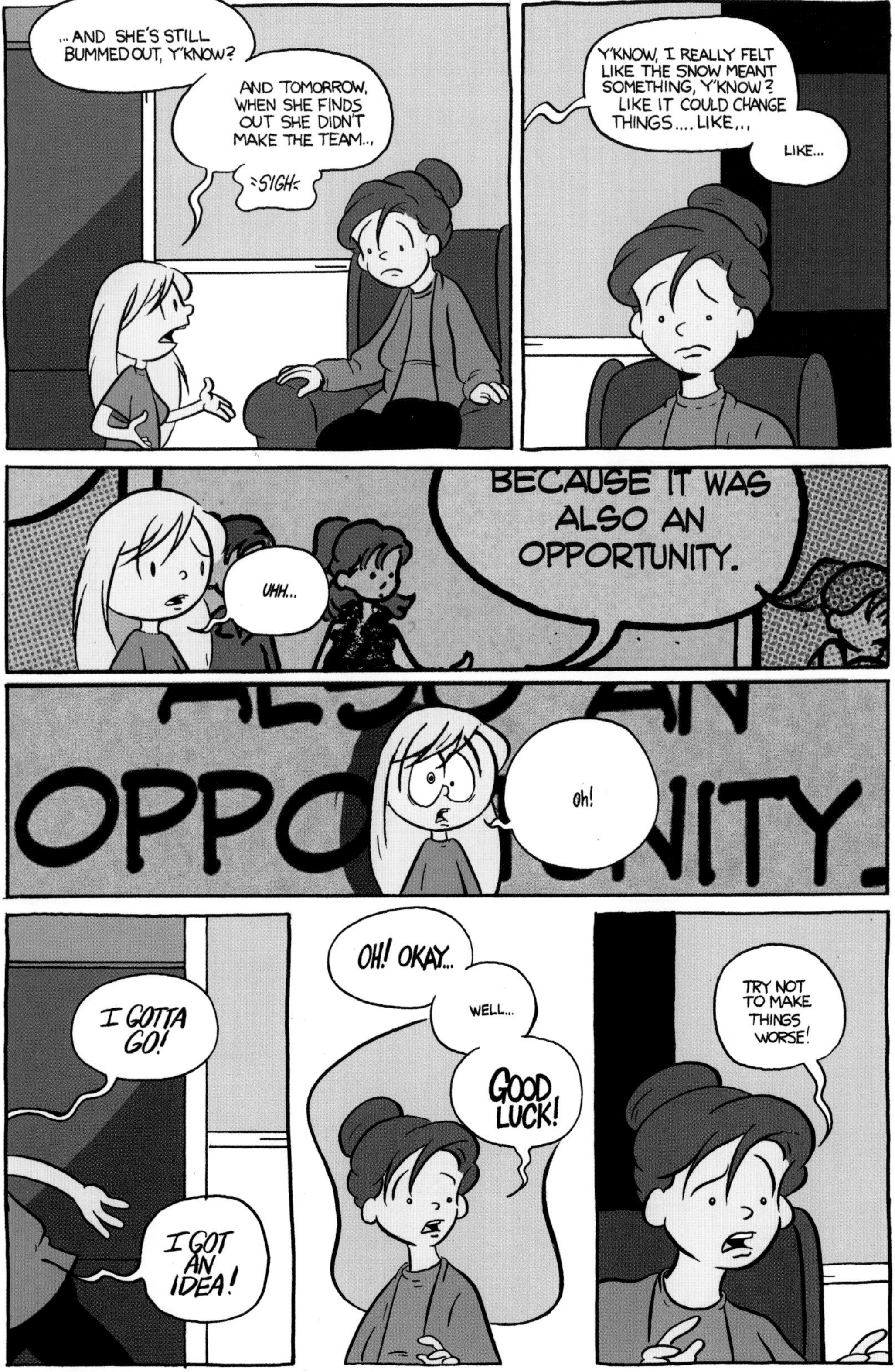

...AND SHE'S STILL BUMMED OUT, Y'KNOW?
AND TOMORROW, WHEN SHE FINDS OUT SHE DIDN'T MAKE THE TEAM...
=SIGH=
Y'KNOW, I REALLY FELT LIKE THE SNOW MEANT SOMETHING, Y'KNOW? LIKE IT COULD CHANGE THINGS.... LIKE...
LIKE...
BECAUSE IT WAS ALSO AN OPPORTUNITY.
UHH...
oh!
I GOTTA GO!
I GOT AN IDEA!
OH! OKAY...
WELL...
GOOD LUCK!
TRY NOT TO MAKE THINGS WORSE!

BUT SUDDENLY IT WAS ALL SO CLEAR. I WOULDN'T MAKE THINGS WORSE! I KNEW JUST WHAT TO DO.

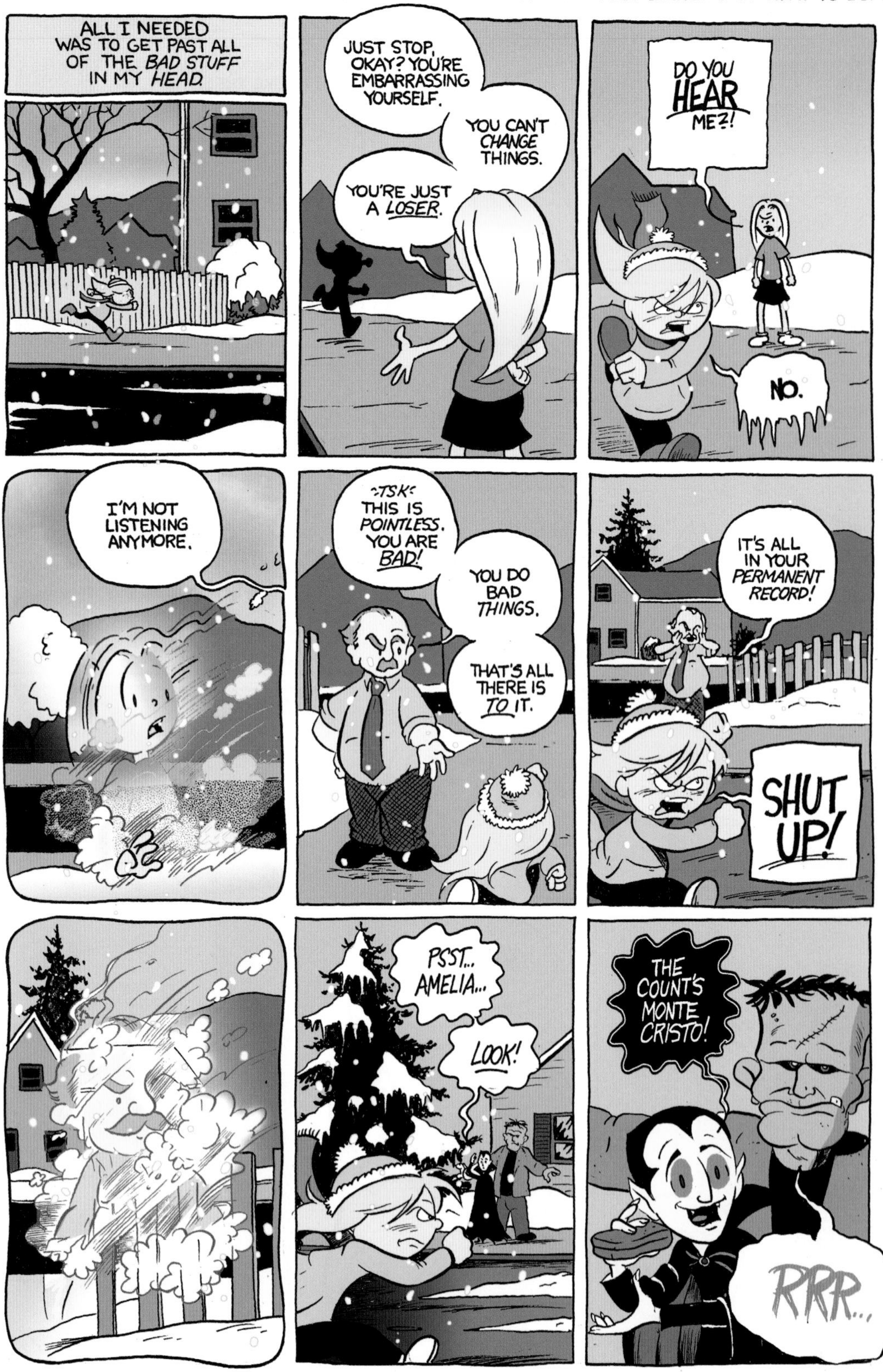

ALL I NEEDED WAS TO GET PAST ALL OF THE BAD STUFF IN MY HEAD.
JUST STOP, OKAY? YOU'RE EMBARRASSING YOURSELF.
YOU CAN'T CHANGE THINGS.
YOU'RE JUST A LOSER.
DO YOU HEAR ME?!
NO.
I'M NOT LISTENING ANYMORE.
TSK
THIS IS POINTLESS. YOU ARE BAD!
YOU DO BAD THINGS.
THAT'S ALL THERE IS TO IT.
IT'S ALL IN YOUR PERMANENT RECORD!
SHUT UP!
PSST... AMELIA...
LOOK!
THE COUNT'S MONTE CRISTO!
RRR...

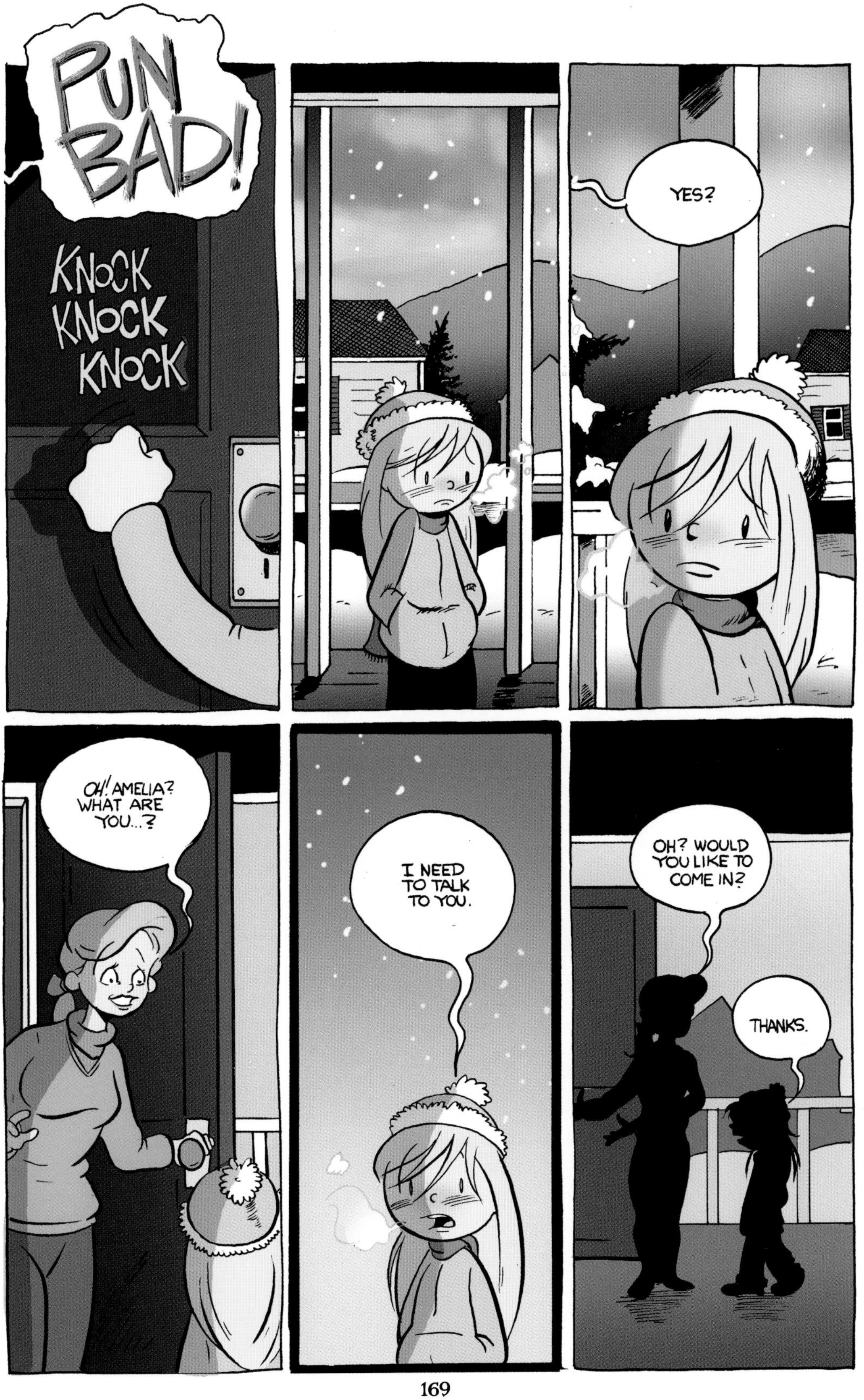
PUN BAD!
KNOCK KNOCK KNOCK
YES?
OH! AMELIA? WHAT ARE YOU...?
I NEED TO TALK TO YOU.
OH? WOULD YOU LIKE TO COME IN?
THANKS.

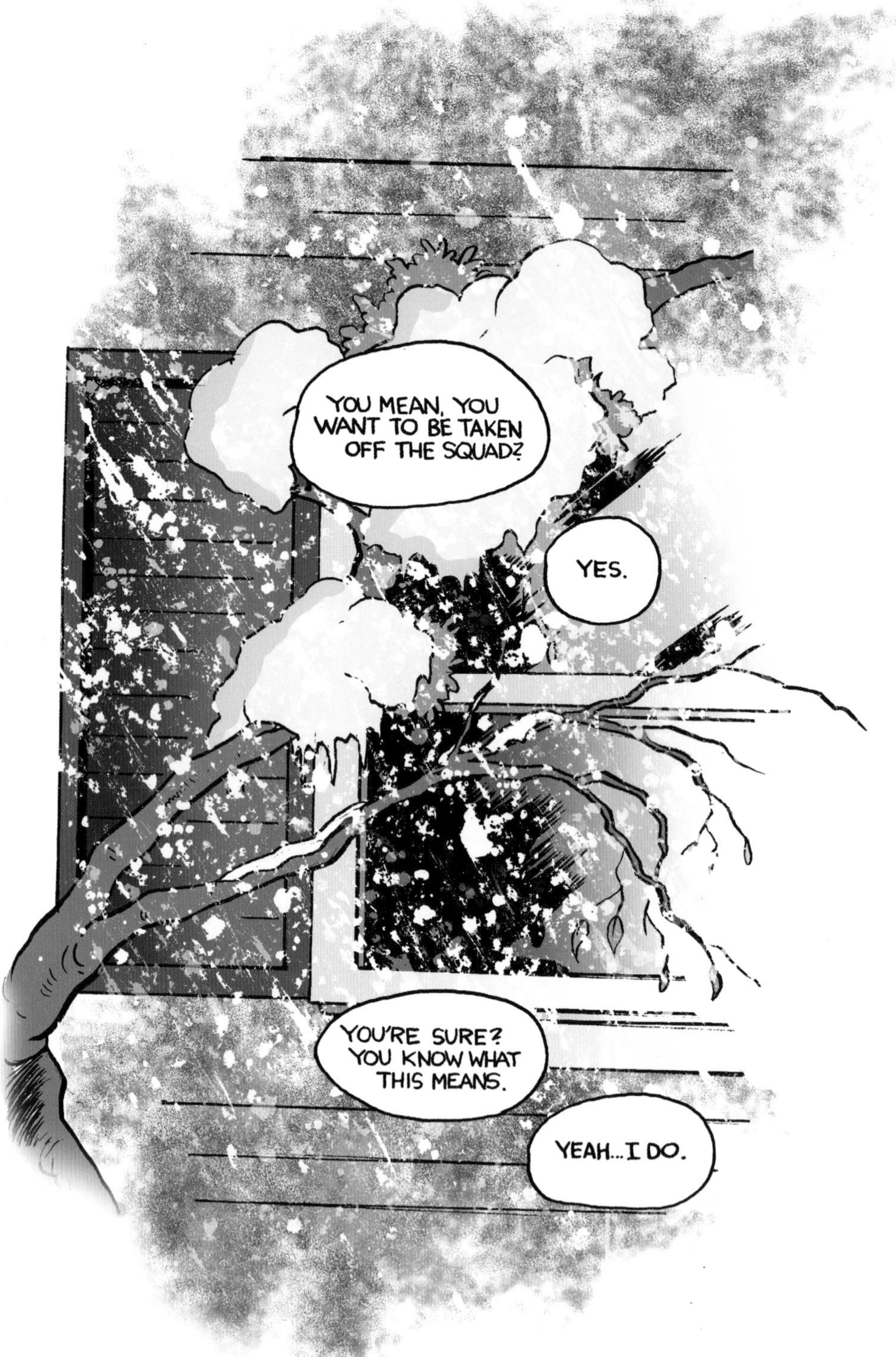
YOU MEAN, YOU WANT TO BE TAKEN OFF THE SQUAD?
YES.
YOU'RE SURE? YOU KNOW WHAT THIS MEANS.
YEAH...I DO.

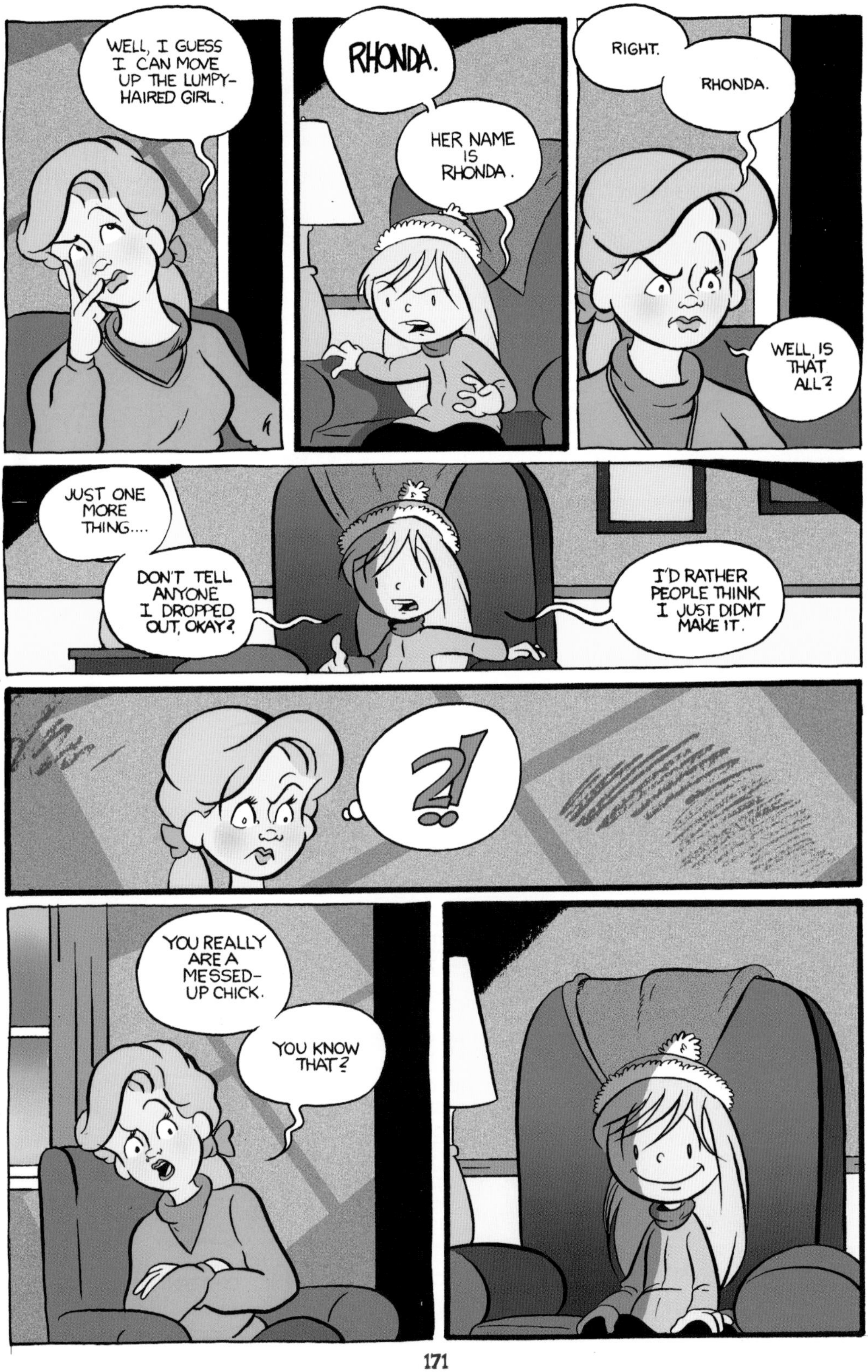
WELL, I GUESS I CAN MOVE UP THE LUMPY-HAIRED GIRL.
RHONDA.
HER NAME IS RHONDA.
RIGHT.
RHONDA.
WELL, IS THAT ALL?
JUST ONE MORE THING....
DON'T TELL ANYONE I DROPPED OUT, OKAY?
I'D RATHER PEOPLE THINK I JUST DIDN'T MAKE IT.
?!
YOU REALLY ARE A MESSED-UP CHICK.
YOU KNOW THAT?

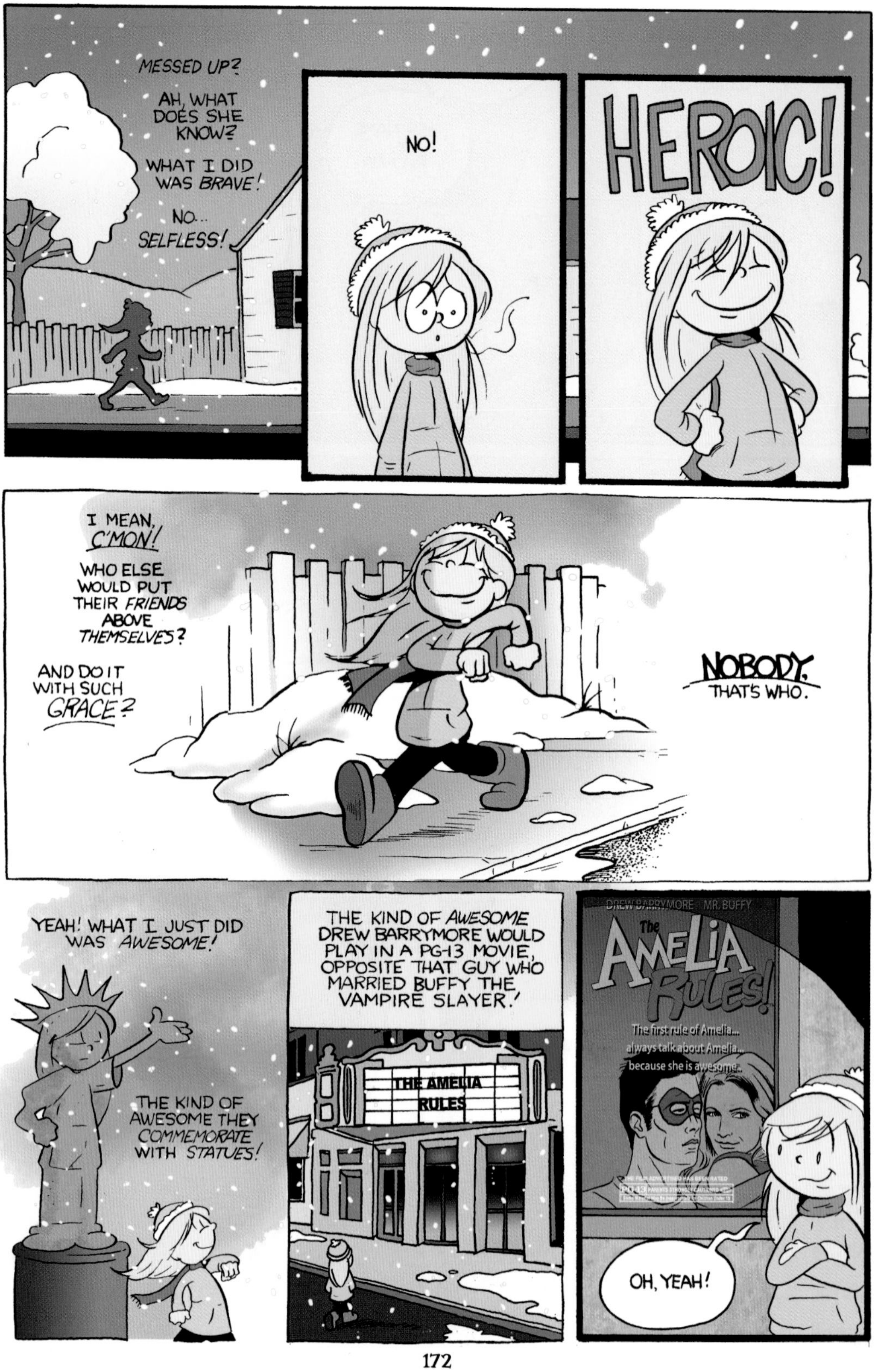
MESSED UP?
AH, WHAT DOES SHE KNOW?
WHAT I DID WAS BRAVE!
NO... SELFLESS!
NO!
HEROIC!
I MEAN, C'MON!
WHO ELSE WOULD PUT THEIR FRIENDS ABOVE THEMSELVES?
AND DO IT WITH SUCH GRACE?
NOBODY, THAT'S WHO.
YEAH! WHAT I JUST DID WAS AWESOME!
THE KIND OF AWESOME THEY COMMEMORATE WITH STATUES!
THE KIND OF AWESOME DREW BARRYMORE WOULD PLAY IN A PG-13 MOVIE, OPPOSITE THAT GUY WHO MARRIED BUFFY THE VAMPIRE SLAYER!
THE AMELIA RULES
MR. BUFFY
The AMELIA RULES!
The first rule of Amelia... always talk about Amelia... because she is awesome..
OH, YEAH!

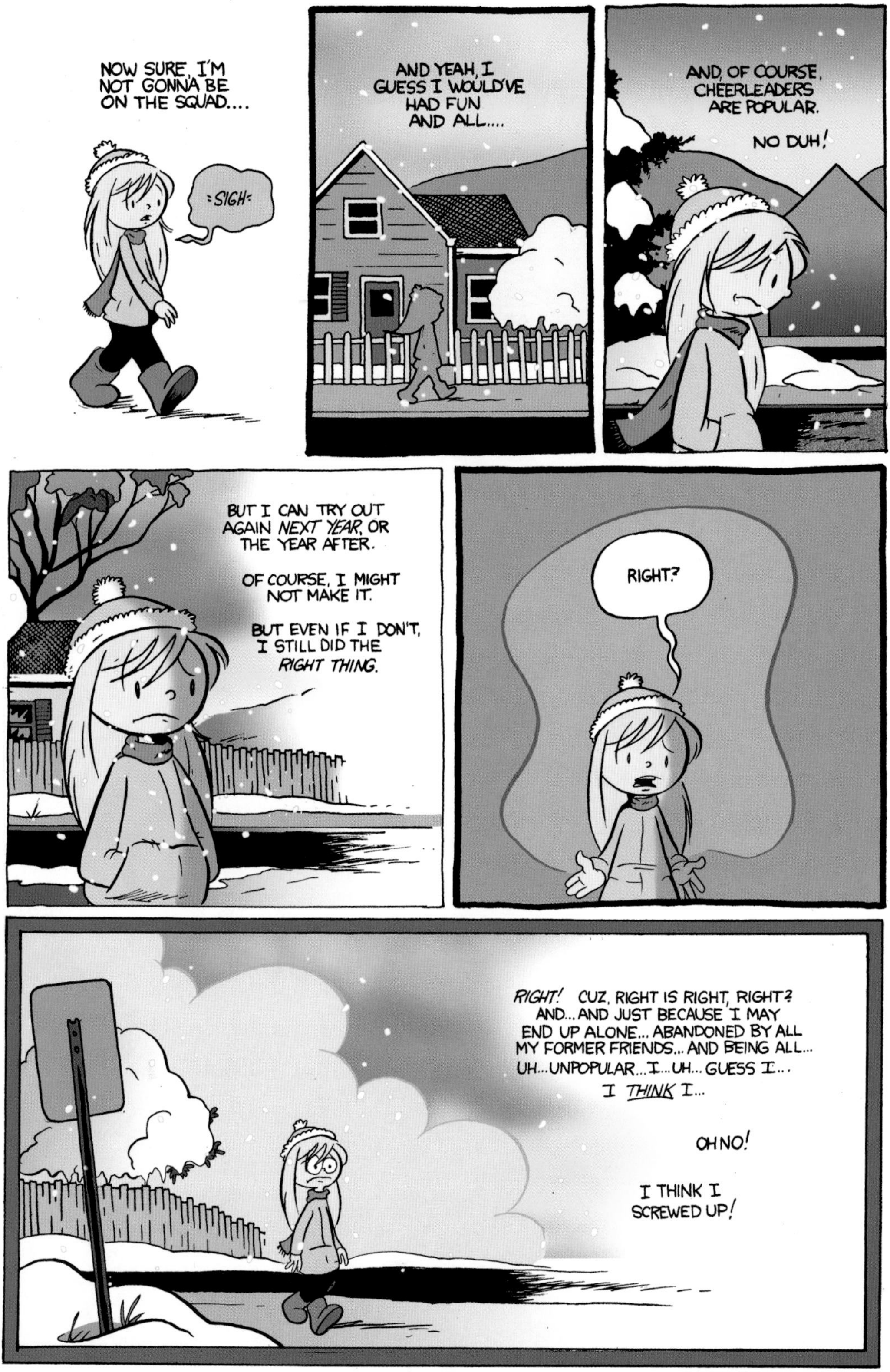
NOW SURE, I'M NOT GONNA BE ON THE SQUAD....
=SIGH=
AND YEAH, I GUESS I WOULD'VE HAD FUN AND ALL....
AND, OF COURSE, CHEERLEADERS ARE POPULAR.
NO DUH!
BUT I CAN TRY OUT AGAIN NEXT YEAR, OR THE YEAR AFTER.
OF COURSE, I MIGHT NOT MAKE IT.
BUT EVEN IF I DON'T, I STILL DID THE RIGHT THING.
RIGHT?
RIGHT! CUZ, RIGHT IS RIGHT, RIGHT? AND... AND JUST BECAUSE I MAY END UP ALONE... ABANDONED BY ALL MY FORMER FRIENDS... AND BEING ALL... UH... UNPOPULAR... I... UH... GUESS I...
I THINK I...
OH NO!
I THINK I SCREWED UP!

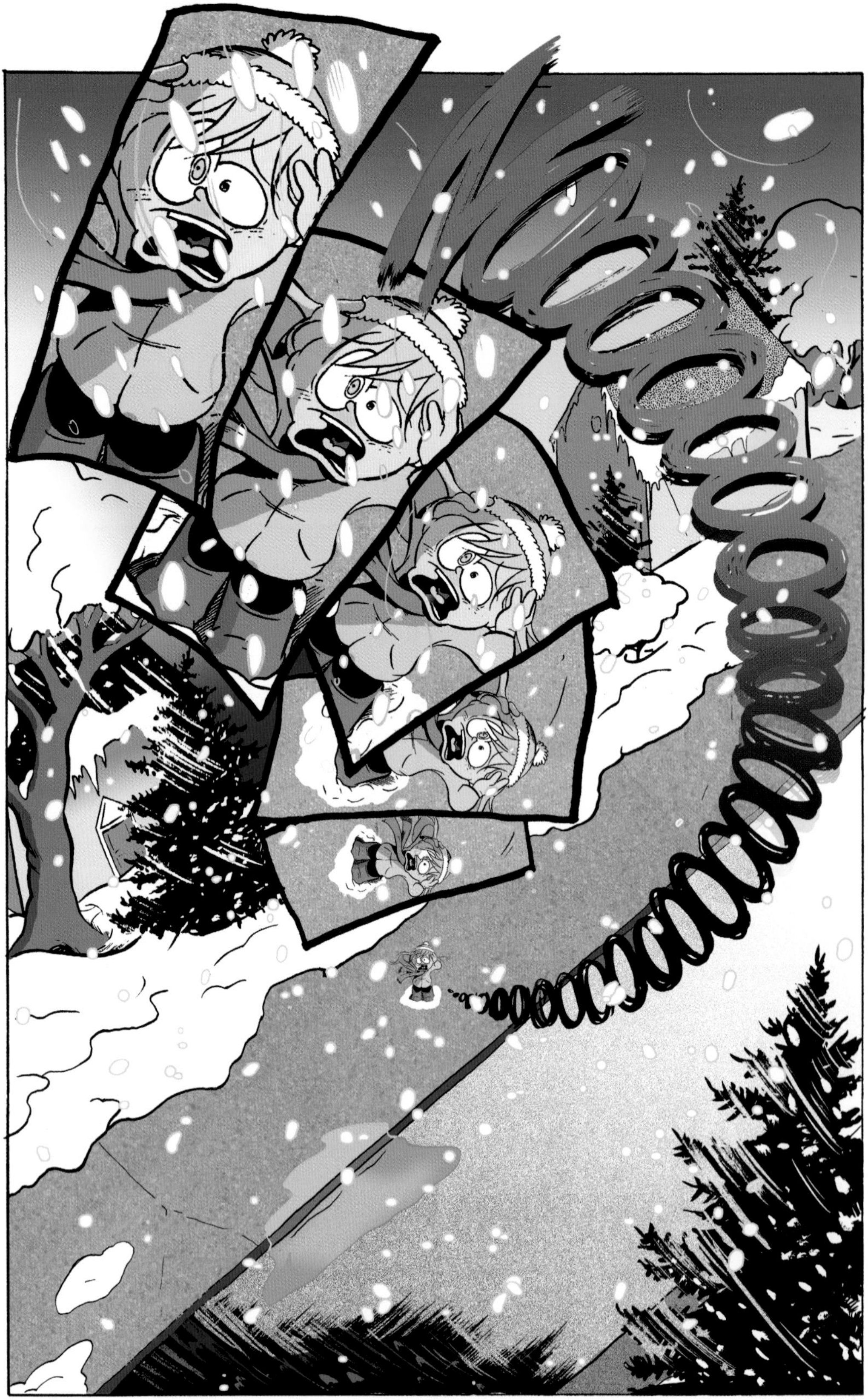
NOOOOOOOOOOOOOOOOOOOOOOOOOOO

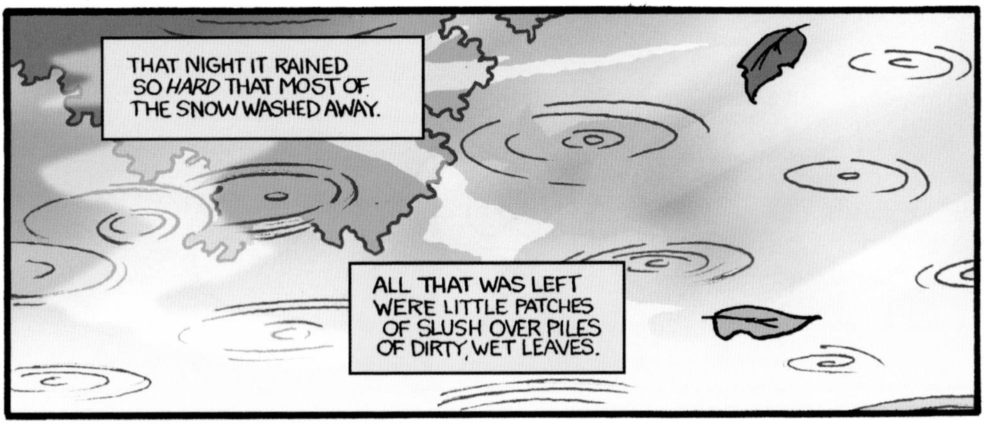
THAT NIGHT IT RAINED SO *HARD* THAT MOST OF THE SNOW WASHED AWAY.
ALL THAT WAS LEFT WERE LITTLE PATCHES OF SLUSH OVER PILES OF DIRTY, WET LEAVES.

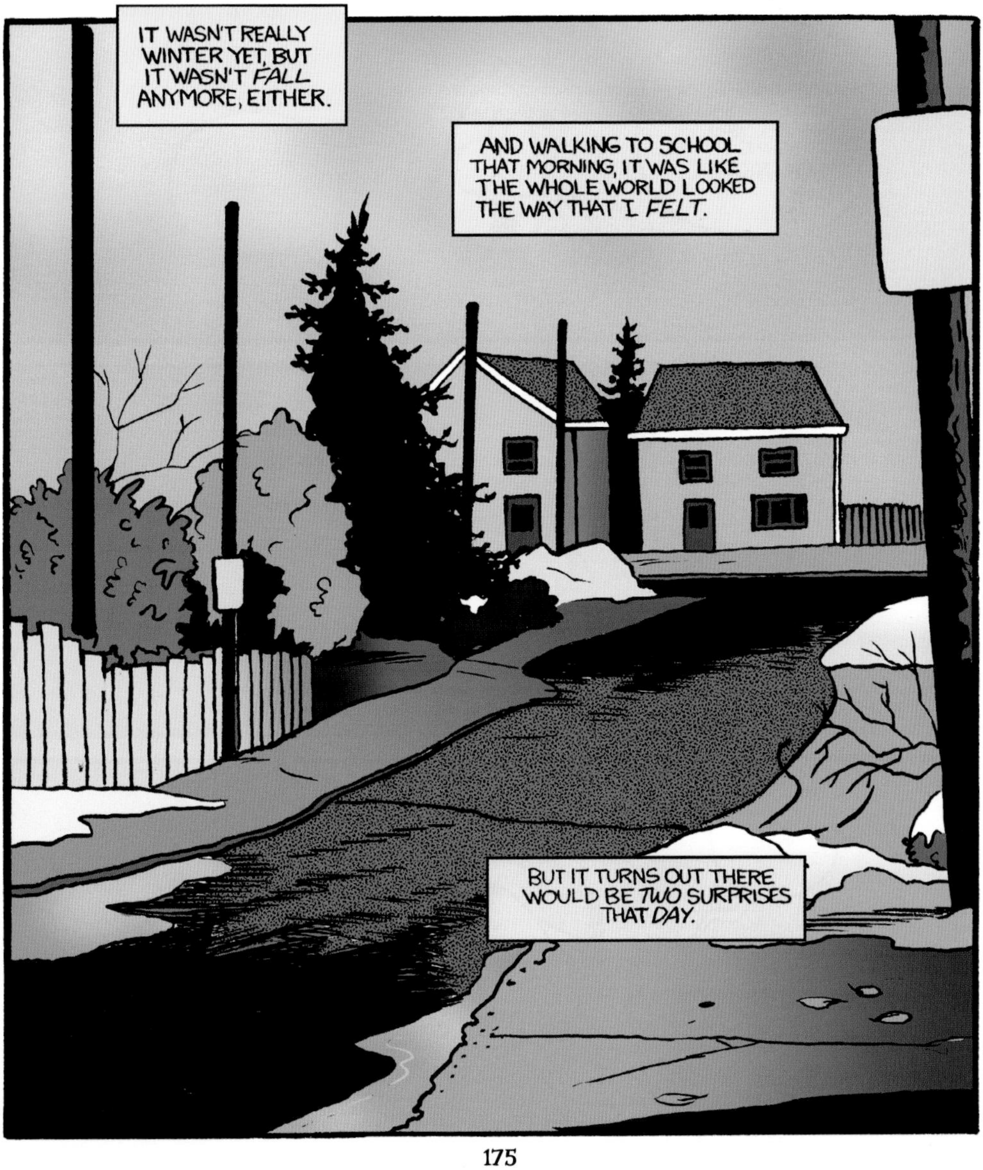
IT WASN'T REALLY WINTER YET, BUT IT WASN'T *FALL* ANYMORE, EITHER.
AND WALKING TO SCHOOL THAT MORNING, IT WAS LIKE THE WHOLE WORLD LOOKED THE WAY THAT I *FELT*.
BUT IT TURNS OUT THERE WOULD BE *TWO* SURPRISES THAT *DAY*.

THE *FIRST* WAS FOR US...

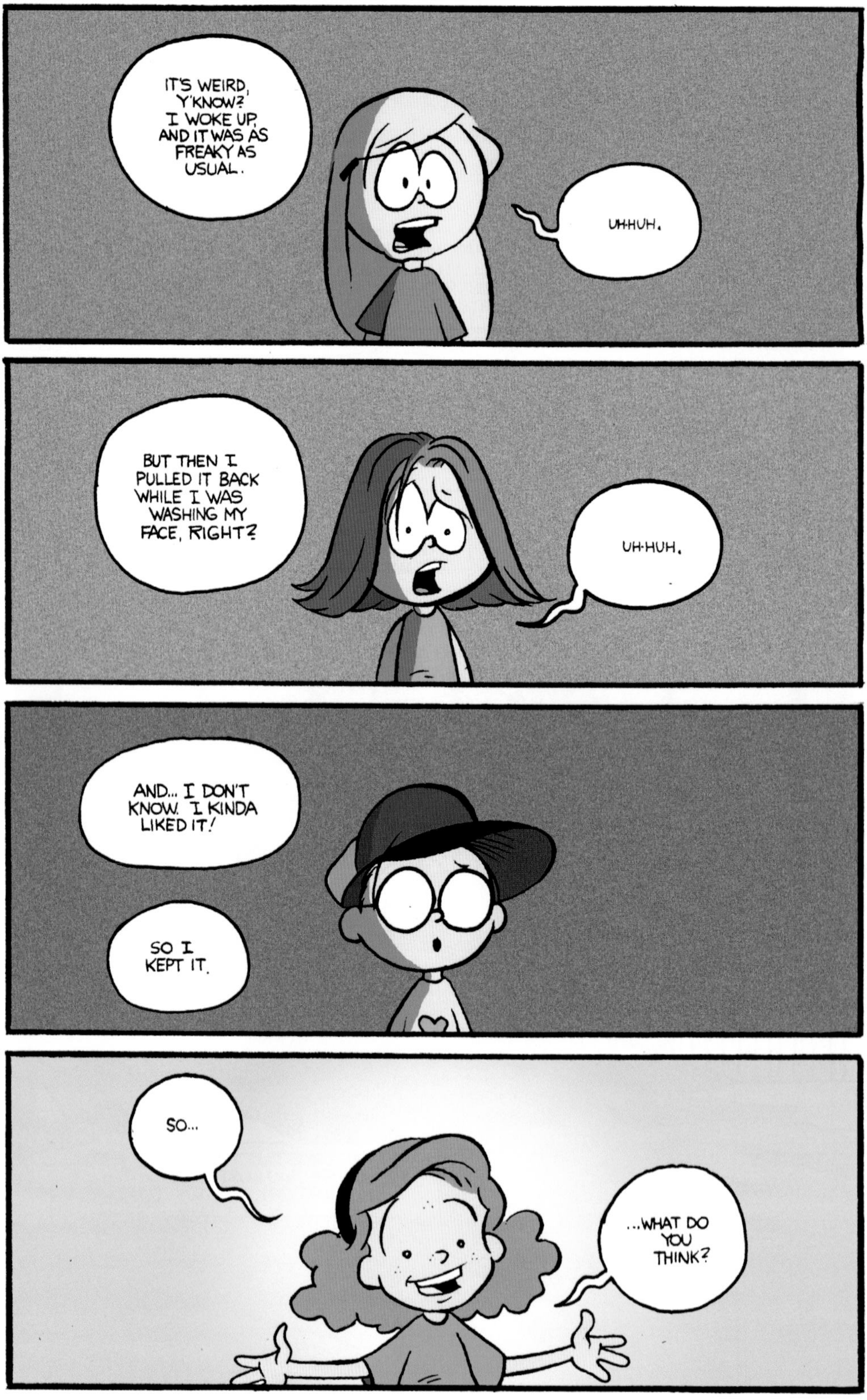
IT'S WEIRD, Y'KNOW? I WOKE UP, AND IT WAS AS FREAKY AS USUAL.
UH-HUH.
BUT THEN I PULLED IT BACK WHILE I WAS WASHING MY FACE, RIGHT?
UH-HUH.
AND... I DON'T KNOW. I KINDA LIKED IT!
SO I KEPT IT.
SO...
...WHAT DO YOU THINK?

AND THE SECOND, OF COURSE, WAS FOR *RHONDA*....

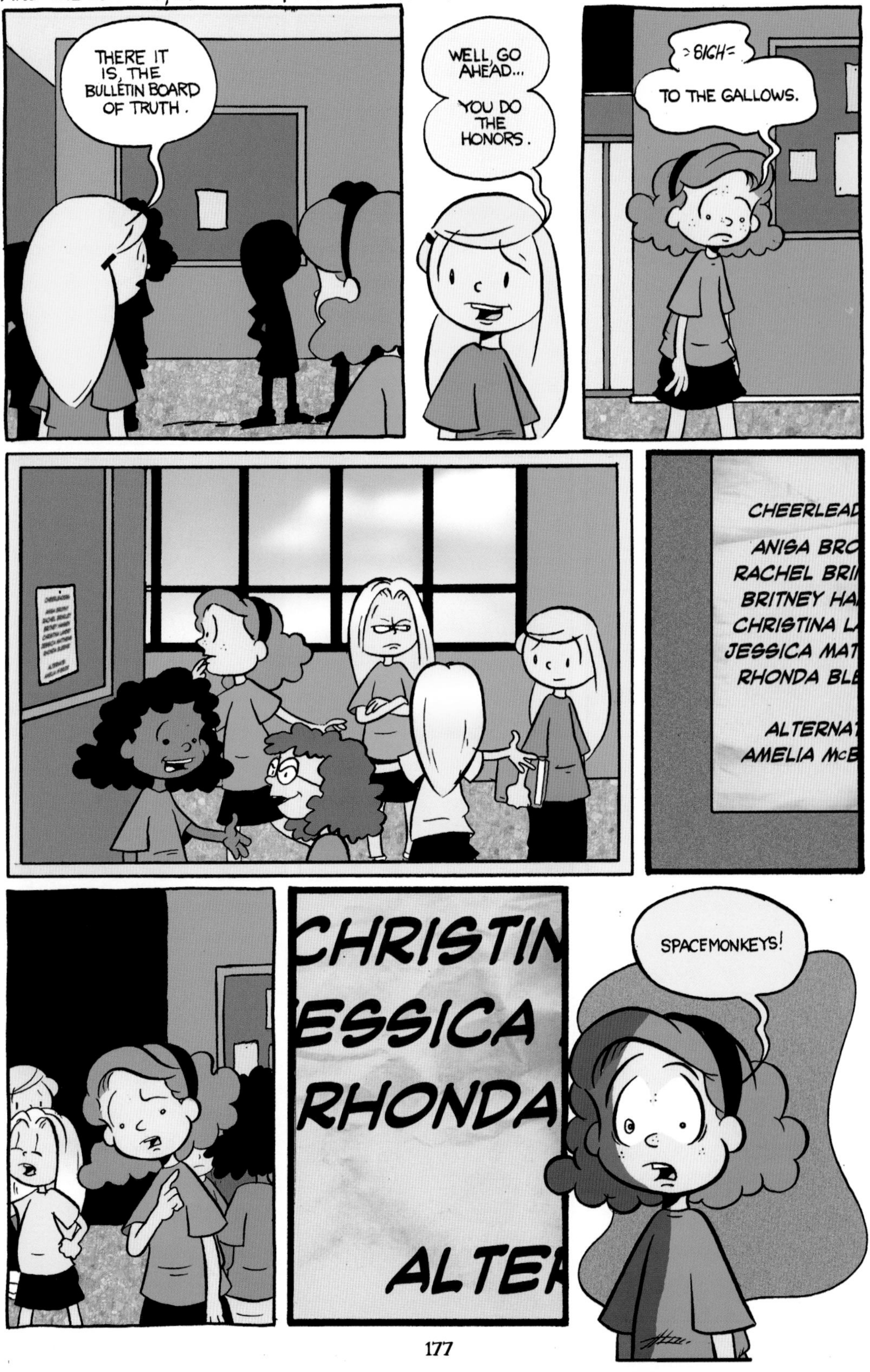
THERE IT IS, THE BULLETIN BOARD OF TRUTH.
WELL, GO AHEAD...
YOU DO THE HONORS.
=SIGH=
TO THE GALLOWS.
CHEERLEAD
ANISA BRO
RACHEL BRI
BRITNEY HA
CHRISTINA LA
JESSICA MAT
RHONDA BLE
ALTERNAT
AMELIA McB
CHRISTIN
ESSICA
RHONDA
ALTER
SPACEMONKEYS!

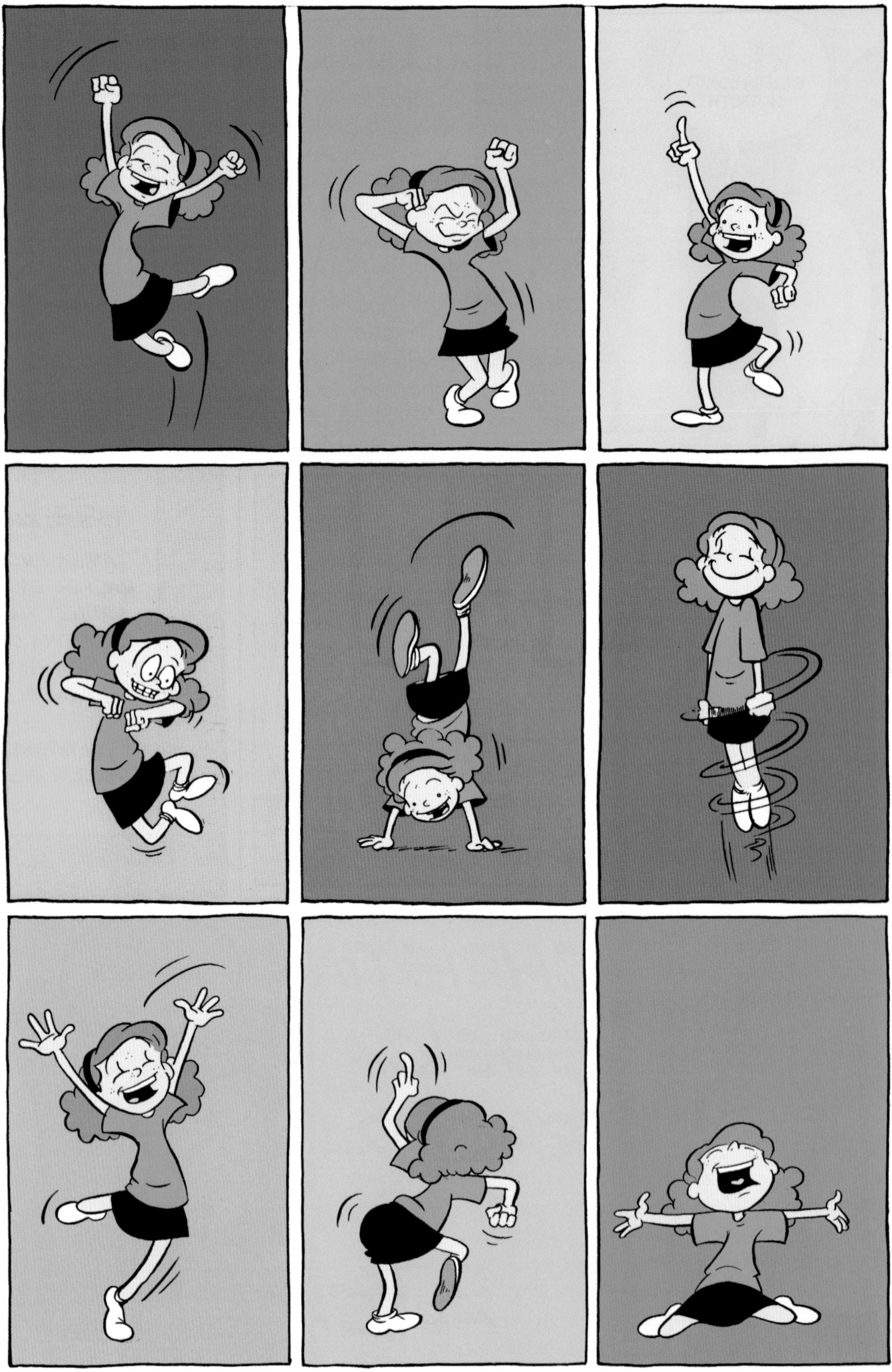

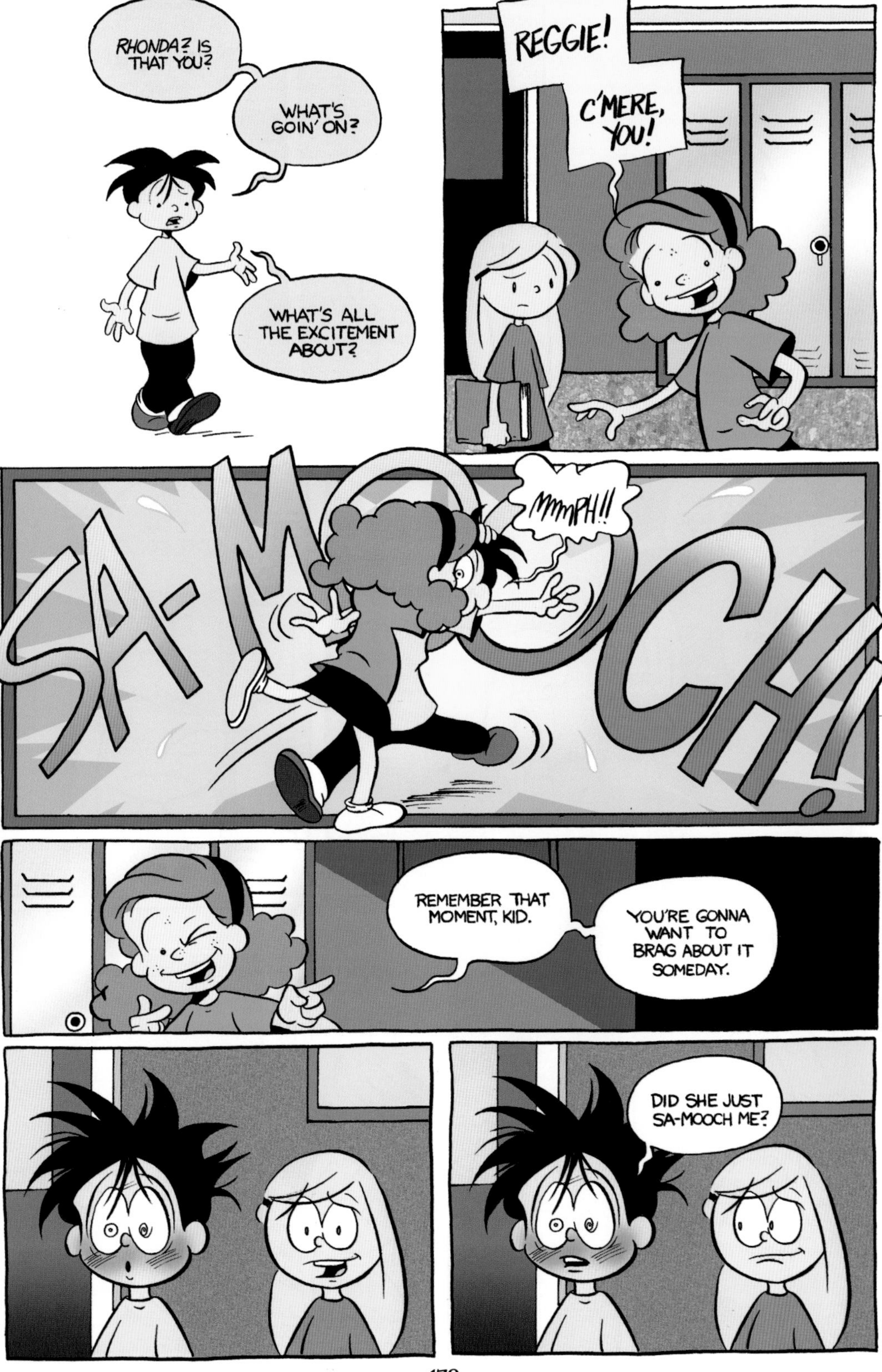
RHONDA? IS THAT YOU?
WHAT'S GOIN' ON?
WHAT'S ALL THE EXCITEMENT ABOUT?
REGGIE!
C'MERE, YOU!
SA-MOOCH!
MMMPH!!
REMEMBER THAT MOMENT, KID.
YOU'RE GONNA WANT TO BRAG ABOUT IT SOMEDAY.
DID SHE JUST SA-MOOCH ME?

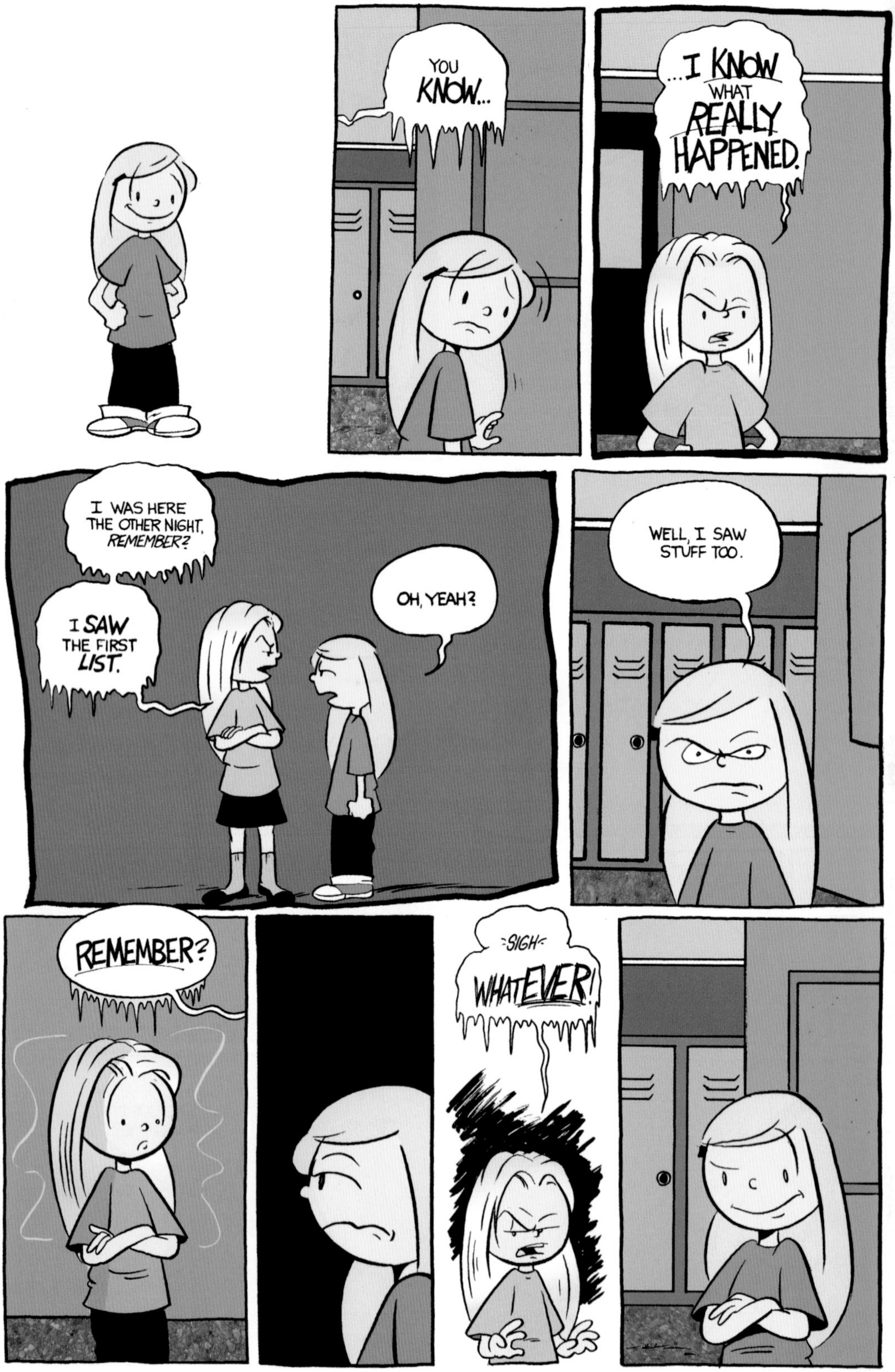
YOU KNOW...
...I KNOW WHAT REALLY HAPPENED.
I WAS HERE THE OTHER NIGHT, REMEMBER?
I SAW THE FIRST LIST.
OH, YEAH?
WELL, I SAW STUFF TOO.
REMEMBER?
SIGH
WHATEVER!

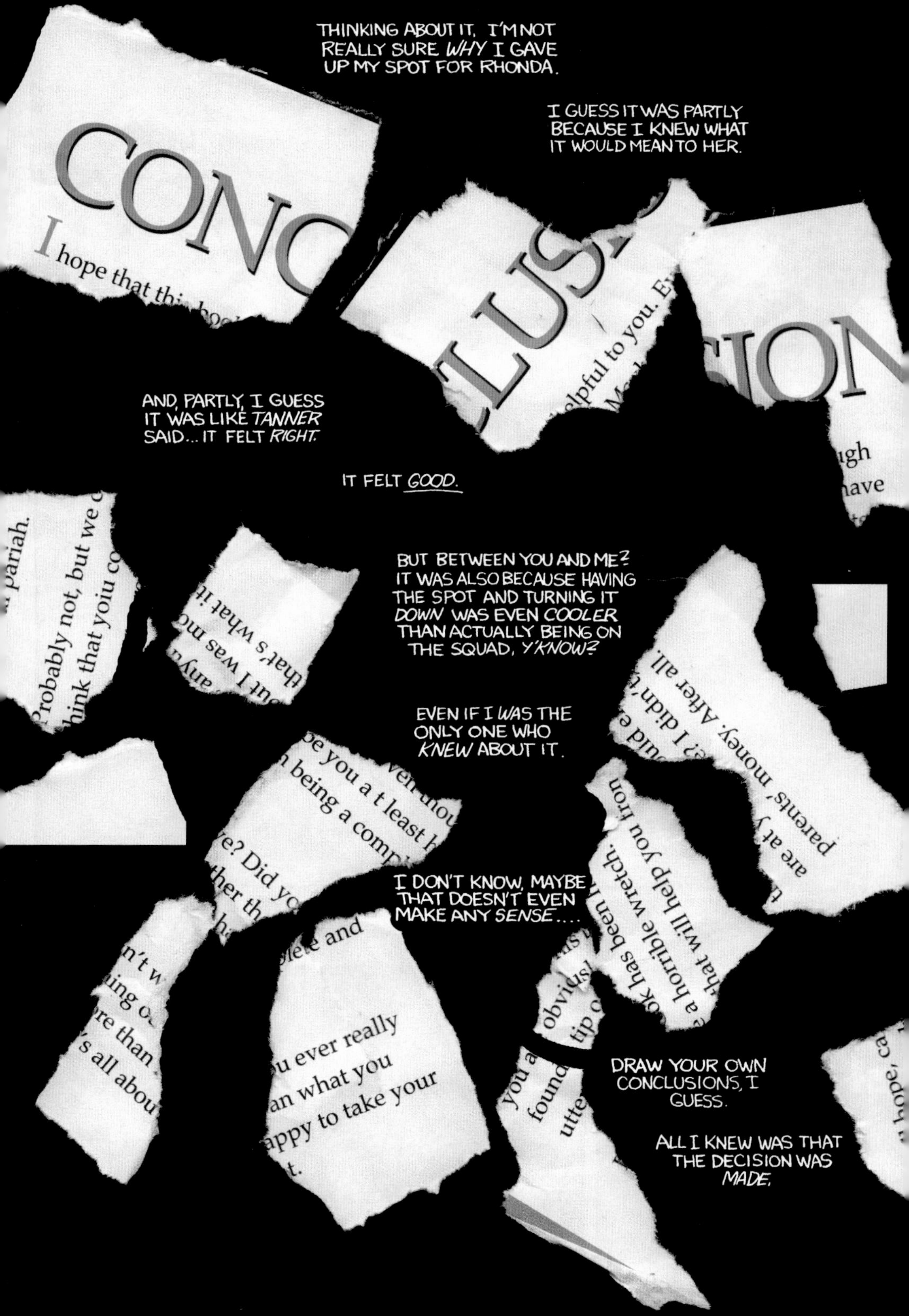

THINKING ABOUT IT, I'M NOT REALLY SURE *WHY* I GAVE UP MY SPOT FOR RHONDA.

I GUESS IT WAS PARTLY BECAUSE I KNEW WHAT IT WOULD MEAN TO HER.

CONC

LUS

ION

I hope that thi...

...lpful to you. E...

...gh

...have

AND, PARTLY, I GUESS IT WAS LIKE *TANNER* SAID... IT FELT *RIGHT.*

IT FELT *GOOD.*

BUT BETWEEN YOU AND ME? IT WAS ALSO BECAUSE HAVING THE SPOT AND TURNING IT *DOWN* WAS EVEN *COOLER* THAN ACTUALLY BEING ON THE SQUAD, *Y'KNOW?*

EVEN IF I *WAS* THE ONLY ONE WHO *KNEW* ABOUT IT.

...pariah.

Probably not, but we c...

...think that yoiu co...

...any...

...out I was m...

...that's what it...

...ve you a t least...

...ver thou...

...id...money. After all...

...are at y...

...parents' money. After all...

...be you a t least...

...being a compl...

...ve? Did yo...

...ther th...

...h...

...n't w...

...ing o...

...re than...

...'s all abou...

...plete and...

I DON'T KNOW, MAYBE THAT DOESN'T EVEN MAKE ANY *SENSE....*

...ok has been...

...s...

...a horrible wretch...

...that will help you fron...

...u ever really...

...an what you...

...appy to take your...

...t.

...you a...

...found...

...obvis...

...tip...

...utte...

DRAW YOUR OWN CONCLUSIONS, I GUESS.

ALL I KNEW WAS THAT THE DECISION WAS *MADE,*

...hope, ca...

...i hope...

AND NOW I HAD TO LIVE WITH MY NEW SITUATION.

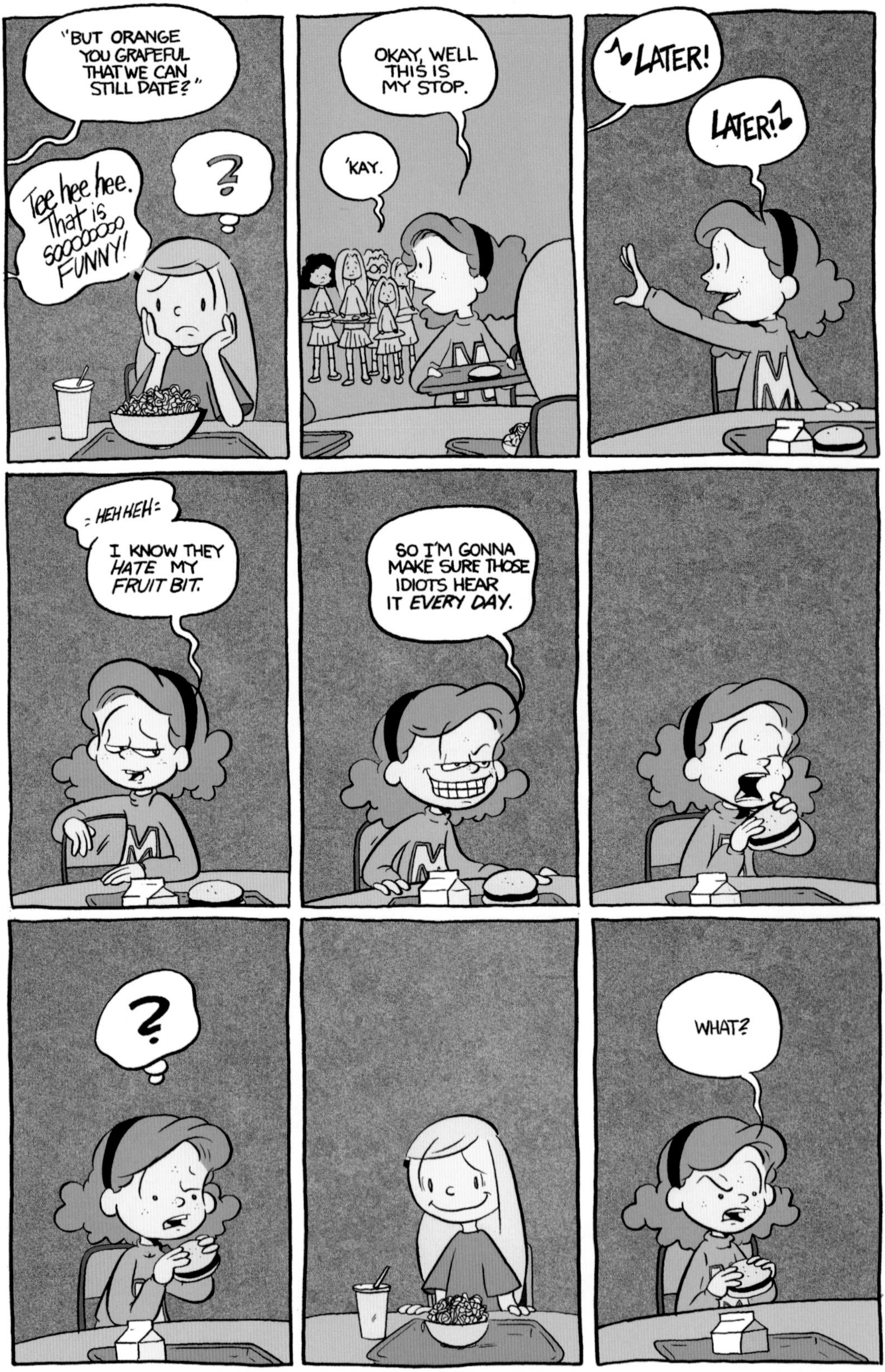

"BUT ORANGE YOU GRAPEFUL THAT WE CAN STILL DATE?"
Tee hee hee. That is soooooooo FUNNY!
?
OKAY, WELL THIS IS MY STOP.
'KAY.
LATER!
LATER!
HEH HEH
I KNOW THEY HATE MY FRUIT BIT.
SO I'M GONNA MAKE SURE THOSE IDIOTS HEAR IT EVERY DAY.
?
WHAT?

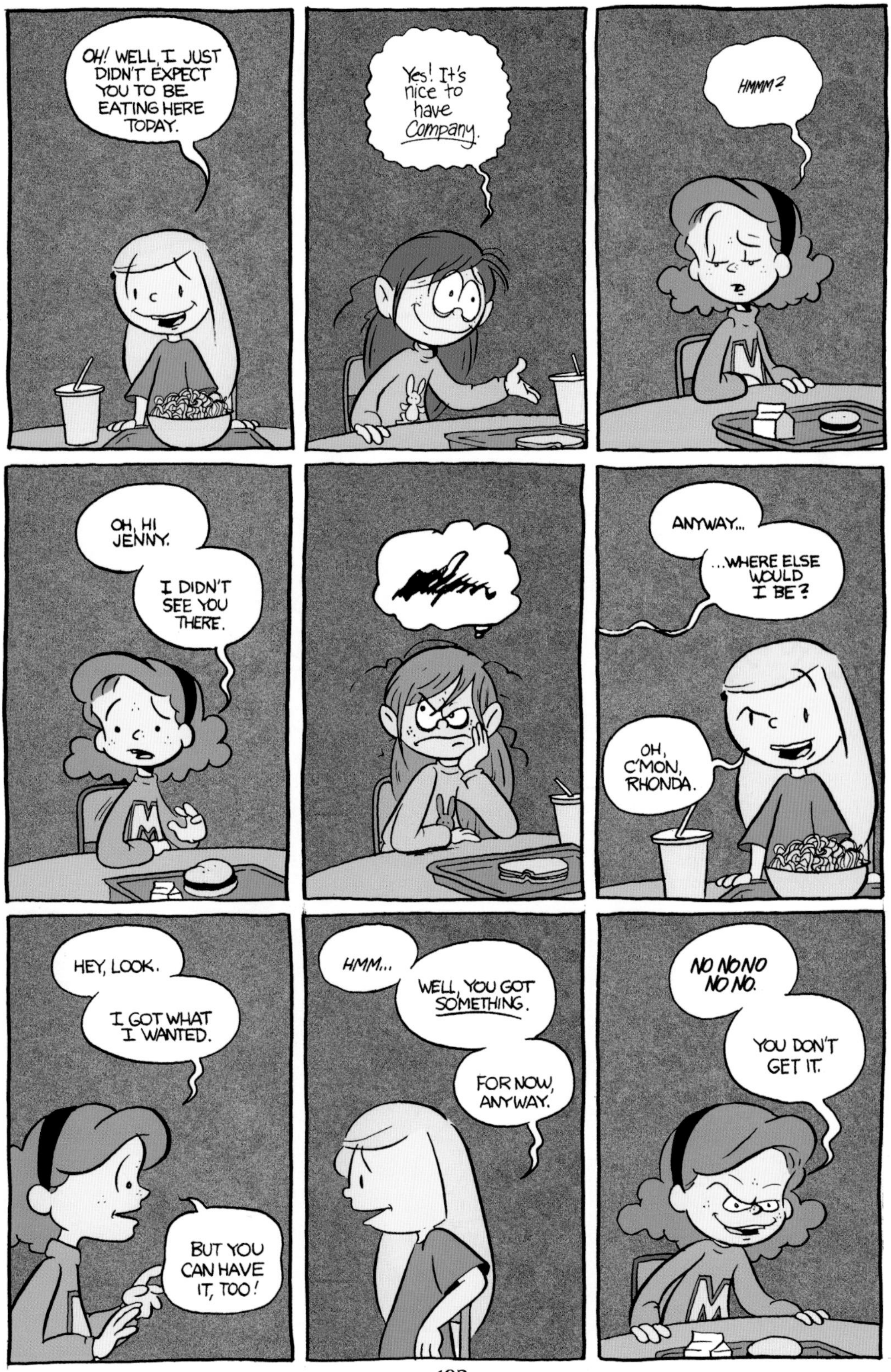

OH! WELL, I JUST DIDN'T EXPECT YOU TO BE EATING HERE TODAY.
Yes! It's nice to have Company.
HMMM?
OH, HI JENNY.
I DIDN'T SEE YOU THERE.
ANYWAY...
...WHERE ELSE WOULD I BE?
OH, C'MON, RHONDA.
HEY, LOOK.
I GOT WHAT I WANTED.
BUT YOU CAN HAVE IT, TOO!
HMM...
WELL, YOU GOT SOMETHING.
FOR NOW, ANYWAY.
NO NO NO NO NO.
YOU DON'T GET IT.

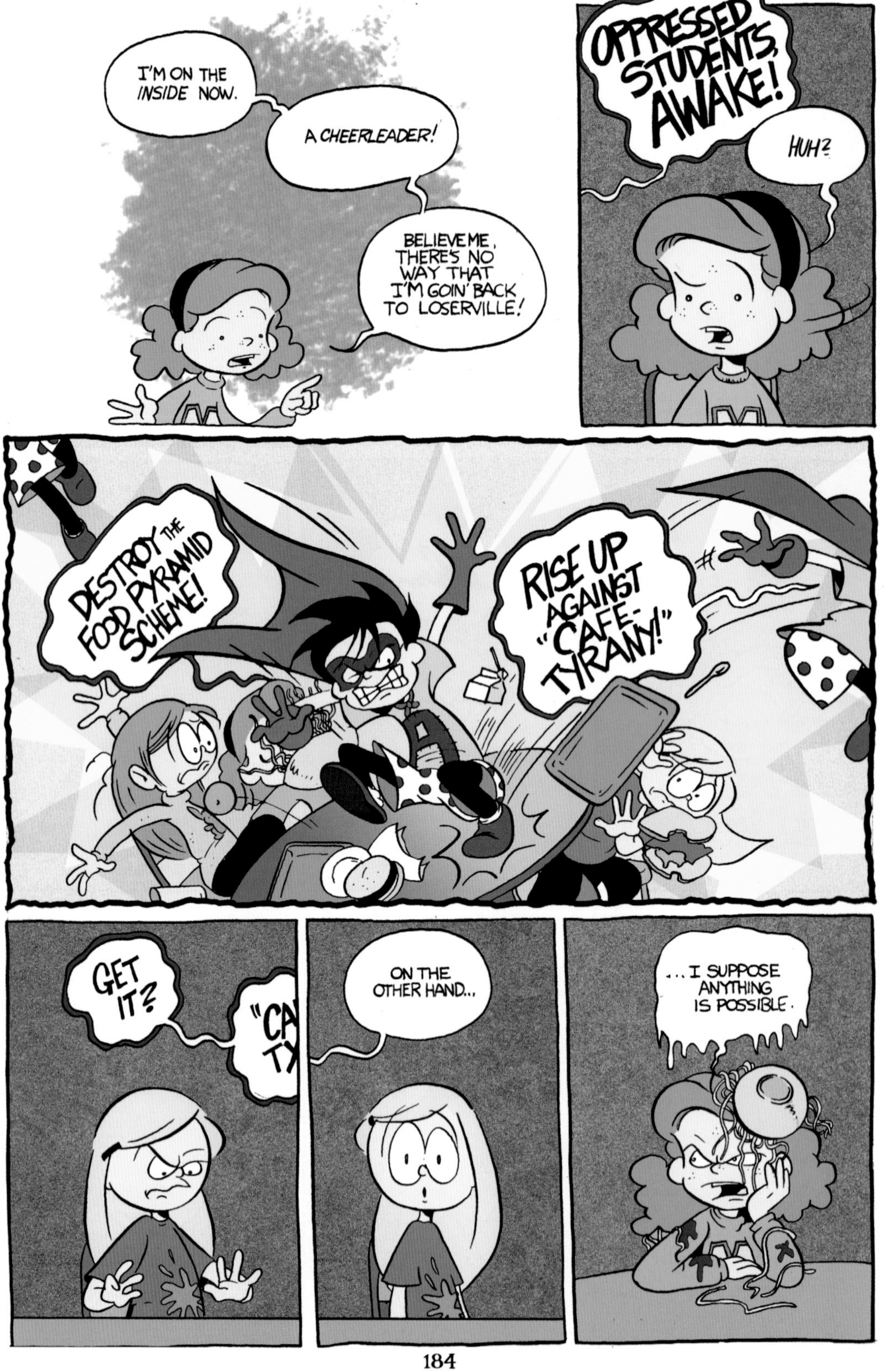
I'M ON THE *INSIDE* NOW.
A *CHEERLEADER!*
BELIEVE ME, THERE'S NO WAY THAT I'M GOIN' BACK TO LOSERVILLE!
OPPRESSED STUDENTS, AWAKE!
HUH?
DESTROY THE FOOD PYRAMID SCHEME!
RISE UP AGAINST "CAFE-TYRANY!"
GET IT?
ON THE OTHER HAND...
...I SUPPOSE ANYTHING IS POSSIBLE.

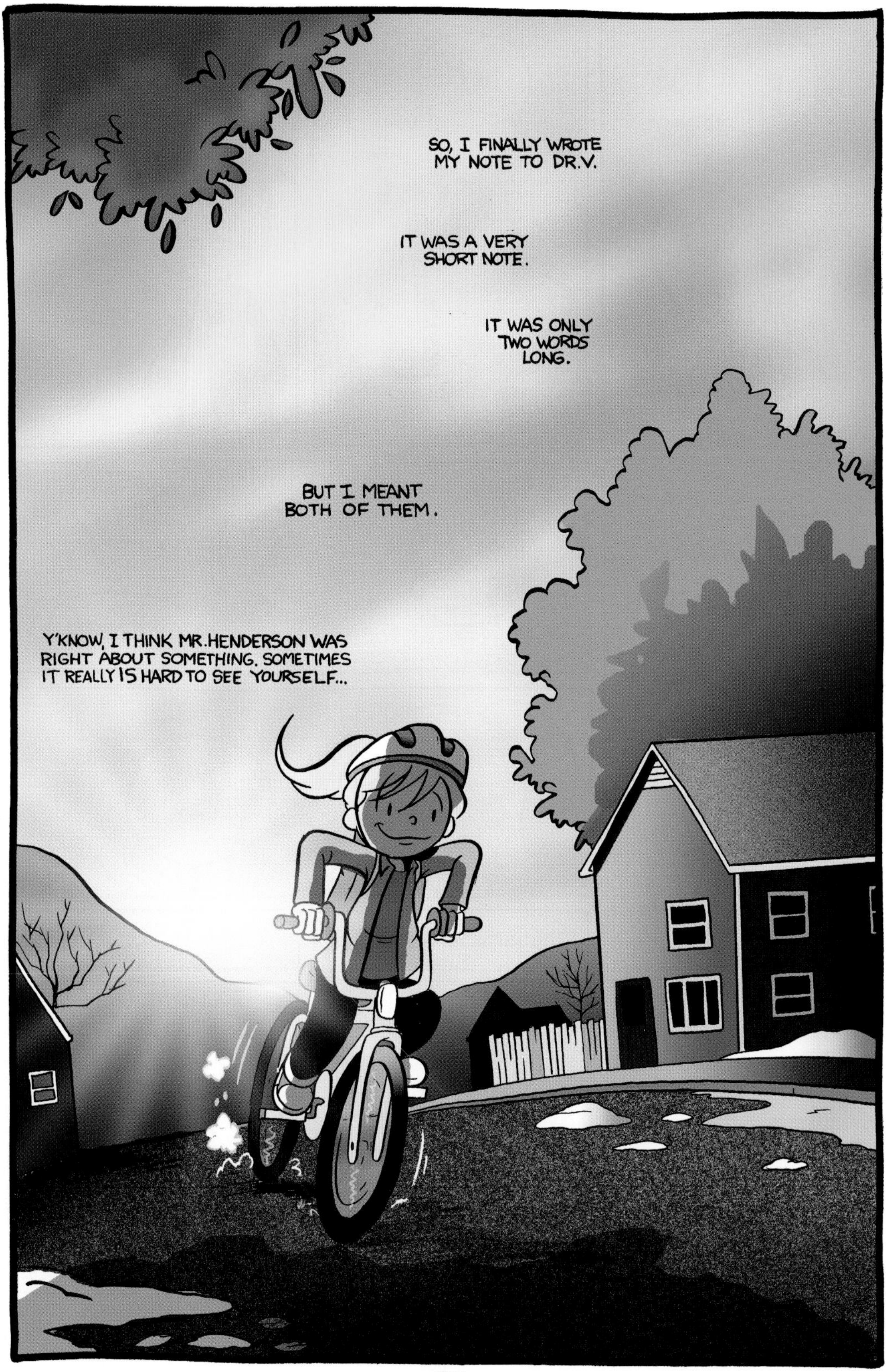
SO, I FINALLY WROTE MY NOTE TO DR.V.
IT WAS A VERY SHORT NOTE.
IT WAS ONLY TWO WORDS LONG.
BUT I MEANT BOTH OF THEM.
Y'KNOW, I THINK MR.HENDERSON WAS RIGHT ABOUT SOMETHING. SOMETIMES IT REALLY IS HARD TO SEE YOURSELF...

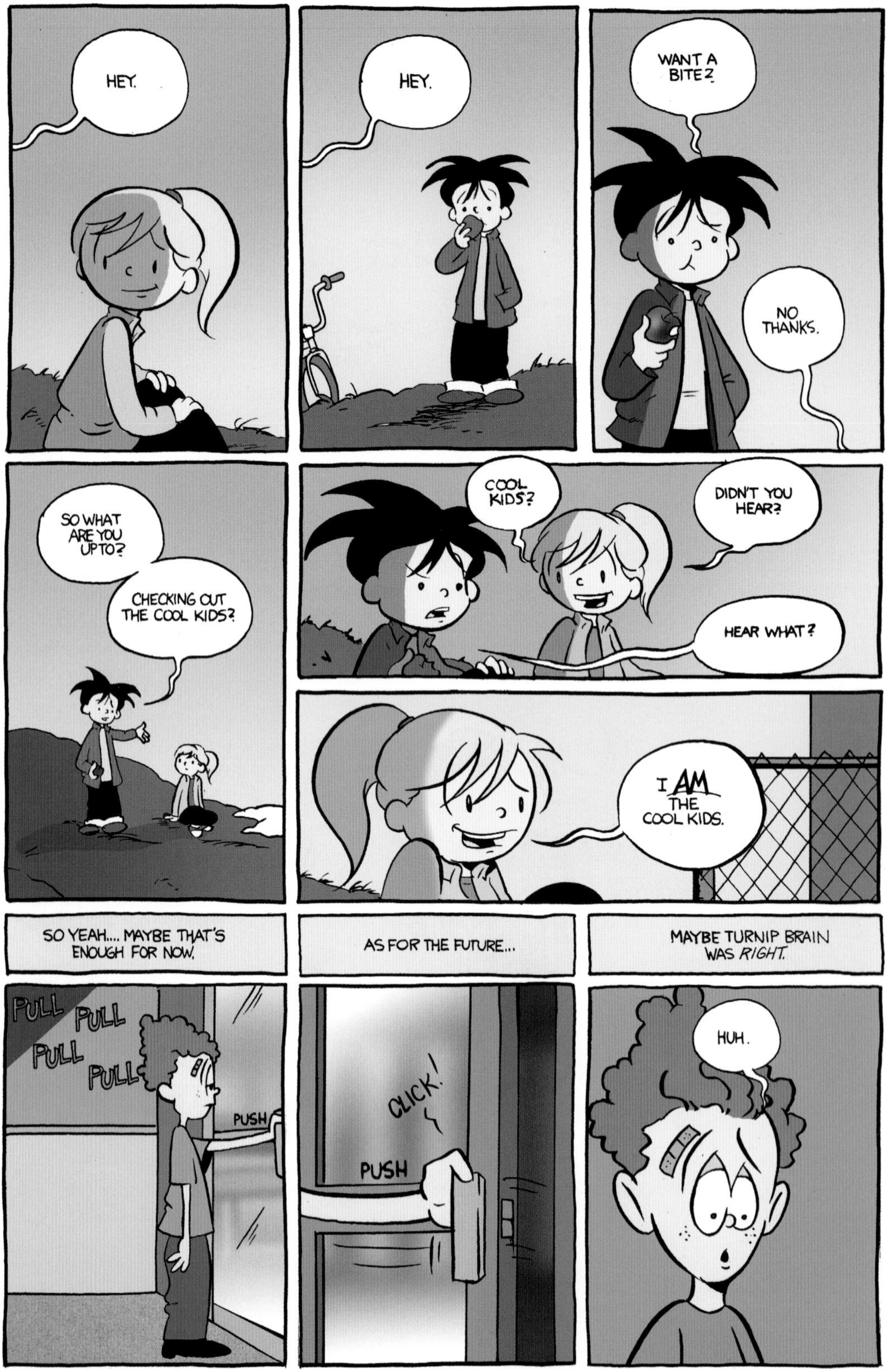
HEY.
HEY.
WANT A BITE?
NO THANKS.
SO WHAT ARE YOU UPTO?
CHECKING OUT THE COOL KIDS?
COOL KIDS?
DIDN'T YOU HEAR?
HEAR WHAT?
I AM THE COOL KIDS.
SO YEAH.... MAYBE THAT'S ENOUGH FOR NOW.
AS FOR THE FUTURE...
MAYBE TURNIP BRAIN WAS RIGHT.
PULL PULL PULL PULL
PUSH
CLICK!
PUSH
HUH.

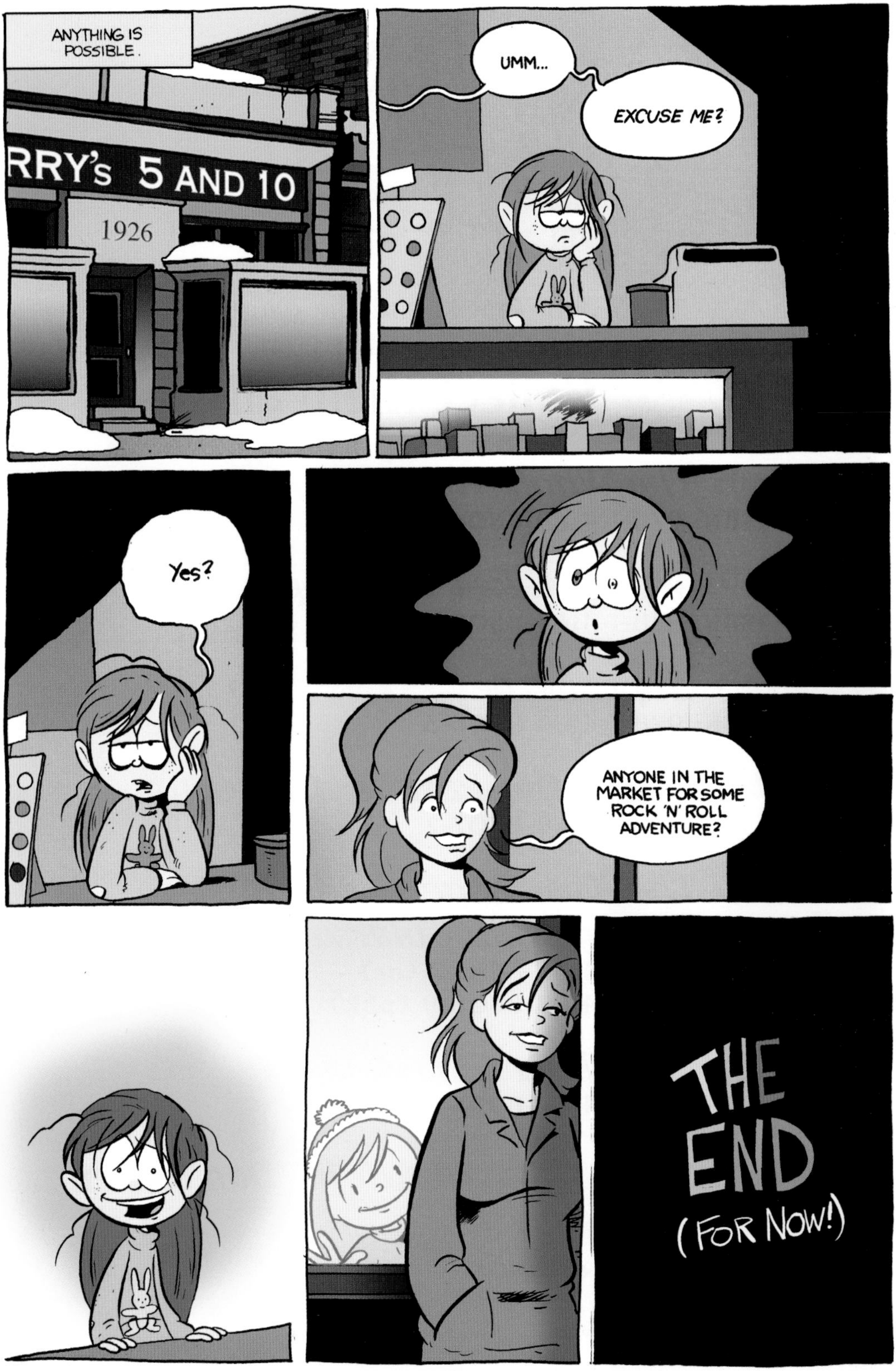
ANYTHING IS POSSIBLE.
RRY's 5 AND 10
1926
UMM...
EXCUSE ME?
Yes?
ANYONE IN THE MARKET FOR SOME ROCK 'N' ROLL ADVENTURE?
THE END (FOR NOW!)

Jimmy Gownley's

AMELIA RULES!™

Join Amelia and the gang for adventures, mishaps, and homework.

Collect them all!